COAL _____

COAL _____

a novel

by Tom Hillstrom

WILLIAM MORROW AND COMPANY, INC.
New York   1980

Library of Congress Cataloging in Publication Data

Hillstrom, Tom.
  Coal.

  I. Title.
PZ4.H6553Co [PS3558.I4535]   813'.54   80-12069
ISBN 0-688-03658-9

Printed in the United States of America

First Edition

1 2 3 4 5 6 7 8 9 10

BOOK DESIGN BY MICHAEL MAUCERI

To my wife, Martha

ACKNOWLEDGMENTS ____

The author wishes to acknowledge the contributions and assistance of numerous persons, especially Rupert and Karen Hitzig, Drew and Carolyn Leckie, Tedda Fenichel, Frederick W. Duff, Cass Vanzi, Joseph O'Brien, Dr. Seymour L. Hess, and two talented and patient editors, James Landis and Meredith Davis.

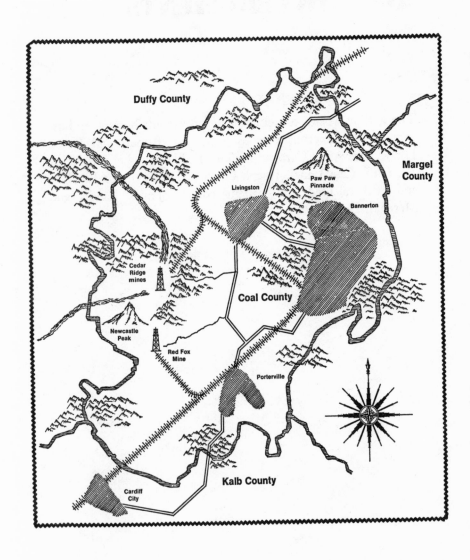

PROLOGUE ———————————

When she was a girl, Bonnie Shaw often hiked to the top of Newcastle Peak. There was a large, flat boulder there that nature had eroded into a thronelike seat. Sitting on it, when the morning fog had lifted, she could view a panorama of almost all of Coal County. The ancient and worn mountains and the long, narrow hollows were spread below like the wrinkled brow of a dying Methuselah. In the late fall and winter the rolling West Virginia foothills were covered with closely spaced leafless trees which appeared from above like the naked bristles of a sea urchin. In the spring the tops of the trees puffed out into an arboreal canopy shrouding the hills like an emerald green fluffy quilt. A railroad track, its steel glistening in the sunlight, skirted the mountainside, clinging to bluffs and snaking through passes as it connected Coal County's three principal communities: Porterville, a company town laid out in rows in two abutting hollows; Bannerton, a onetime boomtown that had evolved into a haphazard middle-class sprawl on the floor of a banana-shaped valley; and Livingston, a mountain-surrounded enclave dotted with the mansions of the county's rich.

Sometimes, as she sat there, Bonnie tried to imagine how it had been when the land was flat, a plane of lush green marshes and verdant rain forests. As she scanned the horizon, she knew it must have been but a relative moment in the span of unmeasured time that the primordial peace was shattered and the earth twisted and turned, pushing upward from the tree stands and sloughs a range of mountains young and regal, their shadows cast imposingly across the furrows left on the earth below. In time, fertile forests of new trees and thick brush edged up the mountainsides to the skirts of the uppermost peaks with their cap of perpetual snowfall. But the great landmasses continued to slide, sometimes quaking in violent spasms that shook the countryside, and the process reversed itself. The long range of snow-topped mountains shrank, consuming in their collapse the hardwood forests and the brush, crushing them into a vast layer of nearly pure carbon which had come to be called coal.

The mountaintop was Bonnie's sanctuary, her secret place in the world. She came there often, seizing its privacy and quiet whenever she felt a need for solitude to sort things out or merely an impulse to witness the tranquilizing display of nature. It was a majestic sight, a sight uplifting to the spirit and soul, and the cool, thin mountain air served as an emotional tonic. Then, one day, it changed. The mountain failed Bonnie and she never again returned.

The change came on the morning she stopped by the Porter Coal Company office and overheard the man she loved disown her, betray her, turn his back on their most intimate moments. James T. Porter II. Jim. She had wanted to believe, to believe it was possible for a woman and a man to bridge a gap that had divided them from their births, that her being a miner's daughter and his being a mineowner's son would mean nothing if both were strong and really cared. When others scoffed at that hope, calling it unrealistic and pretentious, she told them they were wrong, that it could be done, that the chasm could be closed. Then he himself destroyed their dream, denied their love. In that instant Bonnie knew she would forever hate the man.

With pain deeper than any she had ever felt, Bonnie raced to her sanctuary on the mountaintop. The rocks, fallen branches and hidden holes made the trail treacherous in her haste. She was puffing heavily, her feet sometimes stumbling on a sharp-edged stone or skidding on the loose gravel of the soil. More than once the branch of a tree whipped her face, smarting her skin and pushing her closer to the tears she was fighting to control. When she reached the top, no matter where on the horizon she peered, she saw no green, no lushness, no suggestion of life. The foothills appeared gray as steel and cold as the waters of a winter stream. The shadowy ranges in the distance with their towering peaks had the look of prison bars. Her skin flushed. She clenched her fists. The rage rose within her, filling her, recharging her adrenaline, heating her blood. And she remembered an old, stooped miner named Ernie Jason.

"A lad would start out age eight or nine on a breaker," he said. "That was a machine outside the mine that you'd use to bust up big chunks of coal and pick out rock 'fore it went to the coke ovens. About twelve or so and they'd let ya into the mine. And there you'd stay, puttin' in your day, till the years got to ya and yer back and arms and lungs couldn't take it no more. When that happened, back you'd go to the breakin' machine." Jason smiled. "Once a miner, twice a breaker boy."

"Once a miner, twice a breaker boy," Bonnie repeated, the cold wind atop Newcastle Peak stinging her cheeks. Full circle. A revolving cycle. And in the end, nothing is changed.

Bonnie rose from her seat on the thronelike rock, her long jet black hair whipping behind her, her skirt snapping at her legs. She squared her shoulders and turned her green, catlike eyes to the leaden sky. She hated him, yet she wanted him. And all she could do was vow that it would never happen again, that she would never again fall victim to the spell of a Porter.

She started down the mountain.

CHAPTER 1 ———————————————

On the day of his return home from the war, James T. Porter II pressed his face to the train's window, as he had done as a boy, stared blank-eyed at the blur of the passing scenery and wondered what it was he would find when his feet touched the cinder and gravel soil of Porterville for the first time in three years. He was twenty-three, and the war against the communists, for the time being at least, was over.

Officially the fighting had attained not the status of a war but rather a "conflict" or a "police action." At its conclusion, it was unclear if either side could legitimately claim victory. To both soldier and civilian, the announcement of a truce was anticlimactic, and although the end of combat and his release from active duty had at first evoked a feeling of great relief within Jim, this sensation was soon replaced by apprehension at what awaited him back home in Porterville.

Porterville was named after—and had been founded by—his grandfather. It was in the south of West Virginia, thirty-seven miles from the Virginia panhandle. Spiritually, if not physically, it was as isolated as any community in the nation, so much so that except for those residents whose sons, brothers or husbands were conscripted into the fighting, the just-ended warfare had escaped all but the briefest attention. Before the outbreak of combat, few had ever heard of the land named Korea, and still fewer could locate it on a map. The conflict inspired no town rallies. No Porterville women assembled on weekday evenings to roll bandages. And as his train sped toward West Virginia, Jim knew there would be no band waiting at the Porterville railroad station to greet him and no bunting strung out across the weatherworn wooden platform.

He tried to convince himself that he didn't care. For it had been neither heroics nor the threat from an enemy that had prompted him to enlist. His older brother, Peter, had been touched by such noble motivations, and they had cost Peter his life, his blood wetting the soil somewhere deep in France a decade earlier and casting him forever in the valiant role of a Porterville man who had known and met his duty. Jim was no hero and did not pretend to be. His enlistment, in fact, had infuriated his father, who accused him of motives far removed from any sense of patriotism. And his father, Jim readily acknowledged, had been correct.

The train was half full of passengers. As he looked around, Jim saw that several were returning GIs. Their uniforms, once starchily pressed, neatly buttoned and worn with some display of pride, now tended to be crumpled. Except for a slobbering smile on the face of one soldier imbibing from a clumsily held whiskey bottle, their faces bore hollow expressions of numbness or confusion. Returning home was a threatening experience, as threatening, in its own way, as any firefight, and there was an uncustomary silence to the coach car, except for the periodic whistle, passing bells at road crossings and the click-clack of the track, which added its own hypnotic quality to the subdued atmosphere.

Jim stretched, extending his long legs as far as the forward seat would allow him. He was a big man, six feet one, but at 170 pounds, relatively lean. His Roman nose was balanced by a square, slightly protruding chin. This, with his high cheekbones and dark brown eyes, gave his face a sad, sculptured appearance. He ran his fingers through his straight light brown hair, which was long now compared to his combat days. On the way down his fingertips touched a half inch scar that ran diagonally across his right cheek, the result of a grenade's flying shrapnel. As he scanned the car, he acknowledged to himself that he had survived the war well. At least two of the servicemen sharing his coach displayed evidence of wounds more serious than a nearly painless shrapnel gash. One was missing an arm. The other, sitting across the aisle from Jim, cowered in the corner of his seat, his head shaking spasmodically in a violent tic which no doubt was another kind of wound of the war. Jim had seen combat in the Korean highlands and, except for the small piece of grenade, had escaped the lead and steel hurled toward him. This, to his mind, was just one more confirmation that he had made a proper decision to enlist when he did, his father's protests aside.

At the time he had completed three years of study at the University of Virginia and had only two semesters remaining. His father, through deft political maneuvering, had ensured that his student deferment would go unchallenged. There was, as the old man argued, not a reason in the world that Jim should give a single thought to the war. But he signed up anyway, walking to the recruitment office just off the university campus and filling in the forms in their triplicate copies. "Why?" his father demanded, his face reddened and a whiskey glass shaking in his right hand. For just a moment Jim considered trying to explain it but then concluded that no matter what he said, his father would dismiss his action as no more than an ill-advised expression of a young man's rebellion. So he left it an enigma. "For the hell of it,

Pa," was his answer. "That's all I can tell you."

Could Jim himself explain an action that seemed so much the result of careless impulse? He thought so, for the reasoning that had guided him to the desk of the smiling recruiter had been direct and rather simple. Until then, for the two decades of his life, James T. Porter II had yet to make a significant decision. While other young men were deciding whether to continue school or join the work force in the mines, Jim remained in his seat at Bannerton High School, as was expected of the son of a mineowner. And when the others, with paychecks in hand, courted, married and began rearing families, he stood to the side, for no college-bound Porter would enter into marriage before having earned a degree to display behind his desk in the office of the company he one day would manage. Even a choice of university had been denied him, the decision having been reached a generation earlier by his father's enrollment at the University of Virginia, where sons were expected to follow their fathers.

There had been no major forks in the road for Jim Porter, no points in his life where he had had to elect whether to turn this way or that. So he made his appointment at the recruiting office, and when the sergeant ceremoniously handed him a pen and pointed to the official papers, he signed, leaving behind, at least temporarily, the classroom talk of Chaucer's wit and Victorian mores and bisected triangles, topics which at best he found irrelevant and boring. He opted instead for what he hoped would be an adventure—distant lands, camaraderie under fire, the thrill of danger. The war did not quite meet those expectations, supplying instead almost unbearable tedium, weariness and cold that reached to the marrow of his bones, but no matter—he had seen something of life and, most important, for a while he had escaped the gaze of his father.

His tour of duty complete, Jim was hard pressed to explain just why he was returning to Porterville, except that soldiers, when their wars were finished, universally trooped home to their lovers, their families and, if nothing else, their dogs. More than a dozen girls in Livingston would be waiting to see him, and his mother surely would cry when she greeted him. He longed to run his fingers through the furry coat of Samson, his dog, if the ancient mutt was still around, and by anyone's standard he was entitled to a few weeks of hell raising. Beyond that, Jim had no idea what turn his life would next take. He found himself lacking in any impulse to return to the campus. Equally unappealing was the prospect of his taking a formal place of authority in the family company, standing at his father's side, a voiceless lieutenant marking time in the shadows as a patient and unchallenged heir apparent. Perhaps he would join the ranks of the other returning Porterville veterans and line up for work in the mines. His grandfather had dirtied his hands regularly in mine work while developing the business, and his father, too, had been schooled in the rugged labors within the shafts. As for Jim himself, his sole excursion into the mountains had come on a brief coal car ride at the age of twelve. Otherwise, he had little concept of what actually took place in those darkened tunnels, a lack of knowledge he considered astonishing for someone who presumably would one day run the company.

The whistle sounded from the diesel engine ahead as the train wound its way over track cut into and around the mountainsides. Jim loosened his government issue tie and starched shirt collar and slumped further into his seat. His mind was filled with flashes from the past, a parade of faces: his brother, his features a vague outline, the town hero, whose remains were entombed in the churchyard under a marble monument second in size only to that accorded his grandfather; his mother, Sarah, a tall, slender woman with alert, compassionate eyes, who wore her fashionable clothes with the grace of a model; and his father, Major Augustus Porter, the town baron, decent and just when sober, vicious when drunk, class-conscious in either state, his face stern and scowling. Then there were the cheerful faces of the young Livingston women whose affections he had pursued, about half of whom he had known intimately, smiling and seductive, strong in their bearing and possessive. He thought of the family mansion, the hilltop home the size and grandeur of which had been intended for great numbers of Porter offspring but which now was left to shelter only the three of them, Jim and his parents.

Jim felt a tapping on his shoulder. "Can ya spare a butt, pal?" It was the soldier from across the aisle, his tic for the moment subdued.

"Sure. Take a couple," Jim said, pushing a half-empty pack of Camels toward him. The soldier counted out two, handed back the pack and returned to his seat, again to cower in the corner.

The intrusion freed Jim from his memories, and he resumed gazing out the window. His stomach began to tingle as the train closed the miles to Porterville. The train's progress seemed excruciatingly slow. The engine struggled as it pulled from each station and failed to reach normal speed before slowing for the next. The train had entered the heart of coal country, and every time it emerged from a tunnel, timber forest or mountain bend, the top of a mine tipple or coal silo came into view. Freight trains of fifty cars and more idled on sidings, their hoppers overflowing. Soon the stooped old conductor shuffled down the coach's aisle to announce the coming stop as Porterville.

The mining town was only a flag stop on the line. The twice-a-day passenger trains, traveling in opposite directions, usually roared straight through en route to Bannerton or Cardiff City in nearby valleys, but the trains did pick up passengers when the Porterville stationmaster signaled the engineer by semaphore. Similarly, the trains stopped whenever they had Porterville-bound passengers aboard. On such occasions the town was alerted to the new arrivals by the sounds of the engine braking to a halt. This was a rare enough event that it unfailingly attracted dozens of youngsters to the depot, curious as to who the travelers might be.

Jim threw his uniform jacket over one arm and reached for his duffel bag on the overhead rack. He was the lone disembarking passenger. The conductor had his stepstool in place on the track's gravel bed before the train had completely stopped, and his hand was already in a highball to the engineer when Jim hopped off. Jim turned back and, as the train began to pull out, handed the conductor his crumpled pack of Camels. "Give them to that GI back there, would you? You know, the one who sat across from me," he shouted. The conductor took the pack and waved.

The train had left Jim several yards away from the tiny black and white wooden station. He raised the bulging duffel bag to his shoulder and walked up the ties of the tracks. A crowd of excited youngsters raced toward him from the platform, and when they reached him, several began tugging at his uniform. But his eyes were on the fading sign atop the station's shingled roof. "Porterville," it read in partially bleached-out block letters.

A few adults were near the station, but Jim noticed only the children until a hand reached through them and grabbed him by the arm. It was Ernie Jason, staggering slightly as he held onto Jim's sleeve.

"Porter. Young Jimmy Porter. Well, I'll be damned," Ernie said, grinning.

Ernie was a washed-up miner in his sixties who was the town's occasional handyman and most notable drunk. He had among his few duties the handling of the Porterville mail. When the trains had no need to stop in the town, the men in the postal cars kicked out a canvas bag containing arriving mail. At the same time an iron arm device grabbed the departing mail in a sack hanging from a special rigging along the track. Sometimes Ernie, weak-kneed and swaying with the effects of liquor, stood too close to the track and was struck by the tossed bag with sufficient force to slam him to the ground. And more than once he had rigged the outgoing bag upside down. When the iron arm hit the canvas, the sack popped open, scattering mail up and down the right-of-way.

"Ernie, how are you?" Jim greeted him. "That mail been getting you down?"

The stumbling man released his grip from Jim's arm and hitched a thumb under a suspender. "Some. But the way I figure it, the more of you service boys who come home, the lighter those sacks'll be."

"Here," Jim said, reaching into a pocket for a half dollar and pushing it toward Ernie. "Get yourself some 'shine, Ernie."

"Jeez, thanks. Just wait till your pa sees ya, Jimmy. That'll make his day."

Making a fist with his free hand, Jim gently pushed it at Ernie's chin and winked. The old man again displayed his toothless grin. Jim adjusted the duffel bag on his shoulder and continued on his way.

The sun began to disappear in a brilliant blend of fiery reds and yellows behind the foothills in the distance. On Main Street, the town bank and the company store were closed. A light flickered in the small parsonage next to the church. But it was not until Jim passed the church and approached the rows of company houses that he encountered the sights, sounds and smells that told him for certain he was home. In the two- and three-room wooden houses, women bent over pot-laden stoves, preparing evening meals. Outside, smoke curled from blackened tin chimneys. Children and dogs scurried about, and quiet, work-weary men rested on front stoops or gathered around washbasins of sudsy water anchored on makeshift tripods in front yards. To Jim's eyes, the tripods had the look of stacked rifles. He was well known in the company town, and as miners one by one recognized him in his enlisted man's uniform, nearly all waved their hellos. "Welcome home, Jim," each one shouted.

"It's good to be back," Jim answered, keeping an unbroken pace toward the Porter mansion.

The mineowner's house sat on the flattened top of a knoll. Except for the church, it was the largest structure in town. The mansion was a symbol of wealth and authority and in that respect served much the same function as a castle in feudal times. When Jim's grandfather expanded his coal camp, he had set aside a large plot of land for the family home. The original white wood frame house that occupied that spot had served as the family residence for years. In the mid 1920s, the colonel decided that the old structure would no longer do. On a lot adjacent to that of the original home he had constructed a larger mansion, one made from mortar and stone with foot-thick walls and a roof fashioned from sheets of pure copper. An ornate two-story-tall ballroom occupied the entire third floor. All five baths were lined with small tiles imported from Italy. Not trusting local craftsmen, Jim's grandfather had imported a three-man crew from Naples to ensure that the tiles were properly laid. Jim's mother later took up where the colonel left off, filling the mansion's eighteen rooms with imported classic furnishings and European artwork.

When Jim reached the mansion's front gate, a floppy-eared hound approached and growled. It was Samson. The aged dog soon recognized his long-gone master and enveloped him in a flurried welcome of fur, tail and tongue.

"Quiet, boy. Quiet," Jim said, tossing his duffel bag under a bush and breaking into a grin. "Come on now. It'll be good for a laugh." The dog followed him toward the rear of the house.

Dinner had already been served in the Porter household, and Jennifer, the longtime family housekeeper and cook, was busy closing down the mansion's oversized kitchen. A pot of beef stock simmered on the stove, filling the air with a meaty smell. A varied collection of pots, pans and utensils, many of them copper, hung from hooks in the ceiling over a preparation table, which was positioned in the kitchen's center and dominated the room. Off to one side was a chopping block, its surface concave from the pounding of cleavers hanging from its side. In a corner, near the entrance to the pantry, was a newly purchased Frigidaire, which Augustus had managed to buy despite the wartime shortages.

Peeking through a window, Jim saw Jenny walking toward the fridge to replace a slab of home-churned butter. She was a short, pudgy woman with wiry red hair and a perpetually bright pink complexion. Now in her forties, she had emigrated from Ireland as a teenager.

Jim put on his jacket, raised its collar and pulled his overseas cap slightly over his eyes. He knocked on the door.

"Now who could that be at this time of night?" he heard Jenny ask as she set the butter down and walked toward the door. She opened it slightly.

" 'Scuse me, missy, but would ya happen to have a bite for a tired ol' soldier boy?" Jim asked from the shadows.

"What did ya say?" the cook responded, leaning toward him.

"Just a bite or two, cookie. For a starvin' soldier."

"Well, just a minute. You wait right there," the woman commanded, retreating into the kitchen. She returned with a chunk of salt pork and wedge of crusty bread and handed them to the stranger. "There you are, but you git now. The owner here don't like beggars, you hear?"

But Jim didn't leave. Instead, he began to push his way through the door.

"Say, maybe you and me could have a good time," he said. "What d'ya say to that?"

The cook, startled, began to backpedal, her body growing stiff and lungs ready to explode with a scream. But the light of the kitchen caught the visitor's face. She cocked her head and bent forward. Then she was sure. "Jimmy!" she shouted. "It's Jimmy come home!"

Her outburst continued as she rushed toward Jim and wrapped her arms around him. Together they began an impromptu jig around the preparation table, Jim hooting while she shrieked. Jenny's husband, Percy, a slender, balding man who was the mansion's handyman, gardener and occasional butler, was attracted by the commotion and rushed into the kitchen. He was followed closely by Jim's mother, Sarah.

"Jim!" Sarah shouted. "I don't believe it."

"Here, let me take your jacket," said Percy. But Jim had no time to remove it before his mother immobilized him with an embrace, her hands locked behind him.

"My God," she said, stepping back, "let me look at you!"

"No," he said. "Let me look at *you*." He inspected his mother, noting the unchanged gracefulness of her body, his eyes pausing at her glistening blond hair, which was cut short and heavily curled, the envy of every woman who saw it. "You're quite a lady, Ma. Do you know that?"

She ignored the compliment and, dabbing at her eyes, instructed Percy to go to the study for her husband.

From the kitchen, they could hear Percy burst unannounced through the study door and excitedly tell Augustus of the arrival home of his surviving son. In a moment Augustus appeared at the kitchen entrance, walking slowly and straightening his smoking jacket.

"It's Jimmy, Major!" the cook shouted.

Still maintaining his dignified pace, Augustus moved to Jim. Grinning, he shook his son's hand firmly. Then his smile dissolved. "It's good to see you, son, but why didn't you tell us you were coming? We could have been prepared."

Jim felt as if a fist had just slammed into his stomach. In that instant it was clear the passage of nearly three years had changed nothing in his father, that the old man remained the same as always, capable of a smile one second and an ad-

23

monishment the next. To Augustus, Jim would always be
the weaker of his two sons, a wild, reckless, immature adventure seeker who had no conception of the responsibilities
he one day would inherit. His older brother, in contrast, had
displayed good judgment and a no-nonsense business acumen.
In his brief life Peter had set the standard against which Jim
would always be judged, at least by their father, who was apt
to find cause for complaint in anything Jim did, even in so
simple a matter as returning home.

Jim ignored his father's question and turned to Jenny, telling her, "Let's break out some bourbon."

"No," Sarah ordered. "It's a night for champagne. Now
let's get out of this kitchen."

As they moved toward the parlor, Augustus ducked back
into his study, saying he had work to do and would join them
later. Jim stared at the study door as his father closed it.
Then his mother took his arm and led him away. They sat
on a sofa in the parlor, and soon Percy appeared with a
bubbling bottle of champagne.

"All right, son," Sarah said, taking his hand and squeezing
it. "I want you to start right from the beginning and tell
me every little thing that happened to you over there."

It was past midnight when they had finished. Augustus,
meanwhile, remained in his study.

The Porter mansion occupied the highest ground within
the bounds of Porterville, and from it one had a bird's-eye
view of both of the connecting hollows that formed the
town. But it also worked in reverse: The mineowner's house
could be seen from almost any point in the rows of company
homes below it. The Porters lived in a fishbowl, their every
action a subject of discussion among the town's 1,243 residents. The Porters' doings were viewed with scorn by those
who held the mineowning family in contempt for the control
they held over others' lives and with fondness by those who
respected them for the company they built and the jobs they

24

provided. Most Porterville citizens, however, fell somewhere between these two extremes, alternating in their attitudes toward the baronial family with their whims of the moment, the amount of overtime available or the prices at the company store.

Bonnie Shaw had witnessed Jim Porter's homecoming at the train station and rushed home with the news. To her frustration, her mother, Liz, and father, Duke, had already learned of his arrival, the word having been flashed with the speed of a telegraph from household to household up one hollow and down the other.

Generally, Jim's return was well received, for he was remembered as a likable young man, full of hell-raising enthusiasm and missing, as yet, the patina of conceit that seemed eventually to mark all those in the mineowning class. In the first few days after his return, the talk in the barbershop, bathhouse and kitchens of Coal County concerned what the mineowner's son would do next.

"Maybe he'll go back to school," Bonnie speculated as she reached for T. C. Fenner's chest and fastened a button on his U.S. Army shirt.

"Nah," T.C. replied, showing annoyance at Bonnie's meddling with his uniform. "Whatever the hell Jim is, he ain't no scholar." He laughed.

It was the Saturday following Jim's return, and T.C., another Korea veteran, was wearing his uniform because Major Augustus Porter had taken an unusual step: He had declared the day a paid holiday. It was a gesture that had taken the town by surprise—Pugnose Porter, as Augustus was sometimes called by the men who worked for him, was not known for his generosity, and the mines normally would have operated with a full work force. But the mineowner's soldier son had come home, and no matter what his normal disposition, the major had his image to consider. So he declared the holiday.

No one in the town had any illusions about the action.

Most old-timers believed the last time the Porter Coal Company had had a paid holiday was at the end of World War II. Others, however, thought they recalled that Augustus once, in a move as surprising as his current one, had released the work force with pay on the day the deer season opened.

T.C. had been home from a military hospital in Pennsylvania for a month. He had been shot in the back, and the healing wound was still giving him trouble. He took a seat on the sofa in the Shaws' three-room company home while waiting for Bonnie and her parents to get ready for the celebration. The wooden house was poorly insulated, and a draft whistled under a window frame, hitting him on the top of the back. When she saw T.C. grimace, Bonnie had him move to a chair away from the gusting air.

T.C. had light blue eyes and a wide nose. His sandy hair was still close-cropped in the military fashion. Of average height and build, he was, nevertheless, exceptionally strong. His face was rectangular and had a hardness to it—except when he smiled, as he did when Bonnie bent over him and readjusted the Purple Heart pinned to his front pocket.

T.C. and Bonnie had been classmates at Bannerton High School, although he actually was two years older than she. He had been dropped back a grade while she had been moved forward. The son of a miner, he lived in the other Porterville hollow and had been pursuing Bonnie for more than three years. In the month since his release from the hospital, he had been pressing her to marry, but Bonnie had refused, telling him she needed time.

Once, while visiting the Fenner home, Bonnie heard his mother tell of the day T.C. was born. A woman from next door was there, Mrs. Fenner said. And the town midwife. T.C.'s father wasn't allowed into the bedroom, but by God, he never left the house—not even once for the moonshine fortification that was a prospective father's customary due. The labor was long, fifteen or sixteen hours, and comfort came to Mrs. Fenner only in the hot water the women applied and the maple twig the midwife gave her to bite. The cries of her labor shook the fragile company house until they were replaced by a child's scream. The neighbor announced that it was a boy, and Mr. Fenner, a short, stocky man, nearly crashed through the bedroom door. T.C. was his first son, and tears welled in his eyes. He kissed his wife's forehead and squeezed her limp hand. With coal-stained fists large enough to grip a boulder, he reached down, gently picked up the infant and raised him to his chest. For a few moments, he stroked T.C.'s back and then ran the tip of a thick forefinger across the velvet-like skin of his son's face. After Mr. Fenner had left on his long walk to the mine, T.C.'s mother pulled the child to her breast and discovered on the forehead of her baby, not yet a day old, a smudge of coal.

Looking at T.C. as he sat waiting in his slightly tattered uniform in her home, Bonnie smiled at the memory of that story. Like a baby pressed with sacred ashes from the thumb of a baptizing priest, T.C. had been blessed with coal. And that was the problem. Bonnie liked T. C. Fenner, liked him very much. She was attracted to his upbeat nature and rugged masculinity. But weren't the destinies of T.C. and men like him locked up long before their births in the decaying innards of a range of sinking, shifting mountains? Bonnie wanted more from life than that if she could get it. The smudge of coal dust off his father's finger had cast T.C.'s fate, she feared, and it scared her.

Bonnie moved to a corner of the room and reached for her guitar, then sat on the sofa and began picking a soft melody. She seldom ignored a chance to hold the guitar and could be seen playing it whenever she had time on her hands, while monitoring food steaming atop the stove, while waiting for her mother to hand her the laundry or while hitching a ride in the back of a truck to the store in Bannerton. Whenever she wasn't strumming the guitar, it seemed, she was reading, and on the floor beneath her bed were dozens of paperbacks.

"I just reread *The Red Badge of Courage*," she told T.C. "You really should read it. It's all about a soldier's feelings in war."

T.C. laughed. "Me read a book? The boys would never let me live it down."

Bonnie's mother entered the room, her brown hair rolled up into its usual no-nonsense bun. Liz was a short, roly-poly woman with red cheeks and a round nose on a full, cheerful face. As in most mining families, it was she who, in a behind-the-scenes fashion, actually ran the household.

"Maybe you two should go now," Liz said as the sounds of Porterville's five-piece marching band tuning their instruments could be heard from the town square. "How do you feel, T.C.?" she asked, bending to close the damper on the small living-room hearth to conserve the coal still glowing from the morning.

"I'm fine, ma'am," he replied, rising from his chair.

Bonnie tugged at the sleeve of his uniform, smiling. "I'm going to stand right behind you," she declared.

T.C. chuckled. "I just might need you in case I faint," he said, patting her head.

Across the room, Bonnie's father, Duke, struggled with the heavily starched collar of his one white shirt and then clumsily adjusted his unfashionably wide tie. He was unaccustomed to such attire—just as he was unaccustomed to his formal given name, William—and was wearing a suit only because Liz had insisted it would be proper for such a celebration. After passing his wife's inspection, Duke grabbed T.C. by the forearm with his calloused right hand and said, "Well, whatever Porter does, I just want you to know the town is very proud of you."

"Thanks, Mr. Shaw," T.C. replied. "I only hope this back of mine comes around so I can join you in the mine."

Duke, a large man with an unkempt mop of curly black hair, a barrel chest and arms as thick as tree trunks, gripped the younger man's hand. "You will, T.C. In fact, if you get the chance, you might put your bid in with Porter today."

The sky was cloudless and blue, and the sun cast the thin patches of grass in the town square into islands of brilliant green. The warm temperature, company holiday and nature of the occasion had already attracted more than 500 townspeople. Others continued to arrive. The event resembled a church gathering with families strolling as units and greeting others as if they had not seen them only a day or two before. Here and there a dozen young men in uniforms, khaki or blue, their chests thrown out to display medals and campaign ribbons, strutted on this day that had been set aside for them. They were the first of the Porterville men serving in Korea to return home. Among them were two who drew their support from crutches and another who was barely able to move, his belly taped with gauze, an arm hanging from a sling and his once mine-hardened body so dissipated by the starvation of a prisoner of war camp that his musculature surely would never regain its tone.

Porterville had its origin as a coal camp, a nearly inaccessible strip of civilization laid down in some of the most rugged wilderness in Appalachia. The nearest town of significant size was more than thirty miles away. That was a two-day trip by mule and cart until the railroad was extended into the area. Even then it remained a very isolated and mostly self-sufficient town.

Like many mining camps, Porterville occupied two long, narrow hollows that came together in a V. White miners and their families lived in one of the hollows; blacks, in the other. Blacks had arrived in the region in great numbers first when they fled slavery and later when coal companies began "leasing" convict labor from county jails in the Deep South. As in the South, nearly every aspect of life in the coal camps was segregated. Each race had its own church and its own school. And in the long building that served as a camp recreation center, an invisible line separated white from black. But this was changing. Although racial discrimination had hardly disappeared from the coalfields, by the end of the Korean fighting the two races lived among one another in Porterville, and in the mines, white and black men worked side by side.

Wood frame buildings eventually replaced the tents of the coal camp, and Porterville in time instituted at least a token form of democratic government, but its basic layout remained unchanged. Company houses still filled the two hollows in long, monotonous rows. The small commercial area was centered at the point where the two hollows came together. This was also the site of the town square.

The square could more appropriately be called a park since it was little more than an unkempt grassy field across the gravel roadway from the bank, company office and store. When it rained, the patch of sparse turf quickly turned to mud. Two tall logs resembling telephone poles were planted upright in one of the square's corners. On some summer nights a white sheet was strung between them for an outdoor movie. A plate was passed, but the donations seldom equaled the film rental fees, and the local American Legion post, which sponsored the affair, had to make up the difference. In another corner was a cast-iron watering trough, which was fed by a rusty spigot and painted bright red. It was still used by the few horses remaining in the area. In the center of the square was a slab of concrete which served as a dance floor.

Bonnie was smiling as she walked by T.C.'s side, clutching his arm.

"Sergeant, huh? You made sergeant, ya did," said one old-timer, wearing his uniform from World War I and patting the chevrons on T.C.'s arm.

"Corporal," T.C. corrected him. "They needed a cook."

The old man smiled, recognizing the Purple Heart that told a different story.

"Did you ever throw a hand grenade?" one admiring youngster asked.

"Of course," Bonnie answered for him. "And he fired a machine gun, too."

Duke, his bulging forearms and wide shoulders looking out of place in his mail-order catalogue suit, waved and nodded to passing friends but said little. In contrast, Liz chatted enthusiastically with the women they met.

When the church bell rang out noon, the people in the square pushed toward a four-foot-tall marble slab standing off to the side of the horse trough. As they assembled, most of the crowd continued to buzz with excitement and happy chitchat except for one group huddled together, saying hardly a word. The women in this group were dressed in dark gray or black, mourning the six young Porterville men who had lost their lives on the snowy slopes of Korea.

Porterville traditionally sacrificed more than its share in the nation's warfare. The marble slab memorialized nineteen townsmen who were killed in World War I, all but five of them in one disastrous battle involving a unit of the West Virginia Guard. When war again erupted with Pearl Harbor, the military tried to lessen the chances of such losses by separating men coming from the same city or town, but the Porterville GIs were still hit hard. The town, with a prewar population of slightly more than 900, sent 189 men into the ranks. Of these, the names of forty-two were chiseled into the marble tablet.

The five members of the town band, their uniforms a ragtag collection of homemade hats, struck up a march as Major Augustus Porter, accompanied by his wife and his slightly embarrassed uniformed son, moved to a small wooden speaker's stand at the side of the memorial. When the music faded, the Reverend Barnaby Weatherson, the spectacled young pastor of the Porterville First Christian Church, delivered a long and emotional invocation. The remainder of the ceremony moved at a quick pace and was relatively short: The band played the national anthem; a grammar school girl recited the Pledge of Allegiance, and Augustus Porter, dressed in a gray hand-tailored double-breasted suit, removed his homburg hat, smiled and spoke briefly of how proud he, the Porter Coal Company and the community were of the men who had served their nation. The Reverend Weatherson ended the formalities with a brief benediction, and as the band resumed its playing, the crowd began to scatter.

Augustus, trailed by Jim and Sarah, began to circulate, greeting several of his men. "Crawford," he shouted to one of his mine managers.

"Yes, sir?" the short, heavyset Englishman responded with what Bonnie thought was a hint of fear in his voice.

"That was some fine work last week at the Red Fox. That's the kind of tonnage I like to see," the mineowner told him, smiling broadly and pumping his right hand.

"Well, thank you, Major. We'll try to hit it again," Crawford said, obviously relieved.

Augustus spotted Bonnie's father. "Duke, you big bear. How are you?" He draped an arm over the miner's shoulder. Then he saw T.C. "You're young Fenner, aren't you?"

T.C. nodded.

Bonnie observed the mineowner closely, noting the effort Augustus was making to appear friendly. It didn't quite work, she concluded. When Jim moved to his father's side, she sensed that he also was aware of the superficiality of the mineowner's attempt at good fellowship.

When Jim spotted T.C. he greeted him warmly. The two had spent a season as teammates on the Bannerton High School baseball team.

"I heard you got hit, T.C.," Jim said. "How's it coming?"

"Just a little back problem. But I made it. And so did you.

You're looking good, Jim, fit as ever," T.C. replied.

As they spoke, Bonnie's eyes were on Jim. He seemed so tall, so strong, an untouchable figure whose image filled the dreams of rich bankers' daughters curled up on silk sheets in Livingston or debutantes from Philadelphia down visiting their families' investments, but who was beyond even fantasy for young women whose plight it was to be the daughters of mere miners.

As she observed the alertness of his eyes and his smooth manners, Bonnie wondered what it would be like to be married to the son of a mineowner, to live in the big house on the hill and to travel whenever one had the impulse to do so, no matter what the cost.

"What now, T.C.? What do you think you'll be doing?" Jim asked.

T.C. cocked his head slightly and looked sheepishly toward the dusty ground. "Well, once my back gets back in shape," he said, "I was hoping to pick up some work in the mines."

Jim turned to his father. Augustus cleared his throat. "Boy," the mineowner said finally, "when you feel you're ready, see me personally or Mr. Crawford there. The Porter Coal Company always has room for a veteran, especially a wounded one."

"Thank you, sir," said T.C., beaming.

"Come on, Jim," Augustus said. "There's that young preacher there. I'd like to have a word with him."

"See you around, T.C.," Jim said, his eyes catching Bonnie's before he turned to follow his father.

"Yeah. Let's get together," T.C. called after them.

Despite Augustus's words, his company had shown no special preference for veterans after any war. And with the market in a slump as it was, there had been little hiring anywhere in Coal County for several weeks. Bonnie knew this, and it made her suspicious of the offer to T.C.

"That's one thing I'll believe when I see it," she told the others, "old Pugnose Porter actually keeping his word."

33

"Don't talk like that," her mother scolded, her head swiveling abruptly to check whether the mineowner had overheard her daughter's remark. "Whatever Augustus Porter may or may not be, it's him who's providing the pay to put food on our table. We've even got a few dollars in the jar, and that's not too bad for a family that was so poor when it came here it couldn't even buy the shot for a gun."

"You may be right, Ma, but I can't help feeling there's going to be a hitch," Bonnie responded. "These people just aren't like us, and they don't ever do a thing unless it's going to gain them some."

"Now hush," Liz ordered, again checking to make certain the Porters were a safe distance away. In a softer voice she added, "All that matters for us is that our men are working. Don't ever forget that."

"And T.C. just might land that job," interjected Duke, who had watched Augustus closely for years. Back when Augustus was learning how to supervise the mines, Duke had served as a tutor of sorts, introducing him to the fundamentals of mining. Augustus appreciated Duke's sincerity and unwavering honesty and had used him over the years as a barometer of the feelings of his men. From that position, Duke had seen Augustus act very humanely on occasions the other men weren't aware of. "Sometimes," Duke said, "the old guy can be a very decent man."

"I hope so," T.C. said. "I'm going crazy doing nothing."

"When do you think you could start, son?" Duke asked.

"A week. Maybe two. No longer than that," T.C. replied. He slapped his overseas cap on her head and pulled Bonnie toward the dance floor. Liz went off to chat with a group of women, and Duke, rarely a dancer, moved to the side of the band and, with his arms crossed, watched the fiddler.

When the Porters returned to their mansion from the veterans' celebration, Augustus ordered Jim to follow him into his walnut-paneled study. The mineowner fell into a high-

34

backed cracked leather chair; Jim rested against the top of a wide, highly burnished desk which had been hand-carved from the worm-eaten wood of a chestnut tree. At his father's instruction, Jim poured them bourbons. For some time neither man said anything.

As Augustus gazed into the fire Jenny had thoughtfully prepared for them, the flickering light caught the gold ring on his left hand. The ornate letter *P* carved on its flattened surface seemed to glow in the semidarkness. That ring would be his one day, Jim mused, and a chill passed through him.

Jim studied his father's face, the heavily furrowed brow, the dark beard, making its early-evening appearance, and the nose, long and thin, still bent to the side from a brutal fist-fight two decades earlier in a mine shaft. The nose had supplied Augustus with the name Pugnose, but he was never called that to his face. Instead, when he was present, the miners referred to him as the major. This followed a long-time tradition in which miners assigned military titles to their employers. In the days of Jim's grandfather, mineowners had been called colonels. By the end of World War II the office had been demoted to major or still lower to captain. Major was the title Augustus claimed, using it himself, even with the signature on the checks he wrote. He had, however, never been in the military, his brawling injuries having kept him out of war.

It had been inevitable that some title of authority would evolve for Appalachian mineowners, for they controlled not only their companies but also the company towns. And the titles were bestowed with some degree of affection. Most of the mining men making their way from Europe to West Virginia had known only a neofeudal form of government. Democracy, in its purest form, was not a part of their experience, and it seemed natural for one very wealthy and powerful man to exercise autocratic control. In a coal camp, the mineowner was undisputed lord.

After his father had not moved for what seemed several

minutes, Jim cleared his throat to signal his impatience. Augustus finally broke his silence. "And what about you? Of course, you're going back to school."

Jim delayed giving an answer, thinking instead about the two faces of his father—a seemingly pleasant and benevolent man one moment in the town square and, once the first swallow of bourbon touched his tongue, an unyielding, often unreasonable taskmaster who would deal with his son as aggressively as he would the rawest company apprentice.

"Can't go until the fall, Pa. You know that," Jim said, bracing himself for the argument he was certain would come.

"And what about the meantime? I don't want you sitting around moping and wasting yourself."

"I need time, Pa, a little time to think a few things out."

"Ah, bullshit. Things? What things? Here, pour me another drink," Augustus ordered, pushing his empty tumbler toward his son. Jim reached for an imported crystal decanter and refilled the glass. The older man took a long, hard swallow. "You know, before the war—the last war, I mean—the entire United States Navy operated on coal. Every damn ship in the fleet. And by God, it was coal that ran this nation's railroads, coal from right here in West Virginia and a good chunk of it from Porter mines. And now . . . nothing. Not one goddamn boat and not one goddamn train." He paused for another long sip from his glass.

Jim's head was slightly bowed, his eyes staring blankly at the carpeted floor. He had heard it all before, but that did not diminish the truth of his father's statement. It was a painful truth if one gave a damn about the business, but Jim didn't. Shipping and the railroads had almost completed their conversion from coal to oil, and in cities, where sooty coal smoke had once risen in spiraling columns into the air from virtually every building, residential and otherwise, only the puffing discharge from smokestacks atop mills, factories and utilities blackened the skies. These accounted for the coal industry's only major surviving customers.

"The market's shrinking, maybe one-fourth or one-fifth of what it was when your grandfather found the resources to build this house," Augustus continued. "And there's no sign but that it's going to shrink more." He leaned forward, staring at his son for emphasis. "What it means simply is the survival of the fittest—the Porter Coal Company versus all the others. And we—and that includes you—had damned well better be prepared."

Jim refilled their glasses. "I know that, Pa, but—"

"So if you don't want to return to school," Augustus interrupted, "I've been thinking the best experience you could get under the circumstances would be to spend some time with Preston." Lowell Preston was the Porter Coal Company's principal European agent, whose headquarters were in London. "Then, when you come back in a year or so, you could start thinking about marriage. There's nothing like a woman to put some order into your life."

"I think I'd rather spend the summer here, Pa," Jim said, "and maybe put in some time in the mines."

"In the mines! Are you shell-shocked? Someday you're going to take over this company and supervise those men. It's like the military—you can't fraternize."

"But you did it, Pa. And so did Grandpa. That's how you learned mining," Jim said forcefully.

"It was different then. And I was fifteen or sixteen—not twenty-three."

"But the work would be good for me, and it'd give me some time."

His father's reaction came with no warning. Augustus threw his half-empty tumbler across the room; the glass shattered as it crashed into one of the bookshelves lining the walls. "Goddammit, son, you'll never change. Quite frankly, I fear for the future of this company." He glared at Jim, then began shaking his head.

Jim said nothing. After pushing himself from the edge of

the chestnut desk, he walked from the room in retreat from a scene that had been played many times in the past and surely would be repeated on the next occasion that whiskey flowed freely in the Porter household.

"Good night, Pa. I'll see you tomorrow," he said, closing the door gently and moving through the darkened hallway toward the parlor.

A figure appeared from the shadows, startling him. It was Jenny. She looked at him with sympathy.

"I guess my pa's never going to change," Jim commented.

"Your father has his beliefs and sticks to them, son," the cook replied. "Some people admire him for that."

Jenny said good night and departed for the servants' quarters upstairs. Both her husband and Jim's mother had already retired. The mansion was still.

As Jim walked into the parlor, the highly varnished inlaid wood floorboards, in delayed answer to his footsteps, creaked back into their natural alignment, the sounds reverberating in the high chamber. He plopped down on a long fabric sofa and gazed at the huge stone fireplace before him and the oil portrait of his grandfather that hung above it, its canvas wrinkled with age, its veneer cracking. On the fireplace mantel was a small pickax the colonel had used in working his first mine. Engraved on the tool's heavy metal head, in roughly etched block letters, was a motto. Jim couldn't read it from where he sat, but he easily recalled his grandfather's words: *Ex Disciplina Venit Libertas*—"From discipline comes freedom."

"Are you sure, old man?" Jim asked the portrait. "As I remember, it wasn't discipline that got you into the mining business."

The story of how the Porters came into the ownership of their mining property had endured as a local legend. One day in 1894, it was said, sixteen-year-old James T. MacKenna was kicking a soccer ball with some other boys on a playing field of an orphanage in Scotland. He was shorter and lighter than the others but was clearly their superior in skill and speed. Moving quickly, he maneuvered the ball deftly, first with one foot and then with the other, dribbling past each defender in an intricate weave toward the makeshift goal. Then, in a sudden movement almost too fast to see, he lofted the soccer ball with a thump and sent it past the outstretched hands of the diving goalie.

A well-dressed stranger with a snow white handlebar mustache stood with the orphanage headmaster, observing the play from the side. "He's very adept, isn't he?" the stranger commented.

"He's our best," the headmaster boasted. "And probably the most talented player in all Glasgow."

The headmaster summoned the boy and introduced him to the stranger, Mr. George Porter, a gentleman visiting from America. "And he's offered to sign your papers, lad."

"Yes, sir," young MacKenna replied inquisitively, standing straight and motionless except for an almost imperceptible tremor in his hands which betrayed his terror.

"Mr. Porter owns a large coal mine in America, and he wants to take you there."

"But, sir," the boy responded, "I can't go. I can't leave my brother."

The stranger smiled, patting the boy on the back. "He'll come, too. We'll send for him in a month or so. That's a promise."

Although it was not apparent to either the boy or the headmaster, Porter had fallen into ill health. He was a bachelor and, having already made a fortune from his mine, was preoccupied with his lack of an heir. His mother had come from Scotland, and he took his search for an heir to that country. A properly operated coal company needed continuity, and in Porter's view, it would best come from the Scottish heritage he and the boy standing before him shared.

The papers were signed. Jim MacKenna traveled to West

Virginia with his adoptive father, took his name and left his brother behind. Porter, despite his pledge, never did send for the younger boy. And when he died eight years later, leaving Jim his mine, Jim also neglected to send for his brother.

That was the legend. More than half a century later the men working the Porter Coal Company mines under the direction of the adopted boy's son, Augustus, still claimed to hear deep within the mountains the muffled cries of the betrayed MacKenna brother.

As he recalled the story while sitting in the darkened parlor, Jim wondered whatever had happened to his namesake's brother, whether he was still, by chance, alive and whether "discipline" had won him any degree of freedom, economic or otherwise.

"From discipline comes liberty," he repeated. It had the ring of power and, as a result, implied truth. But Jim doubted it, at least for him. As far as he could envision, there was not much he could do—or not do—that would change his future one way or another. His father would one day die, and he would inherit the mines. Like an organism with its own nerve center and energy, the company would move forward. This was his lot, and he felt as trapped by it as any miner's son felt predestined to a life of crawling through coal veins. No, he wouldn't go back to school, and he wouldn't go to London. He was not yet ready to sit behind a desk, chained in place by a heritage over which he had no control.

Hearing the click of a decanter against glass as his father, still in the study, poured himself another drink, Jim raised his long legs onto the sofa. The room seemed overlarge and barren. A chilling breeze of night air came through the flue of the fireplace, causing him to shiver. He curled up into a corner of the soft sofa and closed his eyes. Sleep came within minutes.

CHAPTER 2 ————————

Jim Porter had arrived early. The shift did not start until 8:00 A.M., and the miners were not expected to stand ready at the portal until five minutes or so before then. But Jim had been too excited to wait at home. With his dog, Samson, at his side, he was waiting before 7:00 A.M. outside the locked manager's hut at the Red Fox Mine, his family's major holding and one of the largest mines in the state.

As a boy Jim had been preoccupied with sports, but whenever he wasn't racing around a football field or baseball diamond, he was apt to be found at the Red Fox. He loved to mingle with the miners, and although he wasn't allowed within the mine itself, he tried to make himself useful, fetching water, handing out towels or retrieving windblown mining caps. It was underneath a Red Fox coal car that he had smoked his first cigarette. And it was inside the manager's weatherbeaten shack that he had first made love.

Jim was easily distinguished from the other miners arriving for the shift by the pair of fresh coveralls he wore and his lack of a cap. The Red Fox manager, Henry Crawford, appeared surprised to find the grandson and namesake of the company's second owner standing there. He was further surprised to hear Jim say that his father had agreed to his spending some time in the mine, learning its operation firsthand.

This wasn't quite so. Neither Jim nor Augustus had again raised the subject following their discussion three weeks earlier. Jim had taken it upon himself to make the necessary arrangements at the company office.

"Well, welcome to ya," Crawford said, extending his hand. "Glad to have ya around, Jim, but you be very, very careful, ya hear?" There was a pained expression on Crawford's ruddy face, and Jim knew that the last thing he wanted was for the mineowner's son to start poking his nose around.

"I want to work," Jim told him. "I mean I just don't want to sit around. You treat me as you would any other new man."

Crawford brought his thumb to his chin and cast his eyes downward in apparent thought. Once a boy was put to work at the mines when he was seven or eight. He was sat at a breaker machine and told to weed out the rocks and slate from the coal before it was crushed in preparation for the beehive coke ovens. A year or two later, if his father knew the right foreman, the youth could buy himself a mining cap and work in the shafts as a trapper boy, opening and closing huge air doors for the men moving coal cars in and out. When his arms and back were strong enough, he could purchase a pick and shovel and begin working a vein of coal. More than likely, this would be his burden for the rest of his life until he was too weak and too old to handle a pick and shovel anymore.

But the child labor laws had changed much of that. A youth was at least fifteen or sixteen now before he began part-time or summer work. And the steps of apprenticeship were well established—assignment to a bull gang for general cleanup duties; help with moving and unloading the four-ton coal cars. Not until he had spent at least a year working under the watchful eye of an experienced miner would a newcomer be certified as a qualified miner and be paid a full wage.

"I think maybe it'll be best to put ya alongside Duke Shaw down there," Crawford said finally. "He'll look out for ya, and if I remember right, he once worked with your dad." Jim nodded. "Now, let's see about getting ya a cap."

Crawford stepped into his hut and returned with a cap that was unblemished and obviously new. A modern mine cap was made from plastic, no longer from cloth, and had the feel of a football helmet. Miners had once attached small candles to their caps to provide at least a flicker of light on the inside, but since the turn of the century carbide lamps had been used. Later battery-powered filament lamps came into vogue, but the Porter Coal Company had not yet acquired them in great number. The cap Crawford handed Jim had the traditional carbide lamp. The lamp was in the shape of a tiny coffeepot. Carbide, in powder form, filled the bottom. When water dripped upon it from an upper chamber, the resulting chemical reaction generated a flammable gas. The gas flowed through a bent tube. When ignited, it produced a small bluish flame.

Jim, who had never lit a carbide lamp before, was fumbling with the buckle of the cap's chin strap when a voice came from behind. "Here, let me help you." Jim turned. T. C. Fenner stepped out of the shadow of the huge Red Fox tipple, a wooden structure resembling a railroad trestle on which coal moved in a continuous stream to a loading funnel above hopper cars.

"I guess I'm pretty green, huh?" Jim asked, laughing.

"You'll learn," T.C. replied. "You'll have to if you're going inside."

"How long you been working, T.C.?" he asked.

"A week. Thanks to your father. He's a hell of a man."

Jim didn't know what to say to that. Crawford rescued him when he put a hand on T.C.'s shoulder and asked, "You feel up to taking him in?"

"Sure," T.C. replied. "The back's pretty good today."

"And you'd better show him how to light that carbide." Crawford turned to Jim. "Duke is the best we got down there, and he can always use an extra hand. But look, son, the only way I'll be a party to this is if you promise me you'll follow his every last word. I can't have a Porter getting hurt in there."

"Don't worry, Mr. Crawford. It's my decision," Jim said.

"This way, buddy," T.C. said, pulling the new man toward the portal, which the day crew already had quietly entered while Crawford was issuing his instructions.

The Red Fox Mine was legendary. The vein was first noticed as a small outcropping, a five-foot circular depression in the side of a mountain which occasionally spit chunks of soft coal through a thin layer of shrubbery and vines. A blacksmith who lived nearby collected the discharged pieces to fire his forge. When it appeared the discharge from the mountain would have no end, he began selling the expelled chunks to the other few inhabitants of the remote region for a penny a bushel. Then a passing young mountain man named George Porter spotted the outcropping for what it was—the exposed tip of a sprawling, easily accessible network of bituminous coal. By the time Jim reported for work in the Red Fox it was relinquishing its black insides at rates of up to a million tons a year.

Although he had never before worked in a mine, Jim knew something of the strategy employed in attacking a virgin vein. First a portal was dug at the site of the outcropping, and from it a horizontal shaft—or heading—went straight inside. As the main heading reached more than a mile, other headings were begun at the portal, fanning off to either side. From each heading, the miners turned right and left every twenty yards or so to carve rooms.

After T.C. and Jim walked through the portal, they climbed onto a pair of rail scooters, flat boards with wheels at each end which rode on top of a rail. Jim mastered the movement of the scooter almost immediately. Several times along the way they had to stop, lift the scooters and step to the side to make way for low, flat train tractors, called motors, as they passed with a trailing chain of coal cars. As Jim and T.C. moved farther inside, the sunshine from the portal gradually disappeared, and although a string of direct-current electric lamps provided some illumination through the main heading, Jim had trouble seeing where he was going.

The height of the shaft began to fall below six feet. "You have to bend, so be careful," T.C. warned when they discarded the scooters and turned off the rail line. The ceiling dropped even further as they made their way past the shadowy figures of other miners. When they made their final turn, having traveled two miles into the mountain, the cut's height was less than four feet. Both men dropped from a crouch to their hands and knees.

Duke's eight-man crew was busy a few yards ahead of them, their carbide lights moving back and forth in the dark chamber like streaks of fireflies. Jim watched in amazement as one man crawled soundlessly past them through the water and mud with his dinner bucket hanging by its handle from his mouth.

"Duke!" T.C. yelled, but his voice failed to carry above the ongoing clatter of a cutting machine. He waited until the machine stopped and then tried a whistle. The pounding of pickaxes and the scraping of shovels came to a halt, and Duke's huge bulk, his face, like those of all the men, completely blackened except for the whites of his eyes, moved to the side of the two new arrivals.

In the dim light, Duke failed to recognize the man accompanying T.C. "It's Jim Porter," T.C. told him. "He's going to spend some time in the mine, and Crawford says he wants him to work with you."

Duke turned his eyes to Jim, pausing first at the newcomer's coveralls, store-clean except for the just-added smudges at the knees, and then moving to the young man's face, pale and smooth, devoid of wrinkles and lacking the gray tint of implanted coal dust that years of scrubbing would not erase.

"Well, you're sure welcome here," Duke said, breaking into a smile. "In here, we can use every man we can get, especially one as big as you."

T.C. slapped Jim on the back, wished him luck and left to return to the sunshine outside and the limited duties he had there while recovering from his wound. Duke handed Jim the crew's safety lamp. "We used to use canaries for this," he said. "If the damn bird dropped dead, then you knew you'd better the hell get on out. Now we have this lamp. It tells you the same thing." Jim accepted the handle to the cylindrical lantern and studied the small, flickering flame inside the glass bulb.

"If that flame starts to quit, then we're running low on air and had better have the engineer test the ventilation," Duke explained. "But if it flames up and becomes bright, it's probably from methane. You'll do us all a big favor by getting us out—and fast."

Jim nodded. Four nearby miners, who had watched in silent bemusement the arrival of the mineowner's son to their midst, resumed their picking and shoveling. Tightening his grip on the safety lamp handle, Jim leaned forward and attempted to see through the raised dust and darkness.

A damp, chilling breeze hit his face. With a finger growing numb from the cold, he reached for his eye and brushed away a speck of coal. So this is it, he thought. This is what it's like to be inside the mines. His father and grandfather before him had stooped their shoulders to work the face of a vein, and now, drawn to it for reasons he didn't quite understand, he, too, was putting in his time.

A long, flat machine came into Jim's view. It had an unusual protrusion and looked vaguely like a crab. The machine was relatively new in mining technology. With sharp steel teeth, the device noisily chewed out a cut along the bottom of a face of coal, leaving the remainder hanging from the ceiling. Once the cut was made, the machine moved on to another section of the vein, leaving the actual coal extraction to the time-proved labor of a mining man's arms and back.

Jim watched as a miner, using a long, slender auger, pockmarked the remaining section of the face with deep holes. There were power-driven drills to accomplish this, but the Porter Coal Company had not yet acquired any. The men had to twist the augers by hand. Once the holes were completed, the miner reached for a papier-mâché container resembling a gallon cider jug. It held black blasting powder. After pouring the powder into his hand, he carefully pushed small amounts into each hole. Then, with a copper-tipped probe called a tamping rod, he packed the mounds of powder into the face as far as they would go. This done, the miner inserted pencil-sized squibs into the holes and lit a fuse on each. A squib resembled a three-inch firecracker. When touched off, it shot a fiery wad through the auger hole to the packed black powder. The miner scurried to safety a few yards away after igniting the squibs. Jim covered his ears and pressed himself to the wall of the shaft. The explosion burst the face into a pile of chunky coal. Jim grimaced with the sound of the blast, its reverberations echoing for some time within his head. It reminded him of Korea.

Jim's duties were expanded gradually during his first few weeks of work deep within the Red Fox Mine, but the labor still took a painful toll on his neophyte's body. His service in the army had left Jim trim and in reasonably good shape, but the stooped work in the four-foot vein played havoc with the muscles of his back. He had begun augering holes and helping break large coal chunks into smaller pieces. Duke had yet to hand him a shovel and assign him his own coal car. Judging by the amount of coughing and wheezing car loading seemed to induce in the men performing it, Jim concluded that the worst of his backbreaking labor was yet to come.

The fact that Jim was the mineowner's son and the heir apparent to the company fortune set him apart from the other miners and produced its own tension. At first, it seemed no matter how energetically Jim attempted to share in the work, his bloodline presented a barrier that could not be bridged. This was a new experience for him, and it troubled him. For years he had nurtured friendships among the miners and their sons and felt accepted as one of them. However, upon entering the mine, he had crossed an invisible line, and his motivation was considered suspect by several of his co-workers. Occasionally one would be forward enough to raise the issue during the crew's lunch-break discussions.

"Let me ask ya something," one miner said one day as the crew reclined on the floor of water and mud along the wall of the shaft and ate the hearty lunches packed into their buckets. "Why are you doing this? How come you're here?"

"My family's been mining for three generations," Jim replied, holding his bread in a clean white handkerchief as the men had taught him to keep the dirt on his hands off his food. "I thought it best I learn something about it."

The man laughed. "Do ya really think that working a mine is like goin' to school?"

"What do you mean?"

"Well, to speak frankly, ya can't pull a shift in the mine and then go home to a millionaire's mansion with table linen and servants and roast beef and think that's the life of a mining man."

When that, or the equivalent, was put to him, Jim was lost for a rejoinder. His motives were sincere; he was trying to be honest, and the feeling of animosity and resentment he sensed in some of the miners was painful. But Duke took him under his wing—he was a gentle and understanding tutor—and their friendship was cemented when Duke began inviting Jim to join him and some fellow miners in their Saturday night no-holds-barred drinking sessions.

The group usually gathered for the weekend ritual at the rear of one of their company houses in Porterville and lifted moonshine jugs. But at least once a month they climbed onto the back of an ancient Ford truck and traveled to Bannerton. There they gathered amid the burlap sacks, cardboard cartons and stacked tin cans of a small general store, sharing pitchers of home-brewed ale and passing a jug of prized bootleg whiskey.

The store lacked a formal name. Townsmen generally knew it as Blakely's after the red-nosed round Englishman who managed the place for its banker owner. But the regulars who routinely camped on its sawdust floor one Saturday each month affectionately called it the public, considering it one of the few vestiges of the village life they had known before boarding ships bound across the Atlantic for such ports as Philadelphia, New York and Hampton Roads.

Duke had been among those arriving in Hampton Roads, and in the truck en route to Bannerton he told Jim how his journey had come about.

Times had been hard in his small village in Wales. The local mine had been shut down, and Duke, twenty-four years old and a prospective father, was among the mining men thrown out of work. Merely obtaining food was an almost hopeless struggle, and the prospects of the mine's resuming normal operations were bleak. Then one night a smooth-talking Englishman stopped by the village pub and told of the riches and opportunities to be had overseas.

"It's America, men, a land with no classes and absolutely unlimited opportunity. Believe me. I have no reason to lie," he told them, waving his pint.

When the Englishman laid out a stack of printed contracts on the pub's bar, Duke and his friend Bill Bergen were among the first to queue up to sign them. The documents specified that the Porter Coal Company of West Virginia would advance the men passage to the United States in return for a commitment of no less than four years in the firm's mines.

A huge smile came to his wife's face when Duke told her of the deal he had made. "There's money there, lots of it, and it won't be but two or three months and I'll have enough to send for you," he told her. She was pregnant with their first child.

The voyage across the Atlantic seemed interminable. It lasted nine days in conditions not much different from those endured by African slaves on their earlier crossings. Duke, Bill and seventeen other Welsh miners arrived in Hampton Roads and were immediately put on a train bound for a mining camp named Porterville. His wife and the daughter he had never seen were due to follow soon, arriving in Hampton Roads by cargo ship and then catching the next available train.

Considerably more than two or three months had passed after his arrival in West Virginia before Duke repaid the company for his own passage. It was only by drastically skimping on food, drink and other amenities that he was able to accumulate enough savings to finance his wife's fare. Even then, he needed another company loan to pay for the passage of their few belongings and the purchase of a bed.

Duke waited at the Porterville station three nights in a row before his wife finally arrived. But there was little joy to their reunion after two years—the daughter Duke had never seen was not with her.

"She had taken sick aboard the ship," Duke told Jim. "They said it was the fever. She died and they buried her at sea."

"I'm sorry, Duke," Jim said.

After that, Duke never again mentioned to Jim the death of his first daughter, and there was no discussion of any such tragedy during the high-spirited drinking sessions at Blakely's store. Most of the other regulars had also come from the depressed coalfields of Wales, and like Welshmen around the world who found themselves away from home, they banded together whenever they could for the inevitable Welsh blend of alcohol, fraternity and song.

At Blakely's, the monthly ritual was as precisely defined as any religious service, the drinking and singing lasting well into the night and concluding when, gathered in circles with their arms wrapped around one another, the misplaced men of Wales broke into an ancient dialect foreign to a non-Welshman's ears and sang in complex harmony the sacred anthems of their motherland. The hymns began softly but built to a shaking crescendo, the thin wooden walls of the store vibrating with the final measure while tears fell to the sawdust floor, mixing with the spilled ale and moonshine of the night.

"Duke, my lad, come in, come in," Blakely shouted from behind the counter when the truck from Porterville arrived with Jim, T.C. and the others on the night of Jim's first visit. "Your friend Lou has somethin' to show ya."

"Damn right I do," said Lou Greentree, a short, powerfully built American Indian who worked the Porter mines and was one of the few non-Welshmen granted admittance to the monthly Blakely's ritual. Lou, already well into his drink, turned from the coarse wooden counter, thrust his thick arms toward Duke and nearly tackled him in greeting.

"He's got a piece of Evans's thumb," said another drinking man, who then doubled over in laughter.

"His thumb?" Jim asked incredulously.

"Show it to 'em, Lou," said another.

The heavyset man fumbled in his pocket for a tattered handkerchief which was crudely wrapped around a cylindrical object. As the group around him stood silent and peered at his coal-stained hands, Lou slowly unrolled the fabric, revealing a bloody mess of flesh that indeed appeared to have once been the tip of a human thumb. As Lou related it, a miner named Evans had slipped while working on a mine motor and jammed his thumb into a gearbox. The steel gears ripped off the tip. Lou, in a manner not entirely clear, had acquired the remains.

"It deserves a decent burial, don't ya think?" he asked as Jim stared unbelievingly at the bloody tissue thrust before his eyes.

"A bagpipe dirge at the least," T.C. proposed, inspiring Lou to fall into a fit of hysterical cackling.

"Poor, poor Evans," one of the group shouted in a manner

suggestive of a chant. "He's a poor Welsh coal digger, and now he has no thumb."

"God help his thumb," another miner chimed in, hoisting his mug. "God help his thumb." Soon all fourteen men in Blakely's general store were at it, bellowing their irreverent requiem to Evans's late thumb. Jim, too, joined the chant, rather self-consciously at first. After a chorus more, T.C. cupped his fists to his mouth and hummed the long strains of a funeral dirge. Spontaneously the others lined up behind him and filed in an unlikely procession out Blakely's door, mugs swinging as they circled in the near darkness to a grassy patch at the store's rear. There, with the heels of heavy mining boots, they kicked open a small grave. Lou bent forward and ceremoniously dropped the dismembered thumb tip into the freshly dug crevice. Another mourner used the edge of a sole to scrape a layer of soil and cinders over the grave. T.C. fashioned a small cross from two twigs and poked it into the mound, and the group dispersed in an outburst of shouts and laughter.

Jim had never seen anything like it, not during his drunken escapades at school or even in the army. He liked what he saw —the irreverence of strong, sturdy workingmen who accepted life in its rawest form.

The melody of the dirge had been catchy, and Jim found himself whistling it as he and the others headed toward the front of the store. But his whistling ceased abruptly when he caught sight of a young woman whom at first he believed he had never seen before. She was long-legged and lithe, feline in her movements, with breasts and hips well defined even through the layers of her loose-fitting dress. Her complexion was soft pink in tint and without flaw, and her face was gentle in its curves except for high cheekbones that gave an almost exotic element to her beauty. Her long jet black hair ended just above her shoulders in the softest of curls. Her eyes were green and also catlike and expressive, as they were now in showing her delight at seeing the group of men approaching her. She broke into a huge smile, her face radiating a cheerful glow that communicated her affection for the now slightly drunk miners.

T.C. spotted her and moved quickly to her side. "Bonnie," he asked, "what are you doing here?"

She took his arm with one hand and pointed with the other toward Duke, saying, "It's not you I want but him."

Jim recognized her then as Duke's daughter.

"You," Bonnie said with exaggerated authority, jabbing a finger into her father's chest, "are leaving with me right now."

"But . . ." Duke started to protest.

"Ma wants you home early. No midnight business tonight."

Duke groaned and then shrugged. He turned to the group behind him. "See you later, men." There was a chorus of boos.

Bonnie stood on her toes to kiss T.C. on the cheek and then took her father by the arm to lead him away toward a car she had borrowed.

The Welshmen and their guests, their enthusiasm undiminished by their reduced number, returned inside Blakely's. Fresh ale was poured, and whiskey distributed. Good-natured ribbing and hearty laughter resumed their earlier levels, and the celebrants did whatever they could to make Jim, mine-owner's son or not, feel welcome. But Jim, although he smiled and made token attempts to join in the singing, felt alone and withdrawn. His remoteness stayed with him when, in the truck ride back to Porterville, the other mining men passed the time in a disjointed recital of Welsh ballads. Jim made no effort to join them, his mind preoccupied instead with Bonnie Shaw. He had a vague recollection of her having been in the town square for the veterans' homecoming celebration, but he had taken little notice of her. Now he wondered why. As the image of her beauty lingered, he felt jealous of T. C. Fenner, for obviously the two of them were seeing each other. Maybe they were in love. As his memory reached farther back in time, Jim could recall Bonnie only as a gawky teenager, flat-

53

chested, a bit plain, in fact, and somewhat of a nuisance. But that had been three . . . maybe four . . . years earlier. Obviously she, like Jim, had changed.

"Hey! You gotta sing if you're riding this truck, fella," Lou chided Jim after the seven other men in the cargo bin executed an uncoordinated finale to one of their songs.

"What's the matter with ya, ya too good to try an' carry a tune?" another man slurred, jabbing Jim in the ribs.

"I was just thinking," Jim replied.

"Thinking of what?" another man demanded. "Your ol' man's stocks and bonds?"

Jim stared at him. That was the first verbal swipe at his background the entire evening. "You want to know about stocks and bonds?" Jim asked back. "Hey, Kenny," he said, pounding the rear window of the truck's cab, "turn left at that next intersection."

"But that's Livingston. What the hell do we want in Livingston?" Lou asked.

"You'll find out, the whole drunken bunch of you. Just leave it to me," Jim replied.

The singing resumed, this time with Jim joining in, as the truck bounded over the rough road to Livingston. Soon the village's railroad depot was in sight. The Livingston station was larger and more ornate than the small shack in Porterville, and it summed up the differences between the two communities. Whereas rows of company houses, uniformly white, dominated the company town, Livingston was characterized by mansions as tall as three and four stories. The village claimed fourteen reputed millionaires, most of them mine-owners and the bankers, railroadmen and brokers who lived off them. Their mansions occupied the highest land. Below were the more modest homes of middle-level company managers. Lower still were the simple houses of chauffeurs, gardeners and others who filled the roles of servants in the big houses on the hilltops. There were three post offices in Livingston, one to serve each of the three distinct classes.

Although it was Saturday night, the streets of Livingston were deserted and dark except for the soft glow of light from gaslit lamps spaced several yards apart. Jim shouted instructions to the driver to take a narrow, winding gravel road that led from the depot to the area with the largest mansions.

"Where are we goin'?" someone asked.

"Just sit back and relax," Jim responded, hoping he would find at least one of the mansions free of its occupants for the night.

He grew nervous when he saw lights burning in each of the first three houses they passed, but then they came to a rambling mansion that was entirely blackened. It belonged to a banker, Raymond Baxley.

"Pull in here," Jim instructed. The battered truck moved up a circular driveway to the front portico. "You guys want a time of it, come on and follow me," he said, hopping off the truck and leading the file of staggering miners toward the rear of the home.

Like a silent Pied Piper, he took them across the wet manicured lawn toward the swimming pool. When they reached the water's edge, he stopped and looked at each of them. There were nine of them, counting Jim, and in an exchange of expressive glances they reached a consensus—moving as one, the group lifted Lou's arms and legs and heaved him into the pool. The slap of Lou's muscular body against the surface of the water broke the silence and was followed by an outburst of laughter, jeers and catcalls. Others were shoved or pulled into the water, and in a matter of seconds, all nine men were in the pool, splashing about like toddlers in a wading pond. Lou, playing his role as the "Injun," swam in a dog paddle from one end to the other, carrying a twig in his mouth as he would a knife. Jim, who was proving the most boisterous of the lot, began a series of geyser-producing cannonballs off the diving board. One miner, climbing out of the water, spotted the Baxleys' gazebo off in a corner of the lawn.

"What the hell is that?" he asked.

"A gazebo. Don't you have any class at all?" Jim replied.

"A ma-zee-po?" Lou asked incredulously. "What do you crazy white men do in that?"

"Sit and enjoy our afternoon tea," Jim said, laughing with the image of the nine men daintily cradling cups and saucers while seated on the gazebo's white benches.

The gaiety and horseplay continued, some of the men losing all or some of their clothing, until suddenly two flashlight beams lit up their faces. Like deer caught in a car's headlights, the miners froze.

"All right, get the hell out of that water," came a command. One of the men whispered that it sounded like the sheriff, Thad Carter.

The men, dripping wet and hurrying to dress, stumbled into a group at the edge of the pool.

"You're all under arrest. Jesus Christ, you should know better than to pull something like this," the sheriff said. Then he and his deputy moved forward, flashing their lights in the faces of each of the men. When he came to Jim, the sheriff froze. "Well I'll be goddamned. Jim Porter, what the hell are you doing here with this bunch?"

"They're a bad influence on me, Sheriff. That's the only way I can explain it," he responded with a straight face.

The others, outraged, began jeering and hooting their protests.

"All right, cut the crap," the sheriff shouted. He brought his fingers to his chin for a moment. "Look, why don't you just all climb back into that truck and get the hell out of here? I don't want to remember ever seeing anything here tonight except a couple of squirrels. Okay?"

The men were already racing back to the truck. Their singing did not resume until they had cleared the Livingston village limits and were well on their way back to Porterville. Jim, for his part, just hoped the sheriff wouldn't feel compelled to report the night's frolic to his father.

* * *

Jim and his parents were sitting in the first pew of the Porterville First Christian Church, the pew that had been used by the Porter family since the church was constructed. The Reverend Weatherson had grown more at home in the pulpit over the past few months and had discarded his use of prepared texts. On some Sundays the minister had surprisingly approached a point of eloquence in his sermon, but equally often, as was happening now, his preaching disintegrated into a disjointed harangue about sin, the devil and how badly the parish needed money. The sermon of the moment dwelt upon a number of vices, including illicit sex, infidelity, gambling and liquor. As he spoke, the clergyman repeatedly fixed his gaze on Augustus, and Jim noticed an odd smirk on Weatherson's face when he pronounced that sinners would duly pay for all the excessive drinking common to Coal County.

Jim's mind was not on the sermon. His attention was on the choir and one of its female soloists, Bonnie Shaw. She looked even more feminine and full of life in her church robe, he concluded. When she sang, her clear, powerful voice filled the church and touched every note perfectly.

When the service was over, Jim lingered outside the church, waiting for the choir members to store their robes. When Bonnie appeared at the door, he approached her and said, "I just wanted to compliment you on your singing. Your voice is beautiful. Have you been in the choir long?"

"About a year, I guess," Bonnie replied, looking bewildered at this approach by the mineowner's son.

"I'm Jim Porter," he said, feeling embarrassed as soon as the words left his mouth, for surely she knew who he was. "Can I walk you home?"

"I'd be honored," she replied.

There was an awkward silence as they began walking slowly through the hollow toward the Shaws' company home. Jim was conscious of other people watching them, some displaying envy, others scorn, at the mining girl who had captured the attention of the mineowner's son. A few waved or nodded to her, and she returned their greetings.

"It's a classic West Virginia Sunday morning, isn't it?" Jim said tentatively. "A crystal blue sky, soft wind, the smell of the trees. I wonder how long it will last."

"What does the *Farmer's Almanac* say?" she asked.

"I don't know—didn't get my copy."

She laughed. "Me neither. We can probably thank Ernie Jason for that."

"Did he string the mail bag upside down again?"

"Yep. Last week. The mail was scattered up and down a mile of track," she said, smiling.

Jim chuckled. They walked again in silence for a while. Her hair glistened in the bright sunlight and, when she bowed her head, fell softly over her face. When she looked at him, the green of her eyes seemed to glow, and when she smiled, her teeth were amazingly white.

"You just got back from the war, didn't you?" Bonnie commented nervously to break the silence. "I was at the homecoming celebration, although I doubt you remember me."

"Oh, I noticed you, all right," Jim lied. "You were with your pa."

"Did you have it tough in the army?"

"I'll tell you one thing, it got cold. Sometimes I thought my bones were frozen for good. And I had a first sergeant who wasn't too much of a pleasure. The guy was so strong he could do one hundred push-ups . . . with one arm."

"My pa could do that up until a few years ago. I don't know if he could reach a hundred, though."

"All I know is that I can't do one," he said, then found himself at a loss for more to say. "Actually," he said a few moments later, "the thing that really got to me was the isolation. You'd be on guard duty, say, and there'd be no one else around. The hours would seem like weeks, and you had nothing to do to pass the time except think. Sometimes my head felt like a hollow bowling ball."

Bonnie laughed. "Sometimes I get lonely too. But other times I enjoy being by myself. It's funny, what a difference there is between being alone and being lonely."

They had reached her house. Bonnie asked if he wanted to sit on the stoop awhile. Jim nodded, and they sat down. Bonnie looked wistfully at the mountain range in the distance and pointed to its highest pinnacle, Newcastle Peak. "Every once in a while I take a walk up to that peak," she said. "And whatever may be bothering me at the time just seems to float away."

"I love to be up in the mountains, too," Jim responded. "There's nothing quite like the way the muscles in your legs feel after you've made a climb. I love the smell of the trees and the cool water of the streams, and I tell you, there's nothing in the world like the taste of a brook trout that you stick in a fire minutes after you reel in your line."

"I never did that."

"Maybe someday I can show you how," he suggested.

"I'd like that," she said, smiling.

"Say, why don't you and I head to the hills for some berries? There're still plenty left, I hear."

Bonnie, seeming too excited or flattered for words, nodded energetically.

"Good," Jim said, rising. "Then I'll pick you up next Saturday."

Bonnie stood. Both smiled and, somewhat awkwardly, shook hands.

The forsythia bushes were the first to bloom in the Coal County foothills, painting the countryside with a striking band of yellow. Redwood bushes and maple, dogwood and wahoo trees followed with the subtle creams and pinks of their blossoms. Later came the daisies and lilies of the valley. By late May wild blueberry patches showed evidence of their fruit, and not much later wild strawberries, blackberries, gooseberries and huckleberries began to ripen. Then, the housewives of Coal County trekked en masse to the hillsides to fill their baskets with berries and hickory nuts while their sons and husbands sometimes worked veins of coal directly below. The annual harvest was brief, and with most of it completed, Bonnie and Jim found themselves alone in the foothills.

"Of course, it's too late to get any *decent* berries," the young woman chided as she swung an empty basket and trailed Jim's tall figure up a narrow footpath through the thick underbrush, his dog, Samson, limping behind them.

"Oh, there're still plenty around. You just have to know where to look for them. And good tasters, too," he replied, waiting for her to catch up to him so he could take hold of her arm.

Two weeks had passed since Jim found himself transfixed by Duke Shaw's nineteen-year-old daughter outside Blakely's. She seemed so different from the young women he had known in Livingston, the daughters of bankers, brokers and mineowners he had pursued since his first date as an adolescent.

Bonnie spotted a small patch of yellowed grass among the boulders and thorny brush. "Let's stop for awhile," she suggested. Spreading her plain skirt under her, she flopped down, allowing the still-empty basket to roll to the side.

"I love the summer," Jim said, sitting to the side of her. "It renews the spirit."

"Oh, early spring's the best," she contradicted. "That's when nature comes to life."

"It's too soggy and slow for my taste, and when you look around, you see faces still pale from the long, dreary winter. Humans need sun. Do you know it's not even July and already your cheeks are sunburned?"

She blushed. "Well, yours aren't. Can't you men do something to get rid of that coal from your skin? There's a big black stripe right across your forehead."

Jim was aware of the band of black embedded in his skin. He had noticed it in the mirror, right where the front edge of his mining cap crossed his forehead, and no amount of scrubbing could eliminate it completely. He continued to labor side by side with Bonnie's father and taking what for him was an unprecedented pleasure in the feeling of levity brought on by stiffened muscles and expended sweat. He had begun to relish his daily regimen of manual labor as a source of tranquillity, both physical and mental. He was also learning the business of mining. Now he wanted to learn more about a miner's daughter.

Although it was Bonnie's striking beauty that had first attracted him, Jim now found himself intrigued by her spunk and sense of humor. Her banter revealed high intelligence and a wide-ranging knowledge which far exceeded her schooling.

"Come on, let's climb," he said, reaching for her hand and helping her to her feet. They resumed their walk, climbing upward until, a few minutes later, both were out of breath. They reached an unstated mutual decision to pause again and moved from the shady path to take seats on the trunk of a fallen tree in the middle of a patch of sun. As Bonnie carefully arranged her dress beneath her, Jim studied her face. Her beauty was enhanced by the sunlight, the harshness of which would have betrayed the flaws in a less attractive woman. Bonnie did not rely on cosmetics to provide the smoothness and healthy tone of her complexion.

"I've seen you with T. C. Fenner. Is he your boyfriend?" Jim asked, a bit astonished at his own boldness.

"A friend, yes. And a good man."

"We were teammates once at school. He's a good fielder, as I remember, but I didn't get to really know him."

"Well, he's already asked me to . . . ah . . . go to Philadelphia," Bonnie said, the pace of her words changing abruptly in mid-sentence as if she had wanted to say something and then changed her mind.

"You've never been to Philadelphia?" Jim asked, unsure of what else he could say.

"I'm not the daughter of some rich mineowner," Bonnie shot back, a smile on her face contradicting the biting challenge of her inflection and words.

"What's that supposed to mean?" Jim asked with unconcealed irritation. That the resentment he sometimes encountered in the mine might surface in Bonnie hurt him.

Bonnie blushed. "I didn't quite mean that the way it sounded," she said softly, reaching for a twig to roll in her fingers. "It's just that people with money are so different from my family and me. It's hard for me to imagine what it's like, to eat from imported china and drink from crystal. At my home, we even share the meat knife."

Jim was shaking his head. "We're not as rich as you may think. Anyway, with the state of the economy, mineowners are having their troubles, too. You have no idea what it's like."

"But you'll survive," she said, the belligerence returning to her voice. "And I can't say that much about us—with any certainty, at least."

Her combativeness made her appear even more catlike. Despite the bite of her words, Jim found her aggressive nature appealing. "Can I ask you something?"

"Sure."

"If we Porters are so different, why did you agree to come up here with me?"

She spoke slowly, weighing her words. "I could say, 'I don't know,' but it wouldn't be exactly truthful."

"Then tell me the truth," he said.

"Okay. I've never been approached by the son of a mineowner before. I was flattered . . . and curious."

He reached out and began patting the top of her head as if measuring a punch. "Well, beware, young lady—we sons of mineowners can be very vicious and mean. Why, I've already kidnapped seven women and carried them off to my castle on the hill."

"Now cut that out!" she ordered, chuckling. "Come on, let's go."

They had nearly reached the top of the ridge. As they continued the final few yards toward a plateau, the wind began to kick up, sending Bonnie's long black hair splaying behind her. Jim pulled her behind him, and they trotted through a clearing in the brush to a nearby brook, Samson barking at their heels. The water was less than a foot deep and only fifteen feet or so from bank to bank. As they reached the water's edge, Jim dropped to his knees, pulling her alongside him. He broke a twig from a thornbush and tossed it into the brook. The thin piece of branch swirled in place for a moment and then began to float downstream with the slow current.

"Let's say that's a ship," he said, pointing to the twig. "One of the great oceangoing liners on her way to France. And you and me . . . well, let's pretend it's some twenty years from now and we've been married all that time, with kids, you know, and a dog and a pony—"

"Wait a minute, mister . . . aren't you getting a little ahead of yourself?" she interrupted.

He looked at her with an expression of contrived shock. "What's the matter with you, can't you pretend?" he chided. "Anyway," he went on, returning his gaze to the twig, now several feet away from them, "there, on the first-class deck, that's you and me. We're holding hands, just like this." He tightened his grip. "And I'm in my smoking jacket and you're in your gown. And in seven days, we're going to arrive in France. There'll be dancing in Paris and parties and dinners. And finally, when we're alone—" Jim shot forward suddenly, wrapped his arms around her and kissed her lips.

Bonnie pushed him away. She jumped to her feet. "I'll get you for this!" she yelled in a rage Jim wasn't sure was mock

63

or real. He, too, sprang to his feet and, with Bonnie in pursuit, scampered through the brush, hurdling fallen trees and dodging boulders until he found himself splashing through the brook, its cool water sending chills through his soaked feet. Bonnie, bent with laughter at the sight, stood at the water's edge and derisively pointed toward her prey. Jim began walking slowly downstream. After a few yards he darted out of sight. For more than a minute Bonnie heard nothing.

"Jim?" she called out in almost a whisper. Then louder: "Jim? Where are you? Are you all right?"

As quickly as he had disappeared, Jim sprang from a copse of willows at Bonnie's side, splashing her with water. Bonnie brought her hands to her eyes and screamed. "You're terrible!" she shouted, turning and sprinting back toward the footpath.

Jim easily caught up with her, and as the two of them made their way down the hillside, they were silent, walking hand in hand, the energy of their silliness having passed.

When they had nearly reached the bottom, Bonnie asked, "I heard you won a medal in the army just like your brother. How does it feel to be a hero?"

"I'm no war hero," Jim replied with a pained expression.

"You won yourself a medal, didn't you?"

"But for what? Catching a tiny slice of metal on the side of my face, that's all. Getting a Purple Heart for that bordered on fraud."

"It sounds like you're bitter."

"Let's just say nobody in this country seems to give much of a damn." His eyes grew distant, and he turned his thoughts for a minute to the friends he had lost in combat, the senseless brutality of the forced marches in the cold and the snow. "You know, my mother cared. When I came home, I found a map she had cut from the paper and taped to the door of her closet."

Sarah had drawn a thick red line with a crayon on the

map across the thirty-eighth parallel. From the disjointed wire service dispatches in the Bannerton *Tribune* and the spotty information relayed over the radio news broadcasts, she attempted to plot the progress of the war. But the front moved in wiggly lines without a pattern, up and down and then back up again. Soon the map's midsection became a maze of incomprehensible pencil marks.

"She gave up finally," Jim said, "and decided that the only thing that mattered was whether or not I got home."

"That's the same thing my father told T.C.," Bonnie said. "Individual survival."

"You know, Bonnie, I envy your father."

"What do you mean?"

"It seems like everything in his life is so neat and tidy. He knows exactly what he wants, where he's going and who he's going to take along."

"And you?"

"Right now I don't know what the hell I want to do with my life."

Bonnie laughed. "Me neither, Jim. Me neither." Her eyes widened as she, too, withdrew to her thoughts. Jim stared at her, noticing again how rich her hair was and how totally feminine were her appearance and demeanor. Her bearing, her voice, her movements all told of an inner strength, an awareness and a raw sensuality absent from all those women roosting under dryers in the Livingston beauty salon. On the surface, her likes and dislikes, values and goals seemed as simple as the way of life she was born into, yet he sensed underneath great complexity and ambiguity, a person as challenged and confused by the mysteries of life as he.

Bonnie's voice was soft. She spoke slowly. "Sometimes I fantasize that there I am on center stage in Nashville, singing and playing my guitar and a long, long way from Coal County. And the next minute I'm thinking that it is right here that I belong, washing dishes, raising kids, watching my family grow. It's confusing and frustrating, and sometimes it makes me so mad I want to kick the wall. But I know that one day soon I'll wake up and BANG!" She pounded a fist into the palm of her other hand. "The answer will be there. And, Jim, I bet the same thing will happen to you."

"I hope so." He took her hand and walked her home.

Rain splattered off the wooden roof of the Red Fox Mine bathhouse as Jim prepared for the shift, removing his outer clothing and stuffing them into a wire basket hanging by a chain from the ceiling. The large, flat room was filled with other men doing the same.

"Somebody shot Injun Lou's hound dog last week," said a voice in a corner of the dressing area. "He figured it was this here farmer, and the next night the farmer's barn burned to the ground." There was a soft round of knowing laughter. "The next morning I see the Indian and ask 'im, 'Hey, Lou, you fling a few arrows last night?' He didn't say nothin'. Only smiled. So I asked 'im, 'Well, ya figure that barn makes it even for the dog?' He smiles and says, 'Hell, no. There's still eighteen head of cattle out there that gotta go.'"

The laughter grew louder, Jim joining it, the roomful of men all smiles. "You don't wanna mess with Injun Lou's puppy dog," the storyteller yelled. Several others nodded in agreement, and Lou, who had listened to the tale without changing his expression, was grinning broadly now.

Like an athletic locker room, the mine bathhouse was filled with gossip and good-natured banter, talk of women and gambling and baseball teams, small talk and storytelling that stemmed from blood-thick camaraderie. Although he had yet to take part in much of it, Jim loved to listen, relishing in particular the mixture of diverse accents which somehow came together in a common dialect peculiar to the region. The polyglot mining men had come from almost every nation in Europe—Wales, Ireland and Scotland, England, Spain and Italy, Russia, Poland and Czechoslovakia—and unlike immigrants in New York and the other large cities of America,

Coal County's immigrants intermingled, joining the third- and fourth-generation Virginians already present in the mountains, the Indians who had always been there and the blacks who had arrived on their own accord or otherwise. From this fusion came a vocabulary as rich and colorful as any dialect in the nation. It seemed as if no mining tool, kitchen utensil or flower were without a special name unique to the mountains. The exception was coal. Federal agents were revenuers, and company scrip, flickers, but coal was simply coal. From the many tongues that contributed to the mountain language, none provided a suitable substitute for that short, earthy word.

In the West, cowboys assigned dozens of names to the livestock they handled. Trainmen had a long list of indignities with which they described their locomotives. Soldiers collected a multitude of choice words to salute their enemies. But the mining men of West Virginia did not tamper with the word "coal." Coal was the source of their sustenance, and as such, it commanded reverence, devotion and respect. Nature had laid it into the mountains, and men pulled it out. Simplicity. And it was this—the simplicity—more than anything that appealed to Jim as five and six days a week he reported to the Red Fox Mine.

The work already had inlaid gray and black stains into the skin of his hands, a tarnish which resisted even the bar of Octagon soap he applied nightly. Whether or not his father had noticed the discoloration he didn't know, for Augustus had not again raised the issue of Jim's working in the mine. At dinner, virtually the only time the three family members were together, all avoided any mention of Jim's newfound occupation. But a few times, when Jim and Sarah were alone, his mother questioned him about what he was doing.

"Are you sure it's the right thing?" she asked. "I get worried something's going to happen to you."

"Come on, Ma. I'm in there with people who know what they're doing. Nothing's going to happen," he responded.

Jim's experiment attracted interest and support from one unlikely source: Jenny, the cook. She seemed to understand his motivation.

"I like what you're doin', Jimmy. Does a man good to get his hands dirty, especially when he's young," she told him.

Jim was loading his own coal now, using a pick to bust up the larger chunks and then scooping the smaller pieces into a low, flat railcar, often working from his knees. When the car was full, he reached to the bib pocket of his coveralls for an oversized safety pin holding several round metal tags bearing his work number, removed one and hung it on a special hook at the rear of the car. This was how a miner's pay was determined. After the motorman collected the filled cars and pulled them to the outside of the shaft, the dispatcher or one of his aides removed the metal tags and turned them over to the paymaster. The number of tags accumulated in a week recorded the number of tons of coal a man had removed and, thus, his pay. Although Jim was going through the motions of hanging his tag on the coal cars he filled, as the son of the mineowner he received no pay.

Jim pulled on his coveralls and removed his watch, which he placed between folds of clothing packed into his wire basket. The chain connected to the basket extended in a pulley system across the ceiling to the other side of the bathhouse. He walked to the opposite wall, pulled the dangling end of the chain and secured it to a metal bar with a small padlock. The action raised the basket out of reach toward the ceiling, leaving his personal possessions protected from thievery. The men told him this was merely a precaution, thievery in the bathhouse being virtually nonexistent.

Some of the miners had begun to file from the bathhouse toward the mine's portal while stragglers still went about the securing of their baskets. Jim joined the procession, which came to a stop at a large board just outside the mine's entrance. There were two lights on the board, one red, the other green. The red bulb was burning now, signifying that the mine's safety engineer was still inside, making his daily inspection. Until he returned, the men would have to wait.

It continued to rain heavily, but the men did little to shelter themselves from the downpour, experience telling them they would get wet in the mine anyway. Their caps and thick denim jackets warded off some of the wetness, and their boots were theoretically waterproof. Jim had learned, however, that by the shift's end, he would be soaked to the bone.

As he looked around, Jim noticed that another new miner, Clem Hawkins, had isolated himself from the others, as he had done daily for more than two weeks. Because each man was dependent on the next for the safety of his life, there generally was goodwill within a mine's work force. But sometimes the bathhouse banter went too far, crossing a certain line and leading to fistfights and other violence. Hawkins had been a victim of such a showdown, but it had been his own doing.

A muscle-bound, sandy-haired twenty-two-year-old marine veteran, Hawkins had joined the Red Fox day shift a month earlier, along with Jim and T. C. Fenner, one of the few newcomers. Hawkins had an unconcealed hatred for blacks. Despite this—or perhaps because of it—Crawford's assistant manager had assigned Hawkins to the same crew as Will Thomason, who was black.

Thomason was extremely popular among the men not only because he was very likable but also because he operated a backwoods still which produced a very fine corn whiskey, the best bootleg in the county. He was a veteran at mining, forty-five years old and almost as wide as he was tall, weighing—Jim guessed—at least 280 pounds.

"Nothin' more I like than whompin' the tar out of some damned nigger," the loud-voiced Hawkins declared with a smirk during one of his first days on the job. "They ain't at home 'less they're chewin' bananas and swingin' from trees." Similar barbs followed, all targeted at Thomason, but the big black man let them slide. None of the other miners who heard Hawkins's insults responded, for each knew that when the time was proper, Thomason himself would handle the matter.

"Don't know how much longer Will's going to listen to that crap," Duke told Jim after they had reached their work-site in the mine one day. "I'm going to feel very sorry for that Hawkins boy when Thomason's decided he's had enough."

A few hours later, when the crew reached daylight again, they noticed several foremen and engineers gathered at the cargo bed of a long tractor-trailer truck. Resting on the flat trailer was a new motor for one of the mine's trains. It appeared to weigh 300 pounds or more, and the engineers were puzzled by how to get it off the truck without using a block and tackle, which the poorly equipped Red Fox lacked. Thomason, at last, saw his opportunity. As the day and night crews watched in silent awe, the portly black man gripped the motor in his fat fists, drew a deep breath, grunted loudly, gently lifted the hulk of blue-painted steel off the truck and eased it to the ground. A few seconds passed before he straightened his back. Then he walked directly toward the brash Hawkins, who had been standing to the side.

"That there was nothin', boy, ya see?" Thomason said, a huge grin on his face. "You jist learnt yerself a lesson, understand?"

Hawkins nodded meekly, and in the two weeks since the incident, he said little to his co-workers. Even as the day crew waited silently in the rain, he kept apart—and far, far away from Will Thomason.

The safety engineer emerged from the mine and switched off the red light in favor of the green. The men, many of them climbing aboard coal cars, moved through the portal.

Scooping the coal from a crouched position at first had been brutal to Jim's back, but after a few days his muscles began to adjust. The work became routine, second nature, allowing Jim to muse for long, uninterrupted stretches. What was on his mind was Bonnie. He was unable to stop thinking about her, and each time he conjured up the image of her face and nubile figure, his insides tingled, and he was filled with a longing to see her. No woman had ever affected him in this way.

Jim was on his hands and knees next to Duke and was thinking of Bonnie when another man on the crew prepared to ignite his squibs. Duke had to warn Jim twice to take cover from the blast.

"You can't daydream, son," the older man scolded him, "or you're going to put somebody's life on the line, probably your own."

"I'm sorry. I'll try to be careful," Jim responded, knowing he couldn't very well tell Duke he was preoccupied with thoughts about his daughter.

"My God, Jim, the last time I saw a man daydreaming like that, he went off and eloped the next morning. What's bothering you?"

"Nothing, Duke. Honest."

"Well, let's get to work. Here," Duke said, extending his hand. In it were a half dozen squibs. He then handed Jim a blasting powder bucket and moved away.

Jim, carefully fingering the squibs, broke into a huge grin. His being equipped with squibs and blasting powder signaled that in the judgment of Duke and the other men he was ready for his own share of the face to blast. He had completed his apprenticeship and passed his probation. The mineowner's son was now a fully credentialed miner. But no one offered his congratulations. No one shook Jim's hand. Veteran miners did not get excited over such things, and this day in the mine was to be like any other.

It wasn't for Jim, however. The rest of the shift passed with an agonizing slowness. He longed to tell someone of his just completed rite of passage and to share the good feelings brought by that accomplishment. He needed Bonnie. She was the daughter of a miner and, unlike his father or any of his young, well-heeled female acquaintances in Livingston, was certain to understand the reason for his enthusiasm and pride. The fall carnival was due in Porterville the next day. He would ask her to join him.

CHAPTER 3 _____

The special train assigned to carry the carnival arrived in Porterville from Kalb County shortly after 9:00 A.M. The carnival crews were expert at assembling their rigs, and the carousel, game booths and other attractions all were in place by noon. The carnival was sponsored by the railroad not only for the profits it produced by itself but for the increased ridership it generated as people came from surrounding towns. Passable roads were still few in mountainous Coal County, and those that existed were usually little more than a bed of gravel or two parallel dirt ruts. Equally rare, among the miners at least, were cars. So when the carnival came to Porterville, those coming from Bannerton and other Coal County communities were apt to travel on special shuttle trains scheduled for the day.

The ritual of preparing the carnival remained unchanged from town to town. As the work crews began erecting the merry-go-round and other rides, the carnival chief paid a traditional courtesy call on the local mineowner. In past times this visit had been more than a customary paying of respect, for the chief had to ensure that the mineowner would agree to exchange the company's monetary scrip collected during the affair for federal currency. The negotiating of the exchange rate often involved hard bargaining, sometimes leading to an irreconcilable dispute that concluded with the carnival men's dismantling their gear as quickly as they had erected it and hurriedly departing the town. In those days Augustus Porter, and his father before him, drove a hard bargain, but they always bent sufficiently to keep the carnival in town, each considering it a necessary gesture toward the morale of the miners and their families.

The Porter Coal Company no longer issued scrip, so the exchange rate had ceased to be a consideration, but the carnival chief still reported to the Porter mansion to pay his respects to Augustus. Jim passed him on the porch as he left to pick up Bonnie at the Shaws' home.

At the square, youngsters were already queued up at the ticket stand for the carousel. The merry-go-round was small by city standards, but it was the carnival's main attraction. Activity was brisk at the other rides as well. The townspeople used the carnival as an opportunity to set up their own profit-making booths and contests, and hammers pounded on both sides of Main Street and throughout the square as the one-day entrepreneurs put the finishing touches on their stalls. Judges had begun to assemble at the sites of various baking and handicraft contests. And at the baseball diamond, which was laid out in a farmer's pasture on a small square of flatland in an adjoining hollow, the local Porter team warmed up before taking on their archrivals from the Owens mines. No matter who won, the game was certain to end in a brawl, and already the out-of-town umpire was scanning the spectator area with nervous eyes.

The shouts of the youngsters, the hammering at the stalls and the music from the rides could be heard through the thin walls of the Shaws' home as Bonnie was giving her hair a final brushing. T. C. Fenner had asked her to the carnival, and it had not been easy for her to turn him down. But she did, regretting the hurt that appeared on his face when she told him. To herself, she conceded it was probably a mistake for her to join Jim at T.C.'s expense—Jim's interest in her was surely just a whim, and a sensible young woman would make it a point to be especially careful about destroying a relationship with a man such as T.C., who, in her circumstances, was a good candidate for a husband. As she tried to analyze her reaction to Jim's sudden pursuit of her, she found herself both intrigued by him and flattered—like any other miner's daughter, she had never envisioned herself on a date with the mineowner's son. But more than that, she was very attracted to him, finding him very handsome with his sharp facial features and tall, lean physique, and suspecting he had more substance than a spoiled rich man's boy. She had already opened herself up to him on their excursion to the foothills, revealing her fantasies and thus making herself vulnerable. And her heart told her that this was okay, for he, too, had seemed to be honest in relating his confusion about the future, a confusion she shared.

While Bonnie straightened her pastel blue shirtwaist, she heard her parents having a discussion in the kitchen. Then Duke came into the parlor and moved to his daughter's side. "Do you want to talk about it, honey?" he asked softly.

"Talk about what, Pa?"

"About you . . . and Jim Porter."

"What do you mean?"

Duke raised his voice slightly. "It's not right, Bonnie. I don't want to meddle in your affairs, and Jim seems like a nice lad, but you've got to be very careful—"

"Oh, Pa," she interrupted. "We're not exactly getting married in the morning. I've only seen him once before this. And besides, I'm not a little girl anymore, even if you are my father."

"Listen," Duke said sharply, "I know these Porters well

75

enough to tell you Jim is not at all ready to settle down. He's interested in raising some hell for a while until he gets tied down with the company. He's always been on the wild side, and I don't think it's wise you seeing him."

"I don't agree," Liz declared, entering the room. "If Jim Porter wants to take an interest in Bonnie, then I don't see anything wrong with it. She's old enough to use her head and—"

A knock at the door stopped her. Bonnie smiled in relief and went to greet Jim.

"Hi," she said cheerfully, catching his eyes and then admiring his loose-fitting plaid shirt and khaki pants.

His expression was grave. "I want to apologize to you about the other day and the berries."

"The berries?" she asked, frowning.

"Yes. We didn't find any, did we?"

Her smile returned. "Well, I guess it proves I was right all along. Now don't ask me not to rub it in."

"You do and I'll find a way to get even. We rich are mean and vicious, don't you know?"

"Now stop that," she snapped. "Can't we try being friends and have a good time?"

"That's just what I had in mind," he said, taking her hand. "How about we take a look at the baseball game?"

"Fine. I'm in the mood for a laugh."

Still holding hands, they stepped away from the Shaws' home.

Like many mineowners, Augustus Porter placed great importance on his company's baseball team, assigning team members easy jobs at the mines and occasionally trading with other companies for players in positions that needed to be strengthened. He had just acquired the services of a heralded outfielder from another mining operation 200 miles away in Jackson. Jim told Bonnie he knew without asking that his father undoubtedly had bet heavily on the outcome of the game, his interest boosted by his longtime rivalry with the

Owens company and its owner, John Owens.

The game was a pitchers' duel for eight innings, but in the top of the ninth, the visiting Owens club scored on a play involving a disputed umpire's call.

"Thank God the old man's not here," Jim told Bonnie, "or he'd have that ump lynched before sundown."

When the Porter team failed to match the run in their half of the inning, dozens of raging spectators, many of them already intoxicated, stormed the playing field. Jim pulled Bonnie to safety as the Owens players ran pell-mell from the fists, stones and liquor bottles hurled toward them. As far as they could tell, no one was injured seriously, and Bonnie and Jim were laughing about the predictability of the yearly fracas as they joined the others heading back to the carnival.

The remainder of the afternoon passed quickly, Jim and Bonnie merging lunch and dinner into a series of stops at the variety of food booths. By the time the sun set Porterville was packed with people and the festive sounds of the carnival filled the night air.

"This reminds me of scenes from *Tale of Two Cities* or *Oliver Twist*," Bonnie said as they pushed their way into the crowd. "You know, the narrow London streets full of people. Around here you're usually lucky if you see more than a dozen persons on the streets in a day."

"You're not putting down metropolitan Porterville, are you?" Jim asked.

"No. But it's not exactly Paris or New York." Her voice grew softer. "I know you've been all over the world but I've never been to any city bigger than Bannerton."

"Not even Charleston?"

"Jim, I've never even been out of this county. But some day, if I'm lucky, that's going to change. Anyway, I hope so."

Jim squeezed her hand. "I can tell you one thing—you'd be the best looking lady on Fifth Avenue."

"Thank you, sir. Tell me more." She laughed.

Everyone seemed to know Bonnie, and most waved or

shouted their greetings to her. She, in turn, whispered to Jim who they were. For some reason, perhaps the gaiety of the festivities, there was none of the staring that had been directed toward her the first time she walked side by side with Jim Porter in public.

A fiddle suddenly came to life in one corner of the square. Like a bugle call, it immediately attracted a gathering. The fiddler played a simple four-bar melody and stopped, where-upon another played the same tune right back to him in the first fiddling contest of the day.

"That's nothing," Jim said while he and Bonnie rushed with the crowd toward the fiddling. "Even I could play that."

"Give them time," Bonnie responded. "That's old man Quincy, and there's no one who can touch him in the county."

Bonnie was right. The melodies fiddled by the scrawny and bearded old man grew more and more complicated, and his opponent, a stranger who looked twenty years younger, began to strain to match them. At last the stranger fumbled a melody. Even on a second try he was unable to master Quincy's challenge beyond the third measure. A whoop went up from the partisan gathering, and the old man, emotion absent from his face, nodded in a token bow.

As the next two contestants stepped to the center of the crowd, Bonnie spotted T.C. He was sitting under a tree in a secluded area of the square. From the awkwardness of his movements and the jug sitting at his feet, she judged that he was well into his drink. When he saw her, he glared and turned his head away.

"I'll be back in a minute," Bonnie whispered to Jim. She walked over to T.C., whose face was red from a combination of liquor and anger.

"I don't suppose you care"—he scowled at her—"but I won the damn bird. I did it, goddammit."

"That's terrific, honey," Bonnie said, bending to kiss him.

"I'm proud of you, really I am." She looked up. Jim, appearing irritated, was now at their side.

T.C., his head propped against the trunk of the tree, narrowed his eyes at Jim but then raised his right hand limply and said, "How ya doin', pal? You enjoyin' this here little girl?"

Bonnie turned to Jim. "T.C. won the turkey shoot just like he did last year."

"Congratulations," Jim said, pumping the other man's right hand.

"Yep. I traded in the bird for this," T.C. said, raising the jug slightly. "It's some of Thomason's best." He paused. "What the hell, pal—here, have some."

Jim accepted the jug, curled his thumb into its looped handle and raised it over his open mouth. Three large swallows later he lowered it, wiped his mouth with the back of his hand and returned it. T.C. took a long swig and then looked at Bonnie, his lips growing into a snide smile. He pushed the jug toward her. "Here, drink," he ordered.

Under mountain country mores, a woman who had borne a child could drink or smoke anything she pleased, and it was not unusual to see a matron nursing moonshine while puffing a pipe. But unmarried females were forbidden to touch either vice—except on carnival day, when wine punch flowed freely at the food and handicraft booths. Bonnie had had her share of the punch already and didn't want to drink any more, but T.C. insisted. "Come on, I said, have yourself a little swig," he ordered again.

She took the jug. Following Jim's lead, she tried to hook her thumb into the handle and cradle the container in the nook of her bent arm, but the jug rolled away. So she gripped its bottom with both hands and tipped the jug to her mouth. She hadn't taken half a swallow when she suddenly dropped the vessel and began to gag, bending over with her hands clutching her throat. T.C. began laughing hysterically. Jim chuckled.

When T.C. recovered from his chortling, he rose drunkenly to his feet and placed a hand on one of Jim's shoulders. "Ain't she somethin', my friend?" he asked in a slow, slurred voice. "You know she and me are gonna get married."

Jim's eyes focused hard on the miner. "Think I'll be on my way," he said. "Maybe check some of those booths on Main Street." As he turned to leave, Bonnie grabbed him by the arm.

"Give me just a minute," she whispered.

After Jim departed, Bonnie scolded T.C. "You've had enough, so go home now before you do something you'll regret," she told him.

He stared at her intensely for a moment. "Ah, the hell with it," he said, turning his head. "Go on off and play with that little rich boy." He turned his back and stumbled away into the crowd. Bonnie hurried in the opposite direction to rejoin Jim. She felt both angry and guilty but decided she would sort out her feelings about T.C. later.

"Guess he's been doing some celebrating," Jim commented when she was again at his side.

"T.C. is a good man. He very seldom gets drunk like that," she said, somewhat defensively.

"Well," he responded, taking her by the hand, "T.C. won himself a turkey. How would you like a duck?"

"A duck? What would I do with a duck?"

"What does anyone do with a duck? Wring its neck and eat it," he said. Bonnie cringed. "If you feel that way about it, you can keep it as a pet, a good-luck pet," he went on. "Let's go."

He led her to a roped-off area where a local man named Salerno was barking, "Ducks! Three throws to win a duck." Jim paid ten cents, and Salerno handed him three rings fashioned from stiffened rope. He then moved to a line painted onto the street's gravel and focused his eyes on a wooden trough of water four paces away. Inside the trough were eight live ducks. Whoever managed to throw a ring around a duck's neck was entitled to take the bird away.

Jim studied the nearly motionless ducks carefully for several seconds before, in an underhanded motion, he let the first ring fly. It was well aimed, heading directly for the cluster of swimming birds, but at the last possible moment the appointed target lowered its head abruptly to the water's surface and avoided the oncoming ring.

"Damn!" Jim shouted in mock rage. "We'll get him now."

His second shot resulted in a repeat performance, as did the third. "You know," Jim said, turning to Bonnie, "I think I hate those ducks. Give me another three," he demanded of Salerno.

Bonnie tried to conceal her smile as Jim increased his concentration but to no avail. He spent the next twenty minutes carefully tossing the rings only to have the birds lower their heads. By now a crowd had gathered to observe the mine-owner's son who refused to give up.

"One more time," Jim said, handing Salerno another dime.

His concentration had lapsed—he was clearly angry now—and he threw the rings almost randomly. The first missed the water trough entirely, but the second was right on target. The intended victim, as was now automatic, ducked, but the ring bounced off its back and slipped over the head of an adjacent, unsuspecting bird.

"We got him!" Jim shouted as Bonnie rushed to his side to throw her arms around him. "I won the damn duck!" He discarded the unthrown third ring and waited while Salerno grudgingly went to the trough and removed the unfortunate duck with the ring around its neck. At Jim's insistence, he tied a cord to the bird's neck, and Jim strutted away, to the applause of the crowds, with Bonnie at his side and the duck waddling behind them.

"I told you I'd get you a duck," he boasted, placing his free arm around her shoulders.

"Big deal," she teased.

"Hey," he shot back, stopping. "You don't seem to understand. This duck is going to be your best friend. You can take him with you to Nashville, put him right up there on the stage. Here, take him." He handed her the tether. She accepted it reluctantly, feeling embarrassed at the attention they were still getting from others in the crowded street.

"The way I figure it," Bonnie told him, "you just spent more than two dollars for a duck Salerno probably would have sold you for a quarter at the end of carnival day." She laughed and looked toward Jim—but he wasn't there. In a moment she understood why: Augustus Porter was making his way through the crowd in their direction.

"Good evening, Major Porter. We've got some great pie here, sir, a prizewinner," a woman said to the mineowner from inside one of the baking booths.

"Thanks, but I've already had my fill," Augustus replied, half smiling. "I'm sure it's the best, however."

Bonnie watched him reach into his pocket, remove a silver flask and take a drink. He then made his way to the church booth where Mrs. Porter was assisting other women in the selling of raffle tickets. Bonnie had not noticed the mineowner's wife and wondered if Jim intentionally had avoided that booth. After giving Sarah a peck on her cheek, Augustus resumed circulating through the crowd.

The walk through the carnival was an Augustus Porter tradition. In his younger days he had participated in many of the carnival events, including the baseball game and the turkey shoot. Now he merely strolled, sipping unabashedly from his flask and accepting the greetings from his miners and their families.

"Pssst," Jim signaled to Bonnie once his father had passed. "Let's get away from here." He took her hand, and the two of them fled the carnival area toward the deserted end of Main Street.

"My father looks like he's getting himself into a good mood, but the last thing I need right now is for him to see me walking down Main Street with a duck waddling behind me on a leash," Jim said as they walked, laughing.

She stopped him. "Are you sure it's not that you don't want to be seen with me?"

Jim, searching for the words, did not answer her immediately. "I won't lie to you," he said finally. "Let's just say my father wouldn't be satisfied with me marrying any woman less than a European princess. But that's my worry, not yours." He pulled her forward again.

"In here," he said when they had reached the church. He led her up the wooden steps and through the unlocked door. "He'll never find us in here. My father hates church." She looked at him in surprise but unhesitatingly followed him inside, where he opened a smaller door, revealing a shaky ladder connecting with the belfry. A pigeon flapped its wings loudly as they climbed to the top, Bonnie cradling the duck. Jim took the bird and tied its tether to the ladder's top, and they pushed past the single bell to peer through the belfry's slatted windows. Beneath them they could see most of the carnival spread through the center of town and listen to the sounds of the distant fiddling rising above the rumble of the crowd. Except for that and an occasional rush of wind, the belfry was eerily quiet.

"T.C. said the two of you are going to get married," Jim commented almost matter-of-factly as he continued to stare out the window.

Bonnie turned to look at him. The light from the streetlamps coming through the window was soft and as it passed through the slats painted horizontal shadows across his face. With no one standing near him for comparison, he seemed less imposing than he normally did, and in the yellowish light his face had a boyish quality. He appeared vulnerable, even scared, and for the first time she felt sympathetic toward him.

"T.C. did ask me to marry him," she said, speaking softly and slowly. "Several times, in fact. And I . . . well, I just haven't given him an answer."

Jim's expression remained unchanged. Pointing to a lone figure staggering on the street below, he said, "There he is now." They saw T.C. stumble into a light post and crumple to the ground. Bonnie couldn't watch anymore. She turned her head away and rapped her knuckles against the bronze bell.

Jim moved to her side. He reached into his back pocket and removed a small bottle, which he offered to her. "Go ahead," he said. "It's only wine. You're required to drink wine on carnival day."

The sight of T.C. staggering drunk below them had renewed the feeling of guilt Bonnie had succeeded in shelving while in the park, and she welcomed the wine, allowing the deep red liquid to swirl around her tongue before she swallowed it, and enjoying the sudden warm sensation it brought her stomach. Jim continued to hold the bottle out to her. She took another swallow. He followed.

"Why haven't you given him an answer?" he asked, turning toward the window.

She glared at him, irritated that he was pursuing the question of T.C. and her. "Come on," she said sharply, "do I ask you all sorts of personal questions? And besides, I don't think I can give you an answer. I'm not sure I have one myself."

She was fidgeting with her hands, searching for something more to say. But the duck, its feet caught in its tether, began quacking, breaking the tension. Jim moved to the ladder and freed the bird from its predicament. Stroking its back, he looked toward Bonnie. "He's a fine duck, isn't he? Not just an ordinary run-of-the-mill duck but one with a kind of pedigree. I hope you'll see fit to give him a nice home."

Bonnie shook her head. "For somebody who's rich and educated, you're kind of crazy."

"I suppose you're going to start about that mineowner business again," he scolded. "I'll have you know, young lady, that thanks to your father, I'm now a full-fledged miner. Try to take that away from me."

She didn't know what he was talking about. "You'd better explain that to me."

"Didn't Duke . . . I mean, your father . . . tell you?"

"He didn't tell me anything."

"Yesterday, Bonnie, he let me work a vein . . . all by myself . . . with the blasting powder and everything."

Bonnie stared at him silently. Jim had a look of pride on his face, which struck her as ludicrous, even dishonest. For as long as she could remember, her father had come home from a shift in the mine so tired that he could hardly rise from his chair after dinner, and here was the mineowner's son boasting of his token work at the Red Fox as if he were a Boy Scout showing off a merit badge. "Now just what is that supposed to mean?" she demanded. "You spend a few weeks playing miner, just like you try to make a plaything out of me, and all the world's supposed to forget that it's you, James T. Porter the Second, who'll inherit half the county someday."

Jim's face flushed. "Dammit, Bonnie, can't you take anything at face value? Are you so cynical you can't give me an inch of credit? Can't you see I'm not my grandfather and I'm not my father and I'm sincerely interested in you as a person . . . yes, you, Bonnie Shaw, whether your father's a miner or a banker or the man in the moon?" He was shouting, and Bonnie defensively inched back from him. But Jim said nothing more. Instead, he moved suddenly toward her and began kissing her neck. She stiffened when she felt the touch of his lips, but when he reached for her hands, taking one in each of his, her shoulders untightened.

Jim reached for the buttons of her dress and slowly began to unfasten them from the top. Bonnie's eyes half closed as he reached past the fabric, freed her breasts, then bent to kiss and nuzzle them. With his head still lowered to her breasts, he tightened his grip around her waist and whispered, "I think I'm falling in love with you, Bonnie."

"What did you say?" she asked, her eyes opening.

He looked in her eyes. "I've fallen head over heels for you. And I mean it," he said softly. There was a pleading look on his face. As he embraced her tightly, the two of them fell against the rugged wood siding of the loft and slowly sank to the flooring.

Bonnie still felt the warmth of the wine, and she was light-headed from it, yet at the same time her senses were as sharp as ever. They were entirely focused on Jim. She was aware of his every move, his breathing, his hair flopping over his forehead, the hardness of his muscle-tightened body, the smell of his after-shave. Perspiration formed in droplets on his forehead. When she tasted it, it lacked the salty sensation of sweat and somehow reminded her of the cool, glistening waters of a lagoon on some faraway island. As his hands moved down her body, she became aware only of their touch, losing all sensation of the coarse floorboards and the wall she was braced against. She had no impulse to stop him, no flashes of caution. Bonnie was a virgin, and this was not the struggling, awkward wrestling match to which she was accustomed with T.C. It was, instead, as natural an act as she had ever experienced, almost mystical in its nature. For the first time in her life, she felt whole as a woman sharing with him a most precious communion.

For several minutes they heard no sounds except those of their own lovemaking. As they finished, a burst of hooting and cheers filtered up from the fiddling contest. And as they loosened their embrace and relaxed in each other's arms, the duck tied to the top of the ladder stirred again and let out a quack. They laughed.

Down below, T. C. Fenner struggled to his feet and turned sharply toward the laughter that seemed to come from the belfry.

Bonnie reached up to Jim's face and patted his cheek. "Please don't hurt me," she said.

"Never," he said, bending forward and kissing her gently. "That I promise."

86

As she rested in his arms, Bonnie felt completely complacent, unburdened by thought, and she hoped the sensation of euphoria and total relaxation would never end. But after what seemed only a few minutes, Jim rose to his feet. Handing her the duck, he led her down from the belfry.

As they reached the street, the cool night sent a chill through her body. They were walking slowly back toward the carnival when they spotted a curious crowd forming outside the general store. From inside the square one-story building they heard a shrieking cry.

They rushed to the store's window, pushing others aside to get a view. Bonnie cringed when she saw what was under way inside. Two boys, apparently would-be burglars, were hanging by their hands from an overhead steam pipe. Underneath them, snapping at their heels and growling fiercely, was the biggest dog she had ever seen. The two-inch pipe obviously was red-hot. The two youths kept alternating their hands on the pipe and blowing on their palms. Tears dribbled from their eyes. One boy was weeping loudly; the other was moaning, "Christ! Oh, Christ!" All the while the dog kept leaping at their boots.

In one lunge, the dog managed to reach the legs of one of the youths and sank its fangs into his left calf. The boy screamed in pain. Twisting its head from side to side, the dog ground its teeth into its victim, locking its jaws tightly until the other boy was able to kick it in the head. The dog, slightly stunned, relinquished its hold and dropped to the floor.

"Oh, my God, Jim," Bonnie said, grasping his arm. "That's T.C.'s brother."

Jim spotted Phillip Underwood, the store manager. "Where the hell did that dog come from?" Jim asked.

"Where's your father? I've got to find him," the small, balding man asked urgently.

"Now just calm down and tell me what's going on here," Jim ordered.

Underwood, with a look of fear in his eyes, told Jim and Bonnie how Brutus, the dog, had happened to find a home in the company store.

Jim's father, it seemed, had been having his trouble with the store. One of the Porter Coal Company's major sources of income, the store was well stocked in both staples and luxuries and, of late, had been the frequent target of burglars. Underwood had proposed posting a guard nightly in the store, but Augustus had rejected that, saying it would be too expensive. He decided, instead, to post a dog.

Augustus found the dog he wanted at a local farm and paid a handsome price for it. The animal was not an ordinary dog. It was as high as a man's waist, and its breadth equaled the trunk of a good-sized tree. Its lineage was uncertain, but it appeared to have several traits of a large German shepherd. Muscles rippled up and down its flanks. Most important of all, as far as Augustus was concerned, the dog very clearly hated humans.

Augustus had dragged the balking, muzzled beast into the company store the day before the carnival and instructed Underwood to set the dog free for the weekend when the store would be closed. Underwood accepted the assignment reluctantly.

"As your father left, I asked him the dog's name," Underwood told Jim. "And he replied, 'Don't believe he has one. Why don't you name him after your wife?'

"So I suggested Brutus because the dog is, you know, kind of brutal." Underwood started to chuckle but stopped when he saw the serious expression on Jim's face. "That's the dog in there now. He's got two boys treed. Guess they broke in a few minutes ago, figuring to steal something while the carnival was going on. One's T. C. Fenner's kid brother; the other's Dan Buzek. They're hurtin'."

Another cry came from inside the store. "Oh, my God," said Bonnie, thinking of the pain the two boys must be in. "Do something, Jim."

Just then Augustus strode boldly to the front of the store. There was a slight stagger to his step, apparently the result of his sipping from the flask all day. After suspiciously searching the faces in the still-growing crowd, the mineowner peeked through one of the store's windows. "Hot damn!" he shouted with glee. "That goddamn dog has gotten himself a couple of birds . . . ha, ha, ha . . . he's got the bastards treed right in the store . . . ha, ha, ha."

Underwood approached him timidly. "I've got the keys, Major, so we can go in and get them down."

"Like hell we will," Augustus responded, fire in his eyes. "Damn them, Underwood. Damn them anyway. Those two are probably the same ones who stole those axheads last week."

"What do you want me to do, sir?"

"Nothing. Let them hang and burn awhile." Augustus moved a few steps away from the store. He faced the door, crossed his arms and waited while the cries from within grew louder and more frequent.

"What ya gonna do, Underwood?" someone asked.

"Nothing just now," he replied. "The boss says leave that dog be."

"But they're hurtin', Underwood. And if one of 'em drops, that dog'll kill 'im for sure."

"I know," the store manager said softly. "But the major says it's too bad."

Others joined the onlookers. Among the new arrivals was T. C. Fenner. When someone told him his brother was one of the two boys inside, T.C. exploded in rage. He glared at Augustus, then charged the door. He bounced off the wood and collapsed to the ground.

"My God, Jim, do something!" Bonnie repeated, turning to Jim. But he wasn't at her side. She looked toward the door and saw Jim gently pulling T.C. out of the way. He grabbed the keys from Underwood and began unlocking the door.

Augustus was outraged. "Get the hell away from that door!" he shouted. "Nobody touches that lock until I give the okay."

Jim ignored his father. He opened the door and stepped in. Bonnie watched through the window as Jim, using the steel teeth of a rake as a prod, advanced upon the snarling dog. The dog lurched forward, but the rake stopped it, and soon Jim had the animal backing away, giving the two boys the chance to drop to the floor and scurry to safety outside. T.C.'s brother, his leg bleeding heavily, collapsed as soon as he reached the street. Both boys were barely conscious, their hands burned severely.

"Why? Why?" T.C. asked his brother, raising the youth's head and patting his face with a dampened rag someone had thoughtfully handed to him.

"A few steel bolts. That's all we wanted. Figure to sell them to pay for the movies," the younger Fenner said.

A sheriff's deputy arrived and declared both youths under arrest. He ordered them placed in his patrol car. As he watched this, T.C. bit his lip so hard a drop of blood rolled onto his chin. Jim moved toward him. "I'm sorry about this," he said, attempting to place a hand on T.C.'s shoulder. T.C. pushed the hand away and, head bowed, walked away.

Bonnie had seen enough. With tears welling in her eyes and her fists clutched in anger, she began walking briskly up the hollow. She could hear Augustus shouting at Jim. Then she felt the touch of a hand on her shoulder.

"Bonnie! Please!" Jim said, puffing from his run to catch up to her.

She stopped and turned toward him, seething. "That," she said through clenched teeth, "was the most vicious, barbaric, mean thing I have ever seen. Aren't you Porters at all human? Don't you have any sense of decency? My God!"

Jim reached out for her arm, but she snapped it away and resumed her walk toward her home in a quick, determined pace. Jim kept at her side. "Now listen to me," he shouted.

"I agree with you. That dog was totally uncalled for." She ignored him. "Dammit, Bonnie, my father is not me!"

Something inside Bonnie made her stop. She looked Jim in the eyes. "I'm very sorry that this had to happen and sorrier still that you had to see it," he said, his voice so low she had trouble hearing him. As he spoke, his face again assumed the appearance of innocence, the look of a boy, confused and sad. Without any conscious decision, she fell into his arms and began sobbing.

"Don't cry, Bonnie. Don't do it," he said. "Just give me some time, and this kind of thing will change." He pushed her slightly away. "Now you look me in the eyes and tell me if you could see me ever pulling a stunt like that, disfiguring two young boys."

She shook her head slowly. It was true—she could not envision the man she had just made love to committing any such act of brutality. He reached for her cheek and brushed away a tear. Then, her arm in his, he walked her home.

Bonnie still felt light-headed when she went to bed that night but not from the wine she had consumed—its effects had long before passed. She was spinning with emotions, some of them contradictory, and had a difficult time falling asleep. Although her body felt spent, she lay wide awake, listening to the night wind whistle through the cracks in the walls. Her feelings on carnival day had run the full spectrum from outrage to unrestrained joy, from guilt over T.C.'s condition to a great sense of satisfaction that she had spent the day with Jim. And her thoughts continued to alternate between extremes. One moment she was filled with disgust for the excesses of the Porters, as exemplified by the use of the vicious dog; the next moment she could almost see herself as Jim Porter's wife, loving him and living in his hilltop mansion. She had yet to find anything dishonest about him, and she had found herself attracted to him more than to any other man she had met. She wanted him, of that she was certain, but did she love him? Yes, she decided—yes, she did. And he apparently had fallen for her. So such dreaming was not all that farfetched. She took her projection one step farther and, while fighting for sleep, saw herself on her first anniversary as Jim's wife, living in the mansion, buying art and crystal and real hardcover books, maybe even a new guitar and a piano. The dreary imprisonment she felt in Coal County's hollows would then be behind her and she could. . . .

Bonnie caught herself. My God, she had dated Jim exactly twice, and there were several potential obstacles standing between them before the day they were pronounced man and wife. Still, Jim had asked if he could see her after church services the next morning, and she had agreed.

Thinking of what she would wear to church began to preoccupy her. The practical problem leveled her emotions, and her eyes began to shut as sleep closed in. But then she suddenly sat upright. The duck! What had happened to the duck? The last she could remember was that she was holding it when she and Jim spotted the crowd outside the company store. What happened after that, she didn't know. She must have dropped the bird's tether in her shock at seeing what the dog had done. There was no doubt the duck was long gone, probably swimming in some mountain lake with the leash still tied to its neck. How would she explain this to Jim?

The next morning Bonnie put on her finest white blouse and a blue circle skirt and joined her parents on the walk to the Porterville First Christian Church.

"What are you all smiles about?" Liz asked.

"Oh, I don't know," Bonnie replied. "Just the nice day, I guess."

Liz chuckled knowingly.

As they moved onto Main Street, Bonnie caught a glimpse of Jim. He had just stepped through the front door of the company office. She excused herself from her parents and went after him, hoping to speak to him before the service, to tell him how much she had enjoyed carnival day and how much trust she now had in him.

As she approached the office door, she found it slightly open. She raised her hand to knock but stopped when she heard voices. One was Jim's; the other, his father's. They were speaking loudly.

"What I'm talking about is that young Shaw girl," Bonnie heard Augustus shouting. "I know all about your doings with that young thing." His voice lowered. "They tell me she's very pretty, full of vigor and bounce."

"She's a very fine woman," Jim replied.

"And naturally, since you're a full-grown man now, been to a war and all, you've been thinking in terms of visiting the woodshed and that sort of mischief. Am I right?"

"Get to the point, Pa."

"What I mean is now that you're seeing this young woman so frequently, there's bound to be a natural course to things. I wasn't so bad myself a few years ago, and there weren't many women in these parts when I was your age. And your grandfather . . . well, there were probably six or seven women who remembered him fondly when we laid him to rest. So it's natural, son. But you've got to use your head."

Bonnie felt embarrassed to be eavesdropping, but hearing herself the subject of the conversation, she was unable to leave. She just hoped nobody saw her with her ear pressed to the company office front door.

"Look," Jim told his father, "Bonnie's not that type of girl."

Augustus raised his voice slightly. "The fact is that the two of you will never reconcile your differences. And whether you recognize them or not, there *are* differences. It's a matter of breeding and upbringing, son. My God, you're a Porter, and with that comes—"

"I'm *not* going to stop seeing her just because of her surname," Jim said sternly. "I like her. She seems to like me.

93

And when we're together, I laugh more than I have since I left for that damn university."

Bonnie heard the sound of glass and guessed that Augustus was pouring himself a drink, the fact that it was Sunday morning notwithstanding.

"Now listen here," the mineowner resumed in almost a shout, "I want this to end. It is not to continue, do you understand? It's already the talk of Coal County. And if I have to, I'll do something about it."

"There you go threatening me again."

"Damn right I am. You stop seeing Bunny Shaw, or whatever her name is, or you're through—through with this family, through with this company." He paused and calmed himself somewhat. "I'm disappointed in you anyway, Jim, and you know it. This family has some of the largest coal holdings in the state of West Virginia, and someday they're going to be yours. There's a responsibility that goes with that, but you don't appear to take it at all seriously." His voice changed, becoming softer, almost friendly. "I think maybe what you should do is spend some time in our parlor and take a good, long look at that beaten pickax your grandfather used and the words he himself chiseled on it—'Liberty comes from hard work.' " It was a close, if imprecise, translation of the Latin. "This family has a God-given responsibility."

Bonnie heard Jim groan.

"My God," Augustus continued, "I send you to school, but then you turn your back on it and go to work in a mine. Worse, you fraternize with the men, and you couldn't make a bigger mistake. They're like children, and someday they and *their* sons are going to be dependent on you. But you won't meet that responsibility. When you should be finishing your college education, you're off in a Bannerton store drinking and then traipsing around with the daughter of Duke Shaw, who himself probably knows better."

Bonnie was starting to seethe. The pomposity of Augustus

Porter! Give it to him, Jim. Let him have it! she thought, silently cheering him on.

Augustus could be heard yet again filling his glass. "Look, son," he said gently, "I've given the matter a good deal of thought, and I have a proposition to make. Will you at least listen to it?"

"Okay."

"The coal industry's changing, changing fast, and if all we had was the business in this country, we'd be bankrupt, all of us, inside of a decade. As it is, I've come up with a whole list of austerities I'm going to have to impose if conditions get any worse, and some of them are rather drastic. But I won't go into those now. The point I want to make is that our hope—our only hope—lies with our overseas markets. France, Italy, England and the rest. A company's international trade is going to be the key to its survival." He paused, apparently to take another sip from his glass. "Now we happen to have a good man in London. His name is Preston, and he's as fine an agent as there is in Europe. I've cabled him, and he's agreed. So what I have to propose is this: You go over there and spend a year with him learning the international trade, and when that's done, you come home, and I'll make you a full officer of the company. What do you say?"

"Pa, I just came home from Korea. I was away for three years and—"

"Damn you anyway!" Augustus shouted. Bonnie heard something pound against a table or desk. "You're going to listen to me, and if you don't stop seeing that Shaw girl, I'm going to put you on that boat to England myself. They're all the same, these girls, don't you understand that? Just after your name and money and nothing else. Sluts. Tramps. Whores. They've been around since the first coal camp."

"Okay, Pa, okay," Jim interrupted. His voice was very different. "Let me clear one thing up," he said as if making a confession. "I have seen Bonnie Shaw only twice. Twice, that's all. She is just one of many. You know how many girls I can call up and go out with on a moment's notice. There must be a dozen. I'm not serious, and neither is she. It's what you probably used to call a romp in the hay, nothing more. And to tell the truth—"

Bonnie felt as if a stiletto had pierced her heart. Rage exploding within her, she threw the door open and stormed inside to confront the man she had loved, the man upon whom she had so foolishly bestowed her most precious gift. It was a gift that could not be reclaimed.

"One of many? Is that what you have to say?" she yelled as she advanced toward the two men, both of whom appeared startled. "I trusted you. I believed it could happen. I opened my heart to you, and my dreams and hopes for the future. And you present yourself as such an honest, confused young man in love with the world and everyone in it. And all the while you're playing with a toy, throwing a ring around my neck like you did that duck. You're no different than your father, Jim. You use people. The two of you are the same man."

"Now just a minute . . ." Augustus started to protest, but Bonnie already had turned in place and bolted through the door.

"Hey, Bonnie," she heard Jim shout.

She ignored him. There was nothing he could possibly say now to restore her trust in him and erase the thought, so clear to her now, that she had been had, that she had been used, that a rich boy had found her a plaything. God, how she hated him. And hated his father and hated all the things the Porter family stood for in their greedy race for wealth and power. Bonnie forgot about church and forgot about her parents as she broke into a trot and left the hollows of Porterville for her secret niche on the top of Newcastle Peak.

But the solace she had come to expect from the mountaintop failed her. The sky had grown overcast and the view of the hollows and valleys and surrounding mountain ranges was hostile and cold. In a moment's insight she saw that her acceptance of Jim Porter had been futile, that there were forces at work on her destiny over which she had no control, that hers had been the naïve hope of a nineteen-year-old girl still not ready for the realities of the world. And she cried.

CHAPTER 4 ⎯⎯⎯⎯⎯⎯⎯⎯⎯⎯

With the arrival of fall, Coal County's mountains and foothills assumed a palette of rich reds, yellows and browns. Thick thornbushes turned to the color of rust. Sticky sap began to drip from cuts in the ironwood trees, and the bittersweet darkened and thinned itself out. There was a briskness to the air and a chill to the rocky soil. Later, with the November winds and cold, the trees were stripped of their leaves and the once-colorful foliage darkened. The ridges, in their muted earthy hues, seemed rugged and barren.

Bonnie Fenner swept her fingertips across the window, clearing a transparent path in the layer of moisture that had formed on the inside of the pane, and stared at the mountain ridge in the distance. There was a gap where the window failed to fit its frame, and a harsh wind sweeping down into the hollow whistled through the crack, striking her neck and face and causing her to shiver. The sky was soupy and gray, threatening rain or perhaps snow, and she felt sorry for her husband, who had to travel on foot through the near darkness the two miles to the Red Fox Mine. She knew that once he was there, however, the bitter weather would make little difference, for in the shafts and caverns dug into the mountains, the temperature and humidity remained constant throughout the year. Whatever balminess or raging storms prevailed on the surface had no effect on the miners in their cool and damp subterranean chambers.

They had been married for slightly more than two years, and although their life had fallen quickly into a simple and unceasing routine, she felt she hardly knew T. C. Fenner. Her instincts about him had proved correct—T.C. was a good husband, hardworking, gentle and, as far as she knew, faithful. But they rarely talked to each other beyond the chatter necessary to maintaining their household. Each had fallen into a time-honored role: he the breadwinner, she the devoted wife. In bed their lovemaking had become mechanical, less in frequency and shorter in duration, the laughter and giddiness they once shared at such moments having disappeared. While passion was absent from their lives, its disappearance had also tempered their conflicts—Bonnie and T.C. rarely had fights.

Still, Bonnie considered her marriage a success. She believed herself to be a realist, a tough woman who had learned not to expect too much out of life other than what she earned, at least if it was one's happenstance to be born into a West Virginia miner's family.

As a girl she had read every book she could get her hands on. From them she had come to believe that adventure was to be found in the world, that life could offer anyone who sought it a sense of creativity and fulfillment. Her dreams had taken her to every exotic land on the globe while she clung to the arms of the most handsome, gentle and generous of men. Her singing, too, had been a vehicle to take her thoughts far, far away from the desolate hollows of Porterville and the day-to-day drudgery that marked the lives of most women there. But then time—and a man named Jim

Porter—had forced an end to such imaginary journeys, and her mind remained firmly rooted to the gravel-filled soil of Porterville. During her months of marriage, pregnancy and motherhood, however, she had begun to learn the rewards of economy and persistence and was determined, with their help, to make the most out of what favors God or fate bestowed upon her. No matter that the laughter was gone, she had her health, a home and a family. For these she was grateful.

Despite this optimistic bent, Bonnie and her husband had some real and immediate worries. Their frail two-room company house, a few doors away from her parents' home, was in worse shape than in the previous winter, when the battered wooden structure had actually swayed with the wind. Freezing gusts had passed unhindered through the cracks in the thin walls, and melting snow and ice had dripped from the ceiling. Even the largest and most glowing of the coal fires they had managed to maintain in their tiny hearth had done little to cut the biting cold and dampness, which lingered well into the spring, permeating their clothes, their bedding, their bones. T.C. had appealed repeatedly to the company office for repairs to the roof and walls, but nothing had been done. The company had failed to respond to similar appeals from Duke Shaw and from T.C.'s parents, who lived in the other Porterville hollow. And the signs were that the current winter would prove even more severe.

T.C.'s job also was in jeopardy, or at least that was what they feared. While Augustus Porter had eliminated most overtime and imposed other austerities, he had not yet reduced his payroll. Rumors nonetheless swept through the county that layoffs were imminent. T.C., ranking low in seniority, surely would be among the first to go. Bonnie didn't know what they would do if that happened. She had already seen one effect of Augustus's fiscal actions: The mineowner had cracked down on her father's overdue debt to the company, and the humiliation and pressure to pay had left Duke withdrawn, his self-esteem diminished, if not shattered. That made Bonnie bitter and angry. "A mineowner's true colors," she had shouted at the time. "When the chips are down and they find themselves threatened, they're all the same. They think only of themselves." Her mother, although disturbed, did not share in her bitterness, and Liz had urged Bonnie to hush, reminding her again that it was through Augustus Porter after all that Duke—and T.C., for that matter—had a job.

During the hours she found herself sitting idly by the window, staring blurry-eyed through its clouded panes, Bonnie often thought of Jim Porter. Time had done nothing to dull the contempt she felt toward him. It was a contempt also undiminished by distance, for more than two years had passed since Jim hastily left Porterville and traveled to London.

Sometimes, when she saw the Porter's mansion, she remembered her dreaming of one day living there. Then she thought of the shack that was her own home and laughed. It had been a ridiculous idea.

Occasionally she wondered what Jim was doing in London and tried to imagine what he looked like, wearing a bowler hat and carrying an umbrella like the Englishmen she saw in the movies. That also made her laugh.

Bonnie was haunted by one question: Why had she so readily fallen under the spell of the man? Reliving their moments together over and over, she could analyze it in no other way than to see it as a string of events that had taken a course only natural. She could remember no point which she knew at the time to be an opportunity for decision, for her to say yes or no, not when he kissed her or when he reached for the buttons of her dress or even when he prepared to enter her. This perplexed her. For surely at any moment she could have called a halt to it all, especially in view of the apprehension she felt at being used as a toss-away plaything by the son of a rich mineowner with nothing better to occupy his leisure. She recalled mentioning this to him, raising the issue directly, but even with this fear and her logic throwing up other flags of caution, she had proceeded unashamedly and without hesitation and, she hated to admit, enjoyed it, all of it, the handholding, the banter and, yes, the lovemaking. Why? Was she merely intrigued by it all, a simple mining girl with the rare chance to play with and manipulate one of her aristocratic betters? Or had she fallen under his magic in a net cast by his energy, his manliness, his smile? All she knew for certain was that her hate and resentment remained, gnawing at her insides with as much intensity as they had on the day she climbed to the mountaintop and vowed it would never happen again.

The baby cried out in the bedroom, and Bonnie pulled herself away from the window. She found the eighteen-month-old girl wide awake and kicking in the crude wooden bed T.C. had constructed. The baby needed changing. When she had finished with this, Bonnie held the child up to the light of the bedroom's one window. She did this often, each time inspecting the baby's features closely. The girl's face remained roundish and undefined. She seemed to have her mother's jet black hair, but it was baby hair and could lighten. The child was long and chubby. Her name was Mari.

Bonnie had pledged to herself that her daughter would not grow up to be the wife of a miner. Mari would be the first generation of Shaws—and Fenners, for that matter—to break the chains and earn her own place in the world, even if it meant her leaving the mountains to do so. That was Bonnie's promise, and she was prepared to take any step to fulfill it. Already she was keeping her eyes open for available work for herself, a job to supplement the money brought home by her husband. Her mother could care for Mari, or T.C. could switch to a night shift while Bonnie was working. His income could go to putting food on the table; hers, to Mari's education. Bonnie was determined that her daughter someday earn a college degree, for an education was the key to freedom from Porterville's hollows.

After dressing Mari, Bonnie moved to a small broom closet to get her mop. To get it, she had to move a guitar that was also stored there. The instrument was dusty, its strings loosened. She had not played it in more than two years.

Darkness arrived early. With it came a fall storm that sent rolling booms of thunder echoing off the walls of the hollow and released a heavy rain. T.C. was dripping when he shuffled through the door, bent with weariness from his shift in the mine. Loosening his coat but not removing it, he plopped down on one of the two wobbly wooden chairs at their small dining table. Bonnie handed him a towel and then placed a mug of steaming coffee in front of him. She followed this with a bottle of whiskey, which T.C. tipped generously into his coffee.

Bonnie sat across from her husband. Something was wrong. T.C. normally was not very talkative, and he obviously was tired, so his silence alone did not alarm her. What did was his expression. It was worried, his eyes vacant, his skin drawn.

"What's the matter, honey? Something bothering you?" she asked gently.

"Absolutely nothing," he responded. His voice seemed sullen.

"Okay," she said. "I'm ready to listen whenever you want to talk about it." She rose to begin preparing dinner.

"He's back."

Bonnie paused, her hands resting on the back of her chair. "Who's back?"

"Your friend—Jim Porter."

Bonnie retook her seat. The announcement surprised her. She stared at her husband, waiting for him to continue.

"Saw him this morning. Outside the office," T.C. continued, his voice a mumbling monotone, his eyes still hollow.

"Well, Jim Porter being back doesn't exactly make the world stop spinning now, does it?" she said lightly.

"He looks different. You can't believe how his appearance has changed."

"In what way?" she asked, hoping not to sound too interested.

"His hair was slicked back in some kind of fancy haircut. And he was wearing a suit that surely was hand-tailored and must have cost at least a hundred dollars." Bonnie frowned. She sat back and listened as T.C., in his unchanged voice, continued: "He looks older, not just two years older but maybe five. And there was something different about his walk, real straight, just like his father's used to be. He's got a mustache now, and he was smoking some fancy pipe. But do you know what? He hasn't really changed."

"You just get through telling me how different he seemed and then you—"

"He was standing there right with his father. At first everyone was kind of intimidated by him, afraid to go up to him and say anything. So he went around himself, greeting everybody personally. When he came to me and your pa, he asked all kinds of things: about last summer's berry crop, about his old mine crew and the drinking at Blakely's and you, Bonnie —he asked about you."

Bonnie felt her face flush. She hoped T.C. would not notice it. "What did you say?"

"I told him about our marriage and how you and I are very happy and how we have a child. That's all. He offered his congratulations and said he wished us well. And that was the end of it. He went on his way."

Bonnie wanted desperately to change the subject. "Look at this, would you?" she said, pointing to Mari, who was nodding off on the living-room floor. "She wouldn't take her nap, and now she wants to make up for it."

T.C. leaned forward. He turned and looked directly at

his wife, his eyes focused and alert. "I have to ask you something."

She nodded, suspecting what was coming.

"Does he still mean anything to you, Bonnie? I mean once you really fell for him, didn't you? And he really liked you. I used to see it written right on his face. A couple of mugs of ale, and he couldn't hide it no matter how hard he tried. And you know what, Bonnie? I saw it again today. There was a message in his eyes. He wants you, Bonnie. He still wants you very much."

Bonnie reached out and touched T.C.'s face. She smiled. "I can think of a hundred other things you should be worried about before giving two seconds' thought to me and Jim Porter," she said. "Now listen carefully, T.C.—I hate that man. He used me, made me feel like a fool. And most important of all, he made me hurt you. I'll never forgive him for that. Do you understand?"

He lowered his eyes. She bent forward and kissed him tenderly. "Now go and get yourself out of those wet clothes. By the time you do I'll have dinner ready."

T.C. slowly rose from the table.

Jim Porter was not yet accustomed to his mustache, having begun growing it only four months earlier, but he already had developed a subconscious habit of twitching the ends of its bristly growth, especially when he was thinking. In church at Sunday services two days after his return to Porterville, he had caught himself tugging at it repeatedly. The Reverend Weatherson droned on in a sermon unchanged from those Jim had endured prior to leaving for London. The clergyman's voice was low and there was a hypnotic cadence to his delivery which lulled some of the more bone-weary—or hung-over—male parishioners to sleep. On Jim it had the effect of driving him deep into thought.

This was his second homecoming in three years; what

struck him was the difference in his feelings. Coming home from the war, he had been confused, disoriented and searching. Now, in contrast, his mind was clear, and his feelings were sharp.

His mandatory year in London had passed quickly. To his surprise, he had rather enjoyed it and decided to stay a year more. Lowell Preston, the company's agent, had proved delightfully friendly and interesting, and although Jim once had bemoaned to his father his total lack of wanderlust, he came to relish his stay in the overseas city. When it came time—unlike after the war—he experienced no muddled feelings about where next to go: Porterville was drawing him like a magnet. This perplexed him. When he asked himself why, he came up with an unlikely answer—the company. This perplexed him even more. So he had put the question to Preston.

They sat huddled together over pints of Guinness in a small Covent Garden pub a few days before Jim's departure from London. Their table was a few feet from a wall-sized fireplace, and the heat radiated by the crackling flames caused Jim's cheeks to tingle. Preston, a short man with slightly disheveled hair and a ruddy complexion, was wearing his favorite tweed coat, leather elbow patches concealing some of the wear inflicted by constant use and age. As usual, he found opportunity to raise his mug only when his hands weren't busy in an often-unsuccessful effort to ignite the oily tobacco he packed into his pipe. When Jim asked him about the possible cause of his changed feelings toward his family's company, Preston smiled knowingly, called for another round and fiddled with his pipe and matches.

"I think you can find a simple answer," he said finally. "It's just a matter of your perception moving to a higher plane."

"What the hell does that mean?" Jim asked. Preston had a habit of obfuscating matters by elevating them to an abstraction.

"What I mean is the big picture, as the military chaps

put it. You've gotten the big picture!" The Englishman smiled broadly, satisfied with the precision of his answer.

Jim thought for a few moments and decided that what Preston had told him was true. His view of the company and the business it conducted had considerably broadened. Although he disliked admitting it, his father's instincts had proved valid. Jim had taken his prescribed tonic of time and distance, submitting himself to the tutelage of Preston, and his understanding of the company—and his father—had changed to such an extent that he would never view either as he had before.

Preston's mellowness was deceiving; he was a no-nonsense businessman dependent upon commissions in a marketplace filled with vagaries. When he spotted a potential contract, he dived right in, leaving no weapon untouched while he pursued his prey with the persistence of a foxhound. Jim was astounded at the man's unrelenting drive when on the trail of a customer. He was equally surprised to find that when Preston succeeded, as he usually did, the deals, which involved shiploads of coal, thousands of tons, were apt to be hammered out not in fancy wood-paneled boardrooms or high-priced French restaurants but rather in some whorehouse or private club on the dimly lit back streets of Soho. This was particularly true when the buyer was an official representative of some government, a lowly paid bureaucrat whom Preston plied first with a superficial discussion of business, then with a bout of serious drinking and insightful comment on the regrettable state of world affairs and finally with the finest fifty-quid-a-night hookers London had to offer. Jim once actually observed the formal signing of an inch-thick delivery contract upon the silken sheets of a membership-only bordello.

Preston had no apparent qualms about the nature of his tactics. At his and Jim's quiet victory celebrations, he boasted of the enormousness and importance of his just-completed transactions. This, he said with a smug glow of self-satisfaction, was how the civilized world got its coal, without which there would be no life as we know it. In other words, Jim thought—but didn't say—one lives with the tactics or leaves the business.

Whatever reservations Jim might have had about Preston's techniques, observing the agent in action had altered Jim's perception of his family's company. The point Preston emphasized most was that a coal company is a living organism, fluid in its nature and transitory unless nurtured carefully and constantly. The ownership of a mine is especially deceiving, Preston noted, for coal trapped beneath the rock of a mountain has only a potential value. It produces profit only upon its extraction. And extraction involves a complex process of negotiating sales, organizing men and arranging delivery. The more the Englishman talked, the more Jim began to understand the problems in running a firm like the Porter Coal Company. Until then his comprehension of the company's function had been relatively simple: The coal was in the mountains, the miners extracted it and loaded it onto trains and the trains pulled out of Porterville. He had never given much thought to where exactly the trains were heading or, more important, why. And as he turned in his seat in the front pew of the Porterville First Christian Church and scanned the faces of the mining families behind him, he realized that they, too, seldom, if ever, thought of how the Porter Coal Company came to have any customers. It was a worldwide market, so fickle that the pumping hips of a cockney whore could make a difference in a contract large enough to give 100 miners a year's work. What Jim had witnessed confirmed beyond doubt that this market was shrinking and that unless there were changes, drastic changes involving dozens of nations, there would be casualties, the Porter Coal Company possibly among them.

Thinking again of the miners worshiping behind him, Jim wondered what would happen to them if the company was forced out of business. What other jobs could those coal-stained hands and bent backs possibly perform? And when his eyes caught sight of his father sitting next to him, Augustus's head slightly twisted and his eyes clouded with thought, Jim had some notion of the older man's burden and recognized what his father termed the family's mandate. Jim's only qualifications to that claim were that the mandate was not God-given, as his father insisted, but rather the result of an often unfair, sometimes immoral man-made system and that he, Jim Porter, was a part of it through nothing more than a historical accident.

A glimpse of the Reverend Weatherson staring down at him from the pulpit caught his attention. Embarrassed, Jim fidgeted in his seat, snapping his eyes forward and stiffening his back into rigid attention. Although unable now to see the faces of the mining families to the rear, he felt a flush of fondness for them along with what for him were the curious feelings of being, at last, in the right place and having something of a purpose in his life.

The right front pew of the church was reserved for the mineowner and his family. Traditionally, at the service's conclusion, the congregation remained in place until the Porters had left the church. After Jim and his parents had walked down the aisle and were joined by the other worshipers outside the church, Jim, still moved by the intensity of the emotions he had felt during the service, had an impulse to greet everyone warmly. Understanding their reluctance to step forward, he waded into them like a campaigning politician, a smile on his face, his right hand outstretched. Their response was restrained, even suspicious, but this did not daunt him—until he spotted his father chatting with Duke Shaw and T. C. Fenner. Where was Bonnie? At home with her child, he guessed. And with that thought of her, Jim's enthusiasm suddenly evaporated. When Augustus waved him toward their car, he shook his head. No, Jim told him, he'd rather walk home—alone.

Jim had thought of Bonnie often during his stay in London

and once considered sending her and T.C. a postcard. He ultimately rejected that, fearing that it might appear he was meddling in their affairs. When Jim's mother had written him about their marriage and later about the little girl, Jim, although jealous, acknowledged that maybe T.C., in his simple way, could make Bonnie happy. Jim understood Bonnie's outrage, or at least he thought so. Had he been in her place outside the company office that day, overhearing Augustus's ranting about whores and his own words about her being only one of many, there might have been a conclusion in gunfire. Bonnie had no way of knowing that Jim had denied his love for her only to get his father off his back. He hadn't tried to explain it later because he knew no matter how carefully he fashioned his words, she would never again believe him.

On his last night in London, Jim told Preston of his relationship with Bonnie and how it had come to a crashing end. "Call it love or infatuation or anything you want," Jim said while Preston tinkered with his pipe, "but the fact is that I've seen a dozen, maybe more, women in this city, and there's not been one to interest me the way Bonnie did." Jim leaned across the small table. "And her eyes—she's got these green eyes that haunt you, that hypnotize you until you can't think of anything else." His face grew grim. "I blew it, Lowell. I could have had her, but I played a game to pacify my father, and now she won't have me. And I can't blame her for that."

Preston took a long sip of stout and then began to laugh. "Ah, you young men. We all go through it, lad. Then you begin to mature, and you see there's a great risk certain to arise with the intermingling of the classes. You can't do it, Jim. At least you can't do it without paying a bloody price."

Both men concentrated on their mugs for a while. Then the agent continued. "You've changed a great deal, Jim, and you'll change more, especially when you return home with the knowledge and experience you've gained here." Now Preston bent forward. "I'll give you only one piece of advice:

Choose your marriage partner carefully. Marry one of your own, someone with the breeding and financial resources to help you, to introduce you to the right people, to put forth the image necessary to maintaining a small advantage in this bloody business. The right woman can be a big help to you. When you stop and think about it, almost any marriage is doomed from the start—one partner merely tolerates the other and vice versa." Preston chuckled. "I'm sorry, lad, but that's the way it is in this life. So it would behoove you to forget all these fairy-book tales about romance and handsome ladies imprisoned in castle towers. Instead, find yourself someone who can do you some good."

It was a depressing argument. Whether true or not, Jim didn't care. He considered his pursuit of Bonnie lost anyway. And that was how he emotionally stored it, forcing himself to reduce his brief relationship with the catlike young woman to an instructive but finished experience, one of many life was certain to throw his way. But this bit of emotional handiwork crumbled each time Jim saw T.C. and thought of how happy his and Bonnie's marriage appeared to be, how they had already been blessed with a child and how—who knows?—maybe there would be other children. It made Jim feel empty, somehow, and he came to understand that no matter how he rationalized it, he still was attracted to—and wanted—the woman he had known as Bonnie Shaw.

On his return to Porterville, Jim was impressed to see how the relationship between his parents seemed to have changed. They appeared to be closer than they had in years, reunited by a common problem—the deteriorating condition of the Porter Coal Company. On the nights when Augustus was home, the couple spent long periods in low-keyed discussions in the parlor. Jim sometimes sat with them. He was struck by how tender his mother was to his father. Augustus, in turn, was uncharacteristically soft-spoken and reflective at such moments, sometimes openly questioning his own decisions and actions. From this, Jim concluded that his father, perhaps for the first time in his life, was haunted by a vision of the future and was scared.

"What's happening to this industry, Sarah?" Augustus asked dejectedly after one of the late-evenings discussions to which Jim was privy. "What's happening to us? I can only hope that when it's all over, there'll still be a company and we'll still control it."

"Here, here," Sarah said. "Just put all that out of your mind." Her hand moved to his arm. "The company's still alive, and it's going to grow."

Augustus smiled, looking at her with the face of a young child. "Do you promise?"

"I promise," she whispered, raising a hand to brush his cheek. He grinned and then left the parlor, to return carrying three fresh brandies. The three of them had begun to sip their drinks when Augustus started to chuckle.

"What's so funny?" Sarah asked.

"You . . . and your magic," he replied softly. "One word from you or one touch from your fingertips and I find myself thinking like a fifteen-year-old without a worry in the world."

Sarah and Augustus excused themselves and retired upstairs.

There were legitimate grounds for Augustus's worry. The coal industry had enjoyed a small boom during the Korean War—the fighting had generated a demand for all fuels—but after the truce the marketplace love affair with coal began to taper. As had happened at the end of the previous decade, the price of coal began to fall rapidly. World War II had conditioned the nation's great industries to the use of gas and oil, competing fuels the abundance of which in the West and Southwest was beginning to capture the country's attention. Gas interests began laying larger and longer pipelines to the large industrial centers of the Midwest and East. The thousands and thousands of new houses rising on the rural outskirts of cities were more apt to burn oil for their heat than coal. The railroads, which had lived in a symbiotic arrangement with the coal industry from its beginning, turned to diesel fuel, which came from oil. On a large-scale basis, the coal industry was left to woo only the faithfully hungry utilities and the mills that produced the nation's steel.

As the demand for coal declined, more and more of the smaller coal companies—particularly those with one owner and usually one mine—were forced to the brink of bankruptcy. Larger companies survived by ordering complete shutdowns of some of their mines. To many, this seemed such a waste, the actual sealing of a mine's portal, the removal of its equipment and the appearance of security guards. The coalfields, in their growing idleness, assumed the appearance of a land under attack. It *was* war—economic war—and it was in many respects a war between regions as vitriolic as the Civil War had been. The great oil and gas deposits were being exploited feverishly, and the moneymen behind them talked of reserves that would last a dozen more lifetimes. One motion picture after another glamorized the modern-day gold rush in the oilfields; few depicted the lonely struggle at the face of a coal vein. The preferences of Hollywood were fittingly symbolic.

The oil and gas interests perfected a great national transportation network to distribute their fuels efficiently and cheaply—pipelines and huge ships, trucks and special trains. They took every measure they could to keep the prices of the two fuels down, and in a barrage of advertising and promotion they urged the factory manager and homeowner to make their conversion to oil and gas as soon as possible. Many did.

The bankrupted coalmen and the out-of-work miners in West Virginia and other coal states were united in their feeling of betrayal. Few of them understood the changes which had occurred. The rules of the game had been abruptly amended, and the time-proven techniques for marketing coal did not work anymore. Even the railroads saw the shrinking coal industry for what it was. In time it would require a bottle of top-quality whiskey or a $10 bribe just to get access to a railroad car from a disinterested dispatcher.

The feeling of betrayal intensified when nearly bankrupt coal companies surrendered, agreeing to sell their leases and mines and eventually finding the only ready buyers to be—ironically—oilmen. Did these westerners really believe their own projections of unending gas and oil reserves? Or did they know better?

Men wearing Stetsons and high-topped, richly ornamented leather boots appeared with increasing frequency in the coalfields. They made their pitch in accents foreign to a mountain man's ears and, like blockbusters in a changing city neighborhood, declared that selling out would be best for all. Many mineowners did, relinquishing their properties to the oilmen at the price set by nonnegotiable bids and leaving the coalfields behind for retirement in the Florida sun. Others elected to fight it out, hoping that their industry's slide would prove an economic quirk and that in a nation as vast and as industrialized as theirs, there would be room for all forms of fuel.

The Porter Coal Company had traditionally shipped the bulk of its coal to the railroads. Now it fought for short-term contracts with steel mills, factories and whatever overseas customers it could find. This business, too, was rapidly declining. The drop in sales had not yet reached a point where mines would have to be closed, but it did pressure Augustus to tighten the company's belt considerably. In contrast, Augustus's archrival, John Owens, had a long history of dealing fairly with a group of large utilities and, with their continuing support, was able to keep his firm going without major cutbacks as yet. This galled Augustus. To make matters worse, the Porter company was notorious for its lack of modern equipment, Augustus and his father both believing that the backbreaking labor of extracting coal could be accomplished in the manner it had always been—namely, through the sweat and muscle of miners—without tying up the company's money in unneeded equipment. Now, however, the Porter machinery was antiquated. If developments continued as they had been, the company, after paying the men their wages and meeting other mandatory day-to-day overhead costs, would find little money left for capital expenses. Then it would be all the mechanics and engineers could do to keep the existing equipment in operation—the mine trains, cutting machines and tipple conveyors. Breakdowns would increase, and there would be few, if any, funds for replacement parts. New machinery would be out of the question.

Augustus said the lack of new machines might not have too serious an effect at first, but it would eventually make the company noncompetitive. The oil firms were pouring large amounts of cash into the coal companies they acquired, cash allowing for the purchase of the latest in mining automation. There were modern machines called continuous miners that not only chewed away at a face of coal but gathered up the pieces and delivered them to a car all in one uninterrupted operation. More efficient models were being perfected every day, and it was said just one of them could take the place of seven or eight miners. As the machines became more and more plentiful, Augustus said, they would drive the price of coal down even further. What would happen to the men thrown out of work by the new machines? What would happen to the company? Dejectedly, he admitted he didn't know.

During Jim's absence Augustus had begun fashioning his own set of defenses against his growing financial woes. Jim learned of these measures piecemeal and often accidentally through friends, company workers or his mother. On the whole, they were radical—sometimes ludicrous—responses by his father, sometimes unnecessary and even counterproductive. They painted a picture of a man on the edge of panic, a cornered animal striking out at anything that moved.

Augustus had made his first move at the company store. Phillip Underwood, the frail, spectacled store manager, was astonished when Augustus appeared and asked to see the store's books. The mineowner had not bothered with such things for as long as Underwood could remember. With no forewarning, Augustus demanded to see every current ledger page. He spent three days scrutinizing their figures. When he at last was finished the store had closed for the day and the sun had set, but Underwood, at the mineowner's insistence, remained dutifully at his side.

"It's not bad, Underwood. You show a reasonable profit here," Augustus told him. Underwood sighed with relief. "But I think we can accomplish a lot more," the mineowner added. "It's too bad we can't play with the scrip anymore, but I think we can find a way around that."

In times past, when coal camps were located in very isolated reaches of the mountain ranges, mineowners discounted their scrip in such a way that the coin identified as being worth $1, for example, might have the purchasing power of only 75 cents in federal currency. Changing the discount rate was one way of raising prices in the company store. But laws had been enacted to ban such discounting, and eventually the scrip system was dropped.

The company store still held a monopoly on retail goods in Porterville, Bannerton being just distant enough to make a shopping trip inconvenient for most mining families, few of whom owned cars. So Augustus found his other way: He instructed Underwood to raise the prices gradually of every line of products the store carried.

"If it's done right," Augustus told Underwood, "nobody will notice, and there'll be no squawking or outraged wives breathing down my back."

Having ordered the price increases in the company store, Augustus next turned his energies to another area of finance— the outstanding debt owed to the company by its employees. A week after his meeting with Underwood, he went to his desk in the company office to hold court. His orders had been issued the previous day, and a long line of mining men waited to see him. Some had even been summoned from their work shifts. The line moved slowly as one by one Augustus called in the men, reviewed the amounts of money they owed the company for goods or housing and lectured them on their tardy payments. Some of the men, although not many, were still working off contracts they had signed years earlier before boarding ships overseas to work in the Porter mines. The terms of those contracts had left them with virtually no money, and the need for food and shelter had forced them into debts that seemed to be unending.

Duke Shaw had long before worked off his overseas contract with the company, and he had repaid a loan he had obtained to finance the Atlantic voyage for his wife, but the normal requirements of supporting a family on a miner's pay had kept him in debt. The closest to a friend Augustus had on his work force, Duke nevertheless was among those lined up for a verbal thrashing from the mineowner.

"Duke," Augustus began, "I was really surprised to find your name on the delinquents' list when I went through it. I would have thought better of you."

"I'm behind, Major, and I apologize for that, but I'm not that far behind, and it's been rough just keeping up with everyday expenses."

"These are tough times for everyone, Duke, including the company," Augustus responded. "We can't be a coal company and a bank at the same time, as much as I'd like to help people out. What do you think would happen if we had to declare bankruptcy for this company? Why, you and hundreds of other men would be out of work. So we've all got to do our part."

"Give me some overtime and I'll pull it, Major. I'll get you your money," Duke promised dejectedly.

"I know you will," Augustus said, rising to his feet and slapping the miner on his back. "Send in the next man," he then ordered.

Augustus did not limit himself merely to imposing austerities; he also had a few brainstorms for making money from new sources. One of these came to light on a night shortly after his crackdown on debtors when Augustus and a burly aide named Haggerty climbed into a jeep and drove to Bannerton for Sheriff Thad Carter, who was a good friend of Augustus's. Under a full moon, the three men drove over a bumpy road to a remote section of backwoods five miles outside Porterville. The road was little more than a dirt path. Farther on, as it twisted through the foothills, it degenerated into a pair of little-used wheel ruts. Approaching one bend, Haggerty, who was driving, flipped off the jeep's headlights. A few yards later he pulled the vehicle to the side and stopped.

"I think we'd better walk the rest, Major," Haggerty said, removing a shotgun from the rear of the vehicle.

The three men marched single file through the thick brush until they reached a small tree-surrounded clearing. They were silent, Haggerty motioning to the sheriff to drop behind. Then, pointing to a cluster of bushes in the center of the clearing, he stepped aside for Augustus to take the lead. Leaving Carter behind, Augustus and Haggerty walked slowly on their toes, looking down to avoid stepping on twigs. When they reached the cluster of bushes, Haggerty dropped to a squat and tinkered with a metal handle protruding from the earth and barely visible through the brush. With a quick, sweeping motion and a grunt, he jerked the handle upward, throwing open a trapdoor which the bushes had concealed. Augustus turned on a powerful flashlight and pointed it into the blackened hole.

"All right, Thomason, this is Augustus Porter. Get your black ass out of there."

At first nothing happened. Then the round figure of Will Thomason struggled up out of the hole. He was followed by two other black men. Augustus and Thomason studied each other in silence until the sheriff, who had remained in the background on the edge of the clearing, tapped his boot against a tree trunk to make his presence known.

"How about a ten-cent tour, Thomason?" Augustus said snidely, a smirk on his face. "I've heard a lot about this little still of yours."

The black man did not respond. He glared at the mine-owner, contempt in his eyes, while weighing his options. Then, surrendering, he waved Augustus forward, signaling him to follow him down the makeshift ladder into the cavern dug into the ground beneath their boots. Haggerty and the two Thomason accomplices remained at the top, hovering over the trapdoor. The sheriff still stood in the distance.

When he reached the lantern-lit chamber below, Augustus found that the folklore that had evolved about the Thomason still was justified. The tubes of the immense distilling apparatus appeared to travel everywhere like a disorganized spider's web. What made Thomason's moonshine so tasty and mellow, however, was not evident. That was a secret known only to Will Thomason.

"How many gallons do you produce from this?" the mine-owner asked.

"If thar ain't trouble, we'll get about thirty a week," Thomason replied, his voice almost inaudible in the humiliation of his situation.

"Well, come on. Let's go on up. I've got some business to discuss with you."

After the two men rejoined the others, Augustus laid out his proposal. "Thomason, do you know what those federals would do if they ever found a nigger as big as you running a still? Why, I don't think you'd ever again see the light of a free day or any of those fat, hungry women you seem to favor."

Thomason, his huge bulk stooped, stared at the ground. This was the first time in his experience that Augustus Porter's racism had been so cutting and blatant, although it certainly was always there to be assumed.

"Well," Augustus went on, "I think we can work out something to each other's advantage. You and I are going to be partners, splitting right down the line fifty-fifty. And my friends and I'll make sure you never have trouble from the sheriff. Isn't that fair?"

Thomason still said nothing.

"There's no need even to shake on it, I guess," the mine-owner said. His voice had changed, and he appeared slightly flustered, perhaps feeling guilty at his bullying of a quiet, good-natured man who was liked by everyone, including himself. "We're both good to our word. Just make sure you stop by with my share of the proceeds now and again. And I want you to drop off some of this 'shine—not the stuff you peddle, damn it, but some of the brew you keep for yourself. It's not bad."

Augustus turned and, followed by Haggerty and Carter, began to retrace his steps out of the clearing. Suddenly he stopped and shouted back to the silent group of black men, "And one more thing, Will—let's think some about expanding this operation."

His acquisition of Thomason's heralded still completed, Augustus moved onto his next money-making venture—his club.

There were all manner of excuses offered in the mansions of Livingston on the night Augustus opened his Club Havana: "I've got a meeting with the company lawyers." "We're auditing the account books, probably take all night." "I've got seventeen freight cars missing between here and Atlanta." "I'm gonna meet Stanley and play a little gin."

Fully half of the village's wealthy households emptied of their men, and the parade of luxury sedans and handcrafted limousines formed an unlikely caravan on the road to Bannerton.

Judged by the first night's enthusiasm, the club, Augustus's most outlandish scheme for maintaining his lavish standard of living, was certain to prove successful. It occupied a three-story white Victorian house near the Bannerton railroad station. The building had once served as a railroad hotel, and it still retained a hotel's appearance. When the passage of railroad men in and out of Bannerton diminished, the railroad had closed the hotel and sold the building to a fundamentalist missionary group, which put it to use as a retreat house. In time, the religious group could no longer afford its upkeep, and Augustus was able to purchase the house at a very attractive price.

The prospective members had no illusions as to what new purpose the building would serve. Grinning carpenters and other craftsmen were still putting the finishing touches on the remodeling when the club's opening-night guests began to arrive.

Augustus, dressed in formal attire, stood at the front door to greet personally the three dozen men he had invited and introduce them to Mae Sexton, the club's manager, a gregarious, spicy woman whom a Porter agent had found qualified and available in New York City. Mrs. Sexton—she was a longtime widow, she said—was, as one of the pleasantly surprised guests put it, a "fine piece of work." Well past fifty, she had long bleached hair that when free reached almost to the small of her back, but on opening night it was twisted and curled into an elaborate headpiece resembling a highly complex birdcage. Her bosom, its cleavage well displayed in a low-cut, skintight silken gown, was ample in its size, as was her derriere, also delightfully outlined by the smooth fabric. Mrs. Sexton wore a heavy layer of makeup, including two huge ovals of rouge on her cheeks. She spoke in a low, gravelly voice which to most men inspired visions of unspeakable sins.

As the guests arrived in their hand-tailored suits, they were steered past Augustus and Mrs. Sexton to a receiving line of young hostesses, also attired in long, revealing evening gowns, one of whom then broke ranks to escort the newcomers on a tour of the refurbished hotel. Some of what they saw existed elsewhere only in their most private dreams. The old hotel lobby had been transformed into a well-appointed parlor, warm in its color and textures. In the rear, where a dining room had once been, was a gaming area, paneled in walnut from floor to ceiling and filled with eight-sided tables topped with felt dyed bright green. On the second floor, many of the walls between the old hotel rooms had been broken through to leave large suites, each furnished with a different taste in mind. One had blood-red quilted silk covering its walls and its thick, equally red carpet had the feel of pure cotton to unclad feet. Another consisted almost entirely of mirrors, on both walls and ceiling. One more was hardly furnished at all, its walls, ceiling and floor painted a glossy snow white with a simple, low-lying bed in its center. The opening-night guests were not taken to the building's third floor, where, the hostesses explained, they had their dormitory. The tour over, the men were led to the basement, where the evening's festivities were to take place.

The basement featured a small bandstand. On it for opening night was a seven-piece Dixieland group brought in especially for the occasion from Charleston. Along one wall ran a plushly padded bar. A dozen circular tables were scattered about, each holding a flickering candle within a colored glass chimney.

Drinks, on the house for the opening night, were poured generously and served by the young hostesses in their long evening gowns. By the end of the first hour most of the guests were thoroughly drunk. The music grew louder, and the overhead chandeliers dimmed until only the tabletop candles provided light. Fannies were pinched and breasts fondled without reproach from the young hostesses, who, on the contrary, smilingly teased their guests on. One by one, gowns were yanked from slender waists and discarded unceremoniously on the tiled floor, leaving the room a ballet of bare skin interrupted only by sequined G-strings and silver tassels flapping from pasties attached to bouncing breasts. Soon many of the G-strings and tassels also littered the floor. A young woman, maybe nineteen, with a long, graceful body and dark hair pressed straight in the fashion of a pharaoh, belly-danced in front of the reenergized band, and the guests hooted, cheered and filled the smoky room with rebel yells.

"It's a pleasure to see a face like yours," the banker Raymond Baxley gushed to Mrs. Sexton.

"No wonder you West Virginia men are so frustrated," she replied. "There's so many mountains around here how's a girl gonna find space to lay flat on her back?"

"Hey, tootsie," came a call from a table in the corner. "Come over here and let me guess your weight."

By midnight the basement was half empty, deserted by the guests who had made their way to the rooms on the second floor. Of those who remained, at least a dozen had passed out in various postures on tables, under tables and beneath the padded bar. Two nude hostesses, stepping over and around the supine victims as gingerly as medics on a corpse-strewn battlefield, continued to serve those who still retained the capacity to nurse a drink. Augustus and Mrs. Sexton, sitting at an otherwise-unoccupied table in the rear of the room, scanned the field of desolation as if generals at war and winked at each other.

"You make a good partner," the mineowner told her. "And if you stay honest with me, you're going to end up rich."

"Just so I don't end up dead," she replied, patting his thigh.

By sunrise a poker game was under way in the first-floor gaming room, and it was clear that few of Augustus's guests had wanted to—or been able to—make it home to Livingston on opening night, a fact that did not go unnoticed by a group of outraged Livingston wives. When the hours became proper, the tiny village switchboard lit up in a rush of feminine outrage as the ladies of Livingston tactfully and often circuitously exchanged information. At noon a delegation of them consulted with the town's Episcopal minister, who declared there was nothing they could do about the debauchery they outlined except to pray and perhaps to pay a visit to the clergyman in Porterville in whose congregation Augustus Porter was a member.

Augustus was home by that evening with a massive headache. His eyes looked like red-veined golf balls. He found himself unable to eat, pushing even the soup away. And when Percy announced that the Reverend Weatherson was at the door requesting an urgent discussion, it was with reluctance that Augustus told the servant to show the clergyman in. He met him in his study.

The minister, young, diminutive and hopelessly timid, fingered his glasses as he sought a way to begin.

"Well, what is it?" Augustus asked impatiently. He had opposed Weatherson's assignment to the Porterville church from the beginning and found his sermons generally irritating, but the congregation had been able to locate no other man of the cloth who was willing to accept the Porter-run mining town as his mission.

"Ah . . . I'm not sure how to say this, Major, but some of the area women have asked me to have this talk with you," the minister stumbled. "It's about your new club."

"The Club Havana it's called. What of it?"

"Well, some of these ladies—and they're all good, God-fearing women of the church—well, they feel the club is just not proper for a Christian community and—"

Augustus, his hand to his forehead, interrupted him. "Look, Preacher, I've always been respectful of a man with a collar, both you and that Reverend Starky fellow before you. And you know if my father didn't put up the money long ago, you'd have no church to pray in—"

"I know, Major Porter, but—"

"Now, let me finish," Augustus ordered. "I want to ask you just one question, Reverend: Do you play poker?"

"No, sir, gambling is not my way."

"You might try it. With God on your side, you might win enough to finance a new belfry."

"But—"

"You come around, Weatherson. You come by the club some night. You're more than welcome, and the hostesses there, they're all the churchgoing kind too." Augustus chuckled.

"Please, Major Porter . . ." the clergyman attempted as Augustus placed an arm around his shoulder, leading him out of the study toward the front door. "Major. . . ."

"Now it was very nice of you to stop by. You can tell those concerned ladies that you talked with me and they have nothing to worry about. Just rumors, that's all, and people out to slander me and smear my name." The minister, having already been handed his hat, was eased out the door. "Good night, Reverend."

Weatherson, his round face flushed with frustration, slowly placed the hat on his head and turned to walk away.

"Oh, and by the way," Augustus called after him, "you ever been laid?"

Weatherson quickened his steps down the porch stairs and away from the mansion. It was several yards before he could no longer hear Augustus Porter chortling.

It was the Reverend Weatherson who told Jim about his father's club. As he listened, Jim had to bite his lip to keep from laughing—he had not realized his father was that creative.

"Something's come over that man," the minister declared. "I wish I knew what it was."

Jim decided he had to see the club for himself, and the next afternoon he was sheepishly knocking on the old hotel's locked door.

"Yes, sir?" said a young woman with bleached blond hair, opening the door slightly.

"I . . . ah . . . just thought I'd pay you a visit," Jim replied.

"Are you a member?"

"I'm not sure . . . I'm Augustus Porter's son."

The blonde reacted instantly, opening the door fully and apologizing for the delay. "This way, Mr. Porter," she said, leading him into a parlor. "I'm sure Mae will see you right away."

Mae Sexton, attired in a floor-length, flowing chartreuse dress, appeared suddenly before them, a huge smile on her face. "Welcome to the Club Havana. Can we get you a drink?"

"This is Mr. Porter. He's the major's son," the younger woman told her, a hint of warning to her tone.

"You don't say?" Mae responded, stepping back to inspect Jim. "I guess you do look a bit like him. Come and have a seat."

It was a potentially awkward situation, but Mae handled it with the aplomb of a woman who had finessed herself through many a sticky affair. She ordered the coffee Jim requested, and two delicate china cups and saucers were delivered in a moment. Then each eased back into the sofa they shared.

"What exactly is it we can do for you today?" the woman asked, her expression alert and curious.

Jim laughed. "Well, I'm not here for what you might call business, if that's what you mean." Mae smiled. "I've been in Europe for a couple of years, and when I got home, the first thing everyone started telling me was how wonderful your club is here, so I thought I'd stop by and see for myself."

Mae, seeming relieved, bent toward him and placed a hand

on his knee. "Actually, you're here to check up on what your father's been doing, right?"

Jim smiled.

"You see," she said, sitting back and chuckling, "you can't fool an old lady like me. I've been around and seen it all."

"I bet you have," Jim said. His tone was friendly. There was something very likable about the woman from New York with a little too much rouge on her cheeks. If anyone were in touch with the innermost desires of men no matter what their age and station, it would be a woman like Mae. "How long you been in this kind of business?" Jim asked.

She frowned. "Now what kind of question is that to ask a lady?"

"I'm sorry. I didn't mean it the way it sounded."

She rose and moved to the fireplace a few feet away. "It's a rough life sometimes," she said, staring at the portrait of an unidentified man above the mantel, her voice distant and wistful. "If my mother ever learned I was down here in West Virginia, she'd turn over in her grave." She turned toward Jim. "Let me tell you something. You're a young man. Listen to this, and don't ever forget it: This world of ours runs on sex, money and booze—nothing else. No matter what they tell you in church or school, there's not another thing that makes a penny's worth of difference."

Her spirit seemed to deflate as she spoke, and Jim felt sad for her. "Have you ever married, Mrs. Sexton?" he asked, unable to think of anything else to break the dreary mood her impromptu philosophizing had produced.

"Call me Mae," she ordered, her smile returning. "Yes, I've been married, four times, every one of them a disaster. And that's another lesson for you, young man: Find yourself a woman you can trust, someone you can love and give a damn about, and then never let her go. I lost the only fella I ever really cared about years ago, and life never gave me another shot." She sighed. "Oh, well, that's the way it goes."

"It's funny to hear you say that," Jim said. "A person

whose intelligence and perception I really respect told me just the opposite recently. He suggested I find a woman who has the means to help me out businesswise, someone with breeding and money is the way he put it."

Mae shook her head. "That's crap. You listen to Mae." She took his hand. "Come on now. I'll show you around."

"Thank you, but I think I'd better be going now."

"Whatever you say. But you're welcome here anytime you want to stop by, even if it's just to talk." She escorted him to the door.

Jim shook her hand, again feeling a flush of warmness for the woman whose job was probably in many ways the toughest in the world. "Thank you, Mrs. Sexton. My father made a good choice for his manager."

"I told you to call me Mae," she snapped.

"Okay, Mae." He grinned. "I happen to like you, I want you to know."

She lifted herself on her tiptoes and kissed his cheek. "Now scoot before somebody sees us and the talk begins." She slapped him on the buttocks and closed the door.

By the time Jim had his introduction to Mae Sexton he was officially an executive vice-president of the Porter Coal Company. His father had kept his promise. On the books, at least, he was the firm's chief financial officer. From that vantage point, Jim saw ominous portents of an impending economic scrambling by mineowners. The oil company legmen, like locusts that would not die, continued their intimidating invasion of the coalfields, forcing recalcitrant mineowners and their creditors into tightening circles of resistance. Lights burned late in Livingston's mansions, and out-of-town lawyers were summoned for hurried consultations. There were impromptu conferences in the Bannerton barbershop and soft-voiced discussions in secluded corners of restaurants and banks as Coal County's aristocracy intensified its defenses.

Jim, who understood more now than before of what was transpiring, was a ready participant in such gatherings, but much of what was discussed escaped him. The bargaining between a coalman and a banker was subtle, and the arrangements were complex. Despite his experience in London and the authority of his new title, Jim found himself in over his head. But it hardly mattered—his father still spoke for the Porter Coal Company. Augustus made the decisions.

CHAPTER 5 ⸻

When the baby cried to signal the end of her midday nap Bonnie didn't have to look at a clock to know the hour. Mari functioned on her own internal mechanism which timed her activities almost to the same minute each day. The baby fell asleep at the same hour every night and awakened at the same time every morning. The demands of her appetite met a precise schedule and her nap invariably ended almost at the stroke of 1:00 P.M. Bonnie's response to her child's needs had fallen into the same regular framework, but that was not all that remained unchanged for her from day to day: virtually her entire life had fallen into a rigid routine. T.C. left for work each weekday morning at 8:10 A.M and returned shortly before 6:00 P.M. In between, Bonnie's household chores followed as set a script as a cardinal's High Mass: preparing breakfast, making the bed, washing diapers, sweeping and dusting. Supper seldom took less than forty minutes to prepare. And at night, T.C., exhausted from his shift in the mine, rarely finished scanning the newspaper before he dropped off to sleep.

Bonnie left the house only for brief shopping trips to the company store and, when the weather wasn't too severe for Mari, Sunday church. Except for occasional visits from her mother, she was alone with her baby. In this isolation she sometimes carried on one-sided conversations with the two-year-old child, discussions that often made light of her unceasing routine. "If I extend my arms, maybe I can sweep the floor with seventy-three strokes instead of eighty," she joked one day. "I think I'm going to give you a shot of 'shine to squeeze one more hour out of your nap," she warned on another.

Actually, there was a part of Bonnie that welcomed the routine. Like a nun in a convent, she did not have to worry about what action to take next—it was all laid out for her. The range of her emotions had been compressed, and since she had given up her reading as well as her music there were few influences to stimulate her mind, to start her thinking about her confinement or to remind her of her betrayal by James T. Porter II.

Jim. Except for church she had seen him only once in the six months since his return from London and then at a distance. After church he seemed to rush home with his parents as if he were avoiding her. But that was okay—Bonnie had no idea what she would say to him if he ever approached her to say hello.

Mari's crying grew louder as she protested the delay in Bonnie's giving her her bottle. "Here, here. Such a temper," Bonnie chided as she lifted her from the crib.

She carried the still-crying baby to the rocker and offered her the nipple of the warm bottle. With the touch of the rubber against her lips, the baby immediately quieted and went to work vigorously filling her belly.

For a few moments, Bonnie hummed as she rocked her daughter. Then, as she often did, she began telling a story. "Try to imagine a mountain lake that's so big you can't see the opposite shore," she said, knowing, of course, that Mari couldn't possibly understand. "And think of the water being a cold, dark gray and having as salty a taste as a pretzel. That's the ocean, honey, the Atlantic Ocean. And some day, in not too many years, you're going to be crossing that ocean on a big, magnificent boat. Maybe even the *Queen Mary*. You'll be such a pretty young lady as you stroll the promenade with the most handsome man in the world on your arm. At dinner you'll toast each other with the best of champagne and eat the sweetest, fanciest desserts that the chef can make. And before you know it, you'll be in France. . . ." A gurgling sound from the bottle told her that Mari had finished her small afternoon serving. Bonnie raised the baby to her chest and patted her back until she heard an almost inaudible burp.

Bonnie carried Mari to the playpen T.C. had bought in Bannerton second-hand and then went to the closet for her broom.

"As I was saying," she said between sweeps, "you'll be in Paris, France, on the most wonderful honeymoon a girl could imagine. Each day they'll put fresh flowers in your hotel suite and you'll eat at the fanciest restaurants." She began to move the dust into one pile. "At night, of course, you'll go dancing and you and your man will spin gracefully around the entire ballroom. Just like this, honey—" With the broom as her partner, Bonnie began to waltz back and forth before the playpen. Mari, dropping her rattle, watched with fascination her mother's flowing movements and sudden turns and listened attentively to her melodic humming. Then the sounds stopped. Bonnie grasped the hem of her fading housecoat between her fingertips, bowed her head and dipped in a curtsy. As she did, she spotted her shadow in a square of sunlight cast through the grimy window upon the wooden floor.

It was already May; summer would soon arrive.

When his father, two other mineowners and a group of their creditors drifted together to a corner at a lawn party hosted in Livingston by the banker Raymond Baxley, Jim Porter ignored them. He was not in the mood for business. With his pipe in one hand and a glass of champagne in the other, he wandered over the grounds of the Baxley estate, pausing at a coal-fired spit for one more taste of what remained of the affair's roasted pig, and then circulated toward the dance band at the edge of the swimming pool. It was the same pool that Jim and the other miners from Blakely's store had invaded more than two years earlier. Now it was filled with floating pods of bright red and yellow flowers instead of a frolicking mob of drunken miners. Jim chuckled at the contrast.

As he exchanged greetings with several of the formally attired guests, he noticed a young woman staring at him. She was sitting at one of several white metal lawn tables a few yards away and seemed to have closed her ears to the chattering of her three tablemates, all young Livingston women. Jim reached into his pocket for his gold-plated lighter and was directing its flame at the ash in his pipe when the woman who had been staring at him suddenly appeared at his side.

"Hi," she said, flipping her head almost imperceptibly to bounce her ring of curls. "Bet you don't remember me?"

He didn't. In fact, he wasn't sure he had ever seen her before.

"I'm Anne. Anne Baxley. We haven't seen each other since I was sixteen or seventeen."

"Oh, yes," Jim said apologetically. He did remember her now as the banker's daughter. "Well, you've sure grown up since I last saw you." He noticed her empty wineglass. "Here, let me get you a refill."

As he stood at the bar, he inspected the young woman. She was tall with a high forehead and thin brown hair arranged into a ring of delicate curls hanging just below her ears. Her neck was long and thin, accentuating the size of her head. Her dark blue eyes were small, and her lips, thin, growing taut when she smiled. In all, she was neither especially pretty nor plain but knew how to use what she had. Her grooming was perfect with an overall effect that was pleasing, if suggestive of the artificial beauty of a mannequin. There was a stiffness to her movements, but this deficiency was overcome by her bearing, which suggested a woman who knew what she wanted and usually got it, no matter what the cost.

After Jim returned from the bar, they moved to the dance floor, where Anne exchanged pleasantries with everyone. Her style was polished and effective, and Jim was impressed. She had the charm of someone at ease with persons of wealth, culture and authority. In a matter of minutes she had introduced him to an aide to the governor, a prominent Cardiff City lawyer and three other men whom Jim hadn't known and whose connections and influence might prove useful to the Porter Coal Company one day. As he allowed Anne to open these doors for him, he remembered Preston's advice in London to find a woman with the bloodlines, finesse and intelligence to help his business along.

The band finished playing. Anne's father, a short, balding, puffy man in his early fifties, approached them.

"I see you've met young Porter," he said to his daughter. Then, conspiratorally: "Make a good pitch for yourself—he's a young fella who's going to go a long way in these parts."

"Oh, Father, why don't you stick to your ledger books?" she said, blushing.

Most of the remaining guests, including Jim's parents, were preparing to leave. Augustus beckoned to Jim to join them.

"It was nice seeing you, Anne. I had a wonderful time," Jim said, edging toward his parents.

She placed a hand on his thick forearm. "Did you hear that *Giant* is playing in Bannerton? I really hope I get a chance to see it." It was a bold proposal that left Jim with few graceful options.

"Maybe we can see it together," he suggested.

"How about Saturday. Would that be okay?"

He nodded, uncertain quite what to say.

"The movie begins at eight, I believe. I'll be ready anytime after seven."

During the five days before their date Jim gave little thought to Anne Baxley, except to chuckle about how it was the first time he had been asked out by a girl. Since his return from London he had dated a few Livingston women, but none had captured him as he had once been taken by Bonnie Shaw. Still, he liked Anne Baxley's charm, intelligence and sometimes startling forthrightness, not to mention the carnal impulses he suspected were lurking beneath the pretense of her upper-class manners.

On Saturday night the Bannerton Cinema was filled to capacity, and Jim considered himself lucky to buy two of the last remaining tickets. *Giant* had arrived in Bannerton only six or seven months after its general release across the country, about half the lapsed time for most films making their way there. In response, the cinema owner had doubled his admission price, raising it to $1.

Anne maintained a commentary throughout the viewing, paying particular notice of James Dean's rugged sensuality. She pressed close to Jim and placed a hand in his lap. He took it into both his hands and held it loosely. When the film was over, she suggested that they wait in their places until most of the crowd had made their exit. Only a dozen or so stragglers were on the street as they made their way to Jim's car.

It was chilly, and Jim had to turn the Oldsmobile's engine over twice before it started. The air was misty, a thick evening fog having rolled into the Bannerton valley. Jim switched on his yellow fog lamps and drove slowly, the droplets of moisture on the car's finish glistening brightly as they passed under the streetlights, which were encircled by rainbows. Suddenly Anne shouted, "Turn here!"

"Excuse me?" Jim asked, pushing the brake.

"Don't ask questions," she ordered. "Just pull up into that

small driveway there." She pointed to the right and a narrow dirt clearing leading to a parking area behind the Bannerton barbershop. Jim did as ordered. When they reached the back of the shop, he pulled the car into one of the three spaces as Anne instructed.

"It's the best view in Bannerton," she boasted. "Turn off the motor."

Jim peered through the windshield as he reached for the ignition key. All he saw was a windowless brick wall that was part of Al and Henry's Tool & Die Shop. "I can't see anything but a beat-up old wall."

"That's exactly what I mean," she said, laughing. "Gray mountains, black mine tipples, sooty brick walls—it makes no difference. This is the ugliest land God ever created."

"There're a lot of people who might not agree with you," he chided.

"Yes. And none of them has ever set foot on Park Avenue or driven through Beverly Hills. That's where you find style and beauty in this country."

"Is that what you learned at that college in New England?"

"Are you kidding? You think I learned anything from the fairies and old maids who waste their lives teaching there?" She reached for her purse, opened it and extracted what he recognized in the dim light as a pint-sized silver flask.

"If that's the way you feel, I don't understand why you came back to Coal County."

"Daddy," she replied. "Daddy needed his little girl. Or so he said, anyway. Here, have a slug. It's brandy. Takes the chill away."

Jim declined. "You always carry that with you?"

"Only during inclement weather. And around here that's about all the time. If you won't drink from it, then neither will I. But you'd better do something to chase this cold."

"Like what?"

"Like this," she said, turning her back slightly and snuggling up to him. "Do you think you could turn on the radio at least?"

Jim switched on the ignition key and twisted the controls of the radio to find only one station still broadcasting at that hour. It was playing country and western. The windows had steamed up from their breathing, and only the faint glow of a distant streetlamp provided illumination. Jim placed his right arm around her shoulders. She reached for his free hand and pulled it into her lap. They sat silently listening to the radio for a few minutes until Anne, with a slow, deliberate motion, raised Jim's hand under the folds of her heavy sweater. She guided his fingers from one breast to the other and twisted her head sharply to kiss him. Jim, whose impulses were first stirred by the warmth of her body pressed against him, was once again startled at her boldness, but he accepted her invitation and pulled her around to face him. They kissed again. He continued to knead her breasts until one of her hands found his and she once more guided him, this time down to the hem of her skirt and back up again. Jim had just felt the frilly fabric of her panties when there was a loud thump on the car's hood. The beam of a flashlight suddenly lit their faces through his side window.

"All right, you two. Get the hell out of there. Right now!" barked a voice with authority.

"Stay here," Jim said to Anne. "I'll handle this." He opened the door cautiously, unable because of the mist to identify the intruder.

The stranger, keeping his light in Jim's face, recognized him first. "Mr. Porter! What the hell are you doing here?"

"And just who are you, if I may ask?"

"Oh, I'm sorry," he said, removing the light from Jim. "It's Deputy Mellon. How're ya doin'? Haven't seen ya in some time, couple of years, I guess."

"I've been away. Now I'm just sitting here with my girl, catching up on all the news."

The deputy bent to peer into the car in an effort to see who was inside.

"If you don't mind, Deputy, I think I'd better be on my way," Jim said.

"Why, sure. Just drive careful. It's like soup when you hit the pass. Just came from there and had trouble myself."

"Thanks. And good night," Jim said, not waiting for a response before returning inside the car and starting the engine. As Mellon stood at the side of his patrol car watching them, they drove away.

"Idiot," Anne said, glaring at the deputy through the still fogged-up windows. "What's he going to arrest us for, conspiracy to pet?"

Jim didn't respond. His attention was on the roadway, which, as Mellon had warned, was nearly impossible to see. Almost coming to a full stop at times, he carefully nursed the car through the mountain pass where the road climbed in a series of sharp curves midway to Livingston. With Anne's help, he found the entrance to her driveway and pulled the Olds under the front portico.

"Won't you come inside for a while?" she asked.

"Thanks, but I think I had better head for home."

"If you think I'm going to let you drive through this soup, you're crazy. I had too much fun tonight to see you die like that."

"But I wouldn't want to disturb your parents," he protested.

"Oh, they won't mind," she said, smiling mischievously. "They're asleep already. Come on!" She grabbed him by the arm and pulled him out of the car.

The mansion was dark except for a small light in the foyer. Jim stepped toward the front door, but Anne stopped him. "Not there," she said. "Around the back."

Taking him by the hand, she led him around the side and to the rear of the house. The fog was still heavy, and they could barely see the ground. She urged him to be careful. He understood why when they reached a wooden footbridge that crossed a wide, deep gully carved into a rear corner of the yard. The bridge was hidden by a thicket of tall bushes and brush. On the other side was a small house.

"That's my playhouse," Anne explained. "Daddy had it built especially for me . . . to keep my dolls and things."

The playhouse that Raymond Baxley had built for his daughter was fully three rooms in size, and as large as some of the ancient company houses in the old Negro section of Porterville. It was designed as a chalet, pure white stucco broken by the rich dark oak of its crisscrossing beams and by shutters painted bright green. Inside were a miniature kitchen, bedroom and parlor, all filled with handcrafted furniture. Dolls by the dozens were scattered everywhere, along with the other toys and trinkets that are part of a young lady's life when she is a wealthy man's only daughter.

Inside, Anne pointed to a stone fireplace. "There's some wood there to the side," she said. "Do you think you could start a fire? I'll be back in a minute or two." Anne winked and then slipped out the door. She crossed the bridge to the mansion.

Jim placed kindling and some quarter logs into the fireplace, which he was astounded to find in a playhouse, and expertly started a fire. He took a seat on a crushed velvet sofa, which faced the fireplace. Anne soon returned with two glasses and a bottle of champagne. She opened the bottle with a quickness and ease that suggested experience, poured their drinks and sat beside him, tossing a Raggedy Ann doll out of the way.

"That's Annabelle," she said. "But don't worry—she may see all, but she doesn't tell." Anne chuckled and pressed closer to him. "And this is Franny," she said, lifting a stuffed toy poodle. "Do you have a dog?"

"I did. But when I came back from London, he was dead."

"London? I didn't know you were in London."

"I just came home. Spent the last two or so years there."

"That means I was there for more than a month at the same time you were," she said excitedly. "I went there after graduation. Maybe we passed each other in Trafalgar Square. Do you remember seeing a tall, sexy American girl looking lost among all those dirty pigeons?"

"Unfortunately I never had time for the pigeons. Our agent there kept me too busy."

Anne groaned. "That's the trouble with you mining men. Work. Work. Work. Tons of this and tons of that. And what's to be done about the goddamn union. None of you know how to enjoy life. There's a lot more to living than a filthy hunk of coal."

Jim's impulse was to challenge her, to explain, as he had only recently learned, how without coal he and she and everyone else in Coal County would have nothing, but he stifled the impulse and only smiled. He had heard such ranting from other young Livingston women of his acquaintance. How could they know with their mansions, their servants, their hefty allowances? He reached into a pocket of his sports jacket—a heavy tweed like that favored by Preston—and removed his pipe, intending to fill it. But he found his zippered leather pouch empty of tobacco. "I've got some more in the car," he told Anne. "Would you excuse me a moment?"

"If that's a brushoff, it's not very original," she declared, her face contorting into a pout.

Jim laughed. "No, I'll be back. I promise."

"And don't jump off that bridge," she called after him.

When he returned, Jim found her seated on the thick rug in front of the sofa, facing the fire and wrapped in a heavy Canadian Hudson's Bay blanket. "Take your coat off and join me," she said. "I'll get you warm again after that trip into the fog and cold."

Jim, for the moment forgetting about his pipe, dropped his jacket on a nearby chair and slipped under the blanket. He wrapped his arm around her back and, to his surprise, found it bare. Further exploration revealed that the young woman was entirely unclothed.

"Come closer," she said. "Don't be bashful. Didn't you ever snuggle up to a naked girl before? And I'm twenty-two —I don't need my parents' consent."

Jim rolled onto his side and pressed toward her. The crackling flames from the fireplace cast a reddish tint over them both. He studied her face, noting how young it seemed and how clear her complexion was and wondering how many $100-a-half-ounce French creams were responsible for that. As he reached for her cheek, his eyes caught a glimpse of his own hand, and he was struck by how smooth his skin's texture was, the hand pale and unblemished, the ingrained film of coal dust having disappeared. Bending forward, he kissed her. As their tongues tested each other's, he felt her hands reach for the buttons of his shirt and then travel lower and lower in a tantalizing circular route until they reached his groin. They broke their kiss while Jim's clothes were discarded, and then Anne moved her head down his belly and under the blanket while Jim watched the flames in the fireplace through half-closed eyes. When he could take no more, he pulled her onto her back and rolled on top of her, their bodies entwining under the heavy blanket. Slowly at first, and then fiercely, he made love to her. She responded, slamming her hips upward against him in time to his rhythm until, bridging her neck and locking her legs around the small of his back, she shuddered. In a few seconds he followed. And both retreated onto their backs, his hand grasping hers, the blanket at their feet. Jim reached down and pulled the heavy wool fabric over them, and they listened to each other's breathing, which produced the only sounds in the playhouse except for the snapping of the flames.

Anne's lovemaking had been as pleasurable as any Jim had experienced. He had no doubt of her experience. She knew what she was doing. And she seemed to enjoy it, unlike most women he had known. Unless she had faked it, that is—he had encountered that, too. Despite their pleasurable activity of the previous few minutes, Jim now felt wasted and hollow, a pinch of regret added to his other emotions of the moment. He looked at Anne, and only then did it occur to him that her body was bony and muscle-hard in places that should be pliable and soft. He had noticed no such deficiencies in the frenzy of their lovemaking. Her expertise, her passion and, most important perhaps, her appetite had overcome what nature had deprived her of. Jim was intrigued by this sensual power that lay within Anne much like a clown hidden in a jack-in-the-box ready to be sprung.

"You're good, Jim, as good as they come," she said in a raspy voice while handing him her empty champagne glass. He reached for the bottle on the floor a few feet away and filled it.

"You're not so bad yourself. You learn that in New England?"

"Come on," she scolded, "I told you all those teachers were fairies."

As they lay there, his arm again around her shoulders, Jim had a sudden urge to get dressed. Without explanation, he threw the blanket off him and picked up his scattered clothes. "I've got to be going," he told her. "Otherwise, I'll never get home."

She watched him dress silently, the blanket edge now at her waist, her small, firm breasts exposed to the light cast by the dying fire. When he had finished, she turned her gaze to the wood-beamed ceiling and said, "Come back tomorrow. We'll play some cards or something, and with my parents leaving town, who knows? How does seven sound?"

"Isn't that kind of early? I mean, the servants would still be around and—"

"Let me handle that, sweetheart," she interrupted. "And do me a little favor, and make sure the door's closed on your way out. I'm not moving from here until the morning."

Jim paused at the playhouse door for one last look at Anne.

Her gaze was fixed vacantly on the ceiling. The blanket was still at her abdomen. Sufficient light came from the fireplace to project a grotesque shadow from her nose across one side of her face. The room, despite the smoke from the fire, was filled with the odors of flat champagne and spent bodies, and he longed for a breath of the moist night air outside. "Good night," he said finally, stepping into the cold and fog that still lingered. He shivered once as he walked to his car. The inside of the car was cold, but he opened a window anyway, letting the thick, wet air bathe his face on the drive to Porterville.

Raymond Baxley and his wife were away on a vacation to Florida when Jim returned to their mansion the next night and each following night for two weeks. He lost track of how many times he and Anne made love. They did it in the parlor, in her bedroom and on the floor of her father's den, marathon sessions lasting well past midnight. Anne played him like a finely tuned instrument, employing her full set of predatory instincts and creating in him a need for her which was so subtle and slow in its development that by the time he became fully aware of it, it was beyond any defenses he might have mustered. She identified his strengths and played off them, found his weaknesses and made note of them while carefully concealing her own vulnerability, needs and desires. Most powerful in her arsenal of weapons was her sexuality, and she craftily bestowed her practiced favors when Jim least expected them, withholding them when he most wanted them. By design, she inserted herself into his life until visiting her, wooing her and making love to her became part of his routine. She became a habit but was never without surprises. And when the time was proper, she gradually exposed her own soul, revealing one by one at opportune moments her own expectations and demands, laying the cornerstone of a master plan that went far beyond anything Jim was consciously aware of. To him, she remained a puzzle, a growing enigma whose behavior vacillated from one extreme to another like a pendulum caught in an ever-widening arc. When he searched for a pattern, he found none. As with a battlefield general, doing the unexpected was her most dependable strategy.

Sometimes, however, Anne misjudged her distance and had to retreat hurriedly. Jim usually failed to notice these lapses. But one day in August, three months after her father's lawn party, Anne's self-discipline faltered too blatantly. Her behavior in one careless instant almost put their relationship beyond repair.

Jim had stopped by in his Olds to take her for a ride in the country. Anne met him at the door and looked fearfully toward the sky, which was dark gray.

"I think we ought to postpone this, sweetheart," she declared. "It's going to pour any minute."

"It's been overcast like this for two days now, and it hasn't rained. Besides, we'll be in the car," Jim protested.

"Why don't you just come inside and have some tea? Really, Jim, I don't want to go out into this weather."

But Jim had his heart set on the drive and had selected a beautiful spot near Cedar Ridge as their destination. There was a large pond there, hidden by trees not far from the road, and he knew Anne had never been there. "I thought it might be romantic and you'd enjoy it," he said.

"No, dammit," she snapped. "I'm not going, Jim, and that's it."

The sharpness of her words startled him, and his expression showed hurt and shock. Anne read the situation immediately. She reached through the doorway to take his hand.

"Okay, honey," she said softly with a smile. "Let's take a chance on the rain. Like you say, we'll be in the car. Give me just a minute to get ready."

She returned wearing a chiffon summer dress and a small straw bonnet with a sky blue ribbon tied into a bow. She climbed into the car, sliding to the center of the seat to be next to Jim, and he pulled out of the driveway. He negotiated Livingston's winding streets until they reached the county road, which took them to Porterville and then, two miles farther, past the entrance to the Red Fox Mine. Three miles later Jim took the cutoff to Cedar Ridge and, after several yards, pulled the car to the side. "Come on," he said. "That pond I told you about is only a few yards into these trees."

Anne, a smile still on her face, followed him through the brush. Twice she stumbled on hidden rocks, and once she was struck in the face by a flying branch which had slipped from Jim's hand. But she did not protest. When they reached the edge of the pond, she took a seat on a barkless section of a fallen tree. He sat beside her, pointing out and identifying birds as they circled down to the greenish water, snapped up insects and soared off. Then, suddenly and without warning, it began to rain. It fell in sheets, making it difficult for them even to see. Jim yanked Anne toward the protection of a tree, but the rain shot through the leaves like a spray of shotgun pellets. It was too late anyway—with the suddenness of the storm, both already were soaked. Anne's bonnet was a soggy mess, its brim drooping over her eyes, and her dress clung to her like wet tissue paper. The rain was cold, causing her to shiver and spotting her skin with goose bumps.

"My hair!" she exclaimed, reaching up to feel the dripping strands that a few minutes earlier were carefully ironed curls. "Look at my dress!" she shouted, lifting the hem of the drenched fabric for inspection. "Dammit, Jim, get me out of here!"

He grabbed her hand and led her away at a trot. "I'm sorry, honey. I didn't think it'd break that fast," he shouted. When he looked, he saw her biting her lower lip. She appeared to be crying, her tears mixing with the raindrops rolling down her cheeks. He pushed her into the car and then went to the trunk for a blanket. He wrapped her in it and pulled her against him to keep her warm.

"Forget me, and let's get this thing going," she ordered. "If you'd listened to me in the first place, we wouldn't be here now. Take me home."

Jim started the car and drove as fast as he could over the dirt road, which was quickly turning to mud. Neither of them spoke until they reached the intersection with the county road.

"We're home free now," Jim said, easing the car onto the gravel surface.

The rear wheels spun in place for a moment as he pressed hard on the accelerator. By the time they passed the entrance-way to the Red Fox Mine the speedometer had passed sixty. Jim's side vision caught a glimpse of a bent figure trudging along the side of the road, probably a Red Fox miner, heading for town. Jim slammed on the brakes, coming to a stop several yards past the man, who, seeing the slowing car, broke into a run.

"What the hell are you doing?" Anne demanded.

"There's a miner back there. Thought we'd give him a lift," Jim replied.

"I don't care if he's John the Baptist, dammit," she shot back. "Get moving and take me home!"

Jim stared at her, openmouthed in disbelief. He felt his adrenaline pumping, his anger building toward an outburst in which he surely would tell her to go to hell. But at the same time, his right foot moved slowly from the brake pedal onto the accelerator. The car sped off again, Jim watching through his rearview mirror the man behind them, who had abruptly stopped his running and was staring at the fleeing vehicle.

While Anne muttered to herself beside him, Jim searched frantically for a justification for what he had just done. Unable to find one, he looked accusingly toward Anne. She ignored him. He began to feel embarrassed, a sense of regret and shame rising within him for the cruelty of his action. He was asking himself if it wasn't too late to turn back and pick up the drenched miner when the car hit a water-filled low spot in the road, skidded sideways and slid partially off the gravel, its right rear wheel coming to a sinking stop halfway down the muddy shoulder.

"Shit! What the hell will be next?" Anne screamed, then broke into hysterical crying.

Jim said nothing, concentrating, instead, on extricating the car from the mud. He pressed hard on the accelerator, but the rear wheels merely spun in the mud. He tried switching the gearshift back and forth between forward and reverse. The car rocked but still was unable to make traction.

"We need a push," Jim said finally. "I'll get out. You take the wheel and press the accelerator gently when I yell."

"I don't drive," Anne snapped, her weeping ceasing for a moment. "I don't know a goddamn thing about what you're saying."

Jim sighed and slouched into the seat, frustrated at what next to try. Then he remembered the miner, who should be right behind them. He twisted around and looked through the rear window, spotting the figure of the miner only a few dozen yards away. As the man drew closer, Jim recognized Lou Greentree, the husky Indian. "He's a good man," he told the sobbing woman beside him. "With him at the wheel and me pushing, we'll get out of this in a minute."

"The hell you will, Jim," she said, her expression furious. "You're not going to have that dripping, filthy man sit next to *me*. He works for you, doesn't he? Let him do the dirty work."

"But we already passed him by and—"

"Is it your company or isn't it?" she interrupted. "If you don't have the balls to do it, I'll take care of it myself," she went on. She rolled down her side window, stuck her head out and yelled at the advancing figure, "Hurry it up, would you?"

Lou appeared not to hear her. He slogged through the mud and wet grass up to her open window. "Having trouble?" he asked.

"You work for Porter, right?" she demanded. Lou, confused, nodded. "Well, get in back of this damn car and push."

The miner lowered his head and glanced across at Jim, who was unable to look back at him. "Yes, ma'am," Lou said, his tone razor-sharp with bitterness.

With one push from the burly miner, the car was free of the mud. Jim, now ignoring a protest from Anne, stopped the vehicle, waiting for Lou to catch up to it. "Hop in, Lou," Jim told him.

"No, thanks," Lou responded, glaring. "I'm doing just fine . . . *Captain*." His eyes fired with rage, he walked slowly away.

It was the first time a miner had ever assigned Jim the latest bossman's military title, and there was no doubt about its message, that Lou had meant it derisively. A nauseated, empty feeling came to Jim's stomach.

By the time they reached the Baxley mansion the rain had stopped. The overcast was breaking, allowing the bright midday sun to peek down. Anne, saying nothing, rushed in and upstairs. Jim went inside to use the phone. He was talking to his office on the telephone in her father's den when Anne returned. She had changed into a dark red housecoat, her still-wet hair wrapped in a towel. There was a cheerful smile on her face and no evidence of her earlier crying. With a bounce to her step, she went up to Jim, placed her arms around his waist and nuzzled his neck with her lips and chin. As he continued talking on the phone, she slithered down his body, sinking to her knees. She reached for the zipper to his pants, yanked it down and passed her hand through. Jim, preoccupied with his conversation, attempted to brush her hand away; but she persisted, and he found himself responding involuntarily to her caressing. She went to work earnestly on him, her expertise distracting him so he began stumbling on his words. He cut his call short and hung up the phone, then placed his hand upon her hair.

"Are you crazy?" he asked incredulously. "What if your father walks in?"

"Hmmmmm," Anne moaned, continuing her handiwork. A minute later he braced himself against her father's desk, closed his eyes and emitted a groan.

Jim waited until he had caught his breath. "Anne, there's something I think we'd better talk about," he said, intending to air his displeasure and surprise about the scene back on the road. But she stopped him, hushing his lips with her fingers and following with a series of wet kisses, their intensity exciting him again. Then she stopped.

"I'm exhausted, dear," she said. "Can't our talk wait until tomorrow? I love you, you know." She kissed him again and led him by the hand toward the door. "Oh, by the way, my parents will be having Congressman Runyun over for dinner next week, and we want you to join us. He's a good man for you to know."

Jim nodded, offering a smile to signal his defeat. No matter what offense Anne committed, he still remained under her magical control, enjoying it, he had to admit, because this cunning young woman, so full of energy and devious plans, so passionate and talented in her lovemaking, had somehow won his heart.

Jim checked to make certain he was zipped and then left for his car, the rays of the newly reborn sun forcing him to squint and splashing warmness against his face.

In bed that night he tried to sort it out, this selfish bitchiness that had surfaced so suddenly in Anne balanced against the warm, generously loving body he knew in bed. Sleep came before he found an answer. When he awoke the next morning, what had happened in the rain on the road to Cedar Ridge seemed less important than what he and Anne would do that night when her parents would again be out of town.

Anne never repeated her mistake. In the weeks following

the incident with Lou Greentree, she showed herself to be as democratic as anyone in the county. And Jim had all but forgotten the episode a month later as he dressed slowly in his formal wear a few hours before his marriage to Miss Anne Baxley. He had asked to be left alone—not out of nervousness, for he found himself not nervous at all—but to think—of Anne and their marriage and how it culminated a courtship of less than five months. He had met her in late May; it was now early October. His intellect told him he hardly knew the girl. Strangely, this didn't bother him, for there was something deep within him that told him their impending union was not only proper but would endure. Her selfishness, which had surfaced on their drive to the country, had never reappeared. Jim dismissed it as a fluke. On the contrary, she had been especially generous and undemanding in the weeks that followed, and her lovemaking had remained as proficient and satisfying as usual.

His decision to marry had come after he had taken her to visit the Red Fox Mine. Her smile never left her for the entire hour, and as he introduced her to his onetime coworkers, she was exceptionally pleasant and cordial. He was flattered by how the other men looked at Anne, how their eyes traveled up and down her body and how they reacted to her with a mixture of hunger, admiration and respect. Jim took that as an endorsement of his taste, and it pleased him.

As he dressed, Jim's thoughts jumped back and forth in place and time, and he found himself remembering how he had been stirred from his sleep a month earlier with a vision of Red Fox Mine's interior, lingering from a dissolving dream. At a prenuptial dinner only the night before, someone passed him biscuits, and without thinking he lifted one with his napkin as a miner employs a clean white handkerchief to protect his food in the mine. In the shower once he caught himself humming the dirge they played on the day the Blakely's drinking men buried Evans's thumb. And there came the memory of a walk he had taken into the foothills one summer to hunt berries with a miner's daughter who feared becoming a rich boy's toy and said so. Catching himself, he tried to shake that memory from his head and turn his attention to the cuff link he was struggling to put on.

As Jim moved toward the full-length mirror in his dressing room, he noticed a letter Anne had had delivered to him after he left her home the previous night. He picked up the yellow envelope, smelled its perfume and removed the note from inside. It was written in a feminine script, almost illegible for all its embellishment.

"My dear Jim," it began. "Tomorrow you and I will be husband and wife through the holy act of matrimony. It is to be a blessed day and the highlight of all that is worthy in either of our lives.

"I write this, my dearest, to reaffirm my love and to make of you a request I have difficulty putting into words. I know you will understand.

"Our marriage will be a solemn occasion, and therefore, I believe we must take clearly defined steps to ensure it is launched properly. So when we are at last alone on our wedding night, when all the bothersome relatives and guests finally leave, when the license is officially signed and the festivities are over, would you please, please, Jim, drop your pants as quickly as possible!!! Tee-hee!"

She had signed it "With my love and devotion, Anne."

Jim laughed as he reread the note. That was the way she was, alive and hungry, a female in every respect and, at the same time, sufficiently strong to hold her own with the battle-axes who dominated Coal County's high society, such as it was.

There was a knock on the door. Opening it, Jim found both his father and his future father-in-law, Raymond Baxley.

"Well, well, well," Augustus said, grinning as he entered the room. "It's finally happened—my only surviving son has fallen to the charms of a woman." He grasped Jim roughly by the arm. "Now don't be nervous. In hardly more than an hour, it'll be all over . . . and then you'll know what the rest of us men have been going through." Augustus chortled.

Baxley stepped in front of Jim and, with a serious expression, took his hand. "I just want you to know, son, that I'm very proud of you and my daughter and this Baxley-Porter team is going to turn this county upside down. Welcome to the family, boy."

"Thank you, sir," Jim said, edging away from him.

Anne's parents had seen to it that hers would be a wedding to be remembered. The small Episcopal church in Livingston was bedecked with dozens of white mums and gladiolas shipped from Philadelphia. There were yards of white ribbon, and the white wedding carpet extended past the church's door to the outside, where it was sprinkled with fallen leaves.

Sarah, wearing a huge corsage, was beaming when Augustus led her to their front pew. Across the aisle, Anne's mother, a short, slender woman with prematurely gray hair, was dabbing at her eyes while waiting for the entrance of her daughter and her husband.

Anne wore a satin bias-cut gown with a train fifteen feet long. She carried her mother's white prayer book and with it a white orchid, also imported for the occasion. Her bridesmaids wore velvet gowns, each in a different pastel—pink, blue, yellow and green—and carried long-stemmed red roses. The men were handsome in the black tails and gray-striped pants of their morning suits, and none had a better fit than Jim's.

In forty minutes it was over. Jim had officially taken a banker's daughter as his wife. The celebrants moved to the Baxley mansion for the reception, the wedding party traveling by limousine. At the mansion, the popping of champagne corks filled the ballroom with sounds resembling those of a rifle range, and one toast after another was offered to the newly married couple. The musicians struck up a waltz, and Jim and Anne circled the ballroom floor to the applause of the guests. Augustus Porter had just started for the dance floor to cut in on his son when a butler stopped him to report that someone was asking to see him at the kitchen door.

"He's a Nigra, sir. Says his name is Thomason," Jim heard the servant say.

"Well, I'll be damned. What the hell could he want now?" Augustus asked.

"He didn't say, sir. He only said it was very important."

"You tell that son of a bitch not to bother me on the day of my son's wedding. And you tell him his black ass shouldn't be here anyway," the mineowner said.

"Yes, sir," the butler said, departing. Augustus shook his head, muttered an obscenity and cut in on Jim to dance with Anne. In a minute or two the butler was back beckoning him. Augustus left the puzzled Anne on the dance floor.

"Excuse me again, sir," the butler said, "but the gentleman says it is extremely urgent that you speak to him. He told me to tell you it's about the federal men."

"What federal men?"

"He didn't say, sir. Only that they had paid him a visit and might be looking for an appointment with you."

"Oh, Christ," Augustus said. "All right, tell him I'll be down in a minute. But don't let that bastard into the house until I get there. This is embarrassing enough as it is." He returned to Anne with a bow and an apology.

When the waltz was over, Augustus moved to Jim. "Come with me for a minute, would you? I think I've got some trouble." A servant escorted them to the kitchen two floors below.

Seeing Will Thomason standing at the door, Jim knew immediately that there was trouble because of the still. From the first moment he had heard of his father's acquiring an interest in Thomason's enterprise, he knew it would only be a matter of time before there was trouble—there were too many people involved. He could see the headline in the Bannerton *Tribune* now: "Mineowner Nabbed for Bootlegging."

"This had better be important, Will, or I'll have your ass," Augustus said.

"It's important, Major. I think we'd better do our talkin' private like," Thomason responded, looking at Jim.

"It's okay. I want him here," Augustus said, leading Thomason from the mansion's rear porch and into a walk-in pantry. Jim followed.

"Well, what is it?" the mineowner asked impatiently.

"The federals, Major. They just showed up today and caught me. Took some of the still and wrecked the rest."

"Goddammit!" Augustus snapped in a muted voice, striking the fist of one hand into the palm of the other. "How the hell did they find it? And say, how come you're walking around free? You running away or something?"

"No. They set me free. I don't know how they found it. Followed me from home maybe. And then they say they're gonna send me south for the rest of my life unless I cooperate. 'Cooperate?' I say. 'What the hell does that mean?' And they say they ain't interested in just me. They wanna get a bigger fish. Then they start askin' me all about you."

"Me?" Augustus asked incredulously. "They use my name?"

"Sure did, Major. 'Tell us about Porter,' they said. Course, I didn't tell 'em nothin'. That's probably why they set me free. Told me I could run around thinkin' about all the time I'll have to spend behind bars unless I decide to cooperate. And just as soon as they're through with that grand jury, they say, they're gonna come back to get me. And off I go, 'less I cooperate."

"Sit down, Will," Augustus said, pointing to a cardboard box full of cans. "Let me think about this awhile." He did his reasoning out loud: "Let me see, they could have learned about your still from any of a hundred people who know about it. But how the hell did they know about me? Only ones that knew were you and me, the sheriff and a couple of my men."

He paused for a moment, his fingers rubbing his chin. Then, in a voice louder and sharper, he asked, "Say, those two black-assed partners of yours, they didn't say anything, did they?"

"No way, Major. They're like brothers," Will replied.

"Well, they've got you one way or the other, but we still might find a way to keep them away from me," the mineowner continued. "Now, unless you or one of the others start talking, they've got no witnesses. There're no written records anywhere, thank God for that." He turned to Jim. "Listen, maybe we can get him the hell out of the country, to Mexico or some place."

"Pa, that's not the way to—" Jim began.

"There'd be no way," Will interrupted. "They're already on me like flypaper and maybe even followed me here."

"Here?" Augustus shouted. A cook passing the pantry heard him. The mineowner lowered his voice. "Are you crazy?"

"I thought I'd better tell ya."

"You didn't have to lead them to my door." Augustus paused. He grinned. "Tell you what, Thomason, you and me, we'll make another deal. You take the heat, and we'll work out some payments. But not now. Get the hell away from here, and stay put until I send for you. I'll make it worth your while, so keep your mouth shut."

"Whatever you say, Major."

Sarah was searching for them when Augustus and Jim returned to the ballroom. "Where have you been?" she asked. "Is there something wrong?"

"Nothing, Ma. We just stepped outside for some air," Jim answered. But he knew his words were contradicted by his father's appearance. The mineowner's face was ashen. He appeared stunned. Jim and his mother watched as Augustus, his head bowed in thought, made his way to the bar and ordered straight whiskey, double. After taking the glass in a shaking hand, he found an unoccupied table off in the corner, sat down and slumped over the drink.

"What is it, son?" Sarah asked.

"The damn still. The federals found it."

"Oh, my God!"

He put his arm around his mother. "Now just put it out of your mind and enjoy the rest of the wedding, okay?"

Sarah smiled and touched his cheek. "I'll try."

An hour and several refills later, Augustus's attention was diverted by the clicking of spoon to glass as Raymond Baxley, in his role as father of the bride, called for quiet among the guests for a wedding toast.

"To my daughter, who has matured into a beautiful and polished young woman, and to her husband, a young man from one of our most prominent and respected West Virginia families," he proposed from his position in front of the band. "May they spend their lives together in health and happiness."

Glasses were raised, and there was a round of light applause. Anne kissed Jim, then searched the room for Augustus. It was his turn. The mineowner rose from his table and made his way to Baxley's side. There was a slight stagger to his movement.

"My dear friends," he began. "What an honor and indeed a pleasure it is to be among you today as. . . ." His words trailed off, and he turned his face away from the crowd to conceal a coughing spasm. Recovered, he continued: "My dear friends. . . ." But again a series of violent coughs interrupted his attempt at oration. Jim moved closer to his father. "As I was saying, this is an occasion . . . an occasion of great joy to. . . ." The mineowner's knees buckled slightly, and he lost balance. Gripping Jim's arm, he tried again. But this time his words were hopelessly slurred. Jim cast his eyes downward as a murmur from the crowd told him that it was evident to all how much his father was intoxicated. Still, Augustus attempted to complete his toast, repeating one false start after another until, his eyes half closed, he pitched forward. He would have hit the floor had Jim not grabbed him.

Jim slowly ushered his father out of the ballroom as the band, on orders from Baxley, resumed its playing.

The wedding and reception were organized by the Baxleys, but the honeymoon was Augustus's project. He was not to be outdone. Unknown to Jim and Anne, he had arranged for a month's rental of a Pullman car. It was waiting on a sidetrack near the Livingston station, and a group of boys were at work decorating it with white and blue streamers and hanging an assemblage of tin cans from its rear. Augustus had prepaid the railroad for an itinerary that would take the honeymooning couple first up to Chicago and then west to California.

A photographer from the Bannerton *Tribune* was present to record the surprised smiles on Jim's and Anne's faces when they were escorted to the Pullman car. The champagne drinking, interrupted for the brief trip to the station, resumed inside the car at the urging of a reinvigorated Augustus as the couple's relatives and close friends waited with them for the arrival of the 5:14 northbound train. When it arrived, its crew smiled knowingly when they spotted the streamers and strung cans hanging from the Pullman. The car was coupled, and the newlyweds were on their way, alone now except for the Pullman porter. Augustus, Sarah, the Baxleys and a small group of others stood in a cluster at the station, throwing rice and waving farewell until the train rounded a bend and disappeared.

Inside the car, Anne collapsed into a swivel parlor chair. She smiled broadly. "Jim, wasn't it all wonderful?" she gushed.

Jim walked behind her chair and placed his hands on her slouched shoulders. He bent forward and kissed her neck. "I love you," he whispered.

Removing his hand, still smiling, Anne asked, "Did you see Missy Andrews? Wasn't she cute?" Then, looking at Jim gravely: "But your father. My God, Jim, it was embarrassing. What's come over him?"

Jim moved to a chair across from her and sat down, fingering the stem of his champagne glass. "He's been having his troubles lately. The company's in a crunch. The pressure's getting to him."

"We've all got troubles, dear, but we don't get blind drunk in public, let alone at our son's wedding," Anne said sternly. Then she smiled again and changed the subject. "Did you see Susan Jane and the way she had her hair? It was gorgeous, absolutely gorgeous! And Caroline. . . ."

Jim wasn't listening. He leaned back in the high-backed chair, his hands cupped behind his neck. As his new wife continued with her effusively happy replay of their wedding and, it seemed, each and every guest present, he closed his eyes and listened to the click-clack of the train. The rhythm soothed him, and his thoughts wandered to another train he had ridden. He was a GI then, and there were other servicemen with him, one of whom suffered from a horrible tic. What had happened to that unfortunate man? Then he caught himself, shaking his head because this was not a time for such reminiscing. He turned his attention once again to Anne, who was bubbling about the beautiful white orchid she had carried.

The passing mountains were replaced soon by hills and later by a long stretch of prairie. When the sun dropped below the horizon, they were already in Ohio. Jim was still slumped in his seat, a fist to his chin, watching the farmland pass by. Anne disappeared into the other end of the car to dress for the evening. She returned in a silken white nightgown extending from her neck to her toes and eased herself down on the bed, pulling the sheet up over her almost to her chin and winking at Jim, who suddenly remembered the coy letter she had written.

Jim rose, stretched and walked slowly to the bathroom, where he undressed and prepared for bed. When he returned to the bedside, however, he found Anne already asleep. The sheet had moved downward past her waist, and she lay curled up on her side in a pose Jim found seductive. But he decided not to wake her. It had been, after all, a long and exhausting day.

Jim slipped into the bed quietly, curling up next to her and tuning his ears once again to the clickity-clack of the train.

CHAPTER 6 ────────────

Their vision was blurry, but the game had taken on a new vigor as the players, one by one, shook off the effects of a night's worth of liquor and gained a second wind. Jim rubbed his eyes, which he suspected were bloodshot, and tried to concentrate as he, Augustus and three other men continued the poker game they had begun nine hours earlier. The gaming room of the Club Havana reeked with the odors of stale tobacco smoke and alcohol, and with the absence of windows, it was impossible to tell if the sun had yet risen. The soft chimes of a wall clock, however, told them it was 9:00 A.M.

"Hey, Augie," one of the players said as the cards were being shuffled. "How is it that every time I look at Jim here he's smiling. Can't recall ever seeing him so happy."

"You know how it is with newlyweds," Augustus replied. "All he can think about is bedtime." The others chuckled.

Two months had passed since Jim and Anne's marriage. Half that time they had spent on their honeymoon. Another week was devoted to moving Anne's possessions from Livingston to the Porter mansion. Life in the household had only recently begun to fall into a routine. Anne moved into Jim's bedroom, which was large but not spacious enough to store the assortment of artwork, knickknacks and small pieces of furniture she brought with her. These began to appear in strategic locations throughout the house, occasionally prompting Augustus to protest that some territory staked out by him had been violated. Sarah, however, welcomed the additional female presence, especially since Anne, aside from the knickknacks, was maintaining a low profile, leaving the supervision of the household exclusively to her. Augustus had begun to spend more and more time away from home, most of it at his club. Although Jim worried about this, his concern inspired particularly by his father's increased drinking, he, Anne and his mother felt a sense of relief when Augustus was away.

The wedding and honeymoon—like all weddings and honeymoons, Jim thought—were anticlimactic, and he was having difficulty readjusting to the routine of life in Porterville. The consequences of his decision to marry also had begun to sink in. Although he did not yet have second thoughts, he was nervous about how his life had been abruptly and irrevocably changed.

"You'll have to bring that pretty wife of yours along sometime," another of the players suggested to Jim. Jim wasn't certain whether to answer that as an insult or a compliment. Augustus spared him a decision when he grunted and picked up his newly dealt hand, bringing the attention of the group back to the cardplaying.

Sorting his own hand, Jim said to himself that it was bad enough Augustus's forcing him to sit in at the marathon cardplaying without bringing Anne into it.

"You know, Major, I meant to tell you how I sure do miss that 'shine you were pushing. Too bad about Thomason. You're lucky they didn't nail you," one of the players said.

Augustus shifted in his seat. "It wasn't exactly luck, friend." He did not elaborate.

A few minutes later a hostess walked into the room with a tray of boiling coffee spiked with Irish whiskey. The room's appearance had changed in the past month, when Augustus installed blackjack and craps tables, but the sole source of light as the poker game continued was the single shaded lamp suspended above the players.

"Wonder if the ol' lady missed me any," one of them asked with a chuckle.

"Mine sure as hell didn't," said another. "Been so long now I don't remember the procedure."

"Well, there's plenty of young instructors ready and willin' around this place," said the first speaker.

"He knows that, the phony bastard," Augustus chimed in. "He's spent the better part of the last two weeks with that redhead Gloria." The group laughed.

"What a pair, huh, Dana?" said the first man. "You bury your face in those a bit, did ya?"

"You bet he did," said Augustus.

Despite their light-headedness from the liquor and the lack of sleep, the men played a sharp game of cards between their exchanges of chatter. The long hours of play had ingrained strategy and odds making into their nervous systems so that the choice to be made at any point in the game was almost second nature to them and mechanical. Sometimes, when the cards produced no suspense at the table, the talk assumed a serious tone.

"Did ya hear about the three more families that moved out of the county last week?" asked one man. "Don't know what it'll be like when we lose all our people."

"Yeah, there's a steady parade now to Detroit and Chicago," observed another.

"What bothers me," Augustus said, "is all the outsiders heading here to replace them. All these fast-talking sharpies who think a hillbilly's no smarter than a mule."

"Leroy Brammer had one of those Texans stop in his shop a week ago or so and tried to bargain him down on an addin' machine he was buyin'. Ol' Leroy ended up sellin' him four of the things."

All five players laughed.

When they finished their hand, Augustus called for a brief break, during which each man rose to stretch his limbs with a walk around the room. They returned to the table a few minutes later as one of the players was relating the latest tale about Lou Greentree.

"From what I hear," he said, "that crazy Indian was scared out of his feathers. It was about ten at night, see, and here he was walking along Willow Creek Road and he spots it . . . a coffin . . . lying in the road like it fell from a hearse or somethin'. So he walks over to it and starts to lift the cover when an ol' owl lets out a hoot. They say Lou ran all the way to Bannerton."

"Where the hell did it come from?"

"Damned if I know. I don't think they ever did find out. The sheriff went out there and found the coffin empty. They checked every graveyard in the county but couldn't find no evidence of grave robbin' or nothin'."

"Maybe it was Porter here trying to bury all his money," another player suggested.

"Money, my ass," Augustus shot back. "You know anybody making money these days mining coal? Ask the bankers. They're the only ones left getting rich in this state."

Jim was dealing another hand when the telephone rang at the reception desk just outside the gaming room. Mae Sexton soon rushed into the room, shouting, "Major! It's urgent. There's trouble at one of your mines!"

Augustus took the call. Then he stuck his head through the door and said, "Jim, come on. We've got to go." The mineowner's face was white, and his voice grave. "There's been a bump at the Red Fox. A bad one." His hands were shaking as he slipped into his camel overcoat.

Jim jumped up from his seat. He and his father rushed out of the club and sped to the Red Fox. There they found

Crawford, the mine manager, already organizing a rescue operation while foremen took head counts of the evacuated miners.

"It looks like seven," one of the foremen reported. "Seven unaccounted for and probably buried at the end of that third heading."

Jim took Crawford by the arm. "How did it happen?" he asked.

"A classic bump," the manager responded, relating the details of the tragedy.

The number two heading in the huge mine finally had run its course, reaching the perimeter of the vein. A solid wall of red shale told the mine engineer that nothing would be gained by digging the heading any farther. The rooms carved off to the right and left along the heading's path also had been hollowed out to their limits. The time had come to retreat. The engineer had carefully outlined to the foreman the strategy for pulling the pillars, the removal of the columns of coal that had been left in place to help support the mine's ceiling. The engineer reported that he saw nothing to prevent the roof from falling cleanly in sections as the supporting pillars of coal were extracted. That was what they wanted, clean falls. To begin the dangerous project, crews were sent to the farthest reach of the heading seven miles into the mountain.

Two men from one crew were tinkering with the controls of a cutting machine. The machine had just been returned from repair but seemed to be in order.

"Looks fine to me," one said. The other nodded.

With the cutting machine, they then sliced a wedge-shaped incision along the bottom of the most interior pillar in the heading. A third man augered three holes above the cut and primed them with black powder. The muffled blast sent the outer layer of the pillar crumbling into a pile of loose coal. The men watched the ceiling nervously, but it held—as it was supposed to at this point. After the loosened coal was removed, the first two miners positioned the cutting machine for their next slice into the pillar, while other men jammed thick blocks of timber upright between the floor and ceiling to provide extra support temporarily.

The second and third cuts into the pillar were accomplished without mishap. The ceiling still held. When the engineer completed his inspection, he said there should be no trouble with the next layer as well. Extra men were sent to the site to help shovel the coal that already had been blasted from the exterior of the pillar.

"How is it?" Crawford asked over the mine telephone.

"No problem, Chief. We should get a clean fall," the engineer replied.

The men made their critical fourth cut into the pillar without trouble. The auger holes were bored and packed with powder. According to the engineer's plan, the next blast was intended to take down all except a thin strand of the pillar. As the miners huddled a few yards away in safety, the small explosion, as desired, splintered most of what remained of the block of coal supporting that section of ceiling. Again the men looked apprehensively toward the ceiling. But braced by the timber temporarily shoring it, the room didn't budge. All was going well.

After his inspection the engineer declared that it was time to shoot the timbers—to pull down the shoring and allow one section of the ceiling in heading two to fall down harmlessly. Under the watchful eye of the engineer, one man wrapped a thick chain around the bottom of the timber farthest into the heading and ran the chain several yards to a hand-powered winch. Another man spun the winch handle until the chain grew taut. He stopped, gripped the handle with both hands and turned it slowly. The timber groaned as the chain links dug into its fiber. Then it relented and began to move at its bottom. Its base scraped a furrow in the muddy mine floor as it moved first an inch, then another. Finally, the timber was freed. It fell to the mushy floor with a thump. The men looked to the ceiling. It still held. The first miner grabbed the chain to repeat the process with the next standing timber.

The second timber also fell without a struggle at the winch, and the ceiling still didn't move. But four miles away, on the far side of the mountain, men working in a different heading saw a vertical crack open suddenly in one of the shaft's walls. It was the beginning of what miners call a bump. The shooting of the timbers in heading two had caused pressure to shift to a point far away in the mine. Seeing the crack, the men in the distant heading began fleeing to safety outside. When they reached the portal, they told Crawford, who immediately began cranking the magneto on his mine telephone in an effort to reach the engineer at the pillar-pulling site. But the antiquated phone failed to work, and in the far end of heading two the men were unaware of the developing squeeze. They had already chained a third timber, hoping its removal finally would cause the section of the ceiling to fall. The winch was turned. The timber resisted momentarily before it gave and fell to the floor. Again the roof above it held. But the pressure traveled across the mountain, causing a rumbling above the miners working two miles into heading three. The rumbling grew louder, sounding like two massive stone slabs grating across one another. The miners who heard it snapped themselves from an initial state of shock and began scampering to safety. But it was too late. With a terrifying screech, the sandstone, slate and rock that made up the roof above them strained against themselves and then, as if in slow motion, collapsed into the shaft with the sound of thunder. The shock reverberated throughout the mountain, sending echoes into every heading and room of the mine, and was followed by a silence that carried its own message of death. Crawford raced to his manager's shack and called the Club Havana, where he was sure he would find the mineowner.

* * *

With Augustus and Jim standing behind him, Crawford knelt next to the mine engineer, who had unfolded one of his maps to plot the rescue operation.

"Looks to me like it'd be best digging across from heading four here instead of just digging back through the collapsed rubble," the engineer said.

"It would mess us up in there for the next three months," Augustus said, rejecting the proposal. "Cutting across like that would cause us to lose two—maybe three—rooms of coal."

"But it wouldn't be safe retracing that third heading, Major," Crawford said, siding with the engineer.

"How do you know that if you haven't looked?" the mine-owner shouted. He grabbed a helmet and started walking toward the portal. "Goddamn if I don't have to do everything myself," he muttered.

The night of drinking and sleeplessness still affected Augustus, and Jim noticed that his walk was shaky. "Wait, Pa," Jim called after him. "I don't think you ought to be going in there."

Augustus turned. "You don't worry about me," he barked. "Get on the phone, and start calling the other mines for the equipment we're going to need. Crawford will tell you what that is."

Augustus headed for the portal. Just as he got there, a three-man volunteer squad emerged after inspecting the blockage in heading three.

"Major, you can't go in there," one of them, Duke Shaw, shouted as the mineowner staggered past him. "The roof's shifting all the way in."

"Get out of my way, Shaw," Augustus said, pushing him roughly to the side.

"But I'm telling you, Major, the rest of that ceiling's going to give. It's not safe," Duke pointed out again. Augustus ig-

167

nored him and proceeded into the darkness. Duke weighed the situation for a moment and then turned to follow the mineowner inside.

That was enough, Jim decided. His father had to be stopped. But as he darted for the portal, Crawford put out an arm and stopped him. "Let him go, son," the manager said. "You know as well as me there's no way to stop him."

"But—" Jim was interrupted by a foreman running up to them with the names of the men believed to be trapped in the mine: Skeens, Fife, Payne, Morgan, Cordle, McKinney and Leone.

Jim knew five of the seven. Hearing their names reduced the tragedy from the abstract to something personal. Somehow these men had to be freed. Jim turned from Crawford and the foreman and rushed for the manager's shack to make the telephone call for the extra equipment.

Bonnie Fenner was helping her mother bake bread when they learned of the accident at the Red Fox Mine. The news traveled the rows of company homes in Porterville within minutes of the bump's occurrence. Although an expectation of tragedy was almost instinctive in a mining woman, a constant worry at a subliminal level that continued to tighten her insides even on her miner's off days, Bonnie was shocked by the report. Her body froze while her mind raced for any suggestion from T.C. or her father in the past few days that they would be assigned to heading three. Her mother ripped off her apron and calmly told Bonnie to go get Mari.

With Bonnie carrying Mari in her arms, they joined the procession of grim-faced housewives and children that was moving from Porterville toward the mine. The long line had a funereal silence which contrasted with the quick, determined pace of those forming its ranks, families hurrying to receive the word on whether their men were safe or lost to the mountain.

The scene turned to one of panic and confusion when the

line of women and children reached the mine, the stoic reserve of the women deserting them at the site of the disaster as their fears or hopes took on a reality. Some screamed with relief at finding their men safe; others shrieked with pain and disbelief at learning their husbands, brothers or fathers were trapped inside. Bonnie and Liz searched frantically for T.C. and Duke but saw neither of them. The two women looked at each other, fear in the eyes of both. Then Bonnie spotted T.C. running out of the portal.

Leaving Mari with her mother, she rushed to him and wrapped her arms around him, her head falling to his chest and tears streaming from her eyes.

"Oh, thank God, thank God," she said, squeezing him tightly. "Hold me, T.C. Hold me please."

But T.C. didn't respond to her clutching. Gently he pushed her away. "I've got to rush, honey," he told her in an urgent voice. "They need a bucket of water inside right away."

T.C. started for the tipple, but Bonnie stopped him. Something in his eyes had signaled her that there was more to be said.

"What is it, T.C.?" she asked, gripping his arm. "It's my father, isn't it? Something's happened to my pa."

T.C. looked her in the eyes. He spoke softly. "Crazy Porter went walking into that heading, thinking he could do something. Duke went after him. They made it all the way through to the site of the bump. I think Porter was drunk. He was just standing there, looking at the rock that blocked the shaft. Your father was right beside him. Then Duke heard a rumble or something overhead. He knew the roof above them was going to come down any second. So he dove and pushed crazy Porter out of the way. He did it just in time to save the major but not in time to save himself. A huge slab came down and caught him, Bonnie. Has him trapped by the leg. Another two feet or so, and Duke wouldn't have made it."

It was a familiar story. A collapsing roof often fell in slabs, striking one miner while sparing another less than a yard away. Bonnie's fingers went to her mouth. "How bad is it?" she asked in almost a whisper.

"The doc's in there now. That's why they need the water. I think Duke's okay, Bonnie, but they may have to take off his leg."

Liz began screaming and bolted for the portal. She had to be at her husband's side. But Bonnie grabbed her, and soon other women were there to restrain her. They tried to comfort and calm her while T.C. hurried off for the needed water.

"He's going to be okay, Ma," Bonnie said, squeezing her mother's hand and fighting off the image of a silver surgical saw laid against her father's flesh. Then she spotted the stretcher.

Two men carried it, and a third, whom she recognized as the young Dr. Gordon Spencer of Bannerton, walked at the side, holding an intravenous bottle. As the stretcher approached, her mother released her grip and bent over her husband, taking his limp hand and nuzzling it. Duke was unconscious, his eyes closed, his skin paper white under a layer of ingrained coal. His arms and face were marked by cuts and abrasions, and blood seeped from under the sheet that covered him. Bonnie felt an icy chill. She wrapped her arms in front of her. She began shivering, and her knees felt weak. For a moment she feared she was going to faint. But then a hand took her firmly by the shoulder. It was Jim Porter.

"I want you to know that I am very, very sorry, and we will do everything we can to make sure Duke gets the best in medical attention," he said. Jim continued talking, but Bonnie didn't hear him—her attention was focused on the slumped figure of Augustus Porter, who sat braced against the wheel of a pickup truck a few feet away. With a quivering hand he was guzzling from a pint bottle. He looked stunned.

Bonnie's eyes narrowed as she stared at the slouching mine-owner. Suddenly she broke from Jim and charged his father. "It's unfair!" she screamed, pounding his chest as he tried to fend her off. "Such a waste! My father's leg for you! You're nothing but a shell of a man! An old drunk! I hate you! I hate you!"

It took three people to pull her away and the strong words of T.C. to calm her. As Augustus cowered in his stupor, the others helped Bonnie up into the rear of the pickup truck alongside the doctor, Liz, and the stretcher bearing her father. T.C. hopped aboard, and the truck sped away.

The breeze in the back of the pickup en route to the clinic in Bannerton had a soothing effect. Bonnie gradually calmed down.

"Your husband's going to live, and that's the important thing," the doctor told Liz. "We had no choice about the leg. It was the only way to get him out of there."

Bonnie turned to T.C. "Tell me exactly what happened in there."

T.C. nodded. "The first we knew of it was when the major came running out of the portal," he started, then related what had followed.

Augustus was breathless when he emerged from the mine and ordered Crawford to send a rescue crew inside immediately for Duke. "He's pinned bad," the mineowner said. "Must be ten tons of rock crushing his legs."

T.C. felt sick when he heard it. He rushed inside with the rescue crew and the doctor. If Augustus had planned it, he could not have jeopardized the rescue hopes for the seven other trapped men any more than he did, for the rescue operation now had to concentrate on freeing Duke Shaw, who, in contrast with the others, was known to be alive.

They found him with his head and hair dripping with perspiration. His complexion was chalk white. He was conscious—enough to relate what had happened—but he appeared to be falling into shock.

With pickaxes, long crowbars and sledges, the rescue crew struggled to free him. They worked at the rock and slate one piece at a time. Their pace was feverish, and soon they had uncovered all but Duke's right leg, which remained pinned under what seemed to be a solid block of rock several feet in height.

"Give me a pick," Lou Greentree, the biggest of the men, ordered. He began swinging its curved steel head within inches of Duke's thigh. With each stroke, Lou cut a chip out of the block that had the leg pinned. T.C. joined in, the two men alternating their swings. They grunted, swore and huffed while swinging their pickaxes, but their progress was cruelly slow. It became clear it would take much too long to free Duke in this manner if he could be freed at all.

The doctor knelt to check the trapped miner's pupils. With a stethoscope, he listened to his heartbeat and took his pulse. T.C. fell to his knees and with a handkerchief began wiping the sweat and grime from Duke's forehead. "Don't worry, Duke," he said. "This man's a doctor. We're going to get you out of here, and you'll be drinking at Blakely's like nothing happened."

But the doctor shook his head. "That's enough," he said. "There's not enough time."

"Come on, Doc. We'll get him," T.C. argued.

Lou joined him. "We'll do the work. You just keep him alive."

"No. He'll never survive. He's in shock, and I think he's lost a lot of blood," Spencer said, reaching for his bag. The men knew without his saying anything further what it was the physician felt forced to do.

"Are you sure?" T.C. asked, staring into the doctor's eyes.

"There's no choice. I'll need water."

"I'll get it," T.C. volunteered.

"And let's try to improve this light," the doctor added.

A few minutes later T.C. returned with a bundle of towels

from the bathhouse, a bucket of hot water and a large flashlight. Spencer pulled on a pair of surgical gloves and administered a shot of local anesthetic to Duke's right thigh. Duke was unconscious, and the rate of his breathing had slowed noticeably, a dangerous sign.

Spencer reached for the sterling silver saw a mining physician routinely carries in his bag. As T.C. held the light for him, the young doctor used a scalpel to cut through the skin and muscle just above Duke's right knee. He tied off the major blood vessels and put the saw to the bone. In a few minutes it was over. Duke was free. The men lifted him onto a canvas stretcher and carried him toward the portal.

After listening to the story, Bonnie knew that the doctor was right—she had to be grateful that her father's life was saved, as might or might not prove to be the case with the other seven trapped men. While she held her father's hand and Liz stroked his forehead, Bonnie's eyes clouded with tears. She was full of mixed emotions: grief at what had happened, joy that Duke was alive, affection for T.C. and the other men who had worked to free him and hate for Augustus Porter, the sorry suggestion of a human being whose foolishness was responsible for it all.

While Augustus sat in a state of exhaustion and drunkenness under a tree, still sipping from his flask, Crawford took charge of the rescue operation. Under his supervision, the rescuers had begun to dig a new shaft into the collapsed area from the adjacent heading.

"How long will it take?" Jim asked him.

"If we're lucky and work 'round the clock, maybe three days," he replied.

Jim knew, as did every man on the rescue team, that it was unlikely that any of the seven trapped men had a chance for survival. The odds were that all of them had been killed instantly in the crush of rock. But there was always the possibility that one or more of them had managed to squeeze into a protective pocket as the roof came down, and it was with that hope that the rescuers pushed on.

The families of the trapped men gathered in a group. Some had tears in their eyes, but not one openly cried. The Reverend Weatherson arrived to stand by them. Jim followed him, moving to each of the women and promising that anything that could be done to free the men would be. He was uncertain what else, if anything, could be said to comfort them.

Other women arrived to provide food and coffee for the rescue team as it worked on into the night. Even Mae Sexton pitched in. State mining officials had been notified and soon began to arrive. Not much later came the reporters and photographers, first from the Bannerton *Tribune* and then from newspapers and radio stations as far away as Charleston. By the next afternoon newsmen from the wire services and from newspapers of cities as distant as Atlanta and New York were on the scene.

The wives and children of the trapped men continued their heart-rending vigil, as most of them had throughout the night. A brash young reporter from a radio station in Philadelphia pushed a microphone toward one woman and asked, "What do you think the chances are your husband will get out alive?" A weary Lou Greentree gently but authoritatively escorted him away.

The men worked on the rescue shaft into the third day. For most of the time Crawford was at their side. He was unshaved and bent with fatigue, having managed to catch only an occasional catnap. Finally, the new shaft broke through the coal that had formed one wall of the collapsed heading. The men found nothing but an unbroken mass of fallen rock. They found the same thing even when they widened the connection in both directions. Crawford walked dejectedly from the mine. He was met by the mob of reporters.

"What did you find?" one shouted.

"Anyone alive in there?" asked another.

"They all dead?"

Crawford, ignoring the questions, walked to Jim, who had remained at the mine throughout the attempted rescue operation. "Unless you want to make the decision, you'd better come with me," the mine manager said. Jim shook his head. The two men climbed into a jeep. Crawford told the driver, "Take us to the Porters."

Augustus had not been at the mine since the first night. Pale and still obviously shaken, he met his mine manager and son in the study.

"It shapes up like this, Major," Crawford said. "We've broken through and found nothing but rock, solid rock. Now we could dig through that, but to cover the entire area those men were working in would take us days, if not weeks. I talked to the state people, and they agree. There's not one shot in a million that anyone's still alive in there."

"What do we do?" Augustus asked.

"I don't know," Crawford replied. "That's why I'm here."

Augustus rose from behind his desk and poured himself a drink. "What kind of heat would there be if we called the rescue off?"

"It's hard to say. I think the state would officially agree with a pullout. It's the press and families I'm not sure about."

"There's no chance at all those men are alive?"

"I'm afraid not, Major. As I said, every one of them must have been crushed in the first few seconds. If not, then they've had no food or water for three days and no chance of getting any for at least a day or two more."

Augustus looked in the eyes of his mine manager. "Then call it off. Put the mine back in operation," he ordered.

"Pa," Jim protested. He was shocked. "We can't do that!" He put a hand on his father's shoulder. "We've got to try!"

Augustus stared at his son for a moment. He shook his

head. "I'm afraid we don't really have a choice." Turning to Crawford, he snapped impatiently, "You heard what I said."

"Yes, sir, Major," Crawford replied. He left the mansion.

The Porterville First Christian Church was packed for the service. The next of kin to the seven victims sat in the front, all of the women and many of the men and children dressed in black. Jim, one row behind them with his wife and parents, stared at the back of the women's black veils.

There were no coffins. The seven bodies were still buried inside the mine, apparently to remain sealed there for eternity. The church was quiet except for occasional sobs and the music from the organ, which sounded a lonely requiem.

Five of the seven victims had dressed near Jim in the Red Fox bathhouse, and he strained to recall what they had looked like and how they had talked. What had been their hopes and now what would happen to their families, who were denied even corpses to mourn?

Jim wanted the service to end. He felt awkward, even guilty, as if the mishap, so tragic in its effect on the survivors, had been his responsibility. But it wasn't he who had decided to abandon the rescue attempt which, at the very least, would have recovered the corpses. It wasn't his decision. It had been his father's. When he turned to look at Augustus, he found his father's face covered with perspiration, his eyes staring ahead blankly.

It was the young Reverend Weatherson's first appearance at a mass funeral service. He discarded the text of the sermon he had prepared and, moved by the moment, spoke extemporaneously.

"It was in your wisdom, Lord, to take these men away," he said, "our fathers, our husbands, our brothers. But they also shall live—live in the hearts and deeds of all of us they touched during their struggle. We pray for them."

Hearing the minister's words, most of the widows began

to weep. Two were wailing, their screams only partially drowned out by the organ, which had resumed its playing as the service ended. The sexton rang the church bell in mourning.

The Red Fox Mine was closed for the service; except for a guard, it was empty of people. The next morning, however, a full force of miners was back on the job, and the engineer was down on his hands and knees over a map, plotting how best to remove the valuable coal that still remained in the partially collapsed heading.

When Jim saw this, he felt ashamed. Yet as long as his father still ran the company, he was powerless to make even the smallest change.

CHAPTER 7 ———————

It was said the number of years a man had spent in the mines could be measured by counting his missing or shortened fingers and multiplying by five. Sharp-edged rock, picks, shovels and, in more modern times, continuous miners and other mining machines sliced off a toe or the tip of a finger with sad frequency. A new mine doctor fast became accustomed to dealing with amputations—disinfecting the wound, tying off veins and repairing the stump that remained. He also received a good deal of experience with phantom pain. Dr. Spencer told Bonnie he had seen men as strong and sturdy as the mountains they mined reduced to tears from the intense pain their brains recorded from the tips of toes and fingers they no longer had. As a physician, he understood this, but there was little he could do except attempt to explain it to the bewildered victim as a case of nature crossing its circuits.

Surely, Bonnie knew, her father had experienced phantom pain on occasion during the five years since his leg was severed at the Red Fox Mine, but not once did he complain of it.

Sometimes, as he sat at dinner or rested on the living-room couch, Bonnie noticed his eyes water and face tighten. When she quizzed him at such times, however, Duke denied being uncomfortable. Nor did he give any evidence of the mental depression the doctor had warned her was certain to follow the loss of any limb. Duke did not talk of depression, and if he relived the accident over and over in his mind, as Bonnie suspected he did, he did not burden others with his pain.

In the years since his amputation, Duke had been working in the Red Fox bathhouse as a cleanup man. He had saved Augustus Porter's life, and in gratitude the mineowner had offered him the bathhouse job, beaming in the apparent belief that it was a truly magnanimous gesture. Having no other choice that he recognized, Duke accepted it, chuckling to others that this made him "a second-time breaker boy." Hobbling along on the wooden leg Dr. Spencer had fitted for him, he swept a broom under the miners' hanging clothes baskets, mopped the shower area and kept the bathhouse in good order. It was 1962 and his take-home pay was $14 a day.

The meniality of the job—and its low wage—made Bonnie especially bitter. As she thought of her father sweeping a broom while other men dressed for the more manly task of extracting coal, she wished she could whisk him far away from the Red Fox Mine and Porterville, back to Wales, perhaps, and some peaceful, verdant valley where a man could live with some sense of dignity, even if missing a leg. It was old Colonel Porter who had lured Duke to West Virginia, through his agent, under the illusion that freedom and riches were awaiting him there, and the ruse had taken the life of a child. It was the drunken antics of Augustus Porter that had cost Duke his leg and much of his hope. Still, the Porters weren't finished, for now the mineowner was threatening them again, this time with the loss of T.C.'s job.

Bonnie was thinking of the Porters as T.C. described her father's latest humiliation.

"It amounted to begging," he said, thumping a fist on the

table. "And it's not right. Duke shouldn't have to do it—not for me anyway."

"I guess Pa figured it was the only shot. He had to give it a try," she said, knowing, however, that the making of such a request must have pained her father. Duke had put the question to Crawford, the mine manager, that day.

Monday mornings normally were quiet in the bathhouse. The men usually kept their distance from one another, uncertain just what state of mind the next man might be in after a weekend that probably included at least one night of heavy drinking. Monday morning was when miners were apt to turn on one another, venting some previously subdued rage in a flurry of fists and kicks to the groin. But sometimes Mondays were just like any other working day, and the usual banter filled the room as the men dressed for their shift.

So it was as Duke, his broom in his hand, and T.C., standing next to him, heard a miner ask those around him if they were aware of the latest trouble suffered by Ernie Jason, the usually inebriated handyman in charge of rigging the mail at the Porterville station.

"Seems he had a few and got tired," the man related, "and he decided the best place to sleep it off is on the bottom of some car sittin' on the siding. He climbs in, snuggles in a corner, and the next thing he knows it's the next morning and he's been hauled to Vine County." The group laughed, a couple of men shaking their heads.

"Say, Duke," said one. "Now there's a job you ought to consider. Hang the mail bag in the mornin' and pick up the other in the evenin' and nothin' to do all day in between."

"Naw," Duke replied. "Give me that time off, and I'd be in nothing but trouble. You know my Liz would never stand for that."

"You got somethin' there," the miner who had offered the suggestion agreed. "A married man ain't never again gonna get a taste of freedom, that's for sure."

Duke smiled. He began his chores, sweeping until he spotted the mine manager.

"Morning, Mr. Crawford," Duke said. "I've got to talk to you when you have the time."

"Not now, Duke. I've got to go into that number four heading," Crawford replied. "See me at the break, okay?"

"Sure. But it's important."

At noon, when the lunch whistle sounded, Duke grabbed the mine bucket he still carried despite his no longer working in the shafts, and searched for Crawford. He found him sipping coffee from a tin mug, sitting on a tree stump not far from the portal. "Can I join you?" Duke asked.

"Sure, Duke. Plant your ass right there," Crawford said, gesturing to a thick log lying nearby. "What's up?"

"It's my son-in-law. His name's on that layoff list, but he's been a hell of a worker ever since that back of his healed. You know that."

"He's a good man, Duke. You'll get no argument from me on that."

"But if he gets laid off, all he'll be able to find will be odd jobs here and there, and he'll have nothing to bide his time with. I know others are saying the same thing, but, Mr. Crawford, T.C. wants badly to stay in the mine."

The mine manager took a long sip from his mug and placed the cup on the tree stump. "Now, Duke, you know there's nothing in the world I wouldn't do for you if I could, but my God, a fifth of the men in the county aren't working regular. There're men with families—large families—and we haven't put a new man on for more than two years. The company's got to pull back, and Porter says it's got to be done by seniority. There's nothing I can do."

Duke's eyes were pleading. "He's not a new man. Put in his time, he did, and he's a hard worker. He'd have even more seniority if you people would count the time he put in fighting the war." His voice softened. "You know, to be honest,

Liz and I aren't making it so good with just the pay I get from cleaning this bathhouse. T.C. is helping us out, and he's got Bonnie and a daughter to worry about."

Crawford stood, shaking the remaining drops of coffee from his cup. "Porter set the seniority rule. There's no way I could move T.C. up on that list. The major runs it."

"Oh, come on, Crawford, you and I both know that Porter can—and does—fool with that list," Duke said, his voice rising.

"I tell you what, Duke. I'll try. I'll speak to the major today. But he ain't gonna buy it."

Bonnie felt ashamed of the humiliation suffered by her father, but she also felt pride—Duke, thinking of her and her family, had been man enough to give it a try.

The next day Bonnie waited on the stoop of her parents' home for word on Crawford's attempt to keep T.C. on the work force. She spotted other Red Fox miners walking wearily to their homes. Unless he had gotten a lift from Crawford or one of the foremen, Duke would be a few minutes behind the rest of them, delayed by the awkwardness of his artificial leg. Now, however, he was later than usual. When he finally appeared down the street, Bonnie understood why. Duke, seeing his daughter, glumly shook his head.

Once inside, he joined Bonnie and Liz at the table. "Crawford said he'd tried, but Porter wouldn't buy it. Said there was nothing more he could do and suggested T.C. try Owens, that maybe he would be hiring."

"Owens isn't hiring; he's laying off people himself!" Bonnie quickly retorted.

"I know," Duke replied wearily.

The screen door slammed as T.C. entered the house. "I'm sorry I'm late," he said. "I just needed a few minutes alone." He turned to his father-in-law. "Listen, Duke. You tried. Now it's up to me. I'll just have to figure something out for myself."

Duke shook his head. "There's only one thing left to do."

Bonnie and T.C. both read his mind. "You can't do it, Duke. I won't let you. Not for me," T.C. protested.

Bonnie agreed. "It's bad enough you had to plead with Crawford. You've got too much pride to go down on your knees at the feet of Augustus Porter."

"I don't understand it," said Liz. "You give them the best years of your life, lose your leg even, and all Porter can do for you is throw you a mop for the bathhouse." Bonnie looked at her mother in surprise. The outburst had been one of Liz's rare criticisms of the mineowner.

Duke cleared his throat. "No use in you all gabbing like that. I've made up my mind. I'm going to go."

"Well, if you're going, I'll go with you," Bonnie said.

"You can wait outside if you want but I'm going to face this man myself," her father said.

Bonnie and Duke walked past the rows of company houses and went up the hill to the Porter mansion that night. While Bonnie waited at the foot of the walk, her father hobbled up the steps of the front porch, paused for a moment, then lifted the heavy brass knocker and allowed it to fall, striking the door with a thud. Percy, the Porter houseman and butler, answered the call.

"Yes, sir?" he said.

"I'm Duke Shaw. I'd like to see Major Porter."

"I'm afraid he's retired to his study. Is he expecting you?"

"No, but . . ."

"Well, this seems a bit unusual."

Duke shuffled his feet impatiently. "Look, just tell him I'm here. I'll take only a minute of his time."

The butler hesitated, then nodded. He left the door ajar but pointedly failed to invite the ex-miner in. In a few seconds Augustus was standing in the doorway. Dressed in a silk smoking jacket, he also neglected to invite Duke inside.

"Duke, how are you? What brings you here?" the mineowner asked, pumping his longtime employee's hand and grinning broadly.

"It's about my son-in-law, T. C. Fenner. Mr. Crawford—"

"I know all about it," Augustus interrupted. "Now, Duke, you and I have been around together for a long, long time, and you know there isn't anything I wouldn't do for you if I could. In this case, I can't."

"It's just a job. One job," Duke interjected.

"I know," Augustus said, placing an arm around his back. "But I can't do it. It's a rule."

Bonnie had watched the mineowner with increasing irritation and anger. Suddenly she bolted up the steps, pointed a finger at Augustus and shouted, "It means nothing to you, does it?"

Augustus looked puzzled. "Just what do you mean, young lady?"

"You've forgotten just how it was that my father lost his leg. For God's sake, Porter, he saved your life!"

Duke turned to silence his daughter, but Augustus gave him a patronizing squeeze with the hand he still kept on Duke's shoulder. "That's okay, Duke. I understand. It's frustrating. You'll have to excuse me now, I'm afraid. I've got paperwork waiting." The mineowner stepped back inside the mansion and closed the door. Bonnie glared at the door for a moment before turning and following her father down the stairs.

Duke took his daughter's hand. "I guess there's no man alive who's going to change Augustus Porter. What we have to do now is think it out. We'll find an answer."

The looming layoff of T.C. made real for Bonnie and her family the fears that had been growing since the coal boom of the Korean War had begun to taper off. In Coal County there was no doubt that as the sixties neared their midpoint, the coal industry was depressed and getting worse. The problem lay in the uniqueness of the world's coal markets.

Coal, in one sense, is like Christmas trees. As Christmas approaches, a Christmas tree can sell for as much as $30 in large cities, but once Christmas Day has passed it is next to impossible to give one away. Simply supply and demand. The coal market operates in the same way. Unlike grain or the paper securities issued by corporations, there is no central marketplace for the selling of coal. A coalman usually negotiates a price himself or through an agent or broker directly with a customer. With no board of governors to oversee the competition, the game is often brutal.

To complicate marketing strategy still further, coal loses its purity when it is stored. If coal were piled in the open air for too long after its release from the darkness of a mountain, oxygen would take its toll and the coal drop in grade. Because of this, stockpiling for more than three or four months was avoided. The absence of a central marketplace and the inability to store coal for any significant duration led to two basic strategies: With the first, coalmen sought long-term contracts with utilities and steel mills and then mined their coal to meet the delivery timetables; the second tactic was more speculative, with coalmen scurrying for quick, odd lot orders, a few hundred tons to meet a mill's unexpected need or to fill out a ship bound for overseas. In hard times, coalmen were forced to attempt more of the latter, which they called spot business.

Augustus Porter, having depended heavily on railroad contracts that had disappeared, instructed his agents, both domestic and abroad, to direct all their energy toward obtaining spot orders. But nearly every other coalman in the country was beginning to do the same, and the last-minute orders that dribbled into Porterville now and then were insufficient to keep pace with the quantity of coal coming from the company's five mines. As a result, Augustus began to cut back production, reducing the workweek at each of his mines. No one doubted that he did so reluctantly not because of the threat his action caused to the welfare of his miners, but because it involved a loss of face—the Porter mines had been at a level of full production for the three decades since the Depression.

As for the miner, there was a part of him that welcomed the change from a six-day workweek to one of four or five days. The extra free time gave his muscles opportunity to heal and his eyes time to reaccustom themselves to long stretches of sunlight again. Having seen his children only on Sundays and one or two hours on other days at best, he now got to meet and know them. And the unencumbered time filled the need all men have to withdraw into themselves periodically and think. These were some of the gifts the shortened work-week provided. Beneath them operated a cruel illusion.

The cutback in work hours also meant a reduction in pay, of course. This, coupled with the subtle rise in prices again ordered by Augustus at the company store, put a squeeze on every mining family's budget. In the beginning, when the bowl in the kitchen cupboard was found empty of money pre-maturely, there was a tendency to laugh about it as if the family had unwittingly fallen to some frivolous extravagance. But as time passed and the bowl was found empty earlier and earlier in the week, the enormity of the economics at work became clear. Often the revelation came in an instant of shock, a look in the cupboard and the question "What's happening here?" Couples then huddled apart from children to map new strategies. "The honey's got to go. No more honey." "And tobacco. I'll cut down." "Lucy needs a dress, but I'll fix up that ol' one of Mary's." "Do you think we'll have to go into more debt?"

The women were grateful they had canned as many berries as they had the previous summer, and they made plans for the expanded vegetable garden they would plant in the spring. The men snapped into action from their long hours in easy chairs and, rifles in hand and sons at their sides, headed for the foothills and the rabbit, squirrel, grouse and wild turkey they hoped would be there. With patience, but also with a sense of urgency, they taught young boys how to tie a fly and work a stream for the trout, bass, and bluegills that became an increasing part of the family's diet. And on Sundays, in the churches, the miners bowed their heads not to doze but to pray.

Two weeks after Duke's unsuccessful pleading first with Crawford and then with the mineowner, T.C. was out of a job. At first, he sat around the house brooding, an expression of helplessness on his face, his eyes focused in the distance as if he were looking far, far into a tunnel of time. His behavior worried Bonnie, but she left him alone to his thoughts. She, too, felt the same sense of foreboding. Then Duke stopped by after work one day to tell them of a job possibility Crawford had mentioned. It was only a day's work as a busboy and kitchen helper at a Porter party, but it was still money. T.C., despite Bonnie's reservations, decided to accept it.

Even after he left for the Porter mansion, Bonnie had her misgivings. It was true they needed the money desperately. But at what price in dignity? The thought of her husband, a journeyman miner and decorated war veteran, sweating in the Porters' kitchen revolted her. But Bonnie was powerless. T.C., swallowing his pride, had made up his mind.

Upon his arrival at the mansion, T.C. found the kitchen in a whirlwind of activity, although the party was not to begin for another two hours. The affair was Anne Baxley Porter's annual spring dinner and ball, which this year she called Vernal Vertigo—1962. Anyone of wealth in Coal County was sure to attend, and the Bannerton *Tribune* had dutifully provided full coverage of the plans for the noteworthy gathering. No matter what financial pressures the Porter family might be suffering, Anne had spared no expense in staging the affair. The household staff was bolstered by temporary waiters, assistant cooks and dishwashers.

"We'll fit you with a white jacket later," Jenny, the cook,

187

told T.C. "You can start by giving Lou a hand over there."
She pointed to a stainless steel double-basin sink where Lou
Greentree was already at work on a mountain of greasy and
food-encrusted pans, baking sheets, pots and utensils.

T.C. walked to the sink. "Lou, how the hell are you?"
he asked, smiling broadly at the bulky miner, whom he had
not seen since being laid off at the mine.

"Hi, kid," Lou replied. "Sorry to see you let go like that.
Grab yourself an apron. There's one under that counter
there."

T.C. slipped on the heavy rubberized apron, tied its cord
behind him and pitched in by grabbing one of the dirty pots
and working to remove the burned food on its bottom over
a garbage can. He attempted to make conversation with Lou
but was able to draw little more than a grunt each time he
tried. Lou had never been talkative, but he was more mute
now than ever. T.C. guessed he was embarrassed by working
as a dishwasher.

Even with the two of them working together, T.C. and
Lou were unable to keep up with the growing stack of pots
and pans. Jenny walked over with yet another sheet caked
with the residue of canapes. "Let's get you that jacket now,"
she said to T.C., smiling.

After an hour and a half had passed, the guests began to
arrive. Jenny handed T.C. a highly starched white coat from
a locker in the large pantry. It fitted nicely. "You'd better
get on upstairs and start bussin'," she said. "Those used glasses
will be pilin' up at the bar. The waiters will show you how
to use the dumbwaiter."

T.C. climbed a rear stairway to a service room next to the
ballroom on the third floor. The cook was right—the bartender was busy pouring drinks, and the used glasses had
already begun to fill a tray behind him. The dumbwaiter
operated out of the room at the top of the stairs T.C. had
just climbed. A waiter showed him how to work it, using a

rope and pulley system to lower baskets full of soiled glasses and dishes down to Lou in the kitchen.

T.C. had never before been a witness to one of Anne's vernal balls. Glancing around the ballroom during his trips between the dumbwaiter and the bar, he saw that it lived up to its reputation for extravagance. The room was filled with bouquets of colorful spring flowers. There was an abundance of potted shrubbery and small trees. A pair of live doves flew back and forth overhead. The guests were formally attired, the women in flowing, lightweight gowns costing hundreds of dollars. If there was any evidence of the region's economic depression, T.C. did not see it—although he did overhear a maid observe that one guest was wearing the same dress she had worn a year earlier.

The assistant cooks and servers had prepared an elaborate buffet, at one end of which was a hunk of rare roast beef which was the largest cut of meat T.C. had ever seen. It occurred to him that the beef alone could provide a meal for a quarter of the out-of-work mining families left in Porterville.

A few steps from the bar, two male guests were displaying evidence of their predinner cocktails. "Did ya ever see my balancin' act?" one of them slurred to the other, who shook his head.

"You haven't! Well, goddamn, I thought everyone had seen my balancin' act. A hundred dollars says I can balance a wineglass on the tip of my nose and light a cigarette at the same time."

"And not break the glass, right?"

"Of course not."

"It's a bet. The easiest hundred I'll ever make."

The first man gulped down his champagne to empty the glass, bent backward and placed the crystal on the tip of his nose. It wobbled precariously for a second or two, but he won control. He reached into his pocket and withdrew a cigarette, which he inserted between his lips. Feeling his way with his fingertips, he struck a match and raised it above his head. The flame had just touched the tip of the tobacco when the man jerked slightly. The crystal glass swayed dangerously, first one way, then the other, before crashing to the floor. "Son of a bitch!" he shouted. "I ain't lyin'—that's the first time that ever happened." His friend was cackling. "Here," the frustrated performer said, handing the other a crisp $100 bill. "Hey, boy," the loser said to T.C. "Clean up that mess, would ya?"

The sound of the crashing glass had attracted attention from throughout the room, and it was only then that Jim Porter noticed T.C.'s presence. He appeared surprised to see his onetime high school teammate.

"T.C.!" he shouted while walking briskly toward him. "What the hell are you doing here?"

"Can't you tell?" T.C. replied, lifting the bottom edge of his white busboy's coat. The tone of T.C.'s words offset the smile he flashed simultaneously.

"How are you?" Jim asked.

"I'll survive. But I think I'd better get a mop and clean up this mess." T.C. turned his back to Jim and walked to the service room. Jim watched him until a call from his mother diverted his attention.

From the service room T.C. could hear Sarah tell her son, "Please keep an eye on your father, would you? Let's try to cut down his drinking and avoid trouble."

"I'll try, Ma, but I'm not very hopeful," Jim replied.

Later, when all except a few guests had departed, T.C. was summoned back to the kitchen to assist Lou with his washing. Most of the pots and pans had been cleared away. They were replaced by glassware and towering piles of dishes, all to be washed by hand. Lou asked him to do the rinsing and handed him a platter dripping with hot, sudsy water. T.C. examined the piece of china as if estimating its cost.

Hours later, when the Porter butler doled out the day's

pay to the temporary help, T.C. accepted his $11 without counting it and headed home.

It was after midnight when T.C. returned. Bonnie had waited up for him. He said nothing while removing his shoes, socks and shirt and fell onto their bed still wearing his trousers. Bonnie stepped into the bathroom and dressed in a black nightgown, the only one she owned. Then she slipped into bed next to her husband and began slowly running her fingers through his hair.

"I've never seen anything like it," T.C. said finally in a low, gravelly voice that was almost a whisper. "I got so mad I wanted to hit somebody, the sons of bitches."

"What happened, honey?" Bonnie asked, her tone betraying her apprehension.

T.C., his eyes focused on the dimly lit ceiling, told her of his night in the back rooms of the Porter mansion.

"I wanted to throw the money right back at them," he said when he had finished. "Honey, until tonight I had never seen a hundred-dollar bill in my life. That's enough money to buy food for us for a month. And it's not right that the Porters have china that with just two or three pieces could be traded in for one of those new metal legs for your father. It's not right."

"They've always been rich, and it'll always be the same," Bonnie said gently. "I don't see the sense in getting upset over it."

"Hey, wait a minute—I don't think I heard you right," he shot back. "Can that be my wife telling me not to be disturbed about the Porters?"

She laughed. "What I'm trying to say is don't let them chip you down. Don't let them take your pride and hope and manhood away. You're as good as any of them."

She reached to the bed stand and flicked off the lamp, leaving the room dark except for the glow of moonlight seeping through the curtained window. T.C. still seemed preoccupied with what had happened that night, but she was determined to change that. She reached over to his bare chest and began combing its thick patch of curly brown hair with her fingertips. In the dimness she saw his eyes close. A few seconds passed, and then he whispered, "Bonnie, I'm telling you, you should have seen the size of that roast."

"Hush," she scolded. "Put it right out of your mind."

He smiled and then bent forward to kiss her, his hands simultaneously loosening the top of her gown. The fabric fell away to expose the smooth, creamy skin of her back to the softness of the moonlight. Their kiss was long and full of feeling. Bonnie rolled onto her back; T.C. moved over her to kiss and caress her breasts. She felt her hips and legs involuntarily undulating in an unbroken rhythm, and almost as an observer, she became aware that her hands had moved to her husband's belt. When his trousers had fallen, he moved over her, and she placed her arms around his neck, pulling him toward her. Her legs widened, and as she felt his weight and the tautness of his muscles press against her, she marveled how strong and youthful her husband was. They kissed, their lips locking and their tongues exploring one another, and they made love.

When they had finished, he rolled onto his back, and she rested in his arms. After a few moments T.C. laughed.

"Is it that funny?" she asked.

"No, honey. It's just that you and I haven't made love like that since the day we were married."

Bonnie smiled.

A few minutes later she looked at her husband, expecting to find his eyes closed. But they were wide open and distant, his thoughts far away.

She brushed his cheek with her fingertips. "Don't worry, T.C. I've got a few ideas of my own."

CHAPTER 8 —————————————

Jim was having trouble keeping his mind on the poker game, his thoughts preoccupied, instead, with Bonnie. He rarely saw her since his marriage. Anne had a preference for the Episcopal church in Livingston, so he missed seeing Bonnie at services in Porterville. Other than attend church, Bonnie apparently seldom left her home. Jim's glimpses of her were usually brief and from a distance. On the rare occasions that they spoke, other people invariably were present, and the talk never exceeded a superficial exchange of pleasantries. Each time he saw her, however, he recognized old feelings rising within him.

"Are you in or out?" Augustus snapped, forcing Jim's attention back to the cards.

"I'm sorry," Jim said. "I'm out on this hand, I guess." He folded his hand.

There were seven players in the game, and the smoke from their cigarettes and cigars lingered as a heavy haze in the club's gaming room. As usual, the sole source of light in the windowless room was the lamp with the green conical shade hanging above the playing table. The light cast a ring of distorted shadows of the seven men, giving the room a surreal effect. There was little talk. The only sounds were the snap of cards, the low, almost inaudible declaring of bets, the click of chips and the clinking of crystal when the scantily attired young hostess arrived with her tray. There was a serious nature to the game, and Jim understood why: His father had not arranged it merely to pass the time; it was business, a bold attempt by Augustus to wrest an important contract away from another mineowner.

The game's first two hours had produced no major leaders, but now Augustus and a real estate broker named Delafuente appeared to be sharing the same streak of good luck. Their surge in winnings had come primarily at the expense of an out-of-towner in a seersucker suit named Edward Harrison. Harrison was an official of the Green Valley Light and Electric Company of Pennsylvania whose duty it was to procure the utility's supply of coal. He was in Coal County, as he was regularly, to meet with John Owens about another of the long-term contracts Green Valley had had for more than two decades with the Owens Coal Company. Hardly had Harrison stepped off the train, however, when Augustus presented him with an invitation to visit his lavish Club Havana. It soom became clear that Harrison was a man who enjoyed his drink, and the alcohol had begun to influence his play.

The pot had no limit, and the level of gambling varied widely with each hand. By betting from nearly unlimited resources, Augustus was able to advance his winnings simply by outlasting the others, including the equally lucky real estate man. But Jim knew Augustus did not really want to dominate the play. Or more precisely, he did not want his guest from the Pennsylvania utility to fall on the losing side. There was nothing to embitter a gambling man quite like a long losing night at the poker table. Harrison, in his increasing drunkenness, wagered unwisely, refusing to drop out even when the on-board cards of a stud hand showed him clearly out of contention. As the game's energy and the interest in it began to waver, the utility man's pile of chips eroded to almost nothing. Harrison had to be down at least $5,000. When it was agreed at midnight to go once more with the deal around the table, Jim knew his father would have to do something fast to change the utility man's fortune.

The game went through six more deals with no notable change in the players' winnings or losses. Then came the final hand. The dealer called for five-card stud and, anxious to get the game over, dealt quickly.

By the third card three men had dropped out, leaving Jim, Augustus, Harrison and Delafuente. The betting was moderate. The above-board lays showed Harrison with a pair of sevens and Jim with a seven, a nine and a ten and the potential for a straight. Neither Augustus nor Delafuente displayed any power.

The mineowner decided to raise the stakes of the betting, which had begun at $100.

"I see it and raise a thousand," he announced in a move that immediately scared Delafuente away. Harrison appeared startled by the size of the raise and brought his hand clumsily up to his chin.

"One thousand . . . and again," he declared with a slight slur to his voice. He looked at the pile of chips in front of him and found them insufficient to meet his bet. Without asking for the table's permission, as is the custom, he reached into the pot for three $500 chips to make up the difference, setting them to the side and going light. No one objected. Jim called the bet. So did Augustus.

Harrison failed to catch a king on his fourth card, and disappointment showed on his face. Jim, his luck continuing, was dealt a six, leaving him in need of only an eight to fill his straight. Augustus, whose only visible potential was a heart flush, was dealt a spade. Still, he stayed.

Harrison opened at $500. Augustus matched it and raised another $1,000. Jim stayed. The utility man, seeing his chance to counter his earlier losses, raised back again. So did Augustus. By the time the dealer was set to distribute the final face-down card the pot had grown to more than $12,000.

As the dealer snapped down the final cards, Harrison called for a refill on his drink. His fingers were shaking noticeably when he lifted the corner of his last card for a peek at what it was. A pain seemed to shoot through him. Whatever Harrison had been dealt, it was of no help. He was probably left with nothing more than the two sevens that were showing.

Jim looked at his own final card with disbelief. He had caught the eight to complete his straight. The hand surely would give him the game, especially since the hand dealt Augustus still suggested no power.

Harrison took a long, hard swallow from his tumbler. Finally, he made his decision. Forcing a smile to his face, the utility man declared, "Three thousand dollars." It was clearly a bluff.

Jim was sure the game—with the $12,000—was his, but he saw his father staring at him, the message clear in his eyes. Jim knew what had to be done.

"That's it for me," Jim said, folding a winning hand.

With a jerky sweep of his arms, Harrison collected the mound of more than $12,000 in chips. "It was a good game, Porter," he said to Jim, apparently unsuspecting that Jim had thrown the game.

"Good playing," Augustus said. His smile was forced. The final hand had turned his night's winnings into a loss for him and Jim of more than $5,000, and that was a heavy price to pay to keep a visiting slicker from Pennsylvania happy.

The others decided to call it a night, but Jim, Augustus and Harrison moved downstairs to the basement. Despite the hour, a half dozen club members were still present, unwilling to turn off the liquor while toying with the young hostesses who were in varying stages of undress. A blind musician named Corky played lackadaisically at the baby grand.

The three men sat at a table near the piano but away from the others. At the mineowner's beckoning, three young women joined them. They said nothing while new drinks were poured. Then, after gulping another large swallow, Harrison said, "This is some place you've got here."

"We found a little lady named Mae Sexton in New York City to run it," Augustus said proudly. "We think she does one fine job. Isn't that right, Jim?"

Jim, feeling bored, nodded.

"There's no heat from the police?" Harrison asked.

"Hell, the sheriff's a charter member," said the mineowner.

"I guess I gotta say you folks down here got class," Harrison declared. He reached for the curled locks of the brunette who sat beside him and then lowered his hand to her knee. Working his way up the bare skin revealed by the slit in her tight skirt, he went on, "Once I was in Pittsburgh, and this cabdriver took me to a place on the edge of town. Two or three girls pampered me all night at the bar. They disappeared when they closed the goddamned place, and some bastard the size of a gorilla handed me a three-hundred-dollar bar tab. Wasn't sure I'd get out of there or not. And the girls were drinkin' phony champagne. Charged twenty-seven dollars a bottle."

"There's none of that here," Augustus told him. "The rule in the Club Havana is that a man gets exactly what he wants." Turning to the brunette, he asked, "Isn't that so, Sheila?"

The brunette stretched, thrusting her barely covered breasts forward, and wrapped her arms around Harrison's neck; she planted a kiss on his cheek and then rested her head on his shoulder. His hand, meanwhile, climbed higher on her thigh, and the tight-fitting skirt rode upward toward her waist.

Augustus cleared his throat. Jim knew what was coming. "I hate to bring up business at such a precious and enjoyable moment, but there's something I want to talk to you about," the mineowner said.

"Now, don't go and spoil a fine evening," Harrison responded, his head dropping to the shelf formed by the brunette's ample breasts.

"Five minutes, Ed. No more, I promise," Augustus pleaded. "I want to deal with you on that Owens contract."

Harrison sat upright. There was an aggrieved expression on his face. He took another sip from his drink and lit a cigarette. "Owens has been with us for more than I can remember," he said, now sounding considerably more sober than before.

"I know that," Augustus said, "but there's never anything that can't be improved upon."

"He's been very good to us, very square," the utility man said. "He's dropped his price when we asked him to, and he's never late on a delivery. That's important to us, you know. You can't generate electricity if you're short on coal."

"What figure are you at now?" Jim asked, deciding to give his father a hand.

"Well, the contract that's just ending called for eighteen dollars a ton, but in view of the shakeup in the industry, we're gonna bid him at sixteen dollars."

"I'll give you fifteen-fifty," Augustus offered.

Harrison shook his head. "For half a buck I wouldn't have the heart to do it to the man."

Augustus, winking at Jim, decided to drop the matter for the moment. He grabbed the hand of the bleached blonde sitting next to him and ordered, "Get over here, Agatha. Come talk to your daddy." The girl laughed on cue and collapsed into the mineowner's lap. Augustus folded down the top of her halter and began kneading her left breast. Jim averted his eyes, feeling uneasy seeing his father behave like that.

"God didn't create such things only that they should go to waste, did He, my friend?" Augustus asked.

"That's for sure," Harrison replied, easing the brunette into his lap and throwing an arm around the third hostess, also a blonde. She unbuttoned his shirt and reached past the fabric to rub his chest, while the girl on his lap reached behind her and ran a hand back and forth across his thigh.

Although Jim considered himself hardly naïve, the sight of his father cavorting with a whore less than half his age was too much to accept. Each time he glanced at them, he thought of his mother. "Excuse me, please," Jim said and without offering an explanation, left the table.

As he walked briskly through the door and into the corridor, a woman's voice called him. He turned around to find Mae Sexton.

"Come over here and speak to me, young man," she ordered, taking him by the arm and pulling him to a corner. "You want to talk about it?"

"About what?"

"Oh, come on. I've been around, Jim. I know exactly what you're feeling." Her voice grew gentle. "I know it's not a pretty sight, I mean, the idea of seeing your father in a place like this. But it's business, nothing more. That's the way it is in this life."

"That doesn't mean I have to sit there and watch it," he protested, lowering his eyes.

"You remember what I told you? Sex, booze and money. They run the world. Your daddy understands that, and he's doing what has to be done. He's no less a man for it."

Jim looked at her. Her eyes were compassionate. And she was probably right. She had seen too much to be wrong.

"Now, you get yourself back in there and just remember what this old lady told you, okay?"

Jim nodded, kissed her on the cheek and returned to the table just in time to hear his father ask his guest, "That utility of yours makes a lot of money, does it, Ed?"

"Oh, we do okay. Course it's the damn state that sets the rates."

Jim knew that his father's effort was reaching a critical point.

"You on the road a lot?" Augustus asked.

"It's a rare thing that I spend a whole week at home."

"So here you are, working your butt off all around the country for a company that's really raking it in. Don't you ever get mad about not having a piece of that action?"

The brunette had twisted in Harrison's lap, and he now had a hand up the back of her skirt. "This here's all the action I need," he said, laughing.

"You know," Augustus persisted, "you and I could scratch each other's back, if you know what I mean. Your business would be worth one percent to me. There's a lot of that that goes on, you know. And there isn't a thing wrong with it, getting what one is entitled to."

Harrison's eyes widened. His hands stopped in place. One percent of $15.50 would mean more than 15 cents a ton for him. With the thousands of tons Green Valley Electric consumed in a year, he'd have enough money in his pockets to have no worries about his gambling losses anymore. But he shook his head. "Thanks for the offer, Augie, but that's just not me. With three kids, I can't afford to lose my job."

"Think about it a little," the mineowner suggested, deciding to let the matter ride for now. "Come on, Corky, put some life into that music," he barked to the piano player.

"Yes, sir, Major. Whatever you say," the blind man replied, instantly switching from the soft blues he was playing to honky-tonk.

"Hey, Sam," Augustus shouted to the blonde hanging on Harrison's arm.

"Sam?" the utility man asked.

"Yeah, Sam. She's a Samantha. And wait until you see this little act." He looked at the woman and slapped a fist on the tabletop. "Get on up here, and do your number."

The blonde, who appeared to be about twenty-five and was somewhat chubby, hopped onto the table and began rolling her hips and belly to the piano's quickened tempo. With a smooth, well-practiced motion, she freed her halter and undid her skirt, the shiny silken fabric falling into a pile beneath Harrison's now-widened eyes. Wearing only a scant G-string, she dropped to her knees, her rotating belly only inches from Harrison's face. With the snap of a fastener, the G-string dropped down. The bug-eyed utility man almost cracked his whiskey glass with the tightened grip he applied. Augustus reached into his pocket and pulled out a coin, which he placed on the table, standing it on its edge.

"Come on, Sam. Show my friend here what you can do with a silver dollar."

Jim had observed the feat before, and for him it was more of a clinical interest than sexy; but Harrison clearly held the woman's performance in awe, wondering just how he would describe this act to the boys at Green Valley Electric back in Pennsylvania.

Augustus had tried hard. The effort had forced him to drink enough alcohol to put most men under the table, and it had cost him more than $5,000. But he had failed to win over the visiting utility man. As Harrison moved upstairs to one of the club's special rooms with all three young women, Jim and his father left for home.

On the ride back to their mansion Augustus was uncharacteristically quiet. The worry and aggravation of safeguarding the company in a sliding market had begun to take their physical toll of him. He was sleeping for only two and three hours each night and complained that his stomach churned even when the cook was instructed to prepare the most gentle of meals.

"What happened with Harrison back there, that was a nice try, Pa," Jim told him. "You're good at dealing with these people. I'm not sure I could handle it."

His father merely nodded. The rest of the trip was made in silence, Jim doing the driving and thinking about what it was his father had been trying to accomplish.

There had been a time when he would have protested the attempt to steal a large contract from John Owens by bribing the buyer. He would have questioned the ethics of such an action. But now the company's very survival was at stake and with it the jobs that it provided. After observing the tactics employed by Preston in London, Jim could classify his father's departure from the rules of gentlemanly behavior as mild—and probably justified in the context of his goal.

The sounds of Jim and Augustus entering the mansion woke Sarah, and she joined them in the parlor, where Augustus collapsed into a chair. He asked her gently to fix him a nightcap. When she returned, he took a small sip and then set the glass on a side table, nudging it away from him with his knuckles. He seemed unusually contemplative.

"I now know the weight of an albatross," he said softly in a tone very much out of his character. "It's always there, like a ton of coal tied to your back, pushing and pressing until I wonder just how much a man can take before he breaks. I'm not sure I can stomach it anymore."

"Try not to think about it," Sarah said. "The times will change—they always do."

"I've been thinking about something, and I want to sound out the two of you," he said, sitting forward in his chair.

"What's that, Pa?" Jim asked.

"Simply put, it's selling out and moving to Florida. There're many mineowners who've done it, and most have done all right for themselves down there. Why, that Roy Pruitt of Dillon County even went out and bought himself a boat. A yacht, he calls it. When he came home to close the deal on his house, he was wearing a commodore's uniform, for chrissake. The hat, the white pants, the whole bit."

"Is that what you want, a commodore's suit?" Sarah asked.

"Come on. This is serious. I'm really thinking of moving," he scolded.

Jim was aghast at the suggestion. Certainly there was trouble with the company, and he was worried about its effects on his father; but he knew instinctively that his leaving the coalfields for a life of idleness in the sun would kill Augustus as surely as a well-aimed bullet.

Apparently Sarah agreed with that assessment. "It's an option, Augie," she said gently. "And I'm glad you've given some thought to it. But you've got to think it through. What do these men like Pruitt do with their time? Fish? Play golf? Sail their boats? Is that you?"

Augustus didn't answer immediately. "No," he said finally in a tone of resignation. "I guess not. Coal is all I know. This business is my life."

Sarah took him by the hand and led him upstairs. "You've had a couple of bad weeks, dear," she told him. "You'll feel much better after you get some decent sleep."

Augustus was still sleeping when, shortly after 10:00 A.M., Jim heard the knocker against the front door. He listened as Percy responded.

"May I help you, sir?" the servant asked.

"I'm here to see Augustus Porter," the visitor announced sternly.

"I'm afraid the major has not yet risen for the day."

"Wake him then."

Percy, taken aback by the stranger's brashness, asked, "Whom may I say is calling?"

"Daniel C. Rodgers."

"I'll inform the major, sir, but I'm not sure—"

Jim stepped forward and interrupted the servant. "That's all right, Percy. I'll handle this." He turned to the caller, a tall man, wearing a western hat and cowboy boots and chewing on the stub of a long-dead cigar. Jim had never seen him before. "I'm Jim Porter, the major's son. What can I do for you?" he asked.

"It's what I can do for you," the Texan replied in a changed, cordial tone, extending his hand and smiling. "I'm Dan Rodgers. Won't you invite me in?"

Jim was annoyed at the stranger's intrusion—he was tired and had yet to eat breakfast—but he concealed his irritation and motioned the man inside.

Rodgers was trim to match his height. A shirt that appeared custom-tailored hugged his chest and waist. He wore sunglasses with thin silver rims, which, once inside the house, he left in place. Jim showed him to a seat in the parlor.

"Let me get straight to the point, my friend," the visitor began. "I've done some researching, and I see where you're beginning to struggle, what with oil and gas still drivin' the price of coal down. Quite simply, I'm here to make you an offer—a fair and attractive offer—for every piece of coal property you own."

"The company's not for sale," Jim told the Texan.

"In that case, let me give ya a little warning," Rodgers responded. "It's not a threat from me 'cause I myself ain't gonna do nothin' to ya, but these are changin' times in this country, and there's gonna be plenty of prosperity. Unfortunately—and it is a shame—coal ain't gonna be a part of it. I work for Ferguson Oil Limited, and believe me when I tell you it's gonna be firms like mine calling the shots from now on."

Jim was well aware of the advances the oil and gas industries had been making into the coalfields, and his father had been approached both by mail and through intermediaries to see if he would sell; but now Jim had a face to go with the movement that was threatening family-owned coal companies throughout the region. He felt a sense of revulsion while staring at the tall Texan who lacked even the courtesy to request an appointment. Jim decided to swallow his feelings and keep the conversation relatively cordial, but that didn't mean he couldn't touch upon honesty. "I've heard all this before," he said. "But you can't convince me it's not a money game you're playing, grabbing gullible investors' money like the golden ring off a merry-go-round. And someday they're going to catch up with all of you."

"Suppose what you say is true," the Texan said, grinning. "What's gonna happen to you in the meanwhile? Families like yours are walkin' away from their coal all over the Appalachians, and I wanna tell you their timing is perfect—they're leavin' when they can still get a fair price. But that won't last long. You don't sell now, there'll be a day you won't get ten cents on what you once thought was a dollar's value."

Jim smiled. "We're not selling, Mr. Rodgers. It's as simple as that. But I thank you for your offer." Jim stood to signal an end to the conversation, but the Texan remained seated, one of his legs thrown over the parlor chair's arm. He stared at the mineowner's son, studied him and then shook his head.

"There's no fool like a stubborn hillbilly fool," Rodgers said smugly. "You're makin' a serious mistake."

Jim drew the line with that. He rushed toward the seated Texan, grabbed him by his shirt collar and lifted him from the chair. Just then an arm came between them. It belonged to Augustus.

"Easy, son," he said, pulling Jim off the other man. "You don't have to dirty your hands on such scum." Augustus was unshaved and reeked of alcohol. His shirt was rumpled, and his hair was unkempt. He looked threateningly at the Texan. "I think your little discussion is over, friend, and I'll thank you to leave."

"My strong advice to both you and your son is to consider this offer seriously," Rodgers said as he was being edged into the foyer by Augustus.

"There's nothing more to talk about," the mineowner said, his voice louder. "Now get the hell out of here before I work you over."

Rodgers, his hat in his hand, shuffled backward toward the door. "You're a fool, Porter. And someday you'll be beggin' me to take those mines."

Augustus pushed him through the doorway.

"They'll be worthless then. And so will you."

"Beat it, pal."

"You won't be worth your hillbilly spit, you'll see."

Augustus slammed the door. He stood there for a few minutes to cool down. Then he summoned Percy. "Tell that wife of yours to fix me up a little drink," he ordered. "A good dose of gin in some tomato juice." He turned to Jim. "The hell with that shitkicker. If he makes one more move, I'll have him run out of the county. Let's get us some breakfast now."

Augustus spent most of the day in his study on the telephone. When he emerged in late afternoon, he had a mischievous look on his face and announced that Jim and he would not be home for dinner that night—they had a very special dinner party to attend in Livingston at the home of Jim's father-in-law, Raymond Baxley.

When they arrived at the banker's home, Jim found that the other guests included the most prominent local judge, Sebastian Hemphill, and a man from Charleston whom Jim had never seen before.

It was a tasty meal, duck with a sweet French sauce, and Baxley served the finest of his imported wine. The dinner was dominated by polite small talk, politics, baseball and the ill health of the coal industry. Brandy was poured, and cigars were passed. When the five men rose from the table, Baxley suggested, "Maybe we can step into the parlor for our little talk."

The judge, however, cast his eyes at the house servants still clearing the table and offered a counterproposal: "It might be best if we stepped outside for a minute or two."

As they left the dining room, Augustus apparently had second thoughts about Jim's participation in the pending discussion. "I don't want you involved in this," he whispered. "Disappear for a few minutes, would you?"

The early August air was humid, and sweat coated their faces almost as soon as they passed through the mansion's rear door. Still carrying their brandy glasses, they walked toward the gazebo in a corner of the lawn. Jim lagged behind, taking a seat on the top of a short brick wall that formed the boundary of a patio. From this vantage point, Jim watched the judge sit on one of the gazebo benches. The others remained standing. Their discussion, which was beyond the reach of Jim's ears, did not last very long. The stranger from Charleston gestured as he spoke, and once Augustus raised his voice. The judge rose to his feet and put an arm around the mineowner's shoulder. Augustus listened to the judge and then nodded. The stranger also nodded. Then Jim's father reached into a pocket and retrieved an envelope. He handed it to the stranger, who quickly slid it out of sight into his pocket. The four men were talking of the unbearably hot weather when they returned to the patio.

Back inside, Augustus muttered as he dropped into a chair in the parlor, "Never been late on a delivery." He laughed.

"What'd ya say?" the judge asked.

"Nothing," Augustus responded. "Just thinking to myself about a little matter of a utility called Green Valley."

The conversation turned to the marriage between Jim and Anne, a development that had delighted both Augustus and the banker. Jim paid only half attention, his mind attempting to figure out what conspiracy his father had just fashioned.

There obviously had been a bribe paid to the man from Charleston. The fact he was from the capital suggested he had something to do with the state government. And when Augustus had mentioned Green Valley, that meant the Owens company was somehow affected. Putting these pieces together, Jim had a strong suspicion of what it was his father had done. He didn't like it.

"Do you mind if I ask you something?" Jim said to his father in the car on the way home.

"Of course not. Shoot."

"What is it exactly that the state is going to do to Owens?"

Augustus laughed. "Hey, that's pretty smart of you to

figure that out. Guess that college did you some good after all."

"Well, what is it, Pa?"

"All I'm going to tell you is that come the next few days something is going to happen that will make it very unlikely Mr. Owens will make his next Green Valley delivery on time. And that little failure on his part is going to put that fat contract right in our pocket."

"If you're doing what I think you're doing, Pa, it's not right," he told his father. "It's one thing to square off against Owens himself, but when you throw his miners off the job, then that's another story."

His father's face reddened. "What the hell do you know!" he snapped. "It's something that's got to be done no matter what the cost."

"But to put men out of work at times like these? My God, Pa, a lot of these people are hurting. And I tell you, some of them are starting to get mad. It's not like the old days when you and Grandpa ran these parts like a dictatorship. Times have changed, and now you'd better start watching your ass."

"What do you mean by that?" Augustus asked, sounding legitimately curious.

"You keep it up, Pa, and one of these days these people are going to put you into their gunsights or plant a bomb in your car. You're going to switch on the key, and poof! That'll be it. I warn you."

The mineowner's anger returned. "Look, you leave this Owens business to me, do you understand? I'm disappointed in you anyway. Despite all my efforts and all the training you got in London, you still haven't come around to measure halfway up to the size of your brother. You ought to be taking some of this load off my back. It should be you wining and dining these buyers and getting them laid, for chrissakes. You don't have to be a genius at business to do that."

The car pulled up the Porter driveway. Augustus slid off the passenger's seat and slammed the door.

Since being laid off at the mine, T. C. Fenner occasionally managed to find himself an odd job, usually standing in for Ernie Jason when the old man was too inebriated to perform his postal duties. Most days, however, T.C. spent hanging around the corners of Bannerton with other out-of-work men, keeping their ears open for possible jobs and commiserating with one another over their lack of money and feelings of helplessness. T.C.'s lack of a regular job had affected him deeply, touching even his sense of masculinity. He spoke less than ever. Weeks passed between the evenings on which he and Bonnie made love. Because of this, she had decided against telling him the details of her plan for finding herself a job. She knew it was a heavy burden for a man to see his wife working at the same time he was out of a job, but something had to be done—they were almost out of money.

The Coal County Medical Clinic occupied a dilapidated one-room wooden shack behind the service station in Bannerton. The building had been unused for years prior to the arrival of Dr. Gordon Spencer, a Mississippian who had once passed through the mountainous region and decided he wanted to open his practice there. It was a practice that did not produce much money. The siding of the clinic was so weathered and rotted that a steady breeze swept over the interior floor, and even pouring disinfectant by the bucket did not thoroughly sanitize the floor with its accumulations of hidden mold and vermin. Hopes had once been high that a modern, well-equipped infirmary would replace the aging shack, but the growing depression in the coal markets had blocked that. Spencer had to continue making do with a minimum of supplies and instruments in office space much too small for the number of miners and their families whom he served.

Although it was not yet 9:00 A.M., the small waiting bench

inside the clinic was already filled, and the line of waiting patients had spilled outside the door. Bonnie took her place in
the rear behind a man whose arm was encased in a tattered
plaster cast. More than an hour passed before she reached the
inside and took a seat on the bench, which was separated from
the treatment area by a screen. In a few more minutes the
miner ahead of her appeared with the cast missing from his
arm, and the doctor motioned her to go behind the screen.
As he directed, she took a seat next to his small wooden desk.
Just as he began to speak, the telephone rang.

The doctor listened without comment for a long time to
the caller. Bonnie watched him shake his head.

"Now look, Major, the price of everything is going up. I
don't have to tell *you* that—just look at your store," Spencer
said into the mouthpiece. Bonnie could hear a loud rumbling
at the other end of the line but she couldn't make out the
words. "Okay, Major," the doctor said finally, "we can talk
about it. But I can tell you now nothing is going to change."
Smiling, he slipped the receiver back into its cradle.

"Augustus Porter," he said, turning to Bonnie. "Doesn't
like the way I raised my fees for treating his managers. What
he doesn't realize is that if he'd give us half a hand—find us a
new clinic, for example—I'd treat him and every other member of his management for free."

"I don't think he knows the meaning of that word," Bonnie
said.

"Well, enough of him. What can I do for you?"

Bonnie cleared her throat. "Well, I heard you lost Nurse
Jensen, and . . . well, our family's not doing too well, what
with my husband still out of work . . . and I was thinking
maybe I could help you out. Until you find yourself another
qualified nurse, that is."

The physician rubbed his chin. "Have you had training?"
he asked.

"No . . . not formal training. But you don't live in a

mining family without learning a lot about first aid. And I think maybe a lot of nursing is just plain common sense. Could you give me a chance?"

Spencer pinched his chin. "It's true I do need some help. And quite frankly, I'm not sure we have enough money in the medical fund to pay a full-time nurse anymore. I'll tell you what, let's give it a try, Bonnie—but only with the understanding that if the time comes when I can get a qualified nurse, then we'd have to let you go."

"Oh, thank you, Doctor, thank you," she said, grabbing the sleeve of his white coat. "I'll prove you're not making a mistake."

Bonnie told T.C. the news that night. His reaction was just as she had expected.

"I can't have you working, honey. It's up to a man to bring home the bread," he protested.

"Look, it's just temporary. That's what the doctor agreed to. You'll find work any day now, and as soon as you do, I'll quit. In the meantime, Mari can stay with my mother." She moved to his side and began stroking his face. "Honey, it's no reflection on you. It's just the times. A lot of wives are working."

"Okay," he said in a nearly inaudible voice. "If it has to be."

Mari welcomed the news more enthusiastically than her father; the prospect of spending more time at her grandparents' suggested that she would be getting more freedom. She was a very gregarious and active child of seven, almost the opposite in every respect of what her mother had been like when young. Mari did not read books; she was more apt to be found playing baseball with boys. And she had a propensity for getting into trouble. When a window was broken, it was Mari who was likely responsible. But she seldom got caught, being faster on her feet than even the boys.

Mari also failed to resemble her mother physically. Only their eyes were the same—a deep, penetrating green. Otherwise, Mari's hair was brown. Her features were sharp, especially her nose, which lacked the soft feminine shape of her mother's. And she had even less of a resemblance to T.C.

Bonnie, surprised at how quickly and easily she had gotten the job, reported the next day for work at the clinic, where she donned a white frock and immediately took over Spencer's enormous amount of paperwork. She instituted an appointment system that helped reduce the waiting lines and was careful in keeping the clinic's inventory so that Spencer no longer found himself out of vital supplies. Most important, perhaps, her presence produced a noticeable change in the attitude of Spencer's patients. Bonnie's predecessor, Nurse Jensen, had come from Charleston; Bonnie was a local girl.

In the six years the clinic had been in operation, the doctor had managed to reduce some of the miners' reluctance to accept his services, but there were hints of a suspicion many local families still had toward formal medical care. Until Spencer's arrival, most local residents were unaccustomed to seeing physicians and, in large measure, distrusted them. They had heard too many reports of mineowners hiring company doctors and using them to ground—for fabricated medical reasons—the more militant of union men and others who caused them trouble. Spencer's first patients had been miners hurt on the job, ordered to report to the clinic by their mine managers or, if the company was unionized, their union leaders. They reluctantly permitted Spencer to stitch their wounds, set their broken bones and patch their abrasions. Then they rushed back to work. Spencer, in recounting those early days, told Bonnie what bothered him more than the normal run of mining accidents were the other medical problems he spotted while treating the superficial wounds. It had become more and more clear to him that the physical resistance of the people of Coal County was breaking down. The spotty nutrition, the sleepless nights and the unrelenting stress caused by not knowing whether there would be jobs tomorrow were taking their toll, and, Spencer said, the incidence of stomach problems, alcoholism and weakening hearts was at an epidemic level. But these were hidden diseases. The miners did not complain of them. With Bonnie's arrival, however, he began to treat more and more patients for these types of problems. Under her influence and persuasion, miners and their families began seeking treatment for ailments they otherwise would have ignored. There was, for example, the case of Della Blackwood.

It was only her second week on the job when Bonnie escorted the miner's wife up the wooden steps of the clinic. "This is Mrs. Blackwood," she told Spencer. "She's been feeling out of sorts lately, and I told her you probably could do something about it."

"Let's have a try," Spencer said, watching his prospective patient wrinkle her nostrils at the smell of medicine that perpetually hung in the clinic's air.

The wife of a laid-off Porter miner named Axel Blackwood, she was a short, squat woman of forty-seven. When the doctor asked her what exactly was wrong, she complained of a low-grade pain in her left breast. He lowered the top of her dress and began gently probing the area. Bonnie knew his fingers immediately told him of something, for they lingered in one spot. His expression turned grave.

"Mrs. Blackwood, I want you to bring your husband here," Spencer told the woman.

"What is it, Doc? Trouble?" she asked.

"You've got a growth there as hard as a cannonball. I'm afraid you're probably going to need surgery to get it out."

"You mean chop my breast right off?"

"They might have to remove the breast but—"

"No!" she interrupted, yanking her dress back to her shoulders. "There ain't nobody gonna do that to me."

"But, Mrs. Blackwood—"

"You doctor boys did that to Mrs. Lupkin. Took both of 'em off, and she died the next month. I've got ointment—special ointment—and that lump'll just melt away with no butcherin', thank you, sir." She stormed out of the clinic.

Spencer told Bonnie it was his judgment the woman had less than six months to live without treatment, so it was fortunate her husband saw it another way.

"She'll die without the operation, right, Doc?" he asked after rushing to the clinic that afternoon.

"I'm sorry, Mr. Blackwood, but yes—without surgery, if the growth is a cancer, it will be a fatal disease."

"What do you think, Bonnie?" he asked, turning to her.

"You've got to do something, Axel. Just trust the doctor," Bonnie replied.

"Then it will be done," the miner declared.

"Good. It's best you get her to Charleston. Go to the hospital there. They've got surgeons who do this every day. I'll give you a report to take with you," Spencer said.

"Doc, I gotta ask about the expense," he said as Spencer reached for his pen. "How much will it be?"

"I'm not sure," the doctor told him. "Normally it would probably be a two-hundred-dollar surgeon's fee. But with you out of a job, they'll work something out. They do a certain amount of no-fee work and—"

"Charity!" the miner shouted. "Ain't no Blackwood, workin' or not, that's gonna take charity. My father'd roll over in his grave."

"Look, Axel, you've got to have the operation performed, or you're going to lose your wife," Bonnie said. "Accept the treatment, and then later, if you feel the same way, pay the doctor when you're back on the job. Consider it a loan."

"The hell I will," he said. "Ain't never took a dime and don't intend to now. I'll figure something out."

It seemed as if everyone in the county were aware of Mrs. Blackwood and her panicked flight from the clinic. But they also knew of the subsequent visit of her husband and the trust he instinctively had for the doctor. That trust was contagious. When Spencer arrived for work the next morning, there was an unusually large number of patients waiting for him, many of whom he had never before seen. "This is your doing," he told Bonnie. "You keep it up, and there won't be anyone left out there to work the mines."

Bonnie walked to the window to look at the people lined up at the door. Near the end of the line was Axel Blackwood. She went outside and walked up to him. "Are you here to talk, Axel?" she asked. He nodded. "Come on in. You needn't wait in line just for that."

The miner's expression was serious. His eyes told Bonnie he had somehow found his answer, an alternative to charity. Bonnie ushered him behind the screen to Spencer's desk. The doctor greeted him warmly.

"I owe Porter four months' back rent, Doc. I've remortgaged our furniture and sold all but one of my guns. We've still got two children at home, and with me out of work it's a struggle just to eat. It's tough, but I'm not about to stoop to takin' charity. I gave it a night of thought, Doc, and I've made my decision—I wanna sell one of my eyes."

"An eye?"

"That's right. Either one. They're both better than twenty/twenty, and I read how they're puttin' 'em in blind people now. How much ya think I can get?"

"Axel, there isn't a doctor alive who would take an eye from a living man," Bonnie said. "What you read about are corneas they remove from the dead."

He didn't seem to hear her. "I was thinkin' maybe asking for fifteen hundred dollars. That'd clear up my debt and let me pay that doctor," he said.

Spencer rose from his chair. "Mr. Blackwood, now you listen to me. It would be illegal and immoral for a doctor to take your eye, do you understand? There is no doctor who would do it."

The miner also stood, his face angry. "Maybe you won't do it, but somebody will. And I'll find him, dammit, with or without your help." As Blackwood opened the screen door and stomped down the wooden steps, Bonnie heard him mutter, "Been workin' since I was fifteen. Ain't gonna take no handouts now."

Two days later, the Bannerton *Tribune* carried a page one story bearing the headline: "Miner Offers Eye for $1,500."

Despite the publicity, Axel Blackwood never found any takers, and as he tried one scheme after another to raise the $200 surgeon's fee, his wife grew weaker. In time, Bonnie learned that the woman was unable to rise from bed. But she applied her ointment on the hour and insisted to friends that she could feel the lump begin to melt away.

Christmas came, and New Year's, but it was difficult for the Fenners to get into any kind of festive spirit. T.C. was moping at his inability to find steady work. Bonnie's taking a full-time job had had the effect on him that she feared it would—he felt further emasculated and irresponsible, a failure as a provider to his wife and child. Bonnie's job placed an unmistakable strain on their marriage. He withdrew from her and closed his ears to the occasional comment she made about her work at the clinic. And sometimes he appeared outright jealous—as if they were competitors.

The interior of the Fenners' home was immaculate—Bonnie, despite her job, had seen to that—but its exterior reflected the deteriorating state of the region's economy. Paint peeled from the sidewalls, and the roof was naked of shingles in a growing number of places. The wooden steps of the stoop, for lack of proper preservation, were rotting, and window calking shriveled back from the glass panes it was supposed to hold in place. Here and there in the long rows of company homes, a house stood empty, reeking with the same damp mustiness found in shantytowns and slums. As Bonnie saw it, these signs carried a message. They were portents of yet bleaker days to come, a peek at a future that made it mandatory for them to face squarely the facts of their life in Coal County. The time was approaching for decisions to be made.

Thanks to T.C.'s hunting and Bonnie's canning, the family had been reasonably prepared with foodstuffs for the winter. Still, the pinch of their inadequate income was beginning to be felt more and more. Aside from the few dollars T.C. occasionally brought home from an odd job, the household's income came from the relative pittance Bonnie received at the clinic.

Mari, despite her young age, was aware of the tension the insufficient money had produced in the household. She responded to it in a variety of ways, pitching in when her mother set out to repair and clean the floorboards, for example, and asking an unending number of pointed, sometimes painful questions about why her father was still spending so much time at home. Although her energy had not diminished, Mari was less active with her playmates. She also was getting into more trouble.

T.C.'s parents still lived in their company home in the other Porterville hollow. His father had his job but, with the rising prices, was straining to provide for his household, which still included T.C.'s younger brother and an unmarried sister.

Bonnie's parents also were struggling. To cut waste and save money, they began eating regularly with T.C. and Bonnie. After these shared dinners, Duke and T.C. began to spend more and more time in conversation out of range of the women. Sometimes they lingered at the table after dinner with a pad and a pencil, making calculations they did not reveal. They made it a point to destroy the used paper. Bonnie, however—and probably her mother as well—guessed what the two men were up to. But Bonnie didn't reveal her suspicions. She left them alone, confident that before any irrevocable decision was made, she and her mother were certain to be consulted.

Once, on a winter night, the two men buttoned their coats and carried on a long soft-voiced discussion on the front stoop of the Fenner home, oblivious to the cold. T.C., as had lately become a habit, whittled on a stick with a pocketknife. He reduced it to almost nothing, threw away the remaining strands and picked up another. Although he and Duke spoke in low tones, their voices carried through the thin walls of the house, and Bonnie and Liz, sitting inside, became privy to their conversation.

"Some folks are talking about moving," they heard T.C. say.

"Moving? Moving where?" Duke asked.

"Up North or out West. Big cities like Detroit. They say there's good paying work there in those car factories and the like."

"But these are mountain men, T.C. What would they do for their hunting and fishing up there? A move surely would kill half of them, the men anyway."

"Maybe so," said T.C. "But Sam Singleton says he's already wrote to some cousin. Lives in Chicago. Sam says he's some big-shot foreman."

"Our place is here, son. Here with the coal. Starving or spending, it's all we're ever going to know."

A train whistle interrupted their discussion. The two men stopped talking as the sounds of the slowly moving train came from the track 100 yards away.

"Twenty-three," T.C. announced when the train had passed.

"Twenty-three what?"

"Twenty-three hoppers of coal. Was a day you'd count to eighty or ninety."

"That's a lot of miners out of work," Duke commented.

A boom rumbled in the distance, low in its pitch but sufficiently strong to rattle the windows in the Fenner home. Duke and T.C. ignored it, for such explosions had reverberated through Porterville's hollows periodically for as long as anyone could remember. They were interior blasts fed by accumulated gases in a nearby Porter mine sealed thirty-three years earlier. The explosion was followed by another, lower in intensity as if an aftershock. Again the two men ignored it.

"If Roosevelt were alive, it wouldn't be the way it is today," Duke said.

"Well, this Kennedy seems to be for the workingman," T.C. responded.

"That may be so, but he isn't Franklin Roosevelt," Duke said. Then, in a distant voice: "Sometimes I wonder what went wrong, T.C. It seems like only a week or two ago that Bill Bergen and I were in that pub at home and that stranger started talking of all the riches to be had in America. And we signed up. Now what do we have?"

"One coalfield or another—makes no difference, I guess."

"You're right, son. Rich men the world over exploiting mining men. They set it up so there's never going to be that day you get out of debt. And then the economy turns, and the next thing you know, you're not even working. I wonder where it's going to end."

"I don't know," said T.C. "There's some talk about rebellion. Taking it all over like they did in Russia. But I'll have no taste of that. Don't think it makes a penny's difference who's bossing you when you're a miner."

The two men returned inside, and then Duke and Liz left for their home. T.C. slid into the easy chair where he usually read the paper. He picked up the Bannerton *Tribune* Bonnie had brought home but seemed unable to read it. He was twisting and turning in the seat. Bonnie noticed his discomfort.

"What's wrong, honey? Your back troubling you tonight?" she asked.

"No. Nothing wrong with my body. It's my mind. Just won't leave me alone."

219

Having overheard his conversation with her father, Bonnie knew what was bothering T.C. "It'll work out. You pray to God, and it always does," she told him.

"I know, Bonnie. But it just doesn't seem fair. You work until your hands and arms are numb, and then, when you look to the kitty for food money, there isn't any. That hurts, Bonnie. That hurts a man."

She waited a moment before responding. "Well, we haven't run out of food yet. We've got a healthy family, you, me and Mari, and a nice home in a land blessed by God. And you'll get work any day now, you just wait and see."

She kissed him and then went to the kitchen to finish the dishes. A few minutes later, when she looked back at her husband, he was dozing, free finally from his thoughts.

T.C. and Duke waited for a Sunday to reveal to the family's women the precise subject of their weeks of discussion. The two men had stayed up most of the night, recalculating their figures and considering alternatives. Bonnie sensed that they were close to making their decision, and a certain tension hovered over them as they attended church services. Duke waited until after the early-afternoon Sunday dinner they shared in his home before making his move as the family elder. He summoned them into the parlor.

Even before her father began, Bonnie knew that from this point onward, the family would never be the same. They were caught up in circumstances they no longer had any hope of overcoming unless they themselves initiated a drastic change. As it was with a death, Bonnie thought, something had been irrevocably taken from them, only they weren't quite sure how. Or why. But she knew that if they worked together—and were lucky—they might survive with some of the same hope that had lured her father to a ship years earlier and had charted her family's course to the present day.

"I've given it a lot of thought," Duke began, "and I think the time has come where we have no choice but to make a move." The others listened intently. "It's hard to believe, maybe, but there's no longer a future for us here in Porterville. Like it or not, the coal business is dead. If we're to survive and see any of our dreams come true, we've got to get out . . . and do it now." T.C. nodded.

"You mean leave West Virginia, Pa?" Bonnie asked.

"I'm afraid we have no choice, honey," he replied. "The way I figure it, a city like Chicago would give us the best shot. Sam Singleton, for one, has moved there."

"They got a letter from him a couple of weeks ago," T.C. interjected. "He says there're all kinds of jobs up there, good paying jobs backed by strong unions."

"What's he doing?" Liz asked.

"Said he was working on an assembly line in a place called Cicero," T.C. said. "The foreman's his cousin, and I'm thinking maybe he can get us in."

"What's your plan, Pa?" Bonnie asked.

"Well, T.C. and I have done some calculating, and it boils down to this—by selling a couple of guns and borrowing a little from Bill Bergen we'd have enough for train fare for me and T.C. to head on up there. There'd be enough left over for you to live on until we start sending back our pay. We figured that you, Bonnie, and Mari could move in with Ma for the time being."

"And Sam wrote that there's a great many mountain folks who've moved to Chicago," T.C. said. "In fact, he said they kind of all live together in the same area."

Somehow the talk, which had begun with so much apprehension and gloom, had led to an atmosphere of optimism. T.C. was smiling. Liz no longer rubbed at tears. Everyone laughed when Mari interrupted her silent, serious pose to ask, "What's Chicago?"

Duke turned to his wife. "We could send for you in just a couple of months. What do you think?"

The others were silent, waiting for her answer. For all appearances, men as the breadwinners ruled their families in

Appalachia but in practice, it was the women who usually had the final say, particularly on a decision as important as this.

Liz said she viewed the proposal with mixed feelings. On the one hand, she hated the prospect of losing—at least temporarily—the men of the family. But she had noticed how her husband's eyes were displaying a flash of hope and vitality now that she had not seen since his accident removed him from the mines. There was a sharpness and enthusiasm to his words when he spoke of the life that might be theirs in a city like Chicago. And there was a chance a move might bring an end to their financial troubles.

"You've thought this out well, Duke—you and T.C.—and I can see no other way," she said finally. "You and I made such a decision many years ago, and we never regretted it for a minute, even though it hurt to leave our people back home. We did it then, and we'll do it again. I only wish we didn't have to be apart so long."

"It's just a few months, Ma, and we'll write every day," T.C. said.

"And you, Bonnie, what do you think?" Duke asked, turning to his daughter.

"I only wish I could go with you right away," she replied.

Duke looked at each of them affectionately. "Well, that's it," he said. "T.C. and I will leave Tuesday morning. We'll wrap up a few loose ends tomorrow."

The decision thus made, they then turned their conversation to an energetic appraisal of the possibilities awaiting them.

"Do you think we can buy a car, Duke?" T.C. asked.

"Maybe—but not right away," he replied.

"If it does work out," said Liz, "maybe I can get that china I've always wanted."

Duke smiled at his wife. "We'll put that right at the top of the list," he promised.

As they rose from their seats, Bonnie was grateful that Duke had decided to implement the plan without delay. Postponing his and T.C.'s departure by even another day would surely have dampened their enthusiasm for the move. They were riding on their hopes—and little more.

On Monday, Duke went about closing his affairs with the Porter Coal Company, picking up his pay and making certain Liz, Bonnie and Mari would have permission to remain in his company-owned house. The company didn't mind—it would have been unable to rent the house anyway. Bill Bergen came through with a loan of $175 from money he had managed to save and T.C. sold two guns to the gunsmith in Bannerton. The two weapons fetched less than half of what T.C. had hoped for, but he had only one other shotgun, and he didn't want to sell that.

The day passed mercifully fast with all the busywork. Only when the sun had set did it hit Bonnie that this would be their last night together as a family for some time. All of them tried to keep the conversation light, but none was very good at concealing the heaviness of his feelings. Mari sensed the change in the air. She left most of her dinner untouched and refused to leave T.C.'s side.

After dinner, Duke asked Bonnie to take a walk with him. "I don't have to tell you, Bonnie, how worried I'll be about your ma," he said.

"Don't worry, Pa. Mari and I will take good care of her."

"I know you will," he said, smiling.

"And you take care of that leg. If you're gone more than three months, I want you to promise me you'll have a doctor check it out to be sure it's okay."

Duke thumped a hand on his artificial leg. "As long as you've mentioned it, there is something I want to ask."

"What's that?" asked Bonnie, puzzled because her father rarely spoke about his amputation.

"I was wondering if Doc Spencer ever talked to you about it—I mean, I sometimes wonder if it had to be."

"We discussed it once, the doctor and me," she said, trying to measure her words. "He said you were already in shock when he got there, and the rock had your leg so wedged they might still be trying to get it out. He didn't have a choice."

"I guess I knew that all along," her father said, "but every once in a while I think maybe I could have done more to help myself. Sometimes I feel like only half a man."

"You're no half a man, Pa," Bonnie said, patting his back.

Bonnie and T.C. made love that night with more feeling than in years, each knowing it would be weeks, if not months, before they would lie in each other's arms again. Bonnie slept fitfully. When the first signs of daybreak appeared, she protested to herself that it was much, much too soon. Her parents arrived and as the family ate the extra-hardy breakfast Bonnie prepared, they all seemed to tighten with each tick of the clock, fighting the passage of time that was bringing them ever closer to their farewell. T.C. and Duke managed to squeeze their possessions into one cardboard suitcase. T.C. took charge of that. Liz handed Duke box lunches she had prepared.

As with the ticking of the clock, each step they took toward the Porterville railroad station tugged at Bonnie's heart. She and her mother, less self-conscious than the men, dabbed at their eyes. T.C. stared at the ground as the group moved slowly toward Main Street. He, too, appeared to have been pushed to the edge of his emotions, and one inch more might have unleashed his tears. Duke forced a smile and was full of peppy chatter until the arrival of the train.

Before boarding, T.C. pecked Bonnie on the cheek and squeezed her hand, their eyes locking for several seconds. She pulled him back to her for a long farewell embrace. Duke hugged Bonnie and kissed her cheek and then embraced Liz, while T.C., after lifting Mari in his arms, swung the child around in a full circle, then spanked her behind when he had returned her to the ground. "You be good now, you hear?" he said. And the two men boarded the train.

Bonnie, Liz and Mari left the depot as soon as the train started to roll. To have stayed there watching the train disappear into the distance would have been too cruel.

As they walked through the hollow on the way home, Bonnie felt an impulse to be by herself, to climb the long mountain trail up to Newcastle Peak. She needed an answer to the question of why it had come to this. They were leaving Coal County virtually penniless. What had happened to the dream that had inspired her father and her mother to leave their childhood home and cross the Atlantic? Bonnie needed answers, but she fought the urge to hike to Newcastle Peak. The mountain had failed her once. She wouldn't go back.

CHAPTER 9 ────────────

Augustus Porter's bribery of the mysterious man from Charleston paid off for him a week after the dinner at Baxley's. Through an informant within the Owens Coal Company, Augustus learned every detail of what had happened. When he related the story to Jim, he had to pause several times when his chuckling sent him into coughing spasms.

The stranger from Charleston had appeared at the Owens company's largest mine, the Apache, demanding to see the mine manager. When the manager emerged from the portal to meet him, the man from the capital pulled out a silver shield identifying him as a state mine inspector. "Let's go on in," he ordered.

The manager handed the inspector a safety helmet and pair of coveralls without comment and escorted him through the Apache portal. The inspector insisted on seeing every yard of the main heading and many of the tributary headings and rooms off to the side. His tour lasted nearly two hours. When it was over, he handed the manager his cap and, stepping out of the coveralls, ordered, "Switch on that red light, and get your men out of there."

"What was that?"

"Get your men out," the inspector repeated. "I'm closing this mine."

"What for?" the manager asked unbelievingly. All the Owens mines had a reputation for their record of safety.

"Bad top," the inspector replied. "I don't want you in there until you anchor more shoring."

"You're kiddin' me," the manager said incredulously. "We've got enough timber in there now to feed a friggin' paper mill."

"I'm not going to argue. Just get your men the hell out of there, and call me when you think you have this situation rectified."

He handed the manager a card and an official shutdown notice and departed, leaving the manager standing there, still holding the safety cap.

The inspector's day was not yet over. He paid visits to two other Owens mines, including the small cut at Cedar Ridge, and repeated his performance. By sunset only one of the four mines owned by John Owens was authorized to remain in operation, and his company had a large shipment to fill for Green Valley Electric by the end of the week.

"He'll never make it," Augustus chortled. But John Owens had his own political influence in Charleston, and he immediately headed for the capital. A day later his mines were declared safe and opened as quickly as they had been closed. The Owens firm easily fulfilled the Green Valley delivery.

Augustus was livid with rage when he learned this. He spent the next three nights drinking heavily at his club. Finally, he reached a decision on his next move. It would mean a confrontation, he told Jim, but was worth the gamble. He told his son to meet him at the company office.

The office still occupied the simple one-story building on Main Street. The mineowner's private workroom in the rear of the building, however, was richly furnished, its walls paneled and filled with framed photographs and mementos, and a carpet running from wall to wall. Augustus rarely spent time there, preferring to conduct his affairs from his mansion's study, and Jim was puzzled why his father had summoned him there.

The mineowner kept his son waiting outside his closed door for several minutes. Jim sat on a stiff-backed wooden chair, watching clerks file order forms and worksheets into a bank of metal filing cabinets and secretaries punch out directives on their typewriters to the firm's far-flung network of agents and brokers. At noon the dozen office workers set aside their paperwork, rose from their desks and left for lunch, leaving Jim alone until his father opened the door and beckoned him.

Augustus, dressed in slacks and a sportshirt, took a seat behind his paper-cluttered desk. With him were two men: the company attorney and the chief colliery engineer, who held a rolled three-foot-long surveyor's map.

Augustus nodded. The engineer moved to the desk and unfurled the map.

"It's sticky," the lawyer said. "But if Owens ever went to court with a challenge, we could tie him up for years. The case would probably outlive the judge."

Augustus had summoned the two men because of a problem called a rib popping. One of Porter's older, medium-sized mines, named the Hellgate, was located near Cedar Ridge. The bulk of the coal along one of the main headings had been mined out. The men had been in the process of pulling pillars, removing the last walls of coal that had helped support the mine's ceiling, when the mountain above slightly shifted, causing tons of rock, sandstone, slate and other debris to push through the walls of the main heading and nearly seal off the portal. Fortunately none of the miners was trapped or injured, but the mine's track was ruined. The existing portal could be used again only at great risk. The problem for

Augustus was to locate another entrance for the mine. The engineer suggested cutting one at Cedar Ridge, which would place the portal closer to the unmined sections of the vein.

Cedar Ridge formed one wall of a narrow, elongated valley on land owned by a farmer. John Owens leased the coal rights from the farmer, and one of his smaller mines had its portal cut into Cedar Ridge. Owens also held the cartage rights, meaning he had the right to use the farmer's land to haul away his coal. But the ridge also extended into property owned by Augustus, and there was a question about the precise boundary.

"It's hard to be sure, Major, but there are indications you can cut the portal and still remain on your land," the engineer said. Turning to the map and tracing the projected path of the untapped portion of the vein with his finger, he demonstrated how much easier the extraction would be if a new portal were opened on the southern tip of Cedar Ridge. "It'd be a lot less expensive, that's for sure."

"Is that so?" Augustus asked, looking at the lawyer.

"Can't say it's your land beyond a doubt, Augustus, but I think we could make a hell of a case for it," he said.

Ownership and the various property rights were rarely defined with precision in the coalfields. The same piece of land could have one person claiming its surface, another its coal and still others any gas or oil that might lie underneath. Much of West Virginia was handed out in grants from the British crown in the years preceding the Revolutionary War. Later several of George Washington's highest-ranking officers accepted land parcels in West Virginia in lieu of back pay. Much confusion over boundaries stemmed from those eras. Surveying techniques often were primitive at best in earlier decades with such transitory objects as trees and boulders serving as landmarks. Trees died, rotted and disappeared, and even the largest of boulders sometimes shifted its position over time. As a result, title searches and claims disputes often ended up in legal chaos.

"Let's say for argument's sake that we do in fact own the southern tip of that ridge," Augustus said. "Then what do we do about Lambert Creek?" The creek, although shallow, was wide and at times had the force of a small river. It bisected the long valley at the base of Cedar Ridge, and one had to cross it to reach the face of the bluff where the proposed portal would be dug.

"Owens uses the farmer's bridge," the engineer said. "He runs his track right over it, but I don't know if he's paying for it."

"The hell with him," Augustus said. "Let's get digging that portal." To the lawyer, he said, "You go to that farmer and buy the rights to that bridge. I don't care what it costs. You tie the rights up, and if Owens starts making noises, then we'll kick him the hell off the bridge and let him swim." Augustus chuckled. Then, turning to Jim: "You see, we can kill two birds this way—get the Hellgate back in operation and block Owens off from that bridge. Maybe then he won't meet his Green Valley deliveries so easily."

Jim didn't like the plan at all. The odds were too great that it would lead to renewed feuding between the Porter and Owens families. The bitter rivalry had started when Colonel James T. Porter and Daniel Owens, John's father, battled over which of them would own the largest coal company in the region. After both patriarchs had died and control of their firms passed to their sons, the feud entered a period of dormancy, and most people assumed it was over. In 1939 Augustus and John locked horns, however. They had owned mines adjoining each other in the same mountain, and both raced through the vein for the common boundary. There later was enacted a law restricting mining to a distance several feet from a lease line, but then there was no such regulation. Porter's men arrived first and dug within six inches of what his engineer said was the boundary. By the time Owens's men reached the line Porter's cleaned-out chambers had filled with water. The thin barrier of coal separating the two mines crumbled, sending a flood of water into Owens's property. As a result, he was forced to abandon a large amount of high-grade coal, and the dispute between the two families was ignited again. It lasted until World War II redirected their hostilities. After the engineer and lawyer had left, Jim told his father, "I don't like this, Pa. I don't think it's worth the gamble. You're taking a chance on violence by blocking him from that bridge, and if you lose, then all the money that goes into the new portal will be wasted."

"We won't lose, son. That's the point. We'll get this bastard right where we want him," Augustus said.

"Well, a lot of people know you were behind that mine inspector, and they think it was dirty. And they're going to think this is an unnecessary provocation as well."

"Who gives a damn what they think or say?" Augustus responded. "It's not like it used to be. It's changed overnight. You've got to be cutthroat, or you might just as well cash in and move to Florida. What you can't seem to understand is that it's going to be Owens or me in this county—there's no room for the two of us."

"What will this do to Owens?" Jim asked.

"If he plays ball, nothing."

"And if he doesn't? After all, he's been leasing at that ridge for more than a dozen years now."

"Then we'll fight it out," Augustus said. "It's a business decision, nothing less, nothing more. And whatever happens, well, that's the way it's got to be."

Both were silent for a few moments. Then Jim suggested, "It just seems there must be another way. You know what happens every time the Porters and Owenses go after each other. The bitterness grows and grows until it seeps down the ranks to each man's miners. And then there's bound to be blood. With all the outsiders running around now, you'd think there would be a way for all of us to stick together."

"It's not that simple, Jim," Augustus replied. "You show me a way, and I'll do it. The way it stands now, it's got to be us or Owens—there is no in between."

Augustus rose from behind the desk and went to a cabinet in a corner. He removed a bottle of whiskey and filled a tumbler. Jim slipped out the door.

It was cold and snowing, the wind blowing fiercely down from the mountains, as Jim and his father stepped out of the comfort of the Bannerton barbershop onto the street. Augustus, brushing the snow from his eyes, told Jim he could take the wheel for the drive back to Porterville. They had just turned for their car when they heard a call from down the street. John Owens hurried toward them.

Even by Livingston's rigid standards, Owens presented an exceptionally distinguished figure. He was a tall man, slightly more than six feet in height, with a thick head of hair, most of it gray, and a slender face dominated by a high forehead. He carried himself with the straightness of a military man. Despite this stern bearing, he was known as an often compassionate, yet capable businessman and a gentle and just family man, as honest as any person in Coal County. Unlike his father, he had done little over the years to fan the flames of his family's continuing feud with the Porters.

"Augie, I'd like to have a word with you, please," Owens said.

"John. How've you been?" Augustus responded, smiling and extending his hand.

Owens accepted it and nodded at Jim. "Getting along, I guess. As you may have heard, I had a little unwarranted trouble with a state inspector. But that's taken care of now."

"You don't say," Augustus sympathized. He placed his arm around John's back and began steering him toward his parked car. Jim followed silently a pace behind. "It's never easy when you're dealing with the state."

Owens forced a laugh.

"There's no question but that things are changing," Augustus continued. "We just had some son of a bitchin' Texan name of Rodgers barge in on us and demand we sell out. He hit you, too?"

"Yeah. I gave him a quick boot."

"That's the way to handle it, John."

The three of them had moved about ten yards. Owens abruptly switched from niceties and got to the point. "Augie, about Cedar Ridge. They tell me you've been hauling equipment up there."

"That's right, John. I've put in some. Been thinking about opening that south end."

"That's what I thought," Owens said. The three men continued their slow walk through the snow, the two mine-owners casting their eyes downward, Jim staring at their backs, straining to listen. "But I double-checked, and that entire face is under my lease with the farmer there. I've just come from looking over the official county maps, in fact."

"I checked some myself, John, and I don't want to contradict you, but the way we read it, the line slices off that southern tip."

Owens stopped walking. He turned toward the other mine-owner. "So you're going ahead?"

"Got to, John. Don't have a choice because of a rib popping that's nearly shut me down."

"I'll have to fight you, Augie. You know that. And take you into court."

"I always hate to see trouble between two old friends, John. But if it has to be, so be it. My attorney says you'll never win."

"Let's see what the judge says," Owens replied.

The exchange ended. The two men stood in the middle of the street, staring steely-eyed at each other, their expressions communicating much more than their cautious, overly courteous words, each aware of what a bitter title dispute could mean.

"Nice to see you, Augie," Owens said finally, again offering his hand.

Augustus accepted it. "Say hello to the wife," he responded. Owens turned and walked away.

"The two-faced, sly son of a bitch," Augustus said to Jim when the other mineowner was out of earshot. "He knows goddamned well we have a right to open that portal."

"I still don't think it's worth the risk, Pa. Everybody will lose with a long battle out there," Jim said.

"Look, you head on home if you want. I want to stop by the club for a while. After seeing that bastard face to face, I need a drink."

"Go ahead, Pa. I'll stick around. Maybe poke my head into a couple of stores."

Augustus adjusted his coat collar and headed at a brisk step for the Club Havana. Jim knew his father's "one drink" would consume most of the afternoon, and he'd need help in getting home. Maybe the liquor would mellow him and he'd drop this Cedar Ridge showdown, Jim thought. Then he shook his head, dismissing that prospect as completely out of the question. He turned his face to the wind and began walking up Bannerton's commercial strip past several stores, all of which seemed too empty. He wondered how merchants were staying in business with the region's economy the way it was. When he reached a storefront with a sign saying "Judy's Apparel," he found the display window whitewashed and the door chained shut. Peeking through an unpainted crack in the window, he saw that the store was empty. He guessed that few local women had the money to buy a new dress or coat.

From down the street Jim heard the scratchy sounds of a public address system. He followed the noise to a long, squat aluminum-sided building with an arched roof which had once served as a repair garage for cars, trucks, farming machinery and large mining equipment. It now served as an auction hall. Jim went inside.

The dirt floor of the building was crowded with potential buyers and onlookers. Many were sitting in a section with wooden folding chairs. Others circulated among merchandise displayed at the front and to the sides. Most of the browsers appeared to be from out of town. One woman pointed to an old foot-pedal sewing machine and told another, "Look at that. Now that's an antique, all right." Jim knew that such machines were regularly used by mining women.

An effeminate man accompanied by an obese woman examined a brass lamp. "Junk, I tell you. Not worth a dollar," he declared.

Off in a corner was Ernie Jason, the Porterville mail handler. He appeared bent and dissipated, his eyes glazed, and Jim wondered what he was doing at the auction.

The auctioneer stood behind a microphone attached to a tall, crude podium, holding smaller items in his hands and pointing to larger ones as he urged the bidding on in his staccato voice. In most cases, the items went to the first bidder, but when a piece of art or furniture was especially attractive, antique dealers, out-of-town collectors and others competed against one another with vigor.

In the folding chair section, some buyers sat in such a fashion as to communicate their boredom with the entire affair. Theirs was boredom by design. They lifted only one finger when indicating a bid, fearful that any display of enthusiasm would disclose to others the hidden value of an item they were seeking. Other buyers were less coy and shouted out their bids greedily. And when the auctioneer pointed to an ancient oak rocking chair, Jim smiled as two women literally fell over each other while signaling their bids. He took a seat in the rear row of folding chairs to observe the action.

The rocking chair proved to be a popular item, attracting five bids at the start. The price climbed rapidly. Soon two of the would-be buyers dropped out, leaving three, one of them a woman with jet black hair sitting several rows ahead of Jim with a child at her side. After another round, one more bidder withdrew. The woman and a well-dressed man with the appearance of an antique dealer remained. The bids, which had started at $2, had risen to $14. The dealer placed his bids with no hesitation, having obviously found some concealed value in the old rocking chair. But the woman kept pace with him. When the dealer raised his bid to $15 and the auctioneer proposed pushing it $1 higher, the woman turned to shush her child, who had begun to squirm in her seat, and Jim recognized her as Bonnie Fenner. The child beside her must be Mari. What was Bonnie doing there, and why did she want that chair at a price that already seemed beyond its worth and was growing?

The dealer pushed the bidding to $18, and the auctioneer, enjoying the face-off and the profit it was producing, looked toward Bonnie. The expression on her face begged for time. He gave it to her. She removed a roll of dollar bills from her pocket and counted them. Then, with a look of defeat, she turned her eyes to the auctioneer and shook her head.

"Eighteen . . . we're at eighteen . . . that's where it is . . . is there a nineteen . . . do I hear nineteen . . . a fine chair . . . a steal for thirty, maybe forty dollars . . . do I hear a twenty . . ." the auctioneer babbled on in his clipped monotone. Then he paused. "Going once, going twice. . . ."

"Twenty here," Jim shouted from the back, rising from his seat and waving his hand. The dealer came back with a $25 bid. Jim, in turn, went to $30. The auctioneer was smiling. At $40, the dealer dropped out, shaking his head in amazement. The auctioneer declared the chair sold to Jim and went on to a small wooden jewelry box he held in his hands.

Jim went to the cashier's table and paid for the chair. With the receipt in his hand, he walked to Bonnie, who was speaking softly to her disappointed daughter. Jim touched Bonnie's shoulder. She looked up, surprised to see him.

"This is yours," Jim said, handing her the ticket for the

rocking chair. "I want you to have it. That chair must mean a great deal to you."

Bonnie's eyes lit up. She smiled for a moment but then caught herself. Her lips tightened. Her expression became stern. "It's not my chair. It's Ernie Jason's. You know, that poor old man your father decided to crack down on," she said sarcastically.

Jim was confused. "I don't know what you're talking about. What did my father do?"

"Ernie's brother died, and the benevolent major foreclosed on his debt. He ordered all of the brothers' possessions confiscated to satisfy the lousy hundred eighty-three dollars Ernie's brother had borrowed from the company years ago. Some of us at church took up a collection so Ernie could at least keep one of his possessions, that beat-up old rocking chair. It was their mother's."

"Bonnie, I know nothing about this, believe me I don't," Jim said. It was true—he had nothing to do with his father's management of miners' debts.

Bonnie lowered her eyes. Her fingers began to toy with the receipt.

"Look," Jim said, "Ernie's got his chair now, and when I get back to the office, I'll see what the company can do for him. I didn't know about his brother's death."

"His brother just happened to devote most of his life to the Porter Coal Company, but that didn't stop your father from—" she started to chide him but stopped abruptly. She reached out, touched Jim's hand and said, "What I mean to say is thank you. Ernie will appreciate anything you can do for him."

Jim nodded, then looked to the child beside her. Moving suddenly, Bonnie took Mari's hand. There was a flash of panic in Bonnie's eyes. She pulled the child toward her.

"My, you sure are a pretty little girl," Jim said, ignoring Bonnie's curious gesture. It was true—Mari was very pretty.

As Jim inspected her, he concluded that the child did not very much resemble her mother. Mari was broad in her build and hardly dainty. Her hair color was brown in contrast with the jet black of her mother's, and there were basic differences in their faces, Mari's features more defined than Bonnie's. Their eyes, however, were identical, the child having the same expressive, exotic green eyes that once had so captured Jim.

"Say thank you, honey," Bonnie instructed her daughter.

"Thanks," the child mumbled shyly.

Saying nothing more, Bonnie took Mari's hand and went to claim the rocking chair.

"Who is that man?" Jim heard the child ask as she was being dragged away.

"An old friend, dear. Now come on," Bonnie replied.

Jim's chance encounter with Bonnie at the Bannerton auction haunted him for days. He was unable to put her out of his mind. Later, when he learned that she had joined Dr. Spencer at the clinic, he became even more preoccupied with thoughts about her. His fixation on Bonnie perplexed him, for his marriage to Anne Baxley had fulfilled most of his expectations. Sarah still ran the Porter household, but she was allowing Anne more and more influence in some areas, including the selection of furnishings, artwork and menus. Anne's sexual desire not only remained but had grown. The same was true of her bedroom talents, so Jim had no complaints in that regard, except perhaps that their nighttime exercises sometimes reached marathon proportions which, to him at least, often seemed too theatrical. So he was puzzled by his persistent thoughts about Bonnie, his dwelling on her strength and determination, her beauty and her penetrating eyes. Occasionally his reflections on Bonnie proved so distracting that he was unable to concentrate on his work, and he would leave the desk he had taken in the company office for a walk up and down Porterville's hollows.

These walks usually succeeded in clearing his thoughts of Bonnie, but they were replaced by another growing preoccupation: the worsening state of the Coal County economy.

Despite the winter weather, Porterville was filled with dozens of men standing idly around, their faces marked by bland expressions and their hands whittling twigs to occupy the time or slapping their bodies to chase away the cold. The Porter company payroll had been chopped by a third. Those still holding jobs found themselves reduced to a four-day workweek, which gave a family man enough pay perhaps for bread, beans, milk and sugar on top of his rent and other expenses. The men most apt to see their names on the work rosters were those who still owed the company money. Because of the seniority system that otherwise prevailed, younger men had little chance to work and spent their time hanging out in town. The long-honored chain of father-son apprenticeship was broken.

In the deteriorating company homes, meals that were once varied and nutritious became platters of pinto beans and corn-bread squares. Children reported to school in shoes with soles worn through, patches of cardboard affording at least temporary protection against the snow. Jim noticed these signs of growing poverty, and sometimes, in the early evenings when he passed small groups of huddled men on the stoops of the company houses, he heard snatches of the miners' murmuring discussions: "What are we goin' to do?" "We need the union, that's what." "Maybe the government will come up with subsidies." The discussions, often lasting long into the night, produced no answers. In the mornings, the faces of the out-of-work mining men told of their fruitless search for reason in a chain of events that had forced idleness upon them and allowed toughened arm and back muscles to melt into weakness like shriveling strands of putty. When his eyes met those of an idled miner, Jim found it impossible to keep his there, averting them toward the ground. Seeing their plight, he felt as frustrated as they did. He also felt guilty.

239

On one of his noontime walks, Jim had happened upon T.C. Fenner loitering with a group of other idle men. The sight stunned Jim then, and it did again when he thought about it while having dinner with Anne.

As they ate alone, Sarah away visiting and Augustus having gone off to discuss business with Mae Sexton at the Club Havana, Anne was full of chatter. Jim found himself unable to listen. He excused himself from the table early, his food only partially consumed, and retired to the parlor, where he poured himself a stiff drink of brandy. Later Anne climbed into bed next to him, dressed in her favorite and flimsiest negligee. She began her practiced caresses, but Jim wasn't in the mood. "Come on, honey," she urged him. When he still showed no interest, she became angry. "What's the matter with you?"

"I'm sorry, dear, but I've got something on my mind," he responded.

"And what the hell can be more important than your sexy wife trying so hard to seduce you?"

"Maybe if I poured myself another drink," he said, starting to roll off the bed.

"Just forget it," Anne snapped, turning away from him. "I'm sorry I bothered you."

Jim looked at her. It was typical of her not to inquire about what was troubling him. He didn't blame her for this, however. His usual problems concerned the company, a subject Anne found boring. That he could understand. But now he felt compelled to talk to *someone*, and maybe, just maybe when he related his feelings about how he had stumbled into T. C. Fenner, Anne might understand.

"It's just that a couple of weeks ago I was walking through Bannerton and bumped into the wife of T. C. Fenner," he told her. "He's the son-in-law of Duke Shaw. You know, the man who lost his leg. T.C. and I were teammates on the baseball team in high school, and he used to work at the Red Fox until my father laid him off with all the others." Jim paused, but Anne said nothing. "He's been out of work, and his family is really hurting. Sometime ago I told T.C. I'd see what I could do. I went to Pa and reminded him how Duke Shaw had probably saved his life and all that, but the old man was insistent that we could do nothing, not even for Duke Shaw's relatives. I asked him about the store, maybe putting T.C. to work in the stockroom or something, but he wouldn't hear of that either. I didn't know what the hell to say to T.C. Here I was, a so-called executive of this company, and couldn't even squeeze a friend onto the payroll. Now it's too late. His wife didn't mention it, but both T.C. and Duke have gone to Chicago. They've given up on Porterville." He looked at the shadowy curled figure of his wife. Then she suddenly rolled over.

"You're so damn sensitive sometimes," she said. "When are you going to start thinking of yourself? No matter what I sometimes think of your father, at least he has a pair of balls. And he's smart enough to see what steps have to be taken if the great Porter empire is to survive."

Anne rarely talked like that, and it bothered Jim when she did. But he let it drop. Maybe she and his father were right, and survival in the coalfields had reached a point where one no longer could care about what happened to a T. C. Fenner and what could happen in a bitter, toe-to-toe showdown with another mineowner struggling as much as oneself.

Jim, saying nothing, left the bed, put on his robe and returned downstairs to the parlor. He poured another glass of brandy, collapsed into an easy chair and soon found himself thinking not of T.C. or John Owens or his father but once again of Bonnie.

The showdown at Cedar Ridge came less than a month after the two competing mineowners had met on Main Street in Bannerton. Jim learned of it when he went to the Club

Havana to pick up his father and discovered that Augustus, after several hours of drinking, had rushed out to Cedar Ridge.

Jim sped to Cedar Ridge; a few minutes later, rounding a bend overlooking the narrow, long hollow at the base of the ridge, he got a bird's-eye view of the stalemate shaping up below. Owens's thirty-two miners were clustered in a group, blocked from their mine by the creek and prevented from crossing the wooden track on the snow-covered bridge by a guard cradling a sawed-off shotgun. At the other end of the twenty-yard span were two additional sentries, also armed, and a small crew of men was tinkering with equipment near the ridge's south end, where Augustus planned to sink his new portal. Jim caught a glimpse of his father standing behind a bright yellow excavating machine.

Jim carefully negotiated the zigzagging road into the hollow and drove toward the guard on the bridge. The Owens miners stared blankly at him as he passed.

The guard with the shotgun was tall and very slender. He glared at Jim's Olds with eyes that were set too close to his nose.

He's an ugly one, Jim thought. Probably an outsider with a prison record as the day is long.

He shouted through the window to the guard who was inching toward the car with a menacing expression. "I'm Jim Porter. The major is my father. I'm coming through."

The guard pouted for a moment and then stepped to the side. Jim crossed the bridge, parked the car and moved toward his father.

Another car descended the winding roadway to the floor of the hollow, a long black Continental. John Owens was driving. His wife was at his side.

Owens drove to his gathered miners, and a foreman spoke to him briefly through the car window. Then the Continental headed for the bridge, pulling to a stop just a few feet in front of the guard. The guard, chewing gum vigorously, raised his shotgun and cocked its hammer.

"There ain't nobody crossin' this bridge, mister," he said.

"Says who?" Owens demanded.

"I got my orders from Major Augustus Porter. He just bought this bridge, and he's got the papers to prove it."

Owens's wife tugged at his arm. "Don't push it, John. Let's just go and get the sheriff. He gets paid to settle this sort of thing."

"It's not Porter's bridge, dear, and I'm not going to let him get away with it," John replied. He turned back to the guard. "Now you listen to me, friend. I own the Owens Coal Company, and that over there is the portal to one of my mines. Those are my men, and you're standing on a bridge that I legally lease. Now, I'm going to drive over this bridge as I have for fourteen years whether you decide to get out of the way or not."

Owens put the car in gear and inched it forward. The guard stood his ground. On the opposite shore, Augustus turned to Jim and said, "Let's get the hell on over there."

As the Continental continued to crawl toward him, the guard looked to Augustus for guidance.

"Don't move a goddamned inch," Augustus ordered. "And if he keeps coming, pull that trigger."

"Pa, there's a woman . . . ," Jim began to protest.

"Shut up!" his father barked, his words slurred. "This is my ball game."

The car stopped. Owens leaned out the window. "This is a direct provocation, Porter," he shouted to Augustus. "I can't let it go unanswered, not now with my company already pushed to its knees. I've got to draw the line."

"You advance any further and we'll pepper that nice shiny car of yours with buckshot," Augustus responded.

"Please, John," the woman pleaded.

Owens looked at his wife for a moment. Then he returned

to the window. "Okay, I'll leave this be for now. But you two mark my words. I'll get a court order to clear you the hell out of here, and then I'll sue you for every dime I've lost." He put the car into reverse and backed it toward his clustered miners. "Go home, boys," he told them. "If Porter thinks he can take the law into his own hands, he'll find out differently in court. It might take a day or two but you'll continue to be paid."

Augustus and Jim turned toward the portal. "This is not the way to do it, Pa. There's been too much bloodshed in the past. Isn't there another way?" Jim asked.

Augustus glared at his son. "If you ever interfere with me again like that, boy, I swear to Christ I'll put a gun to your head, too," he warned through clenched teeth. "I should have had the guard blast that fancy car before that fool Owens even opened his mouth."

"And what if he pressed charges?"

"The sheriff's in my pocket, don't you ever forget that, and I—" Augustus stopped when a foreman ran to his side.

"They just called for ya from the office, Major. Said you'd better get out to the Red Fox. There's some union fella headed that way."

"For chrissake! If it's not one thing, it's another," Augustus slurred, stumbling off to a company jeep.

Jim looked accusingly at the foreman. "What the hell did you have to tell him that for? You see what condition he's in."

"But, Mr. Porter—" The foreman didn't get a chance to finish. Jim had raced after his father. He managed to hop into the jeep just as the driver pulled out.

There had been something in Colonel James T. Porter's blood that revolted at the very thought of a union and the prospect of outsiders handing him orders. This enmity had been passed down to Augustus, who believed surrendering to any union man would be a cruel betrayal of his dead father. By keeping one step ahead of unionized coal companies in pay, the Porters had managed to keep the union out of their mines. They and their men had reached an unstated understanding, and no would-be organizers had shown their faces on a piece of Porter property for a decade.

It was a surprise then when the report came of the arrival in Porterville of a union official named Andy LeGrande, whose reputation as an especially effective organizer was widespread in the coalfields of several states. Physically he resembled a bear, a large hulk of man with a sandy full-face beard and brush mustache. He had grown up on a farm in Wisconsin, and his fanatical devotion to the militant labor movement had been nurtured on a college campus, not in a coal mine. He had, as far as anyone knew, never worked in a mine. But he was reputed to have the persuasive powers of a well-spoken courtroom lawyer, and his prolabor arguments had been accepted as truth by unorganized mining men throughout Appalachia. As his trademark he wore a wide-brimmed black felt hat sporting a bright red feather.

When the jeep reached the Red Fox Mine, Augustus jumped off and hurried to the manager's shack. He telephoned his office and learned that the organizer had left Porterville about fifteen minutes earlier en route to the mine. "Probably shooting for five o'clock and the shift change," Augustus said. "That way he can cover two shifts with his bullshit." Turning to Crawford, Augustus asked, "You still got that deer rifle around?"

"Yes, sir," Crawford answered. "Right in the corner by the file cabinet."

Augustus went for the weapon. Picking it up, he stroked its long steel barrel and then filled the chamber to capacity with powerful thirty-aught-six rounds.

"You can't shoot this guy, Pa—" Jim protested.

Augustus jabbed a finger into his chest. "I've had enough of your interfering with me for one day. Now you just shut up."

Jim realized nothing he could say would matter. He moved

out of his father's way as Augustus staggered toward the portal.

It began raining, the rain melting the three-inch layer of snow. Jim was worried as he watched Augustus weave through the slush, pacing back and forth in front of the portal. "The last thing I need right now is meddling from the commie union," he heard his father mutter.

As Augustus had anticipated, LeGrande appeared almost with the blowing of the 5:00 P.M. whistle. He was alone, seeming lost despite his size in a huge poncho. Trying to shield a bundle of leaflets under his arm, he began walking through the cut in the hills leading to the Red Fox portal.

"You stop right there!" Augustus barked from a position just to the side of the mine entrance. "I own this land, and you're trespassing, friend."

The union man halted, squinting through the rain toward the mineowner. "This is a democracy, or haven't you heard?" he shouted back. "I have a constitutional right to speak to your men."

Augustus did not answer. Instead, he raised the rifle to his shoulder, aimed for the ground in front of LeGrande and triggered a shot. The slug kicked up a mass of muddied dirt. The organizer seemed to freeze as the rifle report echoed back from the foothills, but then he relinquished his grip on his leaflets and dived belly down into a shallow gully.

Jim moved toward his father, but Augustus raised a hand. "Don't worry, son. I'm just doing what has to be done. Nobody's going to get hurt," the mineowner said. Jim, noting that the confrontation had seemed to sober up his father, believed him.

When nothing further happened for several minutes, Le-Grande inched up on his knees to peer over the rock toward the portal. Another shot rang out from Augustus's rifle. Again LeGrande collapsed onto his stomach.

The two changing mine crews observed all this in silence, and Augustus instructed his manager to get on with the shift change. The mineowner remained at the side of the portal, triggering a shot each time the union man raised his head.

When the sun set, a string of mercury vapor lamps had come on, casting the area in a tint of purple. The rifle shots added an odor of gunpowder to the chilled air which already had the smell of grease from the heavy mine machinery.

Shortly after 11:00 P.M. Augustus finally walked from his position. "That should do it," he mumbled to Crawford, handing over the rifle. "I think my friend there got the message." He turned to Jim. "You do what you want. I'm going to the club."

With all the gunfire Jim wasn't certain the union man hadn't been wounded. After his father left for Bannerton, he walked to the gully. The ditch was filled with nearly a foot of water from the rain and melted snow. LeGrande, soaked and shivering, appeared exhausted. Blood trickled from a gash in his neck. Seeing Jim, the union man struggled first to his elbows and then to his feet. "You tell that asshole Porter that he did me more good with his little spectacle than harm. His entire work force saw him in action against someone they know is trying to help them," LeGrande said, obviously unaware that Jim was the mineowner's son.

"Are you hit?" Jim asked, helping to steady the union man.

"Naw," LeGrande replied, raising a hand to his neck and then examining the blood on his fingertips. "Just a chip of flying rock."

"We'll give you a lift to Bannerton. You ought to have that cleaned. Go to the clinic. If you're lucky, the doc will still be there."

"Forget the ride," the big man replied. "I'll go the way I came."

"Whatever you say, pal," Jim replied. "But my advice to you is stay the hell away from here and the other Porter mines. We don't want you, and if you keep trying like this, you're going to end up dead."

LeGrande smiled. "You just tell Porter someday I'll have it my way, and he knows it. It may take me five or even ten years, but one by one I'm going to win his men, and in the end, they'll have their say." He reached for his waterlogged hat, straightened the feather and plopped it on his head.

By the next morning, the entire county was aware of the face-off between Augustus Porter and John Owens, and a community-wide tension was already developing around it. Competition between two large coal companies was considered normal, if not healthy, but when the rivalry grew out of proportion, mining men knew it would be only a matter of time before they, too, were caught in the web of hostilities. It had happened before in Coal County when the Porter and Owens families tangled and elsewhere when two mineowners were at loggerheads. Not unlike feudal battle, the animosities spread from the owners' drawing rooms to infect even the lowest of common workers, leading to mass barroom brawls among miners who saw their jobs in jeopardy and extending even to the classrooms, where young boys fell into two sides and waged sometimes bloody combat on the question of which company was right.

"The male ego," Bonnie declared as she and her mother discussed the growing feud at breakfast. "Those two old fools are going to throw the whole county into turmoil just because of their greed and pride."

"I'm not so sure, dear," Liz replied. "Sometimes when you argue about a lease line, there can be a lot of coal at stake. In these times it could mean a difference. There comes a time when a man has got to assert his rights."

"Come on, Ma. There's no reason at all that this couldn't be settled peacefully with some kind of compromise. They'd probably even save money if they worked together."

"Perhaps. But we don't have all the facts."

"We've got enough facts to know that Augustus Porter is half crazy, and before he's finished, this is going to be a ghost town," Bonnie argued. "Can you imagine this happening if those two companies were run by women?"

Liz laughed. "It might even be worse. In any event, we don't know now and won't for as long as I can see. It's going to be a long time before some lady takes over a company the size of Porter's."

"Oh, I don't know, Ma. I think we have a young lady right here smart and tough enough to handle the job," Bonnie said, patting Mari's head.

Liz chuckled. "Maybe you've got something there."

"I don't want to be any coalman," Mari protested. "I'm going to be a doctor just like Dr. Spencer."

"Speaking of him, I've got to be going," Bonnie said. After getting her coat, she moved to the front door to wait for the ride one of the Porter truckdrivers gave her each day.

The driver let her off at the service station, and Bonnie walked the few remaining yards to the clinic. When she turned the corner, she saw a large figure huddled in a crouch on the stairs.

"Not again," she said to herself, thinking it was probably another drunk camped out at the door with the ill effects of some acid-strength bootleg. But when she tapped the motionless figure, his suddenly alert eyes and friendly smile told her he had not been drinking.

"Hi," he said cheerfully. "I'm told maybe I can get some help here for this little wound of mine." He pulled down the folds of his poncho to reveal a blood-encrusted gash on his neck.

"Of course," Bonnie said. "The doctor's not here yet, but I think I can be of help to you. Come on inside."

The big man struggled to his feet and followed her inside the clinic. He appeared to be about thirty-five years old. His eyes were large and blue, and his nose was rounded and wide. He was barrel-chested and reminded Bonnie of a big gentle bear.

She helped him out of the dripping poncho and his lumberjack's flannel shirt, leaving on his blue jeans, bright red woolen socks and scruffy black boots. She motioned him to sit in a chair next to the examining table and went for a bowl of hot, sudsy water and a bottle of antiseptic.

He winced as she touched his neck wound.

"It should sting for only a minute," she said. "How did it happen?"

"Well, there I was, minding my own business when I got cornered like a no-good possum, and every time I raised my head, the good man pulled the trigger."

"What good man might that be? You're not on the lam, are you?"

He laughed. "The only law I broke was that great old principle of common sense. Only a fool like me would tangle with Porter."

"Porter. What Porter?"

"I believe you folks around here refer to him as Pugnose. You know, the ugly, mean ol' polecat who thinks he's some kind of major."

Bonnie had cleaned away the caked blood, leaving the three-inch gash pinkish red. "This doesn't look like a gunshot wound."

"It isn't. One of his shots grazed a rock. It was a chip that hit me, at least I think so."

"And just why was Augustus Porter shooting at you? You fleece his club or something?"

"No, not that. All I did was show my face at one of his mines. You see, I work for the union. Name's Andy Le-Grande." His bare belly rocked with an inexplicable burst of laughter.

Bonnie, like most people in Coal County, had heard of Andy LeGrande, the organizer, but she had never seen him. She had imagined him as a tall, stringy figure with an Abraham Lincoln face and a deadly serious demeanor. "You're kidding me," she said, stepping back and smiling with the belief that this man, whoever he was, was putting her on.

"Honest to God," he replied. "It's me, hat and all."

"Well, if you'll pardon me, I would have expected that a union leader of your reputation would tend to be . . . well, more serious and businesslike."

Andy chuckled. "One of the first lessons a man learns in the field is that you can't be serious and still keep your sanity while dealing with the likes of Pugnose Porter."

"Tilt your head back, please, so I can put on this gauze." She taped a thick wad of cotton over the gash. "You don't need stitches. You're lucky. But you were so wet and cold I'll be surprised if you don't come down with pneumonia. How long were you waiting outside that door?"

He smiled. "Only a woman would ask a question like that. I'm not going to answer it, okay? Because if I did, as sure as I'm sitting here, I'd get a lecture."

"Yes. You probably would," Bonnie said, handing him his shirt. "Let me ask you something else, all right?"

"Sure."

"What made you visit that Porter mine?"

His expression for the first time turned serious. "The Porter Coal Company is one of the last major holdouts in this state. Porter's kept the union away by every cheap trick in the book. Pays his men a nickel more an hour than the union wage, and they think they're ahead. Doesn't seem to matter that there's not one cent that goes to retirement, for example, or medical care." He stood to button the shirt. "So every once in a while we like to let old man Porter know we're still around, that we're watching him like a hawk, and the moment the time is ripe, we'll move in and grab him."

Bonnie shook her head. "I don't think the time will ever be ripe with this company. Porter would rather shut down the company than let the union in. You must know that."

"Of course. But I've heard that plenty of times before. 'I'll kill this company before I ever let a union man in the door,' they say. They never really mean it. They're too greedy and like the feel of all that money coming their way.

Without their mines, these people are nothing, and eventually they come to realize that. So it's a bluff, this threatening to shut down."

"You actually think you'll have a chance with Porter then, don't you?"

He stuck out his chest. "Look, sweetheart, I don't want to sound boastful or anything, but I'm Andy LeGrande. I've seen mineowners in all shapes and sizes, and I've had them for breakfast. Augustus Porter is an old maid compared to some of the whores I've dealt with and whipped into line— uh, pardon my language." He reached into his shirt pocket for a small cigar and lit it.

"Actually it's a question of patience and timing," he continued. "With the coal business shrinking and companies like Porter's laying off a lot of good men there's a resentment building. One by one, we'll win those men and then one day—not tomorrow, perhaps; maybe five years from now— we'll find ourselves with a majority. Then we'll make our move, and I'll put the magic of Andy LeGrande to work. And do you know what? I set the stage for it last night. Do you think I actually enjoy crawling around a muddy hole at some mine, taking a chance on getting shot or losing my nice hat here? But Porter shooting at me like he did probably won me more minds and hearts than anything I might have said to those men at this point."

"Where will you go now?" she asked.

"Oh, I've got a little circuit I make in this part of the country. A few pet projects to attend to. They can hold any kind of rally they want organizing a company, but they never seem to win until ol' Andy shows up. But I'll be in and out of Porterville. You can count on that. I got a long memory when it comes to someone shooting at me."

He slipped back into the poncho. Bonnie handed him his still-soggy hat. He ran a finger over the red feather. With its fibers clogged together in bunches, it appeared ruined.

"That SOB almost destroyed my hat, didn't he?" he complained.

Bonnie reached out to touch the feather. He grabbed her hand. It was ringless—she didn't wear her wedding ring to the clinic. "Can I ask *you* something?" he said.

She nodded.

"Is this the hand of a married woman I'm holding?"

"It is," she said, smiling.

"A miner?"

"Was a miner. He's left town to try to earn us a living."

He dropped her hand and turned his eyes away. "More and more good men doing that. But the fight's right here." He looked toward her again. "Help me get that message across, would you? I mean each time you see a man pushed to his limit and wavering, give us a plug."

"If it means making life just a bit more miserable for the Porters, I'll do anything I can," she replied, her voice betraying her bitterness toward the mineowning family.

Andy picked up on it. "You know, I survive by reading the feelings of people. And what I see in you is a rather strong resentment of the good major. Why?"

"Both the major *and* his son."

"His son? What does he look like?"

Bonnie described Jim Porter.

"I thought so," Andy said. "This guy helped me after the old man got through pinning me down, and I kind of thought there was a resemblance." He paused. "That's good, you know."

"Why is that?"

"The third generation. I love them. Andy LeGrande seldom fails when he's dealing with the third generation." He tilted his head to the side. "You see, if you look at the history of the union, you'll find it consistently moving into a company in the months after the second generation of owner dies. That's because the grandsons are too used to the good life to put up much of a fight. They're not as cocky as their fathers or as tough as their grandfathers, who had to claw their way up and fight for years before they got anywhere. Most of the third generation have never even been in a mine."

He plopped the hat on his head, adjusting it to a rakish angle. "Well, it's time for this Robin Hood to get on with it. I've got a lot of work to do before I leave town." He moved toward the door. "I'd like to thank you for your expert treatment, ah . . . say, I forgot to ask your name."

"Bonnie . . . Bonnie Fenner."

"A man like me is like a circuit rider, Mrs. Fenner. Don't have a wife. Don't have any kids. Have very damn few friends. So it's always enjoyable to meet a very pretty woman like you." He edged closer to her. "Next time I'm in town, do you think we could have another chat?"

"Of course," Bonnie said, smiling. "Why don't you stop by my house and let my mother and me give you a home-cooked meal mountain style, the kind that sticks to your belly?"

He slapped his hand against his stomach and chuckled. "I'm not sure that's exactly what Andy LeGrande needs." Waving, he departed.

Bonnie's encounter with Andy LeGrande left her with a very warm feeling. Twice during the next two days she watched him from a distance as he went to work on Porterville's men.

"We don't need no union," one miner told him. "Porter's taken good care of us over the years."

"You think so?" Andy shot back, his voice strong but calm. "Let me ask you this—you got a company doctor? This major do anything about providing you with medical care?"

The miner shook his head. "Haven't needed any doctor."

"Not yet, maybe. And what about a pension? Porter give you one penny toward the day when you can't work anymore?"

"I'll do okay," the man replied. "And anyway, that union of yours is corrupt all the way down the line."

"That's an illusion, a myth that men like Porter spread around to keep you men from organizing and fighting for your rights." Andy put a hand on the miner's shoulder. His voice was gentle. "You'll see all this someday. You'll find out that what Andy LeGrande is telling you is true. And then you'll know that I'm on your side."

Each time Andy cornered a miner others were soon to gather around. His approach was almost evangelical, and there was a definite charismatic quality to him. Bonnie was impressed. Andy was not an especially handsome man, but he had a powerful physical presence. He was cocky, yet his boasting fitted his style and somehow added to his attractiveness. He was personable and capable of gentleness, humor and honesty. Andy was educated; he had been around the country, unhindered by family or a routine job, and he displayed a sense of independence she found very appealing. Andy represented a freedom Bonnie lacked in her own life, which she had not even dreamed of since her brief affair with Jim Porter had ignited a flash of hope so many years before.

Bonnie relished the warmth Andy LeGrande had so suddenly interjected into her life until she remembered T.C. and his desperate struggle to earn them a living in a city far away. Feeling guilty, she forced herself to shake thoughts of the bearlike union man from her head.

Duke and T.C. were not much for writing letters. When T.C. had been off fighting in Korea, his family had heard from him only every two months or so and then only in the briefest of notes. When the two men departed for Chicago, Bonnie insisted to T.C. that he make an effort to keep her mother and her informed. The envelope she picked up at the postal window of the company store on the day she treated Andy LeGrande told her that her husband had made quite an effort at fulfilling her request; the bulky envelope contained a letter obviously several pages long.

Bonnie left it unopened while she finished work and then rushed home to hand it to her mother, allowing her the courtesy of slitting it open. Liz used a paring knife to perform the task, then handed the still folded pages to Bonnie to read aloud. Bonnie propped herself against the wall near the kitchen stove and, as her mother finished preparing their dinner, read from T.C.'s unusually legible script:

Dear Bonnie, Ma and Little Mari,

Sorry for not writing sooner, but we just got here. It took us three days. We had to change trains twice. The depot here is unbelievable. They call it Union Station, and it has a waiting room as tall as a tipple. We were lost the minute we stepped off the coach. There were so many doors and hundreds of people moving the other way. It was about 5:30, and the place was full of businessmen returning home. We asked a couple of them for directions, but they didn't seem to have the time. They walked right by us. But then we found this woman, and she pointed us to a passageway. It was like a tunnel, and it led to a street called Monroe. There were hundreds more people walking real fast toward the station, and we had to push our way through. We showed the lady the piece of paper with Sam Singleton's address, and she told us to go a couple of blocks east to State Street and catch a northbound bus. But there were so many buses on State Street we didn't know what one to take to Wilson Avenue like the lady said. We asked this man, and he pointed to one bus. We got on, and right away this driver started yelling about whether I was paying one or two fares. Anyway, we sat down and rode this bus for what seemed like two hours. And then it was the end of the line. I asked the driver what had happened to Wilson

Avenue. He just walked away to have himself a smoke. But a lady explained that we had gone the wrong way and were on the South Side. We had to turn around and go back all the way again.

Bonnie, you wouldn't believe all the people pushing and running and how all the trucks and cars blow their horns. It's as noisy here as it is in a mine.

Anyhow, we finally found Wilson Avenue and got to Sam's building. It was already dark. We were starving. It is a big building in the shape of a U. I counted four stories. We found the door with the number 417. There were a bunch of buttons, but not one had his name. A man said Sam was on the third floor. We were hoping he'd be home, so we could get some sleep before taking on jobs the next morning. The first door we knocked on wasn't Sam's. Some man with a liquor bottle in his hand answered. He was mean. And it sounded from his voice like he was a mountain man. We couldn't understand that.

Sam's place was next door. A big fat woman answered. She said Sam wasn't there, but his wife was. So we walked in. What a mess that place was in! Garbage bags all over the place. Empty beer bottles all over the beat-up old dining table. There was dirt all over the room and grease and droppings from paint. Duke and I sat down on a smelly old couch. The place stank. Smelled like old beer and urine.

Sam's wife is named Bobbie, and she's only about twenty years old even though Sam must be thirty-five. You might remember her from Bannerton, Bonnie. Anyway, she was pregnant, really close to the end of her term. When she walked into the room, two kids were with her. She welcomed us, but there seemed to be something seriously wrong. Like there was no life to her voice. Like she was all tired and beat. She told us the other woman was a Mrs. Watkins. She had a bunch of children too, and all of them shared the apartment. Each family has one of the bedrooms.

After about an hour we heard a key in the door. It was Sam. He walked in with a paper bag full of beer bottles. I couldn't believe how Sam looked. He hadn't shaved in maybe three or four days. His hands were filthy but not from coal. All he wore was a T-shirt and baggy old pants. And he had a red scar all along one of his arms. Looked like it came from a knife. He had a big hello for us and then got some cracked coffee cups from the kitchen and poured us some beer.

Duke told him how we planned to work in those high-paying factory jobs he had written home about. But Sam looked kind of strange when Duke said this. He looked guiltylike. Duke and I didn't understand. Then he told us how he had meant to write another letter and just never got around to it. It turns out his cousin, the man who was supposed to be a foreman, wasn't at the factory anymore. Been arrested and sent off to prison for knifing some fellow. I felt like I'd walked into a brick wall. I mean it was Sam's cousin who was supposed to get us those jobs. So I asked Sam about getting work. Then he told us he was having some trouble himself. Could only pick up a job here and there. Duke asked him what we could do, and he told us about these agencies. Places you go to and line up for temporary jobs. He told us to go to the one down the street early in the morning.

That night Duke and I wondered if maybe it just wasn't Sam. I mean like he seemed to be drinking so much. Maybe he just couldn't give a damn about finding a job. There had to be jobs somewhere in Chicago. Duke slept on the sofa, and I tried to sleep on the floor. But I was restless. I decided to look around. Out by the stairs I found a door to the roof. I went out there. The tar paper was sticky despite the cold, but I didn't care. I walked right to the edge. There weren't any clouds, but you couldn't see the stars. Too much haze. Off to the west were these rooftops. All the same height as far as I could see. They had these wooden porches on all the buildings. Every one of them was painted the navy kind of gray. The big buildings are to the south, and this one has a beacon that sweeps around in a circle. Out east is Lake Michigan, but I couldn't see it, only smelled it. The wind was blowing heavy, and every once in a while it carried the smell of fish. To the north you can see planes. Lots of planes coming down in a straight line toward the airport. Standing up on that roof, I could hear the cars honking their horns and drunks shouting at each other and one of those trains that run on elevated tracks. It wasn't quiet at all. And you know what really hit me? No matter which way I looked, everything was as flat as one of your frying pans. There wasn't one damn hill or mountain in sight.

Anyway, I still couldn't sleep, so I wrote this letter. And I'll let you know later about our jobs. Hope all of you are okay.

Love,
T.C.

P.S. Sam says the place we live in is called Uptown. He said the newspapers call it the white ghetto. There are a lot of mountain folk around.

The downbeat tone of the letter caused Liz to stop her cooking and sit down. Bonnie felt very uneasy about what T.C. had written, wondering if it were possible that all the talk of those high-paying jobs was merely a hoax. But she decided against discussing this with her mother, whose expression told of her own growing doubt. The two women had to maintain the pretense of their hope.

"Don't worry, Ma. I bet they found themselves some good jobs that very next morning," Bonnie said cheerfully. "The

259

next letter we get will probably even have some money."
Her mother joined in the charade, breaking into a grin and
laughing at how their two mountain men had found themselves so hopelessly lost on the buses in the city.

Suddenly there was an urgent knock at the door. Opening
it, Bonnie recognized a man from the other of Porterville's
hollows.

"It's Mrs. Blackwood," the man breathlessly reported.
"She's sick bad, and we can't find Doc Spencer."

Bonnie immediately grabbed her coat. "Come on," she
said. "Let's go."

They moved at a near trot past the company homes in one
hollow, through the square and into the other section of town
where the Blackwoods lived. Bonnie was nervous. Because of
the nature of the woman's illness, there would be little she
could do. She didn't even have painkiller to administer. The
only hope was that Dr. Spencer be found.

The Blackwood house was in as dilapidated a condition as
any in town. It was sagging to the side, and much of its
wooden exterior appeared rotten. There were lights in the
windows of the nearby homes. Through them Bonnie saw
the faces of the Blackwell's neighbors curious as to what was
going on.

The ailing woman was in her bedroom. Bonnie asked her
husband, Axel, to remain outside while she examined her. It
took only a few seconds.

"I'm very sorry, Axel. Your wife is dead."

Tears welled in his eyes, but he displayed no other sign of
sorrow. He straightened his back, muttered a thank you to
Bonnie and walked out of the house into the night.

The couple had an eighteen-year-old daughter. "We
prayed, Mrs. Fenner. We prayed so hard," the girl said, sobbing and falling against Bonnie.

"I know you did, dear," Bonnie said, trying to console her.
"You go next door now, and I'll send for the preacher and the
undertaker. Try to get some rest."

Bonnie escorted the girl down the stoop. "The ointment, Mrs. Fenner," she said. "Ma really believed it would work."

Bonnie had noticed the jar next to Mrs. Blackwood's bed. It was half full of a malleable grayish substance. As best as Bonnie could tell, it was acorn paste.

The death of the Blackwood woman might have been unnecessary, and it filled Bonnie with a sense of despair and helplessness as she walked home. She felt lonely and scared. Her thoughts turned to the top of a building in faraway Chicago, and she envisioned her husband standing on a rooftop, looking to the sky for the stars and finding none, searching the horizon for the silhouette of a mountain and finding none, and she knew that he, too, was lonely and he, too, was probably scared. She missed T.C. very much.

CHAPTER 10 _____

In a time of dwindling hopes and resources, Thanksgiving of 1964 had a special importance in Coal County. It seemed as if even the most distressed mining families could find something to be grateful for. They could always think of some other family in worse shape than theirs. But when Christmas came, it was different. Families with laid-off miners found it impossible not to feel the pain of their economic paralysis.

Bonnie and Mari trekked to the hills and found a short but full fir to use as a Christmas tree. After dragging it home, they were at a loss for decorations, not wanting to spend money for popcorn to string, as was a family custom. Instead, they cut paper ornaments from newspapers and magazines. During one lengthy evening discussion, Bonnie and Liz decided to forgo the giving of presents and put their resources, such as they were, into the Christmas Day meal. Bonnie had to travel to Bannerton before she could find a chicken they could afford. Where her mother obtained the pumpkin for her pie Bonnie did not know.

On New Year's Eve, there were few festivities anywhere in Coal County. The only formal local celebration took place in the Porter mansion. There some forty well-heeled couples danced through the night, gulping down champagne punch, eating caviar and flirting with each other's spouses. Paper streamers hung by the hundreds from the ballroom walls, and at midnight Percy pulled a cord to release a net filled with balloons. When the cheering started, Anne turned to kiss her husband, but Jim wasn't there. In a panic she pushed through the crowd in the darkened room until she found him. Jim was standing at the punch bowl, keeping a close watch on his father, who was seated alone in a corner, devoting his attention to the glass of bourbon in his hand.

"Where were you, darling?" Anne asked Jim, wrapping her arms around his neck and planting a long, dramatic kiss on his lips. She held their embrace until Jim, seeing they were the last couple still locked together, edged away.

"You embarrassed me, dear," she whispered. "Standing there by myself when they counted down to midnight. Please, Jim. Don't do that again."

"I'm sorry. I just didn't notice the time," he said.

Taking his hand, she pulled him toward the dance floor. "Come on now," she ordered.

Jim danced with her, as instructed, but his thoughts were not on the music. Scanning the room, he inventoried the food, the decorations and the other forms of lavishness procured for the function and wondered how they could afford them. Each time he heard the pop of another champagne bottle being opened he remembered the price tag of the imported cases and cringed.

Within an hour, Augustus had drunk himself into a stupor and was slumped in a chair in a corner. Sarah was seated nearby. When Jim stopped to talk to her, she seemed unusually wistful. "I wonder what kind of new year we'll have, Jim. I have this very uneasy feeling about what's ahead of us."

"You're wrong, Ma. We're going to have the best year

we've ever had. Count on it," Jim reassured her.

Except for the Porter guests, most Coal County residents stayed home. The firecrackers they had grown accustomed to hearing at midnight were conspicuously absent. Also missing were the spirited gatherings on the streets with the drunken shouting, the snake dancing and the screaming of young women as their behinds were pinched in the darkness.

Bonnie and her mother shared a bottle of homemade dandelion wine which a miner's wife had given Dr. Spencer in lieu of a payment at the clinic. They allowed Mari to stay up with them until about 10:00 P.M. and then over her protests put her to bed. They were sitting quietly sipping the wine when they heard a soft knocking on the door. It was Andy LeGrande, clutching a bottle of cold duck wine.

"I just got back in town and couldn't bear the thought of you ladies being alone on a night like this," he declared, grinning. "Actually, I came across this bottle and didn't want to waste it. Can I come in?"

"Of course not," Bonnie said, waving him through the door.

She introduced him to her mother, and then they set aside the dandelion wine in favor of the cold duck, which Andy expertly opened and poured.

"I figured since your menfolk were still out of town, maybe a taste of this fine bubbly stuff would cheer you up a little," he said. "There don't seem to be too many parties around."

"About the only one I know of is up on the hill in the Porter mansion," Liz commented. "If they're true to form, the shouting and singing will last till sunrise."

"That kind of sums it up, doesn't it? The party on the hill, while down in the hollows people aren't sure what they're going to eat tomorrow," Bonnie said.

"That bothers me as much as it bothers you, but believe me, it's not limited to Porterville," Andy said. "Take New York, for example. I've been there many times, and each time I'm struck at how the rich can live so opulently on Park Avenue and less than a block away you have panhandlers in the streets hustling a handout for food."

"Sometimes I wonder if I'll ever get out of Coal County and see some place like New York," Bonnie said.

"Speaking of New York, let's get that TV going," said Liz. She went to the television and spun its dial until she found a station carrying Guy Lombardo's holiday music from New York City. Andy refilled their glasses, and soon the crowds far away in New York began counting down to midnight. The three of them joined in, their voices purposefully subdued with the hope that they wouldn't wake Mari. At midnight Bonnie kissed her mother, and Andy kissed them both. Bonnie thought that when he touched her lips, he lingered a little too long for the kiss to be purely social. And when a scratchy version of "Auld Lang Syne" came over the flickering black-and-white television, she noticed his eyes searching her body, which sent a shiver of guilt through her.

"It wouldn't be New Year's without a dance," he announced merrily. Then, walking to Liz and extending a hand, he asked, "May I?"

Liz's face flushed. She looked at Bonnie. "Go ahead, Ma. He's right, you know. You've got to dance in the New Year."

Liz rose, and Andy spun her around the room to the sounds of Guy Lombardo. At the song's end he seated Liz and moved to Bonnie, bending in a deep bow and sweeping his hand before her. She stood, dipped in a slight curtsy and accepted his hand. It was a perky, big-beat number, but they danced slowly, Andy pulling her closer. When the song ended and he released her, Bonnie was glowing—it was the first time a man had held her on a dance floor in years, T.C. not being given to dancing. With that, Andy collected his hat and coat and moved to the door.

"I'm afraid you won't be seeing me for a while," he said.

"What do you mean?" Bonnie asked.

"I've got to get back on the circuit, I'm afraid. There're some organizing drives under way in Pennsylvania that can't succeed without me."

"Will you be back?"

He smiled. "I'll be back. In the meantime, the best of the new year to you, ladies," he said, pecking both of them on the cheek. Then, tipping his feathered cap, he departed.

Liz, smiling for the first time since Duke and T.C. had left for Chicago, took Bonnie's hand. "He's right, you know. This will be the happiest, most prosperous year we have ever known."

"You're seldom wrong, Ma, and you know what, I have the same feeling, too."

As the dreariness of winter continued with its unchanging leaden, overcast skies and piercingly cold winds whistling off the mountains, Bonnie and her mother wrote letters to the two men of their family almost daily, each writing a section and then putting them together. They reported in detail on the Coal County happenings and although their stated intention was to be as upbeat and cheerful as possible, their dispatches became more and more discouraging.

If you have any doubts about your decision to leave Porterville [Bonnie wrote in her half of a letter posted in late January], you can forget them. Since Porter cut back on his production, the county is looking like a refugee camp. Either Bannerton or Porterville, it doesn't matter. You find men standing around all day with nothing to do. In the stores you see the women looking but not buying. They just don't have the money. Frank's Ford seems to be the only place that's still giving credit.

It snowed hard last week, and that doesn't help. Nobody's got decent clothes for the kids anymore. I saw one boy with a hole in one knee of his pants the size of a baseball. It was 23 degrees outside.

The Spanglers left last week. Went to Cleveland, I heard. Every other house in town is boarded up now. Some of those who are staying aren't taking it too well. You remember the Gillespie boy? The one who got married young and had three or four kids right off the bat? They found him on Monday. He hanged himself from the Porter tipple out at Cedar Ridge in the dead of night. Don't know what happened to his family.

The sheriff stopped in, looking for me to help treat some prisoner he had. He said he's never seen so much trouble. Someone blew up the Bannerton school bus last Friday. The sheriff said he thinks he knows who it was. Wouldn't say who except that some other kids had been making fun of him for the unmatching shoes he was wearing. Nobody got hurt, thank the Lord.

You'd think that with half the town gone there'd be nobody at church. But it's been crowded each Sunday. Guess when there's trouble, folks start turning to the Lord no matter if they never even observed an Easter before.

Liz, in her section of the letter, told how John Owens had gotten a court order to give him passage over the Cedar Ridge bridge:

People said it made the major furious, even though Mr. Owens said his people could use the bridge, too. Haven't seen too much of the major's son. Jim goes to work in that office and then returns straight home to the mansion. No one is sure what to think of it. We've seen a lot of that wife of his, however. Seems like she's running off to this affair and that in Livingston nearly every afternoon.

The two women ended, as they always did, with a plea for T.C. and Duke to write. They had heard nothing from them since receiving a small card at Christmas. But this time their letters crossed in the mails. Bonnie picked up the Chicagopostmarked envelope on her way home from the clinic. She noticed that T.C.'s penmanship was more shaky and hurried than before and decided to read the letter herself before taking it home to her mother. Standing off in a corner of the company store, she noticed her hands were trembling as she ripped open the envelope. She knew the tremor was not caused by the cold.

After apologizing for not sending a Christmas gift, T.C. told how he and Duke had reported to a real estate agent in a storefront office the day after their arrival in Chicago. For two months' rent, the agent found them available space in an apartment already occupied by two other families. Several wooden partitions subdivided the flat, but they had to share the kitchen and bathroom facilities. They said it wasn't too bad, however, and in any case, it was only temporary.

They had decided to forget Sam's suggestion about visiting the daywork agency and try for some high-paying factory jobs. T.C. scrutinized the want ads in the Sunday papers and then boarded a bus for an area known as Cicero. There one factory after another informed him that there was no work available or, if there was, that he and Duke would need union cards. That night, dejected, they asked Sam the location of the daywork agency.

The agency occupied one large room in a storefront and consisted of a couple of desks and a few rows of benches. T.C. and Duke walked into the place in early afternoon and found it empty except for an obese woman shuffling index cards. She told them to return the next day early, no later than 6:30 A.M. They got there by six. To their astonishment, they found the benches nearly filled with waiting men, most of them identifiable by their accents as mountain folk. T.C. and Duke registered, but by the time their numbers were called all the available jobs were gone. T.C., they said, could come back for another try the next morning, but Duke, because of his artificial leg, would not be needed. They had no work for cripples, the fat lady informed them.

"Can you imagine that?" T.C. asked. "Duke a cripple! My God, he could have lifted that whole building if he wanted to."

T.C. won himself a job the next day—washing dishes at a downtown restaurant. And on most days that followed, he arrived at the agency early enough to obtain some kind of employment—loading trucks, removing rubble, shoveling snow, washing pots and pans. Usually, if he didn't arrive home too late, he and Duke walked down to the corner bar to treat themselves to a beer apiece and listen to the jukebox with its country music. Gradually they befriended the bartender, a man named O'Hagan, and when he heard Duke was looking for work, he helped arrange for him to get a cleanup job at the bar. Duke started his duties at about 9:00 P.M. and ended sometime after the 4:00 A.M. closing. The job paid him $9 a day.

So now, finally, both men were working. Not high-paying jobs as they had hoped for but, nevertheless, jobs producing some money. And they had already accumulated enough to send along a money order for $15. "It's not much," T.C. wrote, "but Duke and I knew you could use it. Keep your chins up. It won't be long before we get ourselves better work. Then the three of you can come along."

Bonnie returned the letter to its envelope and decided, since she was in the store, to cash in the money order at the postal window. She hoped the sight of the $15 in cash would partially offset the gloom her mother would certainly feel in reading the letter.

Again the correspondence from T.C. and Duke dropped off to an occasional line, usually on a postcard every three weeks or so, saying little more than that they both were well. Frustrated, Liz and Bonnie decided to bribe them into writing more often and with more detail. They would do it with ramps.

Ramps are wild leeks, a cross between an onion and garlic.

269

Their smell is legendary. When the sprouts of their long, flat leaves begin to pierce the lingering patches of snow in early March, mountain folk enthusiastically harvest them as their rite of spring.

Bonnie, Liz and Mari were seated in a circle on the floor of their home, sorting the ramps they had picked that morning. "Now be sure to set the biggest ones to the side. Those are the ones to send to Duke and T.C.," Liz instructed.

They shook the soil from each of the ramps, removed its protective covering and sliced off the hairlike roots.

"I wonder what the post office will have to say about these," Bonnie said, chuckling.

"It'll be good for those city people," her mother responded. "Clear their noses and keep them from getting colds." They all laughed.

Bonnie told how Dr. Spencer had put a framed sign in his clinic that read:

Eat leeks in March and ramps in May
And all the year after physicians may play.

It was an adaptation of an ancient Welsh saying and drew knowing smiles from those of Spencer's patients who saw it. In earlier days, before refrigeration, the winter diet of mining families consisted mainly of salted meats, dried beans and whatever game the men were lucky enough to kill. Fresh fruit and vegetables were lacking, so when the humble ramp appeared in early spring, everyone rushed to the mountainsides to garner the first vegetable of the year.

In his training as a physician, Spencer told Bonnie, he had learned how important this vernal ceremony actually was. Any prolongation of the miners' restricted winter diet would have led to scurvy. Ramps, as was later discovered, are full of vitamin C. They are heralded for their preventive and curative powers over disease, and there are some ramp devotees who insist they also are hallucinogenic. The one certain property of ramps is that they smell. It was said in mountain country that one could locate a ramps feast by watching panicky skunks flee the area or by walking to a spot where hungry vultures circled above what they sensed was the smell of death.

The long, slim bulb of the ramp has its own distinctive odor, which is enhanced when boiled or mixed with saliva in an enthusiast's mouth and returned to the atmosphere. It produces a unique halitosis which endures for at least two days. The odor is so bad that supposedly there once existed a law giving teachers the right to dismiss for the day any student who appeared for class with the evidence of ramps on his or her breath.

In Coal County, people began talking by March 1 of the "messaramps" they intended to be theirs. When early searchers found their first green patches of the wild vegetable, word spread quickly. By the next day towns were emptied as whole families climbed to their favorite sites on ridges and in coves for the annual harvest.

For Bonnie, Liz and Mari, this was their first ramps season without T.C. and Duke. It didn't seem right without them as they set out for the hills. They found that the winter had cooperated—the ramps were plentiful. Using a homemade short-handled hoe resembling a miner's pick, Liz gently grabbed the deep green ramp leaves and dug them in clumps from the mat of rotting leaves and soil under the snow. As always, she made certain she left a few ramps behind in each patch so they could propagate the next year. In a few hours their gunnysack was full, and they hiked the four or five miles back home.

That night they nibbled on the smaller of the ramps raw as an appetizer and smacked their lips on the thick chicken-flavored ramps soup Liz prepared. Moonshine, beer and buttermilk all are traditional tonics for washing down ramps, but the favorite of the Shaws and Fenners was tea made from the roots of a sassafras tree. They drank theirs steaming hot.

Their dinner marked only the beginning of the ramps season. For them and others in Coal County the highlight came on a Sunday when the annual ramps festival was held in the gymnasium of Bannerton High School. Veteran road salesmen with sensitive nostrils knew to avoid Coal County on those occasions. The few strangers caught in town on the day of the festival were told simply to follow their noses to the high school for the best culinary treat they would ever experience.

Long rows of tables, topped with white tablecloths, lined the gym. A donation of $1 was requested at the door, the funds going to the local widow and orphans' fund. The food was served from 11:00 A.M. on, and up to 3,000 people would partake of the ramps during the day. The food, dished out at tables cafeteria style, included fried ham, chicken, sausage, green beans, home fried potatoes, corn pone and caramel-covered cakes so fresh they crumbled when touched. Of course, there were ramps as well—ramps offered raw, ramps fried in bacon fat, ramps steamed and served with a hunk of salt pork, ramps chopped and mixed into salads and ramps boiled into soups served in a variety of consistencies. Buttermilk and sassafras tea washed it all down.

With the ramps came a day of tall tales ("He lives so far up in the mountains you can see the current alternate in his light bulbs"). At night, there was gospel singing, knee-slapping bluegrass music, square dancing, ramp-eating contests and the selection of a festival queen, who was crowned as the Belle of Smell. In any given hour, at least three mountaineers would attempt to quote Shakespeare: "By this leek, I will most horribly revenge." The one certainty of the day was that ramps would be consumed by all, for only by eating a ramp could one counteract the smell emanating from others.

Bonnie, Liz and Mari waited until midafternoon to travel to Bannerton. By that time the gym was crowded with ramps enthusiasts bunched at tables elbow to elbow. As with vernal rites around the world and through the ages, there was a spirit of celebration in the air; the economic hardships, ill-nesses and deaths of the winter were temporarily forgotten.

"I posted them," Liz boasted as she, Bonnie and Mari joined the food line. "I wrapped them real tight and put them in the mail. Maybe the boys'll get them by Wednesday or Thursday."

"That's assuming Ernie Jason doesn't smell them and open the package before the train arrives," Bonnie teased.

"I'd wring his neck," her mother said, laughing.

After their plates were filled, Bonnie scanned the room and found the only string of unoccupied seats at a table near the serving area. It was not until they were seating themselves that she noticed the seats were across from John Owens and his wife. Like most mineowners, John never missed the Bannerton ramps festival. Neither did Augustus Porter. Of all the carnivals, dances and other social gatherings of the region, this was the most popular. Mountain people needed ramps to fire them up for spring and the steaming sassafras tea to thin their thickened winter blood.

"Good day for a messaramps, isn't it, Mr. Owens?" Liz greeted the mineowner. He looked up from his platter and smiled. Bonnie guessed it was one of the few times he had smiled in weeks for all the trouble the Owens Coal Company was having with the economy and Augustus Porter.

Mrs. Owens recognized Liz and Bonnie but was unable to remember their names. She smiled at them, especially at young Mari, who took a seat directly across from her. "My, what a pretty dress," she told the girl.

The attempts at conversation that followed were awkward, both parties having trouble bridging their difference in class. Also awkward was the silence between the talk. At last, the Owens couple completed their meal. "It was nice seeing you, ladies," John said. He returned his and his wife's plates to a busing table, then led her toward the gym door. Just then Augustus and Jim Porter, their wives on their arms, entered the gym. Bonnie spotted them immediately. Apparently so did everyone else in the room. The gay chitchat abruptly ceased. There was not one person in the gym unfamiliar with the growing tension between the two mineowning families. All waited to see what form their exchange would take.

The Porters seemed to notice the Owens couple as they stepped into the gym but not soon enough to retreat. The two Porter men led their wives to the long line waiting to be served their ramps. Owens could have circled the large room and escaped without directly confronting the Porters. He chose not to. Throwing back his shoulders, he guided his wife past the serving tables toward the door. When he reached the Porters, he stopped. Others present were not even trying to conceal their gawking now. A great hush came over the gym as everyone took a collective breath in anticipation of the inevitable showdown. But they were disappointed. Owens extended his right hand first to Augustus and then to Jim. He offered slight bows in greeting the ladies. "Enjoy your meal, folks. The ramps are especially tasty this year," he said.

"Thank you, John. Good to see you," Augustus replied.

The Owens couple went their way.

The large room remained quiet for a moment more while onlookers digested what had happened. Then conversations resumed at their earlier lively levels as people refocused their attention on the platters of ramps before them.

"The old fool," Anne hissed to Jim. "Making a scene like that simply to play on people's sympathy. Everyone knows how he's hurting." Jim tried to quiet her. "Don't hush me," she snapped, raising her voice. "I think it's silly we're here anyway, making a production out of eating this smelly weed. It's barbaric, I tell you. The air in the house won't clear up for a week after this."

Bonnie, overhearing Anne's remarks, laughed to herself, enjoying the satisfaction of seeing Jim abused by the yammering of his wife. So this is what you wanted? she asked him mentally. Well, this is what you got.

The Porters moved to seats that had just emptied in a far corner of the room. They appeared to eat in silence. As Bonnie watched them from the corner of her eye, she saw Jim scanning the room between bites. Anne resumed her chattering just as his eyes met Bonnie's. Bonnie turned her head away.

A few minutes later Bonnie picked up Mari's empty plate and headed for the serving line for a refill for her daughter. She was aware of people lining up behind her but did not turn to see their faces. Then she heard a voice: "It's been awhile, Bonnie." She turned to find Jim Porter. "You're looking well," he continued, smiling. "You're one of those lucky women who grow more beautiful with each year of their lives."

The comment flattered her, and she was unsuccessful in suppressing a smile. Despite their past history, she still could be moved by his presence, especially when he was close. He was close to her now, so close she could feel his breath on her neck. In that instant, she wanted to touch him, to hold him. But Jim Porter was not interested in mining girls. He wanted money, class and culture; he wanted Anne. Bonnie began to feel bitter at seeing her onetime lover whose own life was so unchanged while she and her family were struggling to survive.

"I heard about your husband and pa going to Chicago," Jim continued. "Are things okay? I mean, are you getting along?"

Her husband. It was the first time she had heard Jim use those words. It sounded so odd coming from someone who once had claimed to be seeking her hand. She tried to bite her lip, to remain silent, but the impulse to vent her feelings toward him proved too strong. "Since when are you Porters interested in the welfare of any mining family?" she asked snidely.

He stared at her for a moment, then nodded to indicate that he could understand her resentment. "A lot has happened to me in the past year or two," he said softly. "I'm beginning to see some places in my life where I've been very, very wrong—"

"Please stop it, Jim. You don't have to apologize or explain anything to me," Bonnie interrupted. She faced forward again, concentrating on the food table a step away.

Jim leaned toward her and whispered in her ear, "No matter what you say, it must be rough for you. I'd like to talk about it."

She turned to face him, not caring who was watching them. Jim's expression was sincere, and for a moment she felt a flash of compassion for him. But now was not the time to sort out her conflicting feelings.

"I think it best, Jim, that we drop this right here," she declared with finality, turning to the food table and holding out her daughter's plate.

"For the young one, I bet," the server said.

"That's right," Bonnie replied. "To her there's nothing better in the world than a plate of ramps."

The spirit of the ramps festival lasted for days, as did the ramps. For Bonnie, Liz and Mari, ramps formed a course at every meal, and the odor of a thick ramps soup still lingered as they cleared the table after dinner on the Thursday after the Bannerton celebration.

"The boys should have gotten the package today. Bet their faces really lit up with the smell of those ramps," Liz said.

"They probably got so homesick they headed for the first train," Bonnie said, laughing.

"Or maybe the postal inspectors arrested them for ruining the mails," Liz suggested.

They had just started washing the dishes when there was a soft knock on the door. Bonnie grimaced, suspecting it was probably someone seeking medical help. She dried her hands and went to the door. She had opened it only halfway when she froze at the sight of her father. "Ma, come quick! It's

Pa!" she shouted. Liz, shaking the wetness from her hands, rushed to the door, followed closely by Mari. The three women embraced Duke simultaneously, tears flowing down their faces. They had not seen him for more than six months. Then Bonnie realized that Duke had not responded to their embraces. He stood limply, his eyes cast downward, his face empty with defeat.

"Pa, is something wrong? Where's T.C.?" she asked anxiously, stepping away.

"Let's go inside," he said grimly.

Bonnie took her father's arm and escorted him to the sofa. He seemed weak and drowsy. His face was gaunt and pale, his posture slightly stooped. He was unshaved and appeared to have aged four or five years since they had last seen him.

Duke raised his head and, with moistened eyes, stared at his daughter. "I'm very sorry, honey. T.C.'s gone. We lost him."

"Pa?"

"He's dead, Bonnie. He was killed . . . by a knife."

Bonnie, moving slowly, sat beside her father. Liz rushed to her side and placed an arm around her shoulders. Mari stared at the three of them, panic in her eyes.

Duke asked for a beer, and Liz went to the refrigerator to get him one. He guzzled half the can, then set it to the side. "Come here, honey," he said to Mari, patting his lap. The young girl climbed onto him, and he gave her a kiss. Then, regripping the beer can, he took a deep breath and began relating the nightmare that had brought him home.

It was Monday. Duke reported for his job in the Wilson Tavern promptly at 9:00 P.M. T.C., having found no work that day, was with him. Monday was usually a crowded night, but the bar was only half full. It was soon clear why. Caputo, a neighborhood loan shark, was holding court in a corner. Duke and T.C. once had been forced to borrow from him to meet their rent, but they had managed to keep up their payments—that is, payments of interest; they had yet to reduce the principal. Others of Caputo's debtors who were not as fortunate, however, made it a point to avoid him.

Duke tied on his apron and went behind the bar to remove the boxes of empty beer bottles that had accumulated during the day. That done, he grabbed his broom to give the floor an early cleaning. T.C., meanwhile, took a seat at the bar. Duke had hardly begun his sweeping when a shout from Caputo brought silence to the room. "Come here, Turner!" he yelled to a tall, wiry man who had just entered the bar and then turned abruptly to leave when he saw the loan shark in the corner. "You walk out that door and you're a dead man. Do you hear?"

A bluegrass song blaring from the jukebox offered the only diversion to the tension in the bar. Turner walked toward the juice man sitting in his regular booth in his usual pin-striped dark suit. Turner said nothing.

"I'm telling you for the last time, pal, you get the three bills to me before I leave here tonight, or you'll have a pair of broken legs by sunrise," Caputo said in a voice intended to be heard throughout the tavern.

Turner had been drinking. He reached for Caputo's lapels and lifted him from his seat. "Why, you greasy son of a bitch," he said in a slurred mountain accent. "Back home we'd need no more than two minutes to deal with swine like you."

There was fire in Caputo's eyes. In a slow, hardly perceptible motion, he slipped a hand under his coat. Then, with lightning speed, he removed a pistol. The shot hit Turner in the thigh and sent him reeling across the floor. The others in the tavern fled to its far corners—all but T.C., who stayed on his barstool three paces from Caputo, watching every move in the unfolding drama. No one made any move to call the police.

Blood flowed from the wound in Turner's thigh, but he

ignored it. He climbed back to his feet, his eyes never leaving those of the man who had shot him. Caputo again raised his gun as Turner approached him. But this time Turner was faster. Reaching behind him, he drew a razor-sharp hunting knife from his belt. In a sweeping motion that began inches off the floor, he plunged the knife into the loan shark's chest at the moment the gun went off. Caputo crumpled into his booth, his blood gushing into a pool on the floor. Turner did not stop. He dived onto the fallen loan shark and thrust the knife repeatedly into his stomach, his side, his arms, all the while swearing and shouting incoherently. T.C. bolted toward Turner and wrapped his arms around the screaming man, attempting to pull him off his victim.

"Get away, goddammit!" Turner barked, his arm continuing its plunging. T.C. groped for Turner's wrist. Despite his shouts for assistance, only Duke stepped forward to help him. But before Duke could grab one of Turner's arms, Turner, his face contorted with his rage, spun around. "Get away, I told you!" he yelled, his arms flailing like the blades of a propeller. The knife caught T.C. in the abdomen. He fell onto Duke's pile of sweepings on the floor. Turner, stunned by what he had done, froze for a moment and then fled from the tavern, blood still trickling down his thigh.

"I think you'd better call the cops, O'Hagan," someone told the bartender matter-of-factly. O'Hagan picked up a dime from the cash register and walked to the wall telephone.

Duke nervously tended to T.C.'s wound while waiting for the ambulance. T.C. was breathing but his face had grown deathly pale. He felt cool to Duke's touch and appeared to be in shock.

"You'll make it, son. Just hang in there," Duke said, using a bar towel to sponge up the blood flowing from the wound. T.C., his eyes glazed and motionless, didn't respond.

It was more than twenty minutes before the ambulance arrived. The two attendants applied a compress bandage to the wound, lifted T.C. onto a stretcher and placed it in the rear of the ambulance. They stopped Duke at the vehicle's door.

"Can't I go with him? He's my son-in-law," Duke asked.

The attendant shook his head.

"Where are you taking him?"

"Cook County, buddy. What did ya think?"

Duke's hands were shaking. His face was pale. He turned to O'Hagan and asked. "What is this Cook County?"

"Cook County Hospital," the bartender replied. "It's on the West Side."

Duke rushed from the bar and hailed a taxi. When he announced his destination, the driver turned in his seat. "What's the matter, you sick or somethin'?" he asked. Duke shook his head. "Better not be—don't want nobody pukin' in my cab."

Although it was relatively early in the evening, the emergency room at Cook County Hospital was already jammed. Rather, it was still jammed, the staff trying to catch up from the overflow left by the day crew. There was one knifing victim with a superficial wound, several distressed infants, a man and a woman from an auto accident and a collection of alcoholics and drug addicts, most of whom had been waiting for attention for several hours.

"You got a welfare or insurance card?" a clerk asked Duke when his turn came at the reception desk.

"No. I'm here looking for my son-in-law."

"If he's been admitted, you're at the wrong place. Go out this door and turn—"

"I don't know if he was admitted here," Duke interrupted. "All I know is that the ambulance man said he was taking him to Cook County. He had a knife wound."

The clerk was irritated at having been stopped in midsentence. "What time?" he asked brusquely.

"Maybe a half hour ago."

"The name?"

"Fenner. T. C. Fenner."

The clerk rifled through a stack of reports. Suddenly his expression changed. His voice also was different now, subdued, even gentle. "You're his father, is that what you said?"

"Father-in-law."

"I'm very sorry, sir, but your son-in-law was pronounced dead. He was dead on arrival. DOA. He had a fatal stab wound in his abdomen," the clerk said, looking up at Duke compassionately.

"Thank you . . ." Duke muttered. He walked to one of the plastic chairs used by visitors and waiting patients and sat down.

Two burly cops hustled a screaming woman in handcuffs past him. An infant, its head cut, cried in its mother's arms. "A smoke. Anybody got a smoke?" one of the winos asked, waving two fingers in the air.

Duke buried his face in his hands. He stayed like that for an hour, not moving until a security guard twirling a nightstick jostled him and asked if he was all right.

When Duke looked up and said yes, the guard told him he would have to move on. After walking slowly back to the desk, Duke asked the clerk where T.C.'s body had been taken. "To the morgue—it's right next door," the clerk replied.

Duke went to the morgue and claimed the body. A few hours later, at a grimy funeral parlor in Uptown, he arranged to have it sent home. The casket would arrive by train in a day or two.

By the time Duke had finished all three women were sobbing. Bonnie dropped her head to his chest. "That night I went walking along Lake Michigan, doing some thinking," Duke continued. "I must have walked five miles. And in the end it came down to the fact that we'd been in that city for more than six months, away from you, and all we had to show for it were the few dollars we managed to send home.

We didn't even have the money for train fare home. And then T.C. is murdered." He squeezed his daughter. "I'm sorry, Bonnie. I let you down."

Bonnie's mind was racing. She tried to reconstruct her last glimpse of her husband and relive the last time she had touched him, the last time they had kissed, the last time they had made love. But all she could achieve were vague outlines of his face and fuzzy memories of their final moments together. She felt a sense of loss, but she was not distraught. She was confused by her absence of grief. Had she, like other miners' wives, long before assumed that her husband's death would predate her own? Or had her affection for him fallen short of love?

Now Duke, too, was weeping. "I'm sorry, honey, very sorry. It was a terrible, terrible mistake," he said. "We never should have gone up there. That's no place for mountain folks."

T.C. had been dead for more than a month. Except for that first moment when her father broke the news, Bonnie had not cried. The murder of her husband continued to seem anticlimactic, and her grief hollow, most of her sorrow directed toward Mari, who now had no father.

Mari was at Bonnie's side as she stood shoulder to shoulder with the others lining Porterville's Main Street. Normally Bonnie would have been too cynical to pay attention to such festivities, but the flashing knife in a Chicago tavern had taken not only her husband but also her dreams of a life free of Coal County. Now, once again, she was grasping for anything that offered hope.

The presidential helicopter landed on a grassy field on the edge of Bannerton. From there a limousine whisked the President to the Coal County Courthouse, where he met briefly with local elected officials. By the meeting's end two buses carrying the press had arrived. Under the direction of the

Secret Service, a caravan was formed with Sheriff Carter's patrol car, its red lights flashing, in the lead. The President returned to his limousine, and the motorcade moved out over the winding, narrow road to Porterville.

The President had insisted that there be no speeches and no ceremonies—this was a working trip, he said, a field inspection of what his aides called "one of the nation's worst pockets of poverty."

As the motorcade entered town, Bonnie saw some stern-looking and efficient Secret Service agents hop out of their security car and begin running alongside the presidential limousine. The press buses pulled to the edge of the town square and were emptied of their reporters, photographers and television crews. A harried presidential aide carrying a clipboard escorted them several yards past the rubble of company houses to a weather-beaten structure. Bonnie, holding Mari by the hand, followed the crowd to the home of Russell N. Mullins, a thirty-two-year-old unemployed Porter company miner. Russell, his wife and their three young children were gathered on a small stoop at the front door. The media people soon surrounded them. The President, a tall, big-boned Texan, walked through a path cleared in the throng of reporters. Grinning, he thrust a huge hand upward to Russell Mullins and said, "Hi, how ya doin'?"

Mullins mumbled a greeting, but the President did not hear him—an aide was repositioning the nation's chief executive at the bottom of the stairs so that his face was directed toward the cameras. Shutters clicked four and five at a time, and the television film cameras began to roll. Several reporters thrust microphones up under the President's chin.

"You out of work, son?" the President asked.

"Yes, sir," Mullins replied.

"How long has it been?"

"I worked about three weeks last year, sir."

"And what did you earn?"

Mullins thought for a few seconds. "About two hundred twenty-five dollars, I guess. That's after paying part of my debt at the company store."

The President nodded knowingly, an expression of sympathy on his face. "Well, that's not right, son," he said. "And we're doin' somethin' about it. We're gonna wipe out this poverty and get you men back to work." Mullins's eyes were directed at the visitor's feet. His two youngest children clung to his wife's dress. "But you gotta do your part, too," the President continued. "These young uns of yours are the future of this great nation, and you gotta keep 'em goin' to school. Now, you'll do that, won't ya?" Mullins nodded.

The President glanced at his press secretary, who signaled with a finger across his throat to cut it there. The press secretary then announced, "That's it, fellas. Thank you. The buses will leave in five minutes."

The President started to leave, but as an afterthought, he turned back to Mullins. He shook his hand. "Nice to meet ya," he said.

The agents ushered the President back to his limousine, and the long black car pulled away from the Mullins house as quickly as it had arrived. Most of the news people began filing back toward their buses, but one television crew remained. Bonnie watched them. The reporter, a thirtyish woman wearing heavy makeup, told her cameraman, "Let's use the family and this shack here as a backdrop."

Mullins, confused and embarrassed by the previous five minutes of attention, opened the sagging screen door to return inside his house, but the reporter stopped him. "Sir," she called out, "can you and your family stay there? It'll just take a minute or two." Mullins shut the door and returned to his position on the stoop. The cameraman spent a few seconds adjusting his focus and then signaled to the reporter, who began, "The miner's family told the President they were living amid rats in this broken-down shack on a diet of beans and stale bread. This is Linda Farnell, traveling with the President in Appalachia."

The cameraman removed the bulky camera from his shoulder, and the sound man packed his equipment. "Come on before they leave us stranded in this slum," the reporter ordered. The three of them ran toward the buses in the town square. Mullins watched them for a moment and then re-opened the screen door.

"We're gonna be on TV, Pa," his eleven-year-old daughter said.

"Yeah, I guess so," Mullins responded. "I wish we had one."

The President's limousine pulled up behind a security car waiting near the square, and the rest of the motorcade began to form behind it. Before the parade moved out, how-ever, the President noticed the people being held back by Secret Service agents at one end of Main Street. He hopped out of his car and walked to them to shake their hands and ask, "How ya doin'?" Several photographers, who had al-ready boarded their bus, jumped off again, swearing at the press secretary. He tried to stop them, but they insisted on photographing the President's impromptu handshaking. Among those in the crowd was Andy LeGrande. The Presi-dent reached for his hand. "How ya doin'?" he asked, already looking toward the next person down the line.

"Mr. President, what about subsidies?" Andy asked, half shouting.

"Excuse me, son?"

"What about subsidies? The government gives them to farmers and tobacco growers and the Merchant Marine. Why not coal?"

The President offered a sympathetic smile. "Don't worry, son. You and me together are gonna lick this poverty thing." He turned away and walked back to his limousine.

That night Andy joined Bonnie, Mari and the Shaws as they pressed around their black-and-white television to watch how the New York newscasters treated the President's historic visit. Because of the interference caused by the mountains, the TV set could pick up only one network station. The picture flickered badly, and it was sometimes difficult to discern the presidential caravan as the filmed report showed its arrival into Porterville.

As she watched, Bonnie thought of how the town once had been, clean, orderly and almost quaint compared to its condition now as depicted in the brief television glimpses. The company houses up and down the two hollows had been reduced by a fourth. Fires had leveled some to ashes; others had been knocked down for safety reasons. The company store had one of its windows boarded, and the company office had fallen into disrepair, a long crack running across the window in its door.

Bonnie and the others watched in silence as the television network displayed Russell Mullins and his family to America. Only when the cameras moved in closely on the President as he vowed in his low voice that something would be done to end the joblessness and poverty he had seen did one of them speak. It was Bonnie. "What bullshit," she said, shaking her head.

"Bonnie! Don't talk that way—especially in front of a child," Liz scolded her.

"I'm sorry, Ma. And I apologize to the rest of you. But all it is is talk. Politician's talk. They can make all the promises they want, but nothing is going to change. It's a fraud, I tell you, all these hotshot politicians coming down here now like it's the thing to do."

"There's some truth to what you're saying, Bonnie," Liz said. "But at least now we're getting some federal attention. It's the lack of jobs that's at the heart of the problem. And maybe Washington will help there."

"Don't count on that, Mrs. Shaw," Andy said. "You want something out of this life, you've got to take things in your own hands. That's a lesson I learned a long, long time ago."

The newscast showed the reporter closing her report with the Mullins family positioned in the background. "Look at that!" Bonnie shouted, pointing to the picture. "They're treating our people like they're visiting a zoo. Who do they think they are?"

Mari, her face serious and eyes wide, was glowering at the picture and nodding slowly in agreement. "We're different from those people, aren't we, Ma?" she commented.

CHAPTER 11 ⸻

It was 1973. Man had landed on the moon, and a Republican was in the White House. Little had changed in Coal County. Augustus Porter had yet to wrest the lucrative Green Valley contract from the Owens Coal Company, although he continued to fashion conspiracies to do so. Will Thomason remained in prison, as far as anyone knew. Andy LeGrande, despite his boasting, had failed to make much headway in organizing the men of the Porter Coal Company and had quietly placed a moratorium on his efforts pending the death or retirement of Augustus. Andy continued to visit Coal County regularly, however, ostensibly for union business, in reality to pursue Bonnie Fenner, who had yet to submit to his advances.

Billions of dollars had been spent on the War on Poverty, but whatever was spent elsewhere, preciously small amounts made their way to Bannerton and Porterville. A Washington-coordinated national media blitz had made the word "Appalachia" synonymous with poverty, and earnest young social workers had been dispatched to the region under what was called the VISTA program. They were sincere and energetic, but the few sent to Coal County stayed briefly and accomplished little of enduring value. With the exception of those young people, the presence of the federal government remained largely as it had always been—in the form of the Internal Revenue Service, the U.S. Bureau of Mines, the Post Office and the Selective Service. The last of these had been especially active supplying manpower for the war in Vietnam, and as usual, West Virginia sent more than its share of young men into combat. The war provided jobs and, through GI paychecks, funneled some money into the county, but the region paid a price in contributing a disproportionate number to the war's wounded and dead.

One who almost benefited directly from the federal antipoverty program was Augustus Porter. Working through his friends in county and state government, he submitted a proposal for the construction of two tennis courts. His application argued that the project would provide both jobs and a source of recreation for the community. The paperwork circulated in the federal bureaucracy for months and returned approved. If the county provided 10 percent of the cost, the federal government agreed to handle the remainder. Under an arrangement with the county, Augustus himself was to provide the 10 percent share from the treasury of the Club Havana, and the two courts were to be built on a lot next door to the club. But the deal crumbled when the club's working funds fell short of the needed amount.

Augustus and the other mineowners rejoiced when a Republican took over the White House, but Richard Nixon, like Kennedy and Johnson, did not prove a savior to the coal business. On the contrary, the industry remained in as precarious a condition as ever. The economic depression which first struck Porterville and then Bannerton had spread even to the once-wealthy enclave of Livingston. The village had the appearance of a ghost town. Windows were boarded. Paint was peeling, producing long streaks of gray across the sides of the once stately mansions. Large cracks crisscrossed the bottoms of dry swimming pools and weeds pushed their way through. Copper fixtures had turned green. Once carefully manicured gardens and lawns were now overgrown. Most of the millionaire mineowners who once lived there in splendor were gone, and the lawyers, accountants and others who served them had largely disappeared as well. Two of Livingston's three tiny post offices were closed, and it had been more than five years since anyone unlocked the door at the quaint stone train station—Livingston was no longer a scheduled stop for any train.

Augustus, through luck and perseverance, had managed to acquire enough spot order business to avoid a complete suspension of his mining, and two of his mines—the Red Fox and Cedar Ridge—remained in operation. He had closed the other three. The mounds of slag outside their portals stood as if crude monuments to the dead at a primitive burial ground. To a coalman, there is no sadder sight than that of a closed mine. Coal County was seeing them more and more—gates padlocked across portals, equipment removed and stored, sometimes a guard, bored and lonely in a solitary vigil and a silence that was as deceiving as the calm before a storm.

At the two functioning Porter mines activity was severely limited. When there were no orders to fill, Augustus kept token mining crews going through the motions at each site. This was intended more for form than for the stockpiling of coal—he was having enough difficulty obtaining business without bucking the image of a mining operation that was completely shut down.

As Augustus saw it, unless the coal economy changed, his only hope lay in modernization, the acquiring of new machinery that could overnight improve the company's productivity. Then he could lower his price to compete against the cheaper and cheaper bids being submitted from cash-rich companies backed by oil interests. But automation required money, and the Porter Coal Company had none. Augustus dispatched Jim on a money-raising mission, and he spent more than six months traveling through the state and even into Virginia in a search for financing. He met with bankers, brokers and other sources of credit. Without exception, they wanted nothing to do with the struggling Porter company. A few lacked even the courtesy to listen to Jim's proposals. "I'm sorry, Mr. Porter," was the typical response, "but if we bank-roll you on these machines and then you go bankrupt, we're out. There's just no market for the machinery once it's used." Like most coal companies its size, the Porter firm already was heavily financed. With the loss of longtime customers, Augustus found himself unable to meet the payments on out-standing loans. He was often put into a position of begging. For a while the bankers, led by Raymond Baxley, extended a moratorium month by month on his payment of principal. But now even the interest charges were a problem for Augustus to meet. He was pushed against the wall. He had closed three mines and reduced production at the other two. Seeing no other choice, he had decided to take the cutbacks one step farther.

The four Porters ate breakfast in near silence on the day Augustus chose to implement the action he thought necessary. Staring at Augustus, Jim observed that his father's appearance had begun to reflect his sixty-eight years of age. His hair had thinned considerably, and what remained was an unbroken gray. His musculature, once rock-hard from work in the mines, lost much of its tone, and his ramrod-straight mili-tary posture had surrendered to a slight stoop, hardly notice-able but nevertheless there.

"I'd like you to come with me, Jim, if you don't mind," Augustus said meekly as he rejected the coffee offered by Jenny.

"Sure, Pa. Whatever you want," Jim replied.

Sarah walked them to the door. She gripped her husband's arm. "You've analyzed it every which way, dear, and there's no other alternative. You're just doing what has to be done."

"I know. But it doesn't make it any easier," he said, departing with Jim for the company office.

Augustus had called a special meeting. His remaining mine managers and foremen were waiting for him. So were the firm's seven surviving office workers. They waited nervously, anticipating bad news of some sort, for Augustus Porter had never before called such a meeting, at least in any of their memories.

After entering the office, Augustus moved to one end of the large workroom and took a seat on the edge of a table. Jim moved to his side. The others were scattered, sitting either at their own desks or on the tops of others.

"I'm very sorry to have to meet like this and even sorrier to have to tell you of the cutbacks we're being forced to implement," Augustus began. He spoke morosely, his usual forcefulness absent from his voice. "As you know, we've been able to keep two of our mines in fairly healthy production. But we've lost just enough of the small business that we're starting to hurt and hurt bad. We rely on those short-term contracts to fill the gaps in our production schedule. I've held out as long as possible, but we've begun to stockpile too much now. We've got to pull in the reins."

"Are you gonna have to shut down completely?" one of the foremen asked.

"Not completely, I spent half the night working on the figures. We'll have to shut down the Red Fox, at least for a while. Maybe two, three weeks. And we'll probably have to cut back at Cedar Ridge even more than we have. As in the past, the men will be kept or laid off on the basis of seniority. This is a hard decision for me, and I want to be fair. If you have any suggestions on that, I'd appreciate hearing them."

There had been an audible gasp with his announcement of the closing. The Red Fox was the keystone mine of the company, one of the largest in the state, and it had never been closed since a blacksmith in the previous century had begun collecting coal chunks spilling through the cover of vines and brush at its outcropping. It was bitter news.

"What about us?" asked one of the clerical workers.

Augustus's expression was pained. It was evident that he would have rather been anywhere but in the office at this moment. "I was getting to that. I'm afraid there's no way to avoid temporary suspensions."

"You mean we're fired?" a woman interrupted, panic in her voice.

"Not fired. Just suspended until we get back on our feet a little. If there're no orders and a reduced payroll, then you'll have to agree there's little paperwork to perform here. You have two weeks' notice beginning today—all but Charlotte, that is. As my secretary she'll stay to handle what work there is. All I can say is I'm sorry." Augustus, his head bowed, walked quickly from the room. There were tears in most of the women's eyes. One of the foremen kicked a desk.

A short, rotund man known as Fat Smitty rushed out of the office and pursued Jim and Augustus as they walked toward their car. He was a former miner disabled from a lung problem whom Augustus had put to work as a clerk.

"Major Porter! Major Porter!" the round man shouted. Augustus and Jim turned around.

"Yes, Smitty, what is it?" the mineowner asked.

The clerk did not respond. He was staring at Augustus's eyes and the tears that had started to form. Jim noticed them, too, and he was astounded—he had never before seen his father cry.

"What is it, Smitty?" Augustus repeated, impatiently.

"Isn't there any work left for me to do?" the ex-miner asked in a wheezing voice. "You know, clean the bathhouse or somethin'?"

"I'm sorry, Smitty, but you heard me in there."

"But I've got five kids, and ever since my oldest lost his job, it's been rough. What will we do now?"

Augustus stared at the puffing man with compassion. "I

don't know what to tell you, Smitty. Maybe you can give a try for work at the Owens company. I hear he's doing a lot better than me."

Augustus and Jim walked away, the mineowner's shoulders bent and his gait slow. His face had the appearance of a man who had just lost a great deal. Augustus stopped when they reached the car. "That was bad, Jim. And I only told them half the story. The truth is I don't know how much longer we can hang on, even with more spot business."

"It'll work out, Pa. You'll find a way," Jim told him.

Augustus stared at him blankly. Then he said, "You might want to walk home, son. I think I'll be driving to Bannerton now." Augustus was heading for the club.

Augustus did not return to the mansion all day. Concerned about his father's state of mind, Jim waited up for him on the sofa in the parlor. By midnight Jim had dozed off, but about an hour later the sounds of his father noisily returning home awakened him.

Augustus, seeing the light next to his son's chair, staggered into the parlor. He fumbled to return his house key to his pocket. He appeared very, very drunk.

"Good," Augustus slurred, "I'm glad you're up. I wanna have a little talk with you and my lovely missus. And where's that wife of yours? Get her down here, too."

"But, Pa, it's almost one in the morning," Jim protested. "They're both sound asleep."

"I'll do it myself then. I don't give a damn what the hell time it is." Augustus stumbled to the staircase. "Sarah! Anne! Get down here! And I mean right now!" he bellowed out.

A minute later, still fastening the cords of their robes, both women appeared at the top of the stairs, confused and apprehensive. "Get on down here, ladies. We're all gonna have us a talk."

The two women looked at Jim, who, with an apologetic expression, shrugged. They came downstairs and into the parlor, where they took their seats without a word.

Augustus paced back and forth before them silently for more than a minute. "They're out to get me," he at last declared, stalking like a caged cat from one corner of the room to the other. "These sons of bitches are out to get me, and I don't know why or how."

Then, a slur coming in and out of his words, he related the source of his outrage. He was unable to make sense out of it, he said. The assault against him and the company had been going on for years, unfolding like a mountain thunderstorm—an initial bolt of lightning, followed by a period of deceiving silence and then a crescendo of ever-building thunder. First there had been the raid on his still. Who the hell had tipped the revenuers to that? He wouldn't learn the answer from Will Thomason, who was still in a federal prison. Then came the notification that Augustus's tax returns for a three-year period were to be audited. And the taxmen were continuing their assault a decade later. Why, only a night earlier two men wearing gray suits and flashing federal identification cards had visited the Club Havana. Standing outside the main door, they collared each man who left the building and peppered him with questions about membership fees, the charges for drinks and exactly who was the real owner of the establishment, which was listed on tax forms as a nonprofit charitable organization. The raid on the still Augustus said he could accept as probably the work of "one of the three dumb niggers" inadvertently disclosing the location of the underground hideaway. The audit of his taxes also was not out of the ordinary—the IRS had a tradition of maintaining a close watch on the men who owned coal mines. But now, with the club also under scrutiny and the company pushed to its knees, it was all too much of a coincidence to be anything other than a conspiracy—a coordinated and well-planned attack against him. The question was: Who was behind it?

"If you'll listen to a suggestion, I think you've got to examine the situation rationally and logically," Sarah suggested.

"Things don't just happen. You've got to find the pattern." She was trying to avoid antagonizing Augustus further while attempting to steer him away from his anger.

Augustus stopped his pacing. He glared at his wife. "Do you think I'm stupid? I've made a mental list of every enemy I've ever had and gone over it time after time in my mind. At first, I think maybe this bastard did it, but then I think of something that tells me that would be impossible. I go on to the next son of a bitch, and the same thing happens. I don't understand it."

Augustus flopped down in a chair and buried his face in his hands for a moment. Then he bolted upright, walked to the parlor door and began shouting for Jenny, who was asleep in the servants' quarters. The woman, wrapped in an ancient housecoat, appeared in a moment, rubbing the sleep from her eyes.

"Get me a drink, Jenny. Make it a double," Augustus ordered.

No one spoke while he waited for the housekeeper to return with the bourbon. She was followed into the room by her husband, Percy, who also appeared sleepy.

Augustus gulped down the drink and slapped the empty glass on a table. He rose from his seat and stood motionlessly, thinking, until, without warning, he shouted, "Goddammit anyway!" He began stomping in circles around the room, kicking furniture and flinging crystal ashtrays, statuettes and other valuable ornaments off the floor and walls. The parlor was a shambles of fractured furniture and broken glass before Jim was able to subdue his father, convincing him to be seated again. The peace did not last, however. Augustus ordered Jenny to refill his drink. When she returned with it, he told her and her husband to stand before him.

"Excuse me, sir?" the confused woman said.

"You heard me," he replied. "You and that useless husband of yours come over here."

The couple stood side by side before Augustus, who, after

glaring at them, rose and began pacing in front of them in the manner of a marine drill instructor.

"Do you two like working here?" Augustus asked.

"Pa," Jim interrupted, "there's no need for—"

"You stay out of this," Augustus snapped back in a snarl. Turning again to the servants, he repeated the question. Percy nodded in the affirmative. Jenny stared at the mineowner, not moving a muscle.

"I don't hear you answering, Jenny. Do you like working here?" Augustus asked again, his eyes only inches from those of the plump sixtyish woman who had been a Porter employee for more than three decades.

"Of course I do," she finally replied. "If I didn't, I wouldn't be here." Augustus ignored her answer, which had the tone of a challenge. He returned to his pacing.

"When a man hires a servant, he does so on the basis of trust. When you work and live in a household, you're going to be privy to a lot that goes on. Overheard conversations. Letters and documents left exposed. Visitors. Messages. Am I right?" Percy and Jenny nodded. "That being the case, I probably don't have to tell you that there are people after both me and my company. If it isn't some bastard oilman from Texas, then it's someone I don't even know. The one thing I'm sure of is that a lot of personal, private information about me has come into the hands of people outside this house. I'm not accusing either of you, but I just want you to know that if I find out either of you have some involvement in this—"

"Major Porter!" Jenny interrupted. "We've both been here for thirty-two years. And I think it's improper and insulting for you even to suggest we'd be involved in such a thing."

"Shut up, Jenny!" Augustus shouted. "That's exactly what I'm suggesting. There's too great a pattern for it to be someone not close to this household. And I want you warned that if it turns out to be either of you, you'll not only get the boot from this house and this town, but I'll have your goddamned necks broken."

"Enough!" Jenny barked. Her face was as red as her hair. Jim attempted to step between the now-raging woman and his father, but she extended an arm and stopped him. "You don't talk like that to someone who's spent her best years slaving for you," she lectured Augustus. "I'm sorry, but that's outrageous."

"Since when does a servant talk back like that to the man who employs her?" Augustus countered.

"I've had it," the woman responded. "There isn't any amount of money that can force me to work for a beast—and that's what you've become, mister, a mad, insane, drunken beast." Jenny stormed out of the parlor, dragging her husband with her.

"You're fired, Jenny. Do you hear me? Fired!" Augustus, waving a fist, shouted after her. "And get your fat ass out of this county. There isn't a house here that will hire either of you when I get through."

Augustus turned to Jim, who was stunned by what had transpired but had felt impotent to stop it. "You give an ignorant mick immigrant a job for thirty years, and that's the kind of gratitude you get in return. We'll see about her!"

Anne's expression told Jim that she had seen enough. "Excuse me," she said, rising from her chair. "If no one minds, I'll be returning to bed."

Augustus jumped in front of her and stood as if he were preparing to throw a punch. "Sit down!" he shouted. "You're a member of this family, and whether you like it or not, you're going to stay right here until I figure this thing out." Anne, her face contorted with fear, returned to her chair.

"Maybe you should sleep on this, dear," Sarah suggested. "Maybe then the answer will come to you."

"Like hell I will," Augustus said, also taking a seat. For several minutes he ignored the others and began talking to himself, running through his troubles from beginning to end, this time dwelling upon the sorry state of the Porter Coal Company. Finally, his head snapped upright as if serendipity had provided him his answer. "John Owens," he mumbled.

"Who?" asked Sarah.

"John Owens," Augustus repeated. "I discarded him because I didn't think he was smart enough to pull something like this off. Maybe I was wrong." He sat forward on the edge of his chair. "He sure has the motives to do it, being our competition and all, and if he had help—some kind of inside help—he'd try to ruin me, sure as I sit here."

"It couldn't be," Jim objected. "Owens might be your rival, but he's not that type of man."

Augustus acted as if he had not heard his son. "That son of a bitch," he said, his voice rising. "Who would have thought he had it in him? Well, we'll see. We'll see how far he gets with this."

"Pa." Jim tried again. But his father refused to listen.

"Get out of here," Augustus ordered. "All of you. I've got to think."

Sarah, Anne and Jim filed slowly from the parlor. "John Owens," they heard Augustus say again. "If it's dirt the bastard wants, it's dirt he'll get. No one can do this to Augustus Porter."

"What will he do?" Anne asked as Jim closed the tall oak doors to the parlor.

"I don't know. It's anyone's guess," he replied.

"He's crazy," Anne whispered. "That old man has finally lost his mind. The booze has gotten to him. He's nuts, I tell you."

Sarah glared at her daughter-in-law.

Anne Baxley Porter was above all else a member—a member of the Episcopal Church Guild, a member of the Town and Country Garden Club, a member of the Literary Circle and a member of the Coal County Ladies' Association. This last was the most prestigious of all the women's social groups in the region. It included the wives of most of the prominent men in the area, including every major mineowner. While Anne was active in all the groups, it was the Ladies' Association that she valued the most and about which she was the most worried.

Over the years the antics of her father-in-law had drawn attention to the family in a manner not at all welcomed by Anne. His connection with the Club Havana in particular had inspired frequent snickering. In church and at various club meetings, Anne had complained to Jim, she was certain she had heard derisive whispering behind her back. She agonized over this for years before finally deciding her only option was to meet such slander head-on. To do this, she boldy invited the Ladies' Association to meet in the Porter mansion and, with Sarah's help, maneuvered to win herself the role of featured speaker at the same time. All this was designed to set the stage for Anne's eventually becoming one of the club's officers. However, a young woman had to be very, very careful, especially since her father-in-law continued on his alcoholic bender for more than two weeks after the scene in the parlor, and there was no way to predict what further embarrassment he might cause.

Jim watched his wife nervously prepare for the meeting. For two weeks she reviewed the preparations for the affair with Sarah and Marie, the new French-born maid Anne had hired. She insisted that every last detail be in order. That she was both hostess and speaker was a rare double occurrence, a chance for her really to shine and a fact noted in a story appearing on the society page of the Bannerton *Tribune* three days before the club's affair. The folksy newspaper loved to emphasize such social notes.

Anne spent a week preparing her speech. Sitting in the sunny upstairs sewing room, she painstakingly weighed every word of the twenty-minute talk. The trash basket was full of crumpled paper representing the approaches she had rejected. Within an hour of the start of the meeting, she still was not certain she had gotten it quite right. But then she turned her attention to the white, black and gray suit she had selected to wear for the affair and sent the maid to the garden three times before the servant returned with a flower corsage Anne found acceptable.

"Now, Marie," she said to the maid, "I'm counting on you for the next three or four hours. Please give the parlor and dining room one last dusting, and make sure the coffee isn't brewed until the last possible moment."

Jim, standing in the background, saw that whatever apprehension Anne had, it was not noticeable when the guests began to arrive. She positioned herself in the foyer to welcome them. Her face glowed with pride, and her small talk was exceedingly sharp, self-serving while appearing to be self-deprecating.

"Oh, my, Anne, what a lovely bud vase," said one club member, pausing at a small table as Anne escorted her into the parlor.

"Thank you," Anne replied, smiling. "It's part of a crystal set Sarah had imported from Ireland. We weren't sure if we like it, so she's kept the rest of the set packed away. You can't trust anything that's Irish, you know."

"Well, it's lovely," the woman said, returning the small vase to the table.

Even by the most rigid standards of the most conservative, tradition-minded members of the club, Anne's meeting opened as a success. The imported Indian tea proved popular. The coffee, for those who preferred that, had just the right aroma. The cake was so tasty that some members forgot their vanity and accepted second servings. When Anne was introduced as the speaker, she was rewarded with a very generous round of applause from the members, all of whom could appreciate her charm and grace under what surely were difficult circumstances.

Her talk was entitled "What Kind of Club Member Are You?" The subject was well received by her attentive audience. "A good member makes it a point to attend meetings punctually," Anne declared as Jim listened from a corner. "She must ensure that she is well informed on association affairs and should cooperate to her fullest extent with the club's officers." Anne expanded on these and other points and then deftly changed gears, switching from her definition of the ideal club member to a list of the "ten greatest possessions" of her life. These included everlasting devotion to her husband and a striving for not only external beauty but inner beauty as well.

"It is a strong and enviable woman," she said, "who can give of herself relentlessly and with compassion to her husband, her family and—" A collective gasp from her listeners brought her words to a halt. Jim's first thought was that Anne had unknowingly said something embarrassing, but then he noticed the association members all staring at the parlor doorway behind Anne. Anne turned around to see what had caused the distraction and then appeared faint. Augustus was standing at the door. He was unshaved, and his bathrobe, the only piece of attire he wore, was partially open, revealing one of his hairy and pale calves. His mouth was slightly ajar, and there was a look of fierceness to his eyes as he scanned the room of jewel-bedecked ladies.

"It's a strong woman," Augustus declared, mimicking Anne in a syrupy, effeminate voice. "It's a s-t-r-o-n-g woman," he repeated, gesturing with his hand in an exaggerated feminine manner. Then he began howling in derisive laughter, throwing his head back and pointing to various women in the front rows.

Anne, very red in the face, rushed toward him. Jim went to help. They ushered Augustus out of sight. Anne took a deep breath, straightened her shoulders and reentered the parlor. After clearing her throat, she resumed her talk, having decided to ignore the interruption. Although she chose her words carefully and attempted to regain her enthusiasm, her concluding remarks fell flat on her audience. She ended her speech abruptly. The other club members lined up to offer their polite congratulations. Mercifully no members lingered after the official end of the meeting.

"It was embarrassing, Jim, very embarrassing," Anne complained to Jim in their bedroom that night. Her eyes were red from an afternoon of crying. "He had a crazy look in his eyes, and we can just thank the Lord that he didn't do anything more than he did. My God, I shiver when I think what could have happened. How much longer do we have to go on with this?"

Jim, listening to her from the bed, was half asleep. He answered her with a question. "What do you propose?"

"An asylum somewhere. In Philadelphia or some other city far away. Some place where he isn't known. Nobody'd have to know he was there," she said.

"It's something to think about, I guess," Jim said, hoping this would pacify his wife so he could go to sleep.

"And you know, that man frightens me. Sometimes I think he's going to come sneaking in here at night with a knife. Sometimes I get nightmares after thinking about him, and I don't believe it's fair for me to be scared of my father-in-law."

"Yes, dear," he said, pulling he blanket up so that it half covered his ears. Anne continued her talking in the dark, but Jim had dropped off to sleep and did not hear a word. Shortly after 2:00 A.M., however, he bolted upright after being startled from his sleep by a loud boom. At first, rubbing his eyes, he dismissed it as just another of the rumbles from the sealed mine that periodically shook the countryside. But then he heard it again and recognized it as the sound of a shotgun blast.

Jim hurriedly dressed and ran from the mansion. The blasts

continued, and he followed them toward the center of town. Lights were snapping on up and down the rows of company houses, and Jim could hear doors opening as residents emerged from their sleep to investigate. There was another boom, this time followed by the sound of breaking glass. Then Jim, and the others who had joined him, caught sight of a gun-wielding figure. A full moon, breaking through the scattered cloud cover, cast his shadow in a long tail behind him as he raised the weapon to his shoulder and released another blast. When the figure turned, the light caught his face, and Jim recognized him. It was his father.

Jim watched as Augustus patted the shotgun's smooth black barrel, caressed its hand-carved stock and smiled. He then returned the butt of the weapon to his shoulder, aimed it high into the air and squeezed off another shot.

Jim cringed with the blast and rushed forward. "Pa, it's me. Jim. That's enough now!" he shouted.

"Get back, you! I don't care who the hell you are. Get back before I blast you!" Augustus ordered, pointing the gun in the direction of his son. Jim stopped his advance.

Augustus smiled broadly. A sparkle came to his eyes. Turning slightly, he raised the weapon again, pointed it at his own company office and triggered another round. The blast shattered the office's front window, and the buckshot smashed into its weathered wood exterior with a thud. Augustus patted the barrel and prepared to shoot once more, this time taking aim at the water trough at the corner of the park. The shot pitted the heavy metal and sent specks of the trough's red paint flying.

By now a crowd was gathered, many still in their nightclothes. They stared in disbelief at the mineowner, who stumbled drunkenly between shots in the middle of the street. He appeared crazed, the moonlight accentuating the fierce contortions of his face as he fed additional shells into the shotgun's chamber.

"Pa!" Jim shouted. But his father ignored him, turning the weapon toward the company store and almost losing his footing from the gun's recoil as another shot shattered the store's window. An odor of gunpowder pervaded the cool night air.

"Dan Owens, get out here!" Augustus shouted. "Do you hear me, Owens? I said get out here."

"Dan Owens?" the onlookers muttered one after another. Dan Owens was John's long-dead father.

"But, Pa, Dan's dead. He's been dead for years now," Jim said, taking a step forward.

"Dead like hell!" Augustus retorted. Scanning the tops of the nearby buildings, he again shouted, "Get your ass out here, Dan, you goddamned coward. You cheating, scheming son of a bitch. . . ."

Someone tapped Jim on the shoulder. It was Sheriff Thad Carter, who had been summoned from sleep at his home in Bannerton. "What's going on here?" he asked.

"I don't know," Jim replied.

"Your father's been doing plenty of drinking by the looks of it," commented the sheriff. "What the hell set him off like this?"

"He's upset about many things, the company and all," Jim answered, without taking his eyes off his father.

Augustus stared briefly at his son and Carter, then returned his attention to the rooftops. "This is Augustus Porter, Dan, do you hear me?" he shouted. "Answer me, goddammit!"

The sheriff interrupted Augustus's attempted conversation with the dead Owens. "Now you just put down that gun, and we'll talk about this awhile," Carter said.

"Get the hell back, you bastard. Owens has probably got you bought and paid for, doesn't he?" the mineowner responded, sweeping the shotgun in an arc before him. The onlookers fell to the ground, many of them diving for the cover of trees in a panic. Augustus ignored them and carefully took aim with the weapon again. The target this time was the sheriff's patrol car, which was parked nearby.

"No, Major! Don't—" Carter shouted. But it was too late. The blast shattered a side window and peppered a hole in the driver's door.

Carter reached for the handle of his sidearm but then reconsidered and left it holstered. This was no ordinary drunk. This was Augustus Porter. "How many shells do you think he still has?" he asked Jim.

"I have no idea."

"Well, as long as he stays where he is, nobody should get hurt. Let's wait it out," the sheriff said. Turning to the crowd behind him, he ordered, "Now get the hell out of here. Everybody home now. This is not a carnival, and I don't want anyone getting shot." The onlookers responded slowly. Carter began herding them with outstretched arms. Dispersing, they retreated to the nearest houses and watched the remaining action from positions around corners and behind trees.

Augustus released four more blasts of the shotgun, all the time screaming for the dead Dan Owens. Finally, Jim decided he had had enough. "I'm going to end this," he declared, stepping toward his father. Carter reached out to stop him, but Jim brushed past him, moving boldly toward Augustus. The mineowner leveled the shotgun at his advancing son. The whispering in the background ceased, and for a few moments the only sounds came from the crunch of Jim's shoes against the gravel of the street.

"Get back, dammit!" Augustus ordered. But Jim continued to close the gap between them. When he reached within two yards, he stopped. Augustus still had the barrel of his weapon directed toward Jim's chest. The two men stared at one another, Jim's eyes intent, his father's confused.

"It's all over, Pa," Jim said softly, his hand reaching for the barrel. Augustus drew the weapon back but continued to point it toward his son. "Give it to me," Jim said, this time sternly.

"Get back," Augustus responded. "Don't you turn on me, too."

"I'm not turning on you, Pa. I'm doing what's best. Now come back to your senses and give me that gun."

Augustus shook his head violently. He jumped back a step, the shotgun shaking in his hands. "I warn you!" he shouted. "Don't push me."

"Pa?" Jim said, edging forward.

Augustus raised the sights to his eye. The crowd gasped. Still, Jim did not retreat. Slowly but without hesitation he advanced on his father, Augustus's hands shaking more noticeably with each of his son's steps. Finally, Jim extended his arm and grasped the hot shotgun barrel. His father, dropping his head, released the weapon and began quietly weeping. Jim unloaded the gun's chamber, throwing the unfired shells to the gravel.

Carter moved to their side. "It's time to go home, Major," he said in a soothing voice. But as the officer reached to take him by the arm, Augustus exploded into a violent charge, his arms swinging in roundhouse punches and his feet flailing toward Carter's knees and groin. He was still drunk, however, and his blows missed their marks. Jim and the sheriff had little trouble in taking him down. "I'm sorry to have to do this to ya, Major, but it's for your own good," Carter said as he snapped his handcuffs on the mineowner's pinned wrists. "Let's get 'im home."

As they escorted Augustus toward the damaged patrol car, Jim heard some of the comments from the crowd. "Been here forty-seven years and never seen anything like that," said one elderly woman.

"He's gone crazy, that's for sure," another lady commented.

The sheriff drove Jim and his father to the mansion. When Dr. Spencer arrived a few minutes later, he found Augustus's arms pulled over his head, pushed through the spokes of the brass headboard of his bed and handcuffed. He was still struggling, screaming obscenities and attempting futilely to kick his captors in the head. A strong dose of a sedative calmed him.

"How much did he have to drink?" the doctor asked.

"Can't say for sure," Jim replied. "He was off drinking at his club."

"Has he been like this before?"

"He's yelled and screamed some, but nothing like this," Jim said. Looking at Spencer with worried eyes, he asked, "What is it, Doc? What made him act like this?"

"We'll have a better idea in the days ahead," the physician said. "Maybe he's just overworked and tired and drank too much. It can happen."

The doctor left instructions to prepare Augustus a large breakfast and hot bath in the morning and to fill him full of tea. "I'll send over some mild sedatives," he said, adding, "I think he's calmed down enough that you can release him."

After Spencer left, Carter freed Augustus from the handcuffs. Sarah, who had stood nervously in the background, now approached the bed. Bending over her husband, she began running her fingers across his still-perspiring forehead. The expression on her face told of her intense worry. Anne moved to her side and took her arm.

"It might be best if you let him sleep alone tonight," Anne said softly, suggesting Sarah use a guest room. Sarah nodded.

As they left the master bedroom, Jim flicked off the lights. Then, as a precaution, he also locked the door.

Jim was so tired he did not bother with his pajamas. He plopped down in his clothes on their bed, yawned and went to sleep. It seemed as if only an hour or so had passed when Anne was shaking him awake.

"I smell something," she said.

"Huh?" He was rubbing his eyes. "What's wrong?"

"I smell something. I think it's smoke," she said.

Jim took two deep breaths. "Are you sure? I don't smell a thing."

"I'm telling you I smell something very strange in the air," Anne said, irritation thick in her voice.

Jim took another breath. His wife was right. There was smoke in the air. He jumped from bed and ran into the hall. The smoke was seeping from the crack of space under the door to the master bedroom. Jim ran back for the key and then opened the door, coughing from the billowing smoke as he entered the room. He found its source almost immediately—the paper in a wastebasket was burning. He stomped out the flames and went to open the window to air the room. To his surprise, he found the window already open. Then, when he looked at the bed, he found that his father was gone.

"Where is he?" asked Anne, entering the room.

"Your guess is as good as mine. I thought he was so sedated he couldn't move. I'll go outside and take a look."

"Oh, no, you don't," Anne snapped. "You're not leaving me alone with that lunatic father of yours running around loose."

"Look, Anne, isn't there enough of a problem as it is? You can just go back to bed and lock the door. Nothing will happen to you. In the meantime, I want Marie to give me a hand. She can check the gun cabinet while I take a look outside."

Jim saw no sign of his father anywhere on the mansion's grounds. Returning inside, he asked Marie what she had found in the gun cabinet.

"I counted six rifles and shotguns, sir," the servant said.

"Good. Then they're all there," Jim said, sitting on the parlor sofa. "We've got to relax a minute and think this out. He wouldn't have gone to the club, I don't think, because it's surely closed by now."

"Mr. Porter," the maid said, standing next to the mantel. "I think you'd better take a look here." She pointed to a spot above the fireplace. The pickax, which had been passed down from Jim's grandfather, was gone.

"Marie, I'd like you to help me search every square foot of this property."

"Yes, sir," she said.

For the next half hour Marie and Jim searched the mansion's grounds a second time. With a flashlight, Jim even looked under the porch, but failed to find his father. They looked in the three-car garage and the woodshed but found no sign of Augustus. "Where the hell could he be?" Jim asked in despair. "He was so sedated I just don't see how he could go far."

Finally, Jim told the servant to return inside. He followed her and went to the telephone. He had to wait for several rings before someone answered his call. "It's Jim Porter, Sheriff. I apologize for calling at this hour. . . . Yes, I know it's six A.M. . . . But we've got another problem here. . . . No, he's not out shooting up Main Street again. . . . He's disappeared."

Jim hung up the phone and looked at Anne, who had come downstairs. "Carter said he'll be right over. I guess there's nothing more we can do until he arrives."

Nearly an hour passed before the sheriff rang the doorbell. His eyes looked tired, and he needed a shave. He declined Jim's invitation to sit down in the parlor.

"I'm really very sorry to have to call you here, but we've searched everywhere in the house and on the grounds. He was so doped up I'm afraid he just slipped out the window and passed out somewhere. I can't see any way he could have gone far."

"When's the last anyone saw of him?" Carter asked.

"Right when you left. I locked the bedroom door."

"Any indication he's armed this time?"

"No, sheriff. Our guns are locked up. They're all accounted for. An axhead is missing, though."

"An axhead?"

"A small pickax of my grandfather's. It was hanging over the fireplace."

"Did you call that damn club?" Carter asked.

"No. I just assumed it was closed."

"Well, let's check. After all, your father is the principal owner. Where's the phone?"

Carter telephoned the club and spoke with Mae Sexton, who said Augustus Porter had not been there since the previous night.

"Okay," Carter said, rubbing his eyes. "Now we know where we stand. At least he doesn't have a shotgun. That's all I needed was an encore to that performance of his on Main Street. I'm gonna need some help. Have some of your people check each of your mines as well as your office and any other company property he might have headed for. Oh, and you might give a call to that young minister at the church here. If your father was distressed, who knows—he might have gotten religion all of a sudden, as hard as that is to imagine."

"I'll get some men on it. And thanks, Sheriff," Jim said.

Carter started to leave but remembered one more thing. "I think I'd better warn you," he said, looking at both Jim and Anne. "With all the people that are goin' to be involved here, there'll be no way to keep this out of the paper. That is, unless you want to appeal personally to the publisher."

"I didn't think of that," Jim said. "Unfortunately the publisher is no friend of the Porters."

When Carter had departed, Anne looked at Jim with panic on her face. "You mean to tell me this whole thing's going to be splashed all over the front page of the *Tribune?*" she asked incredulously. "My God, Jim, I'll never be able to face anyone again." Her expression turned to anger. "This is it. I've had it with that madman. If we ever do find him, Jim, out he goes. You'll have to make a choice—him or me."

Jim did not have the time to argue. He brushed past her to get to the phone. He called Crawford first. "There's a bit of an emergency," he said. "I'm going to need a few men."

The Porter employees searched every corner of company property, and the sheriff's men checked each of the logical locations in Porterville, Bannerton and Livingston where Augustus might have gone. But there was no sign of the missing mineowner. When Carter stopped by the mansion that night, Jim told him he had begun to worry. "It's cold out there at night," he said. "As far as we can determine, he didn't take a sweater or jacket." The sheriff, however, was thinking of something else.

"The club, dammit. The more I think of it, the more it bothers me," Carter said. "Let me use your phone." He called one of his deputies and instructed him to get right over to the Club Havana. "Don't take Mae's word for nothin'," he said. "Go in there yourself, and eyeball every inch of the place."

An hour later the deputy called back with a negative report. Wherever Augustus was, he had not gone to the club.

The sheriff's expression was grave. "I've got to be honest with you," he told Jim. "I talked to the doctor, and he confirmed what you told me—your father was so doped up that it is unlikely he had the energy to walk ten yards. What that means, I'm afraid, is that we can't rule out some kind of foul play." He looked directly at Jim's eyes. "You would tell me, wouldn't you, if you received some kind of note or telephone call? I mean, if somebody claims they've taken your dad for whatever reason."

"Of course," Jim replied. "But what I don't understand is if somebody kidnapped him, why did he go through all the trouble of sneaking downstairs to take the pickax? And why would he have set a fire? The fire would only steal precious time."

"I know," Carter said wearily. "I can't make one goddamn bit of sense out of the whole thing. Well, there's nothin' more we can do tonight. I think we'd better go back to square one in the mornin' and start right here at your house. I'll get the dogs. And, Jim, we'll need more men."

With most work suspended at the Porter mines, Crawford had no trouble assembling a search party of twenty-eight miners. They were to be paid for their efforts by the company. Early in the morning Carter appeared at the mansion with a man named Hargrave who owned three hound dogs. The dogs were supplied with Augustus's scent from one of his shirts and were led to the area underneath his bedroom window. Despite the time that had elapsed, the dogs had no trouble picking up a trail. But fifteen yards down the Porter driveway, they lost it, and even though they were led in widening circles around the spot, they were unable to pick it up again.

The sheriff summoned Jim away from the other men. "I think we're going to have to assume he's away from the house and start a systematic search through the town and the hills," he said. "Who knows? Maybe the dogs will pick up on him again."

"Whatever you suggest," Jim said dejectedly.

The sheriff organized the men into three groups. He kept one in town and sent the others into the countryside. Later he tacked a map to a wall on the mansion's front porch and marked the progress of the search as it eliminated first one section and then the next. At dusk the men were issued flashlights. When complete darkness came, Carter suspended the search. "We'll try again tomorrow," he told Jim.

The perimeter of the search area was expanded the next day, but again there was no trace of the mineowner. On the third day all three teams of searchers were sent far into the foothills. When that, too, failed, Carter asked again to speak privately with Jim.

Jim knew from the sheriff's expression what to expect. "It makes no sense going on, I'm sorry to say," the sheriff said. "We've covered half the county. If you ask me, I don't think your father's anywhere in these parts. He probably hitched a ride and left town. From my experience in these things, I'd say he'll turn up. It's just a matter of time. Why, you may even get a postcard from him tomorrow. He probably decided he just needed some time to be alone."

The three-day search had sapped Jim's emotions. He felt

numb. "But what if he wandered out to those hills or crawled into some abandoned mine, he'd be dead from exposure by now, wouldn't he, Sheriff?"

"Well . . ." Carter started. Jim did not wait for an answer. Without a word, he turned and walked up the stairs into the house. He was met by Anne.

"Look at this!" she shouted, thrusting the afternoon newspaper before his eyes. "I'm so embarrassed!"

The headline ran across the top of the page: "Missing Mineowner Feared Dangerous."

Andy LeGrande gave the door a token knock and then walked in. Bonnie was helping her mother clear the dinner table. "They called off the search. I just heard," the union man announced. Bonnie wiped her hands with a towel and motioned to Andy to sit on the sofa. In a moment she joined him there.

"I wonder what could have happened to that crazy old man," she said. "Do you think he was kidnapped or something?"

"Oh, I don't know if it's anything all that exciting. You know, in New York or Philadelphia something like this is very common."

"It is?"

"Yea. A man will get tired of his wife and kids. Or maybe his job. He tells his old lady he's going out for cigarettes or something, and then they never see him again. He flees to some place where he has no responsibilities and starts all over again. Maybe Las Vegas or Reno or some place like that."

"Do you think we'll ever see him again?" she asked.

"I doubt it. The odds are overwhelming against it. He's either dead, which I doubt, or long gone on his own volition. As far as people around here are concerned, they might just as well consider him dead," Andy said.

Bonnie's eyes grew distant. "You know, I guess I should be laughing and skipping and dancing for joy. Life has finally caught up with the Porters, and people like me are getting our sweet revenge. But, Andy, I can't do it—I just don't feel that way."

"I can understand that. It's like a kid who waits all year to get a bike at Christmas, and then, when it finally comes, he isn't interested anymore."

Bonnie nodded. Andy had a knack for explaining her often contradictory feelings to her. During his visits to Porterville, he stopped by her house or the clinic frequently, and she had begun to use him as an emotional sounding board, seeking from him the advice and support she couldn't find elsewhere now that she no longer had a husband.

Andy was enamored of Bonnie, attracted to her beauty, her strength and her vitality. She, in turn, was attracted to his intellectualism, self-confidence, idealism and ruggedness and, having been freed by T.C.'s death, no longer felt guilty about her fondness for him. Several times Andy had attempted to entice her to bed, but he didn't press the matter when she said no—that she couldn't handle quite yet.

"What do you think it will mean with Augustus Porter gone?" she asked. "What will happen to the company?"

Andy's face lit up. "Don't you see it? This is exactly the moment I've been waiting for. Don't you remember my telling you that what we union men like to see is the third generation of a family taking over a company? They don't have the ambition of their grandfathers, and they don't have the greed of their fathers. They're too used to getting their own way, handed to them on a platter. Not a worry in the world. And their biggest goal in life is to avoid trouble. It interferes with their backgammon games." His face, slightly tilted, moved closer to Bonnie. "Now comes my time. Now Andy Le-Grande lifts his gun and puts James T. Porter the Second in his sights. All I have to wait for is the company to get back on its feet a little. And it will. With a new man at the helm, they always do."

Bonnie smiled. "There was a time, my union man, when I

would have kissed the ground to hear those words. But right now I don't care. I just don't care anymore. So what if you organize the Porter company? Will that bring back my father's leg? Will it resurrect T.C.? Will it give my daughter a father? So much has happened, so much time has passed, that I just can't see how anything can change our lives very much. The day I die I'm still going to be right here in Coal County and still struggling for the money to buy meat once or twice a week."

"But what about Mari, Bonnie? And all the others of her generation. We're fighting for them. We've got to learn from the past and make sure what happened to you doesn't happen to your daughter and the children she'll have."

Her daughter. Bonnie had almost given up on her daughter. All her plans for Mari to get an education and escape from Coal County and the life it stood for had been abandoned, replaced by the mere hope that somehow the eighteen-year-old girl would learn to cope with just the basic requirements of life. The trouble with Mari had first surfaced in the weeks following her father's murder. Mari was nine then and in the fourth grade, and Andy happened to be there on a night she came home for dinner with her face and dress bloodied and an eye swollen shut.

"What in the Lord's name happened?" Bonnie had asked her.

"Nothin', Ma," the girl responded. But when her mother pressed her, she related how she had been confronted by a lanky schoolmate named Alice Grabowski.

Mari attended the Bannerton Elementary School, and the teachers there had informed Bonnie that her daughter was an exceptionally bright child, far ahead, in her comprehension, of anyone else in her class. This ability elicited a special attention in the classroom from her teacher which did not go unnoticed by other pupils. As a result, Mari was a frequent target of abuse from her classmates.

Mari told her mother that the Grabowski girl had called

her a brownnose for raising her hand in class with answers to the teacher's questions, but she had ignored the taunts and attempted to walk away. Alice, joined by two other girls, then ran up behind her, grabbed her books and tossed them to the road.

"Hey, dope, we're talkin' to ya," Alice declared. Mari stared at her aggressor, who had the reputation of a tomboy, then retrieved her books and tried to walk away.

"You know your family's trash," Alice shouted after her. Mari continued walking. "My mother says you're trash."

With that, Mari turned around, cocked her right arm and slammed a fist into the other girl's face. The punch popped open a small cut in Alice's lip. It began to bleed. The swing of her arm had thrown Mari off-balance, and before she could recover, the other two girls grabbed her from behind and threw her to the ground.

"How come you don't have a father, trash?" Alice taunted. She wiped the blood from her chin and then kicked Mari in the face while her partners held her pinned. One blow caught Mari's eye. It began to puff shut. Another hit her in the nose, causing it to bleed. For good measure, Alice hammered a fist into Mari's stomach before the others let her go. Mari struggled to catch her breath. Her three opponents were chortling as they sauntered away.

"Oh, I'm so sorry, honey," Bonnie said, examining her daughter's blackened eye and injured mouth. "But you gave them a bit of a lick, too, didn't you? Now go into the bathroom and wash up."

The family ate their supper in near silence that night with only Bonnie or her mother at times interjecting a tidbit of gossip or small talk. Liz served her granddaughter an extra-large portion of the stew she had made, the gravy for which was so thick and rich it could have been eaten with the flat edge of a knife. Mari said nothing as she ate it all. Later, however, after Bonnie had poured boiling-hot cups of coffee for both Andy and Duke, the girl asked a question. It was a question she had posed several times in the previous few weeks, apparently never quite able to accept without doubt its answer.

"Ma, Pa really died, didn't he?" she asked. "I mean, he just didn't run away or something?"

"Oh, honey. We've been through this before. Your father was killed, stabbed to death by a very bad man. His body was in that casket."

"Tell me again what happened, Ma."

"Well, your father was trying to stop a vicious fight. He was a very fearless man. And one of the men went crazy and stabbed him. Your grandpa was there."

Duke reached over to Mari and took her hand. "Your pa was a very good man. The army gave him a medal for his bravery during the war, and he was a very strong worker in the mine. You can be very proud that you're his daughter," he said gently.

"But I only wish he was still alive. Some of the kids at school say I never really had a father or that he ran away—because of me. Something I did."

"That's nonsense, Mari," Bonnie said, brushing her daughter's straight light brown hair with her fingers. "I know it's hard, but your pa loved you very much. Now you run along now." The girl scampered outside for one last hour of play before bed.

"It's not easy for her," Duke remarked, spilling some of his still-steaming coffee into his saucer to cool it. "She sure could use a father now."

Bonnie rose to clear the table. She moved to her father and kissed him on the forehead. "Somehow, with God's help, these things always seem to work out," she said.

But the loss of her father remained devastating to Mari, and she was never again the same child. She withdrew into herself, abandoning virtually all her earlier interests. Instead of playing baseball with the boys, she was apt to be found sitting

318

zombielike in front of the television or staring blank-eyed out a window. In school, her grades dropped off. Teachers summoned Bonnie to warn that there was a chance Mari might not even graduate. The chances of Mari's going on to college grew increasingly dim, shattering one of the last dreams harbored by her mother.

Then, one day when she was sixteen, Mari changed. Her spirits improved, and her bitterness softened. Bonnie was delighted. The cause for the change was Ron Handel. He was a sincere young man, a miner's son. Mari had fallen in love. She began acting more ladylike and mature. She contributed more to the running of their household and frequently asked Bonnie questions about what it was like to be married and have children. Then war sneaked up on the country.

The war, which was not even official, sent sons and brothers and husbands to a distant semitropical land called Vietnam. There were echoes of Korea. No bands assembled to march the conscriptees off to their duty, and for the first time in anyone's memory, the draftees missed their reporting dates in significant numbers. The mass patriotism and sense of purpose that had marked the 1940s were missing, replaced by doubts, confusion and cynicism. No Minutemen took to the stumps with their minute-long pep talks on sacrifice and responsibility. AWOLs and deserters set records in their numbers, and at least three Coal County young men were among those fleeing to places like Sweden and Canada. Except for brief attention to the newspaper accounts and the blood-tinted film clips on television, life went on as if there were no war, and the men whose lot it was to fight slipped away as if theirs was a sinful and embarrassing mission.

The monthly draft calls climbed to the tens of thousands; the Coal County draft board was charged with supplying as many as thirty combat-worthy men a month. Among those selected was Ron Handel, high school classmate and boyfriend of Mari Fenner.

At five in the morning on the day he was to report, Mari

joined Handel's family in escorting him to the Porterville train station. The morning fog had yet to lift, and the sun was just beginning to climb above the mountains when he and the other draftees assembled. The station was eerily quiet as mothers, sisters, wives and girlfriends dabbed at their eyes, and fathers and brothers extended their right hands in silent expressions of affection. When the train had left, the families dispersed as quietly as they had assembled.

Mari tried to follow the progress of the war from the news reports, but the fighting showed no pattern. Finally, she reduced the conflict to its simplest terms and merely prayed that Ron was not under fire.

"It's planned, I tell you. The whole thing is planned," she declared one day to her mother.

"What do you mean, honey?"

"They're sitting there in Washington, looking around, and all they see is men laying idle with nothing to occupy their hands. Men with nothing to do have time to think about things. And when you get a whole lot of people thinking, then you got the pot brewing with trouble. Because when they think, they begin to see rhyme and reason in things they once took for granted, and they just might not like what it is they see. Soon the reasoning takes hold of them like a magnet. They move as one. And the boys sitting in Washington got themselves plenty of trouble."

Bonnie was shocked. She had known her daughter was resentful of losing Ron to the army but had had no idea her bitterness ran so deeply. Nor had she suspected that Mari's thoughts about the war were so abstract. "I understand your hurt, Mari, but I think you're seeing things that simply aren't there," Bonnie said.

"Well, just look what they did to Coal County," her daughter replied. "You don't see those young boys hanging around anymore, do you? And some of them aren't ever coming back, don't forget that. They're going to spill their blood fighting for Ky."

Unfortunately Mari's forecast proved accurate. Several of her classmates had been conscripted into the service, and one by one came reports that some of them would not be returning. Each time she learned of another Coal County casualty the news sent Mari into a depression often lasting two or three days. Then came the shocking notification that Ron's name had been added to the list of war dead, that he had been blown into oblivion by a land mine. Mari, having now twice lost the men closest to her in her life, was devastated. At first she refused to talk to anyone. She wouldn't eat. She couldn't sleep. Her hours were filled with her crying. But then the resentment within her grew to a point where she began to explode, striking out at anyone near her, including Bonnie.

"You're too soft," she shouted to her mother. "You've been too nice, and that's why people like the Porters can walk all over us."

"Now, Mari, calm down," Bonnie said. "You're just frustrated and upset. This will pass, and someday you'll forget you ever heard of the Porters or the Vietnam War."

Mari stormed out of the house, the door slamming behind her. Andy, who had witnessed the exchange, stepped outside to talk to her. In a few minutes Mari returned and apologized to her mother. Andy had that effect on her. And as she sat next to him discussing the disappearance of Augustus Porter, Bonnie knew that in many ways Andy had assumed the role of a father for Mari—just as in some respects, he filled the function of a husband for her.

"You know, I find it very hard to believe old Major Augustus Porter isn't around," Bonnie told him. "For the last two days I've been walking around, expecting him to pop out of some bushes or come running around some corner, yelling and screaming and firing his damn shotgun into the air again like a crazy man. Why, it was only last week that Doc Spencer stopped by to see him about his statistics."

"What statistics?" Andy asked.

"The statistics for what he calls the black lung disease," she replied. "It turns out Spencer has been keeping track of these cases almost since he opened the clinic."

"What has he found?" Andy asked, bending forward in interest.

Bonnie told him how the physician had visited the mansion and spoken to Jim about how two of every three miners over the age of thirty who reported to the clinic, no matter what their complaint, showed evidence of serious lung and bronchial disease caused by the accumulation of coal dust. The dust embedded itself in the tissue, turning it dark gray or, in some cases, black. He said there were cases of emphysema, silicosis and tumors of the lung as well as other diseases probably traceable to the reduced oxygen intake that could be blamed on black lung. Spencer wanted the Porter company to take some of the measures that had been found in recent years to reduce the incidence of the disease.

"What happened?" Andy asked.

"Old Pugnose walked into the room, listened for about thirty seconds and then threw the doctor out. He said there was nothing new about lung trouble—it's always been part of the job," she said.

"Bonnie, you should have told me this. I know all about black lung. I'm making it one of my top issues. I had no idea Spencer was keeping those kinds of records. That's dynamite for me. That's just what ol' Andy LeGrande needs."

Bonnie looked at the calculating smile on Andy's face. As she did, she felt for the first time in years the impulse to do something about the selfish excesses of the Porters. Andy was right. A great amount of injustice had been done that could be righted, at least in part, by the organizing effort. The union, which had been there all along, could be a vehicle for revenge, revenge for her parents and her husband, revenge for her daughter.

"Bonnie, what's wrong?" Andy asked, taking her arm. "You look like you're in shock. Your face is so pale."

Her head shook slightly. "Nothing's wrong. Just thinking. Thinking about how I've been sitting around, doing nothing about it. But now that's going to stop." She edged toward him. "Look, you just tell me what kind of help I can possibly provide, and I'll be right there, right there by your side."

Andy laughed. "Well, that brings me again to the subject of our sex life."

"Come on, Andy! I'm serious," she chided him.

"So am I. Just what do I have to do to make you say yes, make a million first?"

She kissed his cheek. "Please. Don't bring that subject up just now."

"Okay," he said. "But I'm never going to give up. Now what is it that you would like to talk about—my good looks?"

Andy was twisting his ring with his thumb, and the sparkle of its gems caught her eye. She had never seen him wearing it before. It was a cross of five diamonds set into a block of onyx. "How can an underpaid union official afford such a nice piece of jewelry?" she asked.

He laughed. "Ah, the lady has an eye for diamonds. The ring was a bequest from a long-forgotten uncle. Come on now, let's go for a walk."

CHAPTER 12 ⸻

Jim Porter would have preferred it one way or the other: his father alive and at home, making all of them miserable, or his father dead, his remains resting in the Porterville churchyard. As it was, with no clue to the mineowner's whereabouts, Jim wasn't certain what action to take. His mother, in her grief, had almost completely withdrawn, confining herself to the master bedroom for most of each day, even taking her meals there. It was the last place her husband had been seen. Despite her despair, however, she remained convinced that Augustus would return to his home, perhaps walking through the front door any moment now. In the meantime, the company's salesmen and agents located enough business to put the Cedar Ridge mine on a full workweek and even to put the Red Fox back into partial operation. Sarah permitted Jim to do this but balked at his making any other changes in the firm's operation—she didn't want to do anything that would anger Augustus upon his return.

After a month had passed, however, Jim reached a painful decision that his father would have to be assumed dead as far as the company was concerned. Otherwise, the lack of decisive control would only add to the firm's list of problems. His decision presented him with a mixed bag of emotions: While he was sad at losing his father and filled with some remorse that he apparently had not filled his father's expectations, he felt a sense of power in stepping in to take over control of the company. For the first time in his life, he had no aggressive, authoritarian figure standing over him, and he relished his sense of independence. But he was frightened, too, uncertain of his ability to handle such a task as saving an already severely crippled business. Sometimes, late at night, he began to dwell on his own mortality—and the lack of children in his marriage. But whenever Jim had raised the subject of children with Anne, she had said no. "I'm not quite ready to behave like a cow," she said. "When I am, I'll tell you." The word had never come.

Jim found that his father had ignored all forms of record keeping during the six months preceding his disappearance. The ledgers were in disarray. It was impossible for Jim even to estimate how much financial trouble the company actually was in. He decided to turn to Underwood, the company store manager and bookkeeper, for help, bombarding him with every threat he could think of to persuade the timid longtime Porter employee to weed through the firm's records in secrecy. It was not an easy task. After two full days of auditing the records, Underwood concluded that Augustus had been raiding the company's treasury, apparently to subsidize his club in Bannerton. The club's records, although also incomplete, revealed that enterprise had lost great amounts of money from the day it opened. Underwood advised Jim that the club's losses were so great that were they to continue at the same pace, they would jeopardize the company's existence. Despite his fondness for Mae Sexton, Jim saw that the club would have to be dumped, sold if possible. He telephoned his father-in-law, Raymond Baxley, and asked for his help.

The banker confirmed Jim's suspicion that Coal County's

surviving aristocracy would not allow the Club Havana to close; the well-heeled boys had grown too accustomed to its high-stakes gambling and corps of willing hostesses. By the next day Baxley had lined up a buyer.

After finding Underwood trustworthy, Jim released him from his duties at the store and assigned him full time to the company books and those of the family. Two weeks after convincing Jim of the need to sell his father's club, Underwood sounded an alarm about Anne's spending. Jim was startled to learn the extent of her expenses, the most recent being her ordering of a new car as a gift to herself for at last learning to drive.

Anne was sitting in the breakfast nook with Marie when Jim confronted her. "Dear, I'd like to have a brief talk with you, please."

"Oh, not now," she responded. "Marie and I are still working out the details of my next tea."

"Anne, I've got to go to the bank to see your father on something, and this will take only a few minutes," he said.

With an expression of extreme impatience, she dismissed the maid. "Will you excuse us, Marie? But don't go far, please—I'll want to get back to this right away."

"Yes, ma'am," the servant said, departing.

Jim took a seat across from her. "Underwood told me about the car."

"Yes?"

"Well, I was just wondering why you think we need a new one—and a Cadillac at that. Wouldn't the Olds still do?"

"That car's two years old now. Can't we do better than that?"

"Of course," he replied. "But you're buying this car on top of all those paintings you decided you liked. We just can't do it, Anne. We can't live like that anymore."

"What are you trying to tell me?"

"The company's been hit hard by the coal recession, you know that. Although we've been able to keep the family's income more or less steady, I'm not sure how long we can do that. The stock market's not too well, either—at least with the stocks Father purchased—and Underwood thinks we'll have to take a significant cut this year."

"He must be wrong, Jim."

"He's shown me the figures. I've seen them myself."

She was in combat now, and her eyes lit up with the challenge. "What it all boils down to, I guess, is that you're telling me you can no longer support me in the manner to which I'm accustomed. Well, I am not going to change my standard of living just because your insane father went through your fortune like wrapping paper at Christmas. If I have to, I'll go to my father. Now how would you like that—a lowly banker supporting one of the legendary Porters?" She was smiling.

Jim decided not to pursue it further. He rose from his chair. "Do whatever you want, Anne," he said, walking away from the table.

"Marie," his wife called. "Marie, please come back in here."

Jim took a file of ledger sheets with him to Baxley's bank. He intended to lay out the situation as openly and as honestly as he could. He didn't have to—Baxley was already well aware of the Porter Coal Company's troubles.

"It's neither your fault nor your father's," the banker said. "Let's get that stipulated right from the start. The country is in a flux, and so is the coal industry. There's nothing you can do to stop that. It's a simple case of old-fashioned policies and techniques not working anymore. You've got to change with it, Jim. You've got to take the initiative and make the reforms."

Jim listened attentively as his father-in-law outlined what would have to be done to preserve the company—a restructuring of management, the purchase of efficient new machines and an infusion of cash to finance them. "Quite frankly," the banker said, "if you don't accomplish this, then you can say good-bye to your company and follow the other mine-owners who wouldn't change right out of the business."

Jim protested that the company had no cash to finance such reforms.

Baxley nodded in agreement. "You have one alternative," the banker said.

"What's that?"

"An outsider."

Before Jim could voice his reaction, Baxley offered his nomination—one Robert Allen. "He's a local boy and is well equipped to handle a company the size of yours," Baxley said, explaining that the thirty-three-year-old Allen was the son of a miner in Grundy County who had earned an engineering degree under the GI Bill, advanced to graduate studies in business administration and was currently in a middle-management position with a large coal company based in Cardiff City. "He's got the experience now, and he's ripe for a change," Baxley said. "I think he's your man."

Later Baxley handled all the arrangements with Robert Allen, the negotiation of his salary, the designation of his title as chief operating officer and the definition of his authority. The first time Jim met him was at a brief formal meeting called by Baxley to finalize the arrangements.

"You're not making a mistake, Jim," Allen said, calling him by his first name from the start. "I promise you that. We can go places working together. Now let's have a look at those mines of yours."

With Crawford driving, Jim took Allen to the sites of the five Porter mines, starting at Cedar Ridge. Allen frowned when he learned that all except two of them were closed. "There's no need for that," he declared. "That's one of the first things we'll change once we get a little injection of cash."

"Cash?" Jim asked.

"Sure. You have no other choice. First we'll incorporate—there's no way you can survive as a sole proprietorship, which is what in effect you are now—and then we'll issue some stock, a lot of it."

"You mean outsiders would be brought in as co-owners?" Jim asked, cringing at the thought of what his father or grandfather would have said.

"Not as owners in the sense that you mean—as stockholders. You'll still retain control. Your family will own at least fifty-one percent of the stock."

"Did you talk to Ray Baxley about this?"

"Talk to him? It was his suggestion!" Allen replied. "You know, I'd also like to have a look at the store. There're not too many coal companies keeping them anymore. And you can forget about the scrip—the day for that phony money is long past."

"We don't use it anymore."

"Good. At least you've made one wise reform," the brash Allen replied.

Allen's ideas left Jim feeling as if he had run into a punch and were struggling to catch his wind. Just who was this precocious young business whiz kid Baxley had unleashed on him? Who did he think he was? Jim knew one thing for sure: He wouldn't trust him, no matter what his father-in-law said.

Despite Jim's initial misgivings, the company's fiscal health improved remarkably in the weeks after Robert Allen's addition to the firm. Although each slightly distrusted the other, the two men found a natural breakdown to their respective duties, Jim specializing in sales and deliveries, Allen handling finance and development. In time Jim found himself actually liking the younger man. He was precocious, but he was also good, and in the few times Jim tested him, Allen acknowledged readily that Jim was the principal owner and had the final say. In Jim's eyes, they made a good team.

Allen had reformed the firm's structure radically, and the ledger books began to reflect it. Instead of the closed family-owned company that it had been since its founding, the firm was now incorporated. This allowed it to raise much-needed capital funds by issuing stock. Allen, with the help of a group of bankers led by Raymond Baxley as underwriters, had issued as much stock as he could without causing the Porters to lose control of the company. Coal exploitation was becoming an attractive issue to wealthy investors seeking tax shelters, and the Porter stock moved quickly at good prices. In the end, outsiders, including Allen himself, held 49 percent of the company's stock; Jim and his mother accounted for the remainder, leaving the family with majority interest.

Allen had instituted other major changes. These included the closing of the company store, which he determined was more trouble than it was worth. Jim's father and grandfather surely would have considered such drastic action unnecessary, if not sacrilegious, but Allen's argument was convincing. In the end, Jim agreed.

Occupied as he was with sales, which were increasing, Jim had not been to the mines in several weeks when he decided one day to drop by the Red Fox. Even from the distance, he saw that the changes since his last visit had been many. The old, rotting wooden shed used by the mine manager had been replaced by an aluminum structure. The bathhouse had been repainted. Heavy three-axle coal trucks lined up under the tipple which once had exclusively loaded trains. The trucks, recently purchased under financing arranged by Allen, were replacing trains for short-haul deliveries.

The mine remained one of the largest in the state. Allen, in a briefing a week earlier, had told Jim that the latest geological and engineering projections were for another three decades of extraction at the very minimum from the huge mine. Specialists using space-age instruments had been able to track the untapped sections of the vein to within a foot as it spread under the mountain. Allen reported that the overhead mountain rock dipped into a shallow depression at the same point where the vein bulged upward. The engineers said it would probably be economical to dig to the coal at that point from above, by a limited use of strip mining which was being done more and more. Coalmen utilized monstrous earthmoving machines to knock off the tops of the smaller mountains and to slice away at the slopes of others until the growing height of the overhead rock made it no longer economical. Then they opened their portal and tunneled on in. Strip mining, however, required an investment in an entirely different battery of equipment. Despite this problem, Jim was enthusiastic about the idea and told Allen to go ahead with an attempt to line up the credit necessary to purchase the modern stripping machinery.

As Jim drove down the winding gravel road toward the Red Fox portal, he saw that the mine was busy. Several workers spotted him and waved to him, some looking surprised at seeing him there. He parked the car and headed for the manager's shack. The door was open. Inside, Crawford was busy with an engineer and two foremen over a map of one of the mine's longest headings. Their discussion stopped as soon as Jim appeared in the doorway. Crawford, appearing stunned at the sight of Jim, raised his head from the unfurled roll of paper. "Ah . . . Mr. Porter," he stuttered. "Good to see ya. What can we do for ya?"

"Little surprised to see me, huh?" Jim asked, laughing. "I don't blame you. Recently I've been too busy to get out here. What I thought was that maybe I could take a look inside."

"Inside?" Crawford asked.

"I'd like to take a little trip maybe two, three miles in. I haven't seen all the new equipment, you know."

Crawford grinned, then called to an aide. "Get Mr. Porter here a cap and coveralls," he ordered. "And tell the dispatcher to hold traffic on track four for a while. We'll be going in."

Jim stepped into the coveralls and borrowed a pair of boots from the engineer. The new lightweight molded plastic safety helmet felt odd to him compared to the heaviness of the cap he had used after the war. He wondered what had become of that cap. Oh, yes, the new maid had thrown it out. Too bad. He could have used it now.

A motorman named Hurley was assigned to take them into the number four heading. He sat in a small cubicle on a flat electric mine locomotive which was little different in appearance from that used when Jim worked in the mine. Jim found that it was considerably faster, however, moving at speeds of up to fifteen miles per hour. After they had traveled nearly five miles into the mountain, Crawford tapped Hurley on the back and motioned for him to stop. "This is as good a spot as any, Mr. Porter. We've got some men working over there." He pointed to a small tunnel in the vein which led off to the left. "Watch your head," he added. The vein was less than four feet high at this point.

Jim followed the manager on his hands and knees several yards through the tunnel, which abruptly widened into an extraction room. Suddenly a thundering roar came from ahead. Jim was startled. Crawford, smiling, turned around and shouted to him, but Jim was unable to make out his words. In less than a minute the deafening sound ended, and Crawford repeated what he had said earlier: "A continuous miner —one of the three we have now." After they had crawled a few more yards, the long, flat machine came into view. Its operator, who normally sat crunched in a tiny cockpit at the side of the machine, was stooped in front, making an adjustment. Jim and the supervisor nodded their greetings to the man.

"These here dig into the face like it was ice cream," Crawford said, pointing to the row of disks with steel teeth at the front of the machine. He explained that the disks chipped at the coal and then flung the loosened pieces into a boxlike receptacle. There armlike devices swept the coal into a conveyor system, which in turn poured it into a shuttle car. "Seven tons every forty seconds," Crawford boasted, obviously proud of the machine. "The only problem is the dust.

We've got to shut it down every half hour or so to let the dust settle. Let's have a look at it in operation."

The supervisor signaled to the operator, who climbed back into his cockpit and started the machine. Jim held his hands to his ears as he watched the spinning disks attack the jagged face of coal. Crawford's assessment had been correct—the machine sliced through the coal like a knife on butter. Jim was amazed. How out of touch he had been with the technology. One machine now did the work of a full crew of eight men. He asked Crawford the price tag. Crawford answered: "More than fifty thousand dollars."

A small two-man helicopter was landing in a nearby clearing when Hurley eased the train through the portal and back outside. Robert Allen hopped out of the chopper and walked toward the manager's office. When Allen caught sight of Jim, he changed direction abruptly and headed toward him.

"Jim! What the hell are you doing out here?" he asked, shaking hands energetically. The noise of the helicopter taking off prevented Jim from answering. "Glad you're here," Allen shouted after the chopper was airborne. "Got some figures to show you." He ushered Jim into the aluminum shack.

Jim didn't like what he had just seen. It was true the company's sales had improved substantially and productivity was up thanks to some of Allen's innovations. But only Cedar Ridge and the Red Fox were in operation, the other three Porter mines still being idle, and the coal economy remained depressed. The fancy equipment the firm had procured was heavily financed, and the company really didn't own it. Jim was not sure it was a time for renting helicopters.

"About that chopper there. . . ." He started to raise the subject. But Allen interrupted him, explaining that he had rented the helicopter for an inspection flight over a potential mining property to the north in Rocky Gap County.

"It's something I planned to talk to you about later," Allen said. "Not for tomorrow, of course, but our picture's been improving so much that it's not inconceivable to me that we'll be seeking a new mine or two in the not-too-distant future. I thought I'd get a head start on my homework." Until then Jim had had no idea that Allen was thinking in terms of expansion. The idea was premature, he thought, and it frightened him.

"You're not committing us in any way, are you, Bob?" he asked.

"Not at all. It's just that we have this heavy investment in modern equipment, and it won't be too long before we reach a point of diminishing returns out at Cedar Ridge. It might prove better to acquire a lease elsewhere rather than allow the machines to sit idle or put them up for sale." Allen smiled, cocksure of himself and proud of the progress the firm had made under his influence. "Anyway," he added, "what I wanted to talk to you about is a couple of more long-term borrowings. I think we're ready for them, and we could use another six continuous miners. Six at the minimum." He opened a briefcase and removed a collection of charts, graphs and ledger sheets. He had begun arguing his case that the time was proper for the company to borrow more money when there was a knock on the door.

It was a foreman. He motioned Crawford to step outside. In a minute Crawford stuck his head through the door and told them, "There's been an accident. We lost a man. I'll be back in a few minutes."

Jim and Allen both left the shack and followed Crawford, but the manager stopped them at the portal. "I won't allow either of you in there until I find out how bad it is," he told them.

Jim started to protest, but Allen silenced him. "Crawford's right," he said. "It could be dangerous."

It was nearly a half hour before the mine manager returned. His expression was sad and his voice almost inaudible as he related how the Red Fox had claimed another man.

While the company executives were huddling in the manager's shack, the mine dispatcher had instructed Hurley, the motorman, to return into the mine with his train. Hurley, a veteran miner with a ruddy face and a large beer belly, hopped back into his cockpit on the six-car train and guided it past the portal into one of the mine's major headings. The track ahead of him was supposed to be clear, and he pressed hard on his accelerator, the empty cars banging loudly behind him and the train's wheels emitting a piercing screech on every curve. He had passed the five-mile marker when suddenly he engaged the brake with as much force as he could muster. The train strained against its inertia and came to a halt just a few feet before an intersection in the track. Hurley jumped off the motor and walked to the edge of the cross track. He stared at a small pile of rock rubble lying across the ties. Falling to his knees, he peered up at the ceiling. He shook his head. Stooping because of the low ceiling, Hurley then made his way along the track in the direction of the portal until he came to one of the mine's telephones. He cranked the magneto and called for the dispatcher.

According to the surveyor's tags hammered into the roof, the intersection was at marker 147, but the spot was more commonly referred to as the waterfalls, a designation derived from the trickle of water dripping down a wall at that point.

"I'm at the waterfalls, Chief," Hurley shouted over the primitive phone to the dispatcher, a Swede named Nelson. "I ain't goin' through. . . . What's wrong? The ceiling, that's what. . . . There's already a small pile of it on the track. . . . You can swear all you want, but I ain't goin' across that track. . . . You do whatever the hell you want to. . . . Yea, I'll wait right here." He slammed the receiver back into its cradle and returned to the train, which he backed several yards away from the intersection.

It was about fifteen minutes before the dispatcher arrived. Nelson was livid when he jumped off his one-man car.

"Goddammit, Hurley. What the hell is wrong with you?" he shouted as he approached the man sitting on the track. "You've stalled yourself here, talkin' about a weak ceiling, and you've got traffic stopped up and down the entire heading. Dammit, Hurley, I've got coal to move!"

"I tell you there's somethin' wrong, Boss. That roof's gonna go, and I ain't gonna be under it when it does," Hurley responded, his voice equaling Nelson's intensity.

The dispatcher glared at him. Then, muttering to himself, he walked in a stoop to one of the steel beams shoring up the ceiling near the intersection. He tested it first with his hands and then with a kick. The steel held its place. After stooping still lower to avoid the ceiling, Nelson climbed over the cross track and tested the shoring on the other side. He found it also firmly in position. Bent so low he was almost crawling, he moved back to Hurley's side.

"You're crazy, do you hear me? The timber's fine," he told the motorman. "That rubble means nothin'. Now get these cars out of here!" Hurley shook his head. Both men were angry. They glared at each other like gunmen facing off for a draw. "You're warned, Hurley. Consider this a warning," the dispatcher said finally to break the standoff. "I'll do the goddamn job myself."

Nelson slammed himself angrily onto the seat of the cockpit and opened the throttle. The track groaned as the empty but still-heavy train began to move, its hollow cars clanging at their couplings. There was no warning. Just as the motor reached the track intersection, the mine's ceiling dropped with a heavy thud, crushing Nelson under tons of pressure from the mountain above. The movement of the train had created just enough vibration to free the overhead rock. He never had a chance.

Hurley, his face white in shock, raced to the phone and called outside. Within seconds the entire work force had heard of the disaster. Crawford rushed to the accident site. Surprisingly the rescue crew had little trouble removing enough of the fallen rock to free Nelson's body. They couldn't immediately locate his head, however—it had been sliced from his torso as cleanly as if a cleaver had done the job.

Jim cringed when he heard Crawford's report. One of his hands involuntarily moved toward his neck. "Did Nelson have a family?" he asked.

"Yes. A wife and three kids. I think the youngest is nine," Crawford replied. "They live by themselves up near Paxton's Point."

Two men passed, carrying a thick plastic sheet bearing what remained of the decapitated dispatcher. Jim took a quick glance at the corpse, turning his head in revulsion when he saw the mass of shredded tissue, blood and splintered bone.

"There's no way we could have prevented that," Allen declared. "That heading was inspected just this morning."

Crawford nodded. "Guess I'll go do my duty," he said.

His duty was to notify the dispatcher's widow of his death. There was a longtime custom that such news was taken to a victim's home by the mineowner. Jim's father and his grandfather both had performed the function many times. But in the months before his mysterious disappearance, Augustus had rarely visited the mines and, at the Red Fox, Crawford had taken over the dreaded assignment.

"Dodson, can you drive me?" Crawford shouted to a nearby miner while stepping off toward a company jeep.

"Wait," Jim said, grabbing the manager's arm. "I'll go." Crawford looked surprised.

"Good idea, Jim. You're the owner. I've got some business to attend to anyway. We can talk later," Allen said.

Dodson drove Jim to the Nelson house, which sat high in the foothills about five miles outside Bannerton. The last mile of the trip was over a rugged, winding dirt road. The hills blocked the house from their view until they pulled around the final bend and found themselves practically at the Nelsons' front door. Jim was surprised to see how weather-beaten the house was. It sagged badly at one end and appeared never to have had a paint job. Black coal smoke curled from the bent, rusting pipe that served as a chimney.

As Jim slid from his seat in the jeep, he saw that a woman —obviously Mrs. Nelson—was waiting at the door. He searched for words as he walked toward her, but after he climbed three rotting steps to the door, he found that he did not have an opportunity to say anything. The woman spoke first.

"Come in, Mr. Porter. The coffee's ready. We've been expecting you," she said softly, holding the door open for him.

Jim was stunned. According to the custom, once a mine-owner had notified a widow of her husband's death, she made a pot of coffee for the two to share. From Mrs. Nelson's words and the strong aroma filling the shack, Jim knew that the coffee had been brewed already. It occurred to him that there was no way the woman could have seen his approach over the meandering, hidden roadway. Yet she clearly knew of her husband's death. How? There was no telephone line leading to the house; Jim had looked for one. And there wasn't a neighbor in sight. Mrs. Nelson and her youngest child were the only persons present.

The woman walked to her coal-burning stove. She removed a dented metal coffeepot and poured two steaming cups, which she carried to a table. She motioned to Jim to sit down.

"How did it happen?" she asked, no trace of emotion in her voice. Jim told her, softening the details as much as he could while remembering that he was talking to a veteran miner's wife. She knew the work—no sense in lying to her.

"Mrs. Nelson, I'm very, very sorry," Jim said. He brought his cup to his lips but found the coffee still too hot for sipping. "Look, I'm told you have children. It may not mean much at this moment, but I want the company to take care of those youngsters. We'll find you a house in Porterville and set up some sort of pension."

"No, Mr. Porter. I think we'll stay right here. But thank you," she said.

"The money, then. I'll take care of the pension. And if there's anything you ever need, you call me—I want you to promise me that." The woman nodded. Jim found nothing more to say. He had to get out of there. Finally, he gave up on the still-steaming coffee. "Thank you for the coffee, but I think I'd better go," he said.

The woman accompanied him to the door. After he stepped off the porch, Jim turned back. "Do you mind if I ask you a question?"

"No, Mr. Porter. Of course not."

"How did you know? How did you know your husband was dead?"

She spoke softly. "I can't answer that, Mr. Porter. It was shortly after one o'clock—I just got this funny feeling. And then I put on the coffee."

Jim nodded in farewell to her and walked back to the jeep. "Dodson," he said to the driver, "what time was it when that ceiling collapsed on Nelson."

"It was one-oh-four, sir. Precisely at one-oh-four. That's what Mr. Crawford wrote on the report. I saw it."

Jim shook his head. Seeing the widow and her young child intensified his sadness about Nelson's death. It seemed such a waste. As Dodson put the jeep into gear, however, Jim also felt a great sense of satisfaction. For the first time he had played a role assigned by tradition exclusively to a mine-owner, a rite of passage not unlike his assignment to work his own face of coal years earlier. And as had happened then, he felt a need to share the experience with someone. He thought of his wife and her probable reaction to the events of the past two hours. His lips drew into a sad smile.

"Where to, sir?" the driver asked.

"Just head for Bannerton, and drop me off at that club, would you? I promised a fellow I'd meet him for a couple of drinks."

*   *   *

Jim hesitated before opening the door to the Club Havana.
He had not been there since he sold it to Lamon C. Hubbard,
a local lumberman. Before that Jim's visits had been rare,
usually the result of his father's orders. But Andy LeGrande
had insisted on meeting there. What he had to talk about was
best discussed over drinks, he had declared. Normally Jim
would have declined Andy's request for the meeting, but
he had been watching the organizer's flashy style and the
following he now seemed to be winning. The last thing Jim
needed was labor trouble. So he agreed to sit down with the
union man.

The dimly lit interior of the club appeared unchanged
from earlier years, probably reflecting the influence of Mae
Sexton, who still served as manager. He hadn't seen her in
years.

Andy was waiting at a table in the basement dining room.
It was apparent that he already had charged himself for the
session with several drinks.

"Jim, my friend, how are you?" Andy bubbled, pumping
his right hand vigorously.

"Sorry I'm late."

"That's okay. I understand how tough it must be, owning
a mine. Sit right down and let's get you something to drink."

While Andy was trying to get the attention of a hostess,
Jim studied the barrel-chested labor leader across from him,
noting that Andy had called him by his first name and
wondering what this suggestion of familiarity might portend.
They had met face to face only once, when Jim had helped
him out of the rain-filled ditch at the Red Fox mine. There
was something about Andy, a quality Jim could not pinpoint,
that made him very suspicious and distrustful of the man.

Jim scanned the room. He recognized few of the patrons,
a reflection of the new owner's policy on membership.

Coal County occupied an area of West Virginia in which

the lumber industry overlapped the coalfields. Coal and lumber were the state's two most important industries. While the coalmen were mining within the mountains, the lumbermen were above them harvesting trees. The two groups usually lived in harmony with one another, but occasionally they were at each other the way cattlemen and farmers once were on the ranges out West. After Hubbard, a lumberman, bought out the Porters' controlling interest in the Club Havana, he opened the membership to many of his associates in the lumber industry and its allied fields. Some old-time club members feared this would lead to inevitable trouble, but as it developed, there was little as the entire membership pursued the common interests of gambling, marathon drinking and women. Taking over the club, Hubbard had concluded that the chief reason for its losing so much money was that the size of its clientele was too small. Simply put, the hostesses weren't busy enough. So he opened up the doors and, at the same time, added a number of new, sometimes exotic attractions such as regularly scheduled striptease shows.

Despite Hubbard's open-door policy, the one group that did not seem to belong to the Club Havana was union officials. What was Andy LeGrande doing there, mixing with men who supposedly were his adversaries?

"What I'm curious about," Jim said after his bourbon was served, "is just how you get in this place."

"Oh, they love me here," Andy replied. "After all, in a way, I'm a kind of celebrity." He chuckled. Jim didn't respond. "And Lamon C. Hubbard, a fine, fine gentleman, is a longtime friend. Don't ever let him know I told you, but a few years ago I helped arrange some financing for him just when he needed it. He never forgot."

Jim didn't doubt the claim. It fitted perfectly with the assessment he was making of the man sitting across the table.

Andy went on to tell a story about one of the club's recent innovations, a weekly showing of pornographic films. On these nights, he said, the club was packed wall to wall, and the titillating nature of the films inspired a heavy demand for the use of the rooms on the second floor. To run the projector on those nights, Hubbard hired Fat Smitty, who Andy noted was a former Porter employee.

As Andy related it, there was no hint of trouble until midway into the second reel. Two couples were engaged in a variety of contortions on the screen when Fat Smitty dropped his head in a spell of dizziness. The film was so engrossing that no one in the audience noticed his distress until the 280-pound man slumped to the floor, taking the projector with him.

"Turn on the lights!" someone shouted. Another man yanked the projector's electric cord to stop the film from spilling all over the floor.

"Get some water," said another. But Fat Smitty was already dead.

"Can you imagine that," Andy said, chuckling, "dropping stone dead from a dirty movie?" He guffawed.

Jim didn't laugh. He had known of Smitty's death but not the details.

The waitress served them another round. The dining room had begun to fill with its evening crowd, mostly the boisterous lumbermen, merchants and politicians whom Hubbard had added to the membership roll. Andy talked of sports, politics and the weather. A third round of drinks was served. They still had not gotten to the purpose of the meeting. Jim, bored with the small talk, became irritated. "Forget the weather, and get to the point, LeGrande, would you? Why did you want to see me?"

The union organizer laughed heartily. "Can't get your mind off business, huh? Well, they're going to have a little show here in a while that'll help relax you. Just you watch these girls, and you won't give a damn about coal."

"I mean it, LeGrande. I don't have the time to waste. What do you want?" Jim insisted.

Andy looked directly into Jim's eyes. "As long as you're so rushed, let me start reviewing a little history—a little *labor* history." He took a long sip from his glass. "Now you may think you're unique because you're a Porter, the grandson of a man who helped settle this region and all that crap. But let me tell you something—people like you are a dime a dozen."

"Wait just a minute, friend—"

"No, you wait and listen me out. You and me are going to be very clear with each other," Andy shot back. "When you peel away the layers of bullshit, all you got is a relatively small family company. Nickel-and-dime stuff. One of a hundred such firms in this corner of the state. And look at them, Porter. One by one they've been organized. That's what I mean by considering a little history." Jim was glaring at him. "You're a smart enough fellow to know that it's only a matter of time before we move in on you. For chrissake, ol' Andy LeGrande already has the loyalty of half the men in Coal County. The only remaining question is which way it's done." Andy picked up his glass.

"What the hell's that supposed to mean?" Jim asked. "You trying to threaten me?"

"It's not a threat. I'm simply presenting the facts. The transition can occur real nicelike with me ushering the union in like a gentle midwife. Or, if you prefer, it can be done the hard way—with lost production and destroyed equipment. That can cost you a pretty piece of change."

Jim sensed LeGrande's intentions. He began to smell the scheme. It amounted to extortion.

Andy's voice grew calmer. "You know, your father was a very intelligent and astute man. I respected him despite our differences. And let me tell you something, if he were here today, he'd know how to—shall we say—grease his friendship with the union leadership in a kind of working relationship."

"If it's a payoff you're talking about, LeGrande, forget it. You can go to hell. I won't deal with scum and won't waste any more of my time and reputation sitting here with you," Jim said. He started to rise, but Andy reached across the table and pulled him back down.

"All I'm trying to say is that life is complicated, and sometimes you have to scratch each other's backs in order to survive." Jim slid back into his chair reluctantly. "Let me tell you a few things," Andy said, pausing for another sip from his drink. "There's a lot of trouble for people like you on the road ahead and—"

A loud burst of cheering cut Andy short as a line of three young women filed onto a stage at the front of the room. Their dress consisted of G-strings and tassels.

Andy bent forward and raised his voice in an attempt to be heard above the applause and hooting. "What I'm trying to say to you, Jim, is that it behooves you to have the union leadership on your side, if you know what I mean." But Jim wasn't listening. He had tuned out the fast-talking union man and was concentrating on one of the women standing on the stage.

The MC, a dissipated middle-aged man who chain-smoked, attempted a few corny one-liners, which drew more boos than laughs. His effort at comedy over, he summoned one of the women, a redhead, to center stage. After introducing her as Bunny, he stepped to the side and threw a switch which triggered a loud and distorted blast of recorded rock music from two speakers. The redhead began gyrating to the beat of the music and thrust her chest forward, a gesture that drew a chorus of approving cheers and whistles from the darkened tables. Her oiled breasts glistening from an overhead spotlight, she soon moved down a ramp off the stage to a table at the front. Entwining her hands over her head like a pair of embracing snakes, she pushed her writhing hips to within inches of a patron's leering face. The patron, a fat, crew-cut lumberman, bent forward and, with an obscene contortion of his face, stuck out his tongue.

Jim was probably the only man in the room who wasn't

watching the redhead. His eyes were focused instead on one of the two women waiting in the background for their calls. He was staring at her face. Her hair was brown, long and straight, and her features, including the roman nose, were sharp. Her shoulders were broad for a woman, and when the light caught her eyes the right way, Jim was sure they were green. It couldn't be, he thought. But then he was certain —one of the dancers waiting for her turn was Mari Fenner.

Jim jumped to his feet and left the table.

"Hey, where're you going?" Andy shouted after him.

Jim didn't answer. He rushed up the ramp toward the rear of the stage. The dancer stopped. Then there were no sounds in the room except for the thump of the recorded music.

"What's your name?" Jim demanded of the young woman waiting her turn to dance. Appearing astonished, she didn't answer. "I said what's your name? Are you Mari Fenner?"

"Get away from me!" she snapped.

He took her arm. "How old are you? Maybe eighteen? Or nineteen? Whatever it is, you're not old enough for this place, and I want you out of here right now."

She struggled as Jim pulled her off the stage. The crew-cut lumberman approached them, but Jim waved him back. "Just mind your own business, chum," Jim warned him. The man stopped his advance.

"Leave me alone! Let go of me!" Mari protested. But his grip tightened, and he dragged her out of sight of the audience and into a hallway. "Does your mother know you're doing this?" he demanded.

"That's none of your business," she shot back.

"I'm making it my business. And if I have to, I'll go right to Mae Sexton to see you're never allowed back here again. Now go get dressed, and get out of here!"

"Damn you! Damn you anyway!" she said, trying to push past him. "Just who do you think you are? You're not my father."

"Why in the world do you go debasing yourself like

that?" he asked, grasping both her shoulders.

"Money, asshole," she responded. "Money for some friends of mine that you don't need to know a thing about. You'll find out soon enough anyway," she said, sneering.

"Where are your clothes?"

"In there," she said, pointing to a nearby door.

"Well, get in there and change."

She did, slamming the door behind her. In a moment she was dressed in her man's white shirt and blue jeans and rushing past Jim out the door.

The first Jim learned of the fair was when he spotted a large white banner stretched between two lampposts on Porterville's Main Street. "The Faith, Hope and No Despair Arts and Crafts Fair," the sign read. In the square were a dozen wooden tables filled with a variety of goods and several persons clustered around them. Curious as to who had organized the fair, he approached one of two women who were standing behind a table stacked with handmade belts, wallets, purses, dolls and woodcarvings. Both had their backs to him, one talking to a customer, the other arranging the merchandise.

"Excuse me," Jim said to the latter. The woman turned around. It was Bonnie Fenner.

"Bonnie! I didn't recognize you."

She stared at him for a moment and then said, "I guess the world is full of surprises."

Jim had rarely seen her in recent months and couldn't recall talking to her in more than a year. As he studied her in the soft afternoon sunlight, he reaffirmed his earlier observation that she indeed was a woman whose beauty improved with age. Her face had retained its smoothness and character, and her hair remained jet black, thick and luxuriant. Her eyes appeared young and alert, clear windows to her soul. Her body was still youthful, and when she threw her head back, as she did periodically, her hair fell over her shoulders in a manner unfailingly seductive, at least to Jim. Of one thing he was certain: Bonnie didn't look her age, which was thirty-eight.

"These are terrific belts," he said, picking up one of the samples. Fingering its intricate design, he asked her about the fair. In a cool and distant voice, she explained that the event had its origins indirectly with a pair of VISTA workers sent to Coal County as part of the antipoverty program. They were long gone, but they had fostered a spirit of self-help that fitted right in with Bonnie's own thinking. She and a group of other women had organized the fair. Their thinking was that the industry and self-sufficiency of mountain people had produced skills that might well be exploited as a source of family income. All that was needed were a production organization and a marketing mechanism.

Working through the Porterville church, Bonnie and her associates had spent several months urging local residents, men and women, to pursue their handicrafts with an eye toward selling them. Now their initial production was on display: tables of attractive leather goods, finished wood-carvings, bright quilts and handicrafts of many varieties. A group of housewives also had set up food tables, offering cakes, pies and other baked goods. With a sunny sky and unusually warm weather for an October day, the square had the flavor of one of the carnivals of earlier years which no longer came to town.

"How have you been?" Jim asked, continuing to finger the belts.

Before she could answer, a male voice called out, "There you are, you sweet thing."

Lamon C. Hubbard, ignoring Jim, moved to Bonnie and lifted her hand in his. "I just had the feelin' that I would find you here today and knew that just seein' you would give me the lift I needed." Bonnie blushed. Hubbard pretended suddenly to notice Jim. "Oh, Porter. How ya doin'? You don't mind if I have a few words with this pretty nurse here, do ya?" He edged Bonnie away.

Jim couldn't hear their discussion, but it was clear that Hubbard, a widower, had solicited Bonnie's interest before. That was understandable. She was beautiful—and she was available. To Jim, it was a painful sight, Hubbard pawing at her arms and shoulders, Bonnie smiling and responding to him. Could she really be fooled by a man like Hubbard? Or had she changed so much that she could now be enticed by money? The one certain thing was that she would have nothing to do with Jim. She probably still hated him. And he couldn't blame her. He was the one years before who had uttered the words that separated them, even if he hadn't meant them.

Hubbard at last departed, throwing a salute to Jim as he turned his back. Bonnie returned to the table.

"A friend of yours?" Jim asked.

"Mr. Hubbard? Oh, he's a very decent gentleman," she replied, offering no further information.

"I was asking you how you're doing."

"I think you know the answer to that," she said cryptically.

"What do you mean?"

"Well, I'm working at a medical clinic that is broke because your company won't help it, and my pa who lost his leg saving your father's life is back sweeping the dirty floor of the bathhouse at a boy's wage."

Jim fingered his chin. "To be honest, with all the other problems the company has, I forgot all about your dad. Let me make some arrangements to get him a raise," Jim said.

Bonnie grinned. "You'd better do it right away while you still can."

"Here we go again," Jim said, more to himself than to her. "Just what do you mean by that?"

"Well . . . if I were bitchy, I could tell you that the Porter Coal Company is about to become a unionized company. Andy LeGrande is already making the arrangements to see to that."

He moved closer to her. "Look, Bonnie, you know what's happened to the company and my family. We still don't know whether my father is alive or dead, and it's taken me months to get my feet on the ground with the responsibility of running the operation. I can take only one step at a time." His voice changed, becoming softer. "My father was old-fashioned. He made a lot of mistakes, especially in the past few years. And now that I've taken his place, I intend to make changes, a lot of them, and one thing I'm not sure of, even now, is whether we're going to survive. To be honest with you, there are some days when I think letting the union in would be a damn good thing for the firm as well as the men. But I need time. I know without asking her that my ma feels the same way my father did—or does—and I've got to wait for the proper time to broach the subject with her."

Bonnie seemed moved by his sincerity, even embarrassed at her earlier lack of courtesy. "I wish you luck, Jim," she said. Then, changing the subject: "Would you like to buy one of these belts? They're all handmade."

Jim took another belt and wrapped it around his waist to test its size. "How's your daughter?" he asked as he worked the buckle.

Bonnie pointed to the other woman working behind the table. Jim turned his eyes to her. It was Mari, her long hair tucked under a wide-brimmed floppy felt hat.

"That's Mari?" Jim asked, feigning surprise after deciding that he would not let on to Bonnie of his meeting two days earlier with her daughter.

Bonnie nodded.

"My God, she's full-grown now," he said, inspecting the young woman whose resemblance to her mother still stopped with the color of her eyes.

"Mari, come here and say hello to Mr. Porter," Bonnie said.

Mari moved reluctantly toward them. She was pouting, her eyes glaring at Jim, her expression one of disgust, if not disdain. He offered her his hand. She refused it.

"Mother," she said, turning to Bonnie, "I don't have anything to say to this man." She turned her back and walked away.

"I'm sorry," Bonnie told Jim, who felt embarrassed. "She's young, and she's got a lot of ideas about a lot of things, including some thoughts about the Porter Coal Company. She doesn't mean it personally."

"I understand," Jim said, trying to forget what just happened. "Maybe she and I can sit down and have a talk someday." He chuckled. "I can't be that bad." He looked at his watch. "Oh, I didn't realize it was so late. I'd better be on my way. It was nice seeing you, Bonnie."

"Don't you want a belt?" she asked, smiling sheepishly.

"Oh, of course. You pick one out for me, size thirty-two."

She selected a wide belt with a simple design. It fitted perfectly when he tried it on. He paid the $4 price, thanked her and began walking away.

"Jim, just a minute," she called after him, leaving her station behind the table and walking toward him. Her face was serious, and her voice softer than before. Her eyes met his briefly then focused on the ground. "I just wanted to tell you that although my family and I have had some complaints against the Porters over the years—legitimate complaints, I think you'd agree—I have some notion of what you're going through. I mean, the financial troubles with your company. And I think you should know that most people around here are pulling for you. No matter what happened in the past, you and your family are mountain people, not some outside oil company." Her eyes turned toward him. "That's all. That's what I wanted to say."

Jim was moved. "I don't believe you said that, Bonnie. Not you. Why?"

She smiled. "I guess I'm getting mellow in my old age."

He took her arm. "Thank you. I mean that sincerely. We need all the help we can get, and quite frankly, it often doesn't look very good."

Her expression changed yet again, this time growing stern, and Jim wondered if she wasn't now regretting what she had just said. "You're still going to have to accept the union, Jim. The people will draw the line with that."

"We'll work it out," he said, squeezing her arm and leaving for the office across the street.

Sitting behind his cluttered desk in the otherwise-deserted office, he realized that he and Bonnie had been waging parallel battles all along, different only in technique and scale. While he struggled to preserve his company, she fought for survival for herself, her daughter and her parents. The two goals were much the same.

Jim was sitting in the parlor, turning the pages of the Bannerton *Tribune* when he came to the society news section. "Mrs. Anne Porter Chairs Fund Raiser," read the headline over a boxed story in the middle of the page. "Mrs. Anne Baxley Porter has been selected chairwoman of the . . ." the story began. How many times had such a sentence been printed in the Bannerton *Tribune*? he thought, raising his eyes from the page to look at his wife, who, sitting across from him, was talking about a cruise to Brazil. She was thirty-five, and the years had not been good to her. Despite her use of the most expensive lotions and creams Paris had to offer, she had lost her youthful appearance.

"The Jacksons say Rio is marvelous this time of year," she was saying. Jim turned his attention to the newspaper and a section that ran the lists of marriages and divorces. In the edition he held, the list of divorces was half again as long as the list of marriages. Jim smiled. This had been the trend in recent years. If it kept up, there would be no surviving marriages in Coal County.

Jim had almost finished leafing through the paper when he noticed a short item he had missed before. "Coal County Man Freed," read the headline.

> Will Thomason, a former Porterville resident, was paroled yesterday from the federal penitentiary at Lewisburg, Pa., after serving a term of 10 years for moonshining and flight from justice.
>
> Thomason, a former employee of the Porter Coal Company, was arrested by federal agents in Mississippi several years after he fled from West Virginia.

A chill went through Jim's body. He had forgotten all about Will Thomason. Jim never had been privy to the arrangements made between Will and Augustus. If the mineowner had been making payments to him, there was no written record of them. Or maybe Augustus had stiffed his former business partner. Would Will return to Porterville to seek his revenge? Or had Augustus promised him a lump sum in compensation upon his parole? Would Will return now to collect that?

Jim folded the paper and looked at Anne, who was knitting. "It says here Will Thomason was paroled from prison."

Anne grunted. "They should have thrown away the key."

Jim looked at the clock above the fireplace. It was almost 10:00 P.M. "Excuse me, dear," he said, rising. "I think I'll head up."

Upstairs, Jim could hear his mother moving about in the master bedroom. She still spent most of her time there, either sitting in her rocking chair or staring out the window. She continually referred to Augustus in the present tense, and Jim, at times, was sufficiently worried about her state of mind to consider seeking psychiatric care for her.

He entered his bedroom, undressed and put on his robe. From the bottom drawer of his dresser he removed a well-worn book with a greenish brown cover. *A Colliery Empire*, it was entitled. Bearing a copyright in 1922, it told the history of Colonel James T. Porter's expansion of the company.

When Jim opened the book, an aging yellowed envelope fell out. It was a pay envelope which Jim, while hanging around the Red Fox as a boy, had found in 1938. For some reason, he had kept it.

The envelope had been issued to a motorman's assistant who was paid by the hour rather than by the ton. His empty envelope recorded pay at $5.80 a day for six days for a gross of $34.80. Out of that came deductions of $1.60 for insurance, $16.83 for rent on his company home and $1.50 for the recreation club. At the end of the six-day workweek, the miner was left with $14.87 in cash, and out of that he had to deal with his debt at the company store.

Jim shook his head. It hardly seemed worth it. But the man probably had been unable to find work in his European homeland. At least in Porterville he had food to put on his family's table.

The book's text was sparse and loosely written. As he leafed through it while reclining on his bed, Jim concluded that the company's history was better reflected in the accompanying photographs, full-page halftones of stern-faced men posed in front of freshly dug portals, of soot-covered miners wielding shovels at the side of wooden coal cars, of a slender black man sweeping a thickly bristled broom at the base of a tipple. A formal portrait of his grandfather opened the book. At the end was another picture of Jim's namesake, this one depicting him cradling his personal pickax, on which he had carved his Latin motto.

Jim stared at his grandfather's eyes, noting the sense of determination they conveyed even at the age of fifty or so when the photographs were taken. There was not the slightest hint of mellowness or compassion in them, yet by all accounts, his grandfather had been respected as much for his fairness as for his aggressiveness and determination.

The faces of the pictured miners showed no such determination but rather submission. Still, there was a calmness in them that contrasted with the despair and fear common to mining men of the current day. To Jim, this was at least partially understandable, for in those earlier years, matters tended to be much more simple.

Anne entered the room and disappeared into the bathroom. Jim, paging through the musty book, hardly noticed her arrival, but she caught his attention when she returned wearing a sheer black nightgown cut provocatively low.

"What's the matter with my honey?" she asked flirtingly, easing herself onto the bed next to him.

"I was just wondering what Grandpa would . . ." he started to respond, but she placed a finger over his lips and shook her head sideways.

"Hush, hush," she instructed. "You don't have to tell me. Whatever it is we're going to chase it right out of your mind."

She stroked his face with her left hand while her right undid the sash of his robe. She pulled the garment off him and then lay across his chest, kissing him forcefully while guiding his hand to her breasts.

As always, Anne knew what she was doing, and Jim, even if he wanted to, would have been unable to thwart her caressing. After her hands and lips had succeeded in exciting him, she withdrew to remove her gown and rolled to her back to receive him. But Jim moved to the side of the bed and swung his legs to the floor, burying his head in his hands.

"That's not exactly big league, is it?" she protested.

Jim said nothing.

"I tell you what," Anne said cheerfully. "I'll go break open a bottle of champagne, and we can have a party. Maybe we'll even last until sunrise the way we used to. When's the last time we did that?"

Jim lifted his head and stared at the ceiling. "Please, not just now. There're too many things weighing on me."

Anne gave an exaggerated sigh. She pulled her nightgown back over her and slipped under the covers.

"Let me ask you something," Jim said. "Suppose you were in a situation where you had two choices. With one, there'd be a rough time of it with a lot of risk that you might fall on your face. With the other, there'd be a greater chance of success without as much effort, but you'd cause harm to another person, great harm, let's say. What would you do?"

Anne had turned on her side away from him, and her response was partly muffled by her pillow. "Jim, what in the hell are you talking about? You're sounding as crazy as your father."

"What I mean is that I thought I learned something in London," he said. "I came home with the understanding that running the company was a terrible responsibility not only for your own sake but for all of those who worked for you. And it's been only since Pa disappeared that I've come to see it just isn't that clear-cut and easy. It seems there's no decision you make that doesn't have an adverse effect on somebody: the people you compete against, the men who work for you or these new investors who've trusted you with their money. It's like you're in the middle of a triangle, and each time you move toward one side, you move away from the other two." He was still seated on the edge of the bed, staring distantly toward the ceiling.

"Just before you came up," he continued, "I was looking at some old pictures of Grandpa, and I got to wondering how he'd handle this sort of thing. Everybody knows he was a son of a bitch, but at the same time he took care of his people. He put men to work, and no matter how much he exploited their labor, at least he gave them the means to put food on their tables, something they couldn't do in the old country

355

and something, dammit, we haven't been doing today. Do you know what I mean?" He looked at her. Anne was sleeping.

Jim rose from the bed and turned off the light. He went downstairs to pour himself a drink, knowing that without it he would be unable to sleep. He drank the bourbon straight, no ice, no water, and the first few swallows felt warm in his stomach. The thoughts that had haunted him since he had picked up that ragged, musty company history book began to loosen their hold on him during the fifteen minutes it took him to empty his glass. He refilled it and slouched in one of the parlor's easy chairs.

It was not unusual for Jim to have a nightcap before retiring, but it was rare for him to go beyond that, as he did now, drinking by himself in the darkened parlor for more than an hour. When he had consumed the last drop of what had remained in the bourbon bottle, he returned upstairs, stumbling twice as he made his way to the bedroom.

From the sound of her breathing, Jim knew Anne was still sleeping. He walked to their bed and stood over her, looking down on her shadowy curled figure in the dim moonlight seeping through the window. His vision was blurred from the bourbon, and he swayed back and forth. There she was, the banker's daughter. Not a worry in the world except, perhaps, what she would wear to the next tea. Children? Too much trouble. Purpose in life? Finding a man to support her in the style to which she was accustomed. Coal? Live off the profits but never give one thought to the problems of mining it or selling it. She didn't respect coal, nor the men who gave life and limb and breath to extract it. Not a chance. In many ways, he had used her, just as his tutor Preston in London had instructed. But she had used him. She had set a trap. With neither protest nor hesitation he had fallen into it. And this, the figure nestled into the sheets before him, was what he had got for it.

He unfastened his robe and let it fall to the floor. With an intentional lack of gentleness, he threw back the sheet and blanket and fell into bed next to Anne. The movement startled her from her sleep.

"What are you doing?" she asked in an urgent and confused voice.

He paid her question no attention and ripped off her nightgown. When she attempted to protest, he covered her mouth with the palm of his hand. He rolled on top of her, using his feet to scissor open her legs, and forcibly took her in a frenzy of violent movement.

When he had finished, he remained on top of her. Then a curtain of gray fell over him, uncoupling one thought from the next until his eyelids felt heavy. He dropped off into an alcohol-induced stupor and was only vaguely aware that Anne had pushed his nude body off her, reached down for the blanket and covered them both.

Bonnie and the doctor were treating an injured miner when they heard the door to the clinic open. In a moment a face appeared around the screen that blocked off the treatment area.

"Excuse me, Doctor, but I was wondering if we might speak for a few minutes," Jim said. Snowflakes lingered in his hair and eyelashes and his nose was red with cold, but his face was drawn and pale. It looked as if he were lacking sleep.

"Of course," Spencer replied. "We'll be free in a moment or two. Mr. Vickers here got too close to one of those continuous miner machines, but the cut on his arm looks worse than it actually is—didn't cause any lesions to the muscle tissue."

When he had finished, Spencer surveyed the waiting area. There were two patients seated on the bench. "There's nothing that looks too urgent out there," he said to Jim. Motioning toward a chair at the side of his small desk, he added,

"Why don't you take a seat there and we can talk?"

Bonnie was cleaning the examining table. "I'll be out of your way in a minute," she said.

"No," Jim said. "Please stay—that is, if the doctor doesn't mind."

Spencer shrugged. Bonnie moved behind him, resting against a cabinet, and inspected Jim. The years had produced no hint of a stoop to his posture. Despite his weariness, he appeared as imposing as ever. And also as strong. Jim probably could still pull his share of work in a mine shaft. The scar on his face from the war was barely visible, and although there were the beginning of crow's-feet at the corners of his eyes, they added to his rugged handsomeness. His hair was as full and lustrous as it was the day he came home from the war.

Bonnie felt embarrassed in his presence, regretting her encouraging words to him at the arts and crafts fair. She had dropped her defenses and spoken without thinking, and almost as soon as she had uttered her words urging him to save his company, she regretted them. Now, each time Jim glanced toward her, she averted her eyes.

Vickers had finished putting on his shirt. "I suggest you stay away from work for a few days, Mr. Vickers, and give that wound some clean air and sunshine to help it heal," Spencer told the middle-aged miner.

"Can't, Doc. Can't do that," Vickers said.

"Why not?"

The miner looked sheepishly at Jim. The presence of the mineowner obviously made him feel awkward. Bonnie became angry. By all rights, the doctor should have asked Jim to leave, giving the miner the privacy that was his due. But then it struck her that Spencer knew what was coming and wanted Jim to hear it.

"Why not, Mr. Vickers? Why can't you stay out of the mines for a day or two?" the doctor asked.

"I can't afford it, Doc. You know that. If the work's there,

I've got to take it. Otherwise, we don't eat."

"What'll happen if he works with his arm like that?" Jim asked Spencer.

"Most likely an infection. At the very least, the cold and damp air will extend the healing period by weeks," the physician replied.

Jim hesitated for a moment, then turned to the miner and said, "Mr. Vickers, you take the time off like the doctor instructed you. You don't want to jeopardize that arm—if you did, you'd be of no help either to yourself or to the company."

"But, Mr. Porter, I told you I can't afford it. We're in debt up to our eyeballs already," Vickers protested.

"You don't worry about that. You leave that to me," Jim said, authority in his voice.

"I don't understand. . . ."

"You'll be paid, Vickers. Don't worry now. Just get your arm back in shape. Then I'll get my dollar's worth out of you."

Vickers appeared stunned. He walked from the clinic, shaking his head as if trying to snap himself out of a dream.

"We can hold the other patients now," Spencer said after Vickers had departed. The doctor and Bonnie both looked at Jim, waiting for him to state the reason for his unprecedented visit.

Jim cleared his throat. "Do you remember once you went to my father and showed him some records you were keeping about what you called the black lung disease?"

"I do," Spencer replied. "I remember it well, and I can tell you the statistics haven't changed. In fact, there's even a more significant trend now. I can show them to you if you'd like."

"That won't be necessary. I don't need exact numbers. I just want you to explain the disease to me. For what I have in mind, I want to be fully briefed because of the arguments I'm sure to get."

"Better than my just talking, let me show you," the physician said, rising and walking to a wall-mounted cabinet. Inside was a large bell jar which was tightly sealed and filled with formalin. It also contained the remains of a tarlike lung Spencer had removed in autopsy from a man afflicted with the miner's disease.

Bonnie watched Jim's face twist into a grimace when he saw the specimen. Observing his revulsion, Spencer spared no punches in repeating the pitch that had failed with Jim's father. "As you can see, the coal dust works its way right into the tissue. In a healthy person who doesn't smoke, this lung would be almost pink. But the embedded coal particles push themselves right into the cells. The cell becomes disabled, another cell the miner can't use. He literally suffocates—very slowly. In the end, his lungs struggle to breathe, but he gets little oxygen from them . . . and he dies."

The ugliness of the specimen and the horror of the disease it symbolized were having their impact. Jim stared at the jar, twisting it in a complete circle before returning it to the doctor. "I believe you told my father there were some measures that could be taken concerning this disease," he said.

"That's right. We still can't reverse the damage, but once the disease is spotted now, we have more and more techniques to halt its spread and train the miner to breathe more efficiently with what healthy tissue he has remaining," Spencer said. He then described briefly some of the new devices that had been developed for inhalation therapy.

Jim still had questions. "What can be done in the mine itself?"

Spencer told him there were experts who could be consulted in this area but he himself was aware of two precautions now being taken in some mines. "The new machines spray water in front of them, as I'm sure you know, but that's not enough. In some mines they periodically spray the entire working area with water. But that requires first a more elaborate water distribution system within the mine and also the shutdown time for the actual spraying."

Jim rose from his chair. "I want to thank you. I expect that Bob Allen will give me an argument on all this. You know, 'cost analysis.' That's what he calls it. Will you sit down with him if I need you?"

"Certainly," Spencer said.

Jim stopped when he reached the door. "I don't want to make you any promises, Doctor," he said, "but we seem to be getting our company back on its feet. Work is picking up, and if this trend continues, we might be able to give you some help in getting yourself another building." Jim didn't wait for a response. He simply nodded, closed the door and went on his way through the falling snow.

Spencer and Bonnie looked at each other. "I don't believe I heard that," she said. "And even though I did hear it, I don't believe a word of what he said. A Porter doesn't do anything unless there's some self-serving motive behind it."

"Oh, I don't know," the doctor replied, walking her out of earshot of the two waiting patients. "I've been hearing things that tell me Jim Porter is not at all like his father, quite the opposite in fact."

"Like what?"

Her tone was challenging. Spencer smiled at her. "My, you are the suspicious sort."

"And with good cause," she shot back.

"Well, first I heard he made arrangements for some kind of pension for that Nelson family. You know, the fellow who died in a roof collapse."

"Big deal," Bonnie said. "The public relations value of that gesture alone offsets the few measly dollars he's probably sending that widow."

"And then I heard that once a month a mysterious envelope arrives at the county old folks' home for Ernie Jason. The director told me it contains cash to give the old guy some spending money, and there's never a return address on the envelope. The director's sure, however, that it comes from Jim Porter."

Bonnie thought of Ernie Jason. He had become almost totally disabled with lung trouble and had been confined to the county home for more than six months. Bonnie had visited him two or three times, and the attendants had told her she was his only visitor. Everyone else in town had forgotten him, everyone, that is, except the anonymous donor, who apparently was Jim Porter. Maybe Spencer was right. Maybe Jim, unlike his father, backed up at least some of his promises with action and did so without seeking adulation and glory. But then she thought of other Porter victims: T. C. Fenner, bent in shame at not having a job; Duke, struggling to master an artificial limb; Liz, her expression permanently etched with worry; Mari, a child asking what had happened to her father; Lou Greentree, Will Thomason and a hundred other good men stripped of any say in the course their lives had taken; and finally herself, a woman whose girlhood hopes vanished on the day she overheard a conversation and came to understand that she had been betrayed. "No," she said to the doctor, "I don't think anything has changed with the Porter family."

She leaned against the window sill. "I never told you this before, but seeing the snow out there reminded me of it," she said. "It was right after I started working for you. At night I used to wait outside the company store in Porterville for my pa to come home from the mine. Sometimes Crawford would give him a lift to town and let him off at the store. That's what happened that night. Well, it was snowing like it is now, and the snow made it tough for Pa to walk, and with the wind we both had trouble seeing. We had just turned the corner to walk up the hollow to home when we noticed a woman on the railroad tracks. She had a thick scarf wrapped over her head and around her chin, and she was wearing a heavy winter jacket. Her dress came to just below the knees and was flapping in the wind. Bright red stockings protected her lower legs. She didn't notice us as we watched her walk along the rails, reaching through the snow for small chunks of coal that had spilled from the trains. She dropped them into an old banged-up bucket, and the pail was nearly full. It was so heavy she tilted to the side, and since she had no gloves, we knew that freezing handle had to be cutting into her bare hand. It was not until we got within about ten yards of her that Pa and I simultaneously recognized her." Bonnie paused. "It was my ma."

She turned away. "My pa couldn't believe it. 'What are you doing?' he asked. My mother told him that we were running low on coal, and she thought she'd get some, that's all." Spencer moved to Bonnie's side and placed a hand on her shoulder. "Can you imagine that? Scavenging for pieces of coal in the heart of the richest coalfields in the world?" Her voice changed; her tone became stern, almost hostile. "Maybe Jim Porter did give the Nelson widow a pension. Maybe he does send Ernie pocket money. Maybe he does want to do something about black lung disease. But somebody must pay a price for a century of exploitation and neglect. And something must be done to make sure it doesn't happen again."

They stared into each other's eyes for a moment. Spencer squeezed her shoulder. "Come on," he said. "We've got patients waiting. Work before vengeance."

She smiled and then walked to the screen to summon the next patient.

CHAPTER 13 ─────────────

Jim was in a hurry at breakfast. He had a luncheon appointment scheduled later at the new Coal County Trap and Skeet Club, and a pile of work was waiting for his attention at the office before that. He was almost too preoccupied with thoughts of business to notice that Anne was not herself. She was much too considerate and pleasant in a way he had not seen since the very early days of their marriage.

"Did you sleep well, darling?" she asked when she joined him at the breakfast table. He looked at her quizzically. She was smiling.

"Fine, dear. Just fine," he said.

"Marie," she called to the maid, "Mr. Porter is ready for his juice and coffee." She turned to Jim. "How would you like your eggs today? Is scrambled okay?" Jim nodded. "Marie, make it scrambled for Mr. Porter. And a good helping of that Canadian bacon we bought last week."

Jim rubbed his eyes. He was not yet fully awake and was

confused about his wife's unusually good nature. Normally she sat mute at breakfast, unless she had a complaint to raise or a warning to issue.

"Darling, I was planning to go into Bannerton this morning for a meeting with the florist. I have some arrangements to make for our club. Is that okay with you?"

Jim stared at her suspiciously. "Of course," he replied, thinking surely there had to be an angle. Anne seldom did anything without having an angle, but he couldn't guess what this one might be.

He finished his breakfast and politely declined the maid's offer of another cup of coffee. "I've got some business to attend to," he told Anne. "I'll be at the office most of the morning."

"Come here, Jim," she said. He hesitated, but she continued, "Oh, come on over here next to your wife for a moment." When he moved to her side, she reached up and gently pulled his face to hers. She kissed him on the cheek. "Have a good day, dear. I'll see you tonight. Maybe we'll get together, if you know what I mean." She tried to smile seductively.

When she released him, he nodded and fled from the breakfast area. Whatever she was up to would have to wait—there were too many other problems to deal with. And although his curiosity was aroused, he really didn't care what Anne did anymore. Their marriage had grown irrevocably shallow and mechanical, and there was no hope of restoring any meaningful communications between them, except, perhaps, during their less and less frequent sessions in bed. Anne still knew what she was doing.

The luncheon meeting at the Trap and Skeet Club had been arranged by Raymond Baxley, who was a charter member. The club was created by a group of oil company men who had moved to the area to oversee the coal properties taken over by their firms. Baxley, who could not be present for the meeting, arranged for Jim and his two guests, mine-owners from Cardiff City, to have full membership privileges, and the three of them spent the first hour of their get-together at the range.

"Pull!" Jim shouted. From beneath a cluster of small bushes, a black and yellow clay pigeon shot into the air. He raised his shotgun to his shoulder, followed the disk as it spun higher and higher and then triggered a shot just as the target reached the apex of its arc. The circle of buckshot was right on target. The pigeon disintegrated, sending a spray of splinters and chips to the snow.

"Pull!" Jim shouted again, and blasted another of the disks for a total of twenty-four hits in twenty-five throws.

"Not bad. Not bad at all," said one of the mineowners, Red Hanley.

"That's for sure," said Vance Jackson, the other.

The three were about equal as marksmen and had shot well that morning.

The club operated out of a plush lodge where members could pass the day playing chess, checkers or gin rummy. Or they could participate in any of a variety of shooting activities. In the fall, pheasants were stocked along a course that tested a marksman's alertness and agility. There were two target ranges, one inside for handguns and the other outside with provision for both short- and long-range shooting. There also was the large trapshooting range where the three were shooting, Jim recording the best score.

"Come on," he said. "Let's get a bite to eat."

The group handed their weapons to a staff member for cleaning and walked to the lodge. They took seats at an isolated table in the small dining area, a high-ceilinged room with walls of logs and a large stone fireplace in which a wood fire smoldered. Wild game dominated the menu, and the three agreed as a group to try the pheasant with wild rice. "Just watch out for the shot," Jackson warned. "I once almost lost a tooth that way."

Jim had enjoyed the shooting, but he was not under the illusion that recreation was the reason they were at the club on this day. The meeting's purpose was business. "These men have a proposal for you," Baxley had told him. "I'd suggest you give them a listen."

For the times the meeting was not unusual. In barbershops and mansion ballrooms, country clubs and churches, once fiercely independent mineowners were sounding one another out carefully as potential allies in a fight for their collective survival. At first the encounters involved little more than a sharing of information—how to deal with the invading oil-men and what pitch to give the union in the face of massive cutbacks. These hundreds of two- and three-man meetings led to a common line of defense that worked only briefly. When it failed, the talks took a different turn, and a new word began to dominate the industry's vocabulary: consolidation. By merging their operations in the rapidly shrinking market, mineowners could cut their overheads by thirds or halves while simultaneously pooling their sources of credit. As often as not, these mergers between two giant coal companies were accomplished by no more than a handshake at low-keyed conferences that had the pretense of being accidental. Ultimately, however, consolidation meant incorporation and other complicated forms of business financing and structure. This opened the door to at least minimal government monitoring, and for the first time in the coalfields, it seemed the lawyers and accountants controlled more of a company's direction than did its owners. This rubbed against the grain of many of the old-time owners, and they rejected it, opting instead to wage battle alone. Jim was in that category, but the two men from Cardiff City had a proposition for him that they insisted could prove worthwhile to all.

"I think it's time that each of us has to face the facts," said Jackson. "The domestic market is down, and there's no sign of it improving."

"That's for sure," Hanley agreed. "And the hell of it is

that it's not only gas and oil. People are talking of the age of nuclear energy now. If you believe them, someday there'll be no more coal-burning utilities."

Jackson took over again. "There are certain indicators that can't be ignored. Consider, as just one example, that before World War II we had a navy that moved on nothing but coal. Now you can't even sell the navy one stinkin' ton of coal." Jim smiled, hearing echoes of his father.

The pheasant had been served. Hanley finished cleaning the strands of dark meat from a small legbone and said, "What it means is a smaller pie for the entire industry. If each of us is going to survive, we'll have to fight for our rightful share of that pie. Now is there any sense in my fighting each of you?"

The discussion paused while the white-coated waiter served coffee.

"What I want to talk about here is Green Valley Electric," Jackson resumed. "We all know the amount of business that goes to that utility, and from what I hear Owens is in trouble with the contract. He apparently still has that Harrison fellow sewn up, but the rumor is there're rumblings back at his home office in Pennsylvania about the prices other utilities are getting while theirs is falling but only slowly."

Jim, who had remained silent throughout most of the discussion, was impressed with how articulate and crafty the other two men were. Although he had limited experience in such bargaining, he sensed his two visitors were about to unload their proposition.

Jackson cleared his throat. "Now the three of us are among the largest independent owners left in the state," he said. "We could bid against each other for Green Valley and cut our own throats while one of these oil companies sneaks in and steals the contract."

"That's right," Hanley interjected.

"What I have in mind is to enter bids and schedules at three different levels, hope one can win Green Valley and then share the work with each other," Jackson said, delivering his punch line. He paused for the idea to sink in. "A snake divided is a snake that's dead. My God, this is the way our country was founded. The key is cooperation."

Cooperation—or conspiracy to eliminate competition and fix prices? Jim asked himself. There was no denying the Porter Coal Company was still in trouble, and a long-time contract like Green Valley's would do much to stabilize its operation. But the morality of the proposition bothered him.

"What about John Owens?" Jim asked.

The two Cardiff City men appeared shocked. "I didn't think I'd ever see the day when a Porter would be concerned about the welfare of an Owens," Hanley said.

"But he's a local coalman. He didn't come from the oilfields," Jim protested.

"He's out of it anyway," Jackson quickly asserted in an effort to recover his momentum. "The Green Valley home office won't have him. It's just a question of whether some coalmen are going to get that business or those goddamned Texans who've been in here snapping up leases at bargain prices." He looked at Jim. "What do you say?" he asked, extending his hand for the handshake that, under mountain country mores, would seal their proposed agreement with more authority than that offered by any paper contract.

Jim refused the hand. He shook his head. He was repulsed by what he had heard, considering the proposed arrangement grossly unfair, if not illegal and immoral. "You've got the wrong Porter," he told the two other coalmen. "Maybe my father would have had a hand in this, but not me. I'll survive without stooping to such tactics." He rose from the table and tossed down his napkin.

"It's them or us, son," Hanley offered meekly as Jim walked away.

Jim thought of John Owens on the drive back to Porterville. Owens was not the scrapper that Augustus had been. He would not retaliate in kind. Even without the Porter company's participation, Jim suspected the conspiracy would succeed in stealing the Green Valley contract from Owens. The only question was whether Owens could survive it. Jim didn't know.

Jim slipped in the side door of the mansion. He was heading for the stairway to check on his mother when he passed the door to the parlor and heard Anne in soft conversation with a man. Moving toward them, he recognized the visitor as Andy LeGrande.

"Jim, darling, I didn't expect you home quite so soon," Anne said, rising from the sofa which she shared with the union man. "This is Andrew LeGrande," she said, sweeping a hand toward the visitor. "He's an official of the union."

"We've met," Jim said as Andy rose and extended a hand.

"You're a hard man to get to see," Andy said. "Your office hangs up on me each time I call, so I decided to try you at your home. I stopped by last week but missed you. Didn't Mrs. Porter tell you?"

"No, she didn't," Jim said coldly.

"Oh, I'm sorry, honey. I was busy choosing our new piano that day, and it completely escaped my mind," Anne said. "Well, I'll leave now so you two can conduct your business."

Jim motioned to Andy to sit and took a seat in an easy chair across from him. "What is it, Mr. LeGrande, that you want from me?" he asked sarcastically. "You can't even leave me at peace in my own home, can you?"

Andy stroked his beard with his fingertips. "Remember our last little talk, Porter, and how you walked right out on me? Well, the chickens have come home to roost. You might say I'm here simply out of courtesy."

"Go on," Jim ordered, his eyes never leaving those of the visitor.

"Andy LeGrande is about to begin his formal drive to organize your company, and from the feedback I've been getting, I don't think I'll have much trouble in getting the support I need. I'm giving you one last chance, friend. From what I know of your financing, I'm not sure your creditors would be happy about an outbreak of labor trouble. On the other hand, you and I could be sensible men and work out an amicable solution."

Jim knew there was enough anger and resentment among Porter miners now for LeGrande to win a substantial following. If so, he would in short time have the power to hamper operations at the Porter mines, if not close them down entirely. And the history of the labor movement in the coalfields made it inevitable that there would be violence and bloodshed of some sort, the only question being to what degree. Perhaps accommodating the union would be the best answer.

"I'm not about to put you on my payroll, LeGrande, so let's get straight on that from the beginning," Jim told him. "However, if you're talking about my stepping aside and permitting a simple certification election, then maybe we have something to talk about. There's nobody who wants to avoid a confrontation more than I do, but there are other considerations that you aren't aware of. I'll need some time to—"

"We don't need any time," a voice snapped emphatically from the parlor entrance. Jim and Andy turned toward the doorway. It was Sarah.

Wearing a long housecoat, her hair wrapped in a towel, she strode boldly toward the two men, her head held high and cocked slightly to the side. As she brushed past him toward Andy, Jim caught a whiff of her perfumed shampoo. She stood directly in front of the union man, her hands on her waist, and stared unblinkingly into his eyes. "There has been enough of this kind of talk in my house, young man. I am asking you to leave right now."

"Mother . . ." Jim said, but she raised a hand and stopped him.

Turning toward her son, she snapped, "I'm ashamed of you, son. Your father never would have allowed such a man in this house." She turned back to Andy. "My husband was against you people from the start, and even though he's gone, nothing's changed. There will be no union in the Porter Coal Company." She paused for effect, her posture and expression frozen. Andy shifted in his seat. "I think, young man, that it's best you leave."

Andy looked to Jim, who nodded. The union man rose from his seat slowly and ambled toward the door. There he turned around and said, "I understand your feelings, Mrs. Porter. But times have changed. Good day to you."

Sarah slammed the door behind him. "He may think he's smart, but he'll find out," she declared.

"Mother, I'm not sure it isn't time to—" Jim tried to say, but again she stopped him.

"There's nothing to discuss, son. And I'm still surprised at your even giving that man your time. Since your father left, I've stepped back and given you free rein to run the company. But I have to draw the line when it comes to this. We're not going to tarnish your father's memory by opening the door to that corrupt bunch of bandits." Jim's eyes widened in surprise, not at his mother's stance on the union issue—that was understandable—but at her reference to Augustus as if he were dead. It was the first time.

Sarah returned to the parlor. "Anyway," she continued, "we're especially not going to entertain any notion of the union on a day John Owens goes under."

"Ma, what do you mean?"

She sat and took a deep breath. "Ray Baxley called while you were out. The bankers met today. They pulled the rug from under Owens."

Jim knew, without elaboration, what bankers she was talking about. Five of them, each representing a different bank in the region, met periodically. They viewed this as normal business, although others with suspicious leanings might view their sessions as collusion bordering on criminal conspiracy. The practice had had its origin in the Depression, when the moneymen got together regularly to decide which banks would fold and which would survive.

"Ray said he opposed it, but the other four were unanimous that Owens had gone too far to recover," Sarah went on.

Jim could picture it, the bankers shaking their heads gravely while deciding John Owens's future. A vote for foreclosure, the calling in of the loans they had extended to him. If this were anywhere but Coal County, that might be the end of it. But mountain country businessmen never left a man with only one option. Formal foreclosure would be messy, not to mention embarrassing. There was no need for loss of face. Instead, Jim was sure, the bankers had found a buyer for the Owens firm before even beginning their discussion.

"Who's getting the company?" Jim asked.

"Lamon C. Hubbard," his mother replied.

"Hubbard? The lumberman?" Jim couldn't believe he had heard his mother right.

"Ray insists he's a good man."

"That may well be. But what does he know about coal? I don't think he's been near a mine in his life."

"Well, Ray says Hubbard's interested in coal, and with his timber operation, he's diversified enough so that he can get a very good credit line," Sarah said.

Jim was still stunned. "In effect, what they've done is kick out Owens for a man who wouldn't know soft coal from cotton. That's not right. I don't care what kind of trouble Owens was in. He's a coalman, dammit."

Sarah leaned forward. "I don't think we should be worrying about John Owens," she said. "Ray also warned me that some of that banking group aren't looking too kindly on us. He told me to be very, very careful."

But Jim's mind was still on Owens. So that's how it ends. A secret meeting of five bankers, a murmuring discussion leading to a consensus and a man was out of business. A coalman did not own his mine; the bankers did. It was they who ultimately decided who would survive. It had always been this way since the first bearded, toothless mountain fool put his pickax to the side of a hill. Even in death, the bankers were there to keep tabs on their investments. Whenever an old-time mineowner died, the creditors were massed at his home even before a casket was measured, probing with delicate questions to determine if his heirs were capable of carrying on. But they retained the pretense of being gentlemen, no matter how sharp their pencils. They always made it a point to take care of the widow.

John Owens was out of the coal business. It seemed impossible. In a very real sense his departure marked the end of an era. Owens's father and Jim's grandfather had been responsible for the development of the region. They had taken the risks and withstood the pressures while nurturing their fledgling companies into large, successful enterprises which provided jobs for hundreds of others. Now only the Porter dynasty remained.

The bankers no doubt had seen to it that Owens would get a fair price. But they had stripped him of his company. For many coalmen, that was as good as taking their life.

"What are you up to, Andy? You look like a banker," Bonnie said when she walked into the Bannerton union office and found the organizer sitting behind a desk, holding the *Wall Street Journal*.

"Just some more news from our friends at OPEC," he told her.

OPEC. A few months earlier, Bonnie had never heard the term. A group of nations, mostly Arab, had banded together as the Organization of Petroleum Exporting Countries. The newspapers referred to it by its acronym—OPEC. Television newscasters pronounced it "oh-peck." Few Americans had ever heard of it, and of those who had, few paid it significant attention. The Middle East was so far, far away. What possible effect could those strange men with wrappings around their heads have on the life-style and economy of this country?

Andy knew otherwise. What struck him first, he told Bonnie and anyone else who would listen, was that the organization was really a cartel. It would be comparable to the governors of West Virginia, Pennsylvania, Virginia and Indiana meeting monthly to pursue the common interests of coal-producing states. The words "common interests" really meant money, and Andy had warned that it would only be a matter of time before the oil cartel began subduing competition among its members and inflating prices. Then it happened. The Arabs instituted a smoothly organized embargo. Oil prices soared, and "oh-peck" entered the world's everyday vocabulary.

Andy talked incessantly about the Arabs and their action, but few who heard him were interested.

"So the price of gas goes up. With my old heap, it makes no difference," one miner told him.

"You listen to Andy LeGrande," he shot back. "You fools haven't seen anything yet. Someday it isn't going to make any difference how many aircraft carriers you have, how many tanks, how many rockets. If you don't have the gas, you're going to be at the mercy of those steely-eyed bastards with their adolescent mustaches and the pillowcases on their heads."

He warned that when it came to basic commodities, no market was isolated. Whether it was wheat, iron ore, coffee or coal, regional markets were intertwined, worldwide in their scope, and what happened in Iran might well have an effect in Toledo, Ohio. There had been an economic basis to both world wars, Andy declared, and the action by the Arab world frightened him; whenever world markets shook from some party's unilateral action, bloodshed seemed destined to follow.

Listening to Andy's raging on the subject, Bonnie drew a vengeful satisfaction from the country's energy predicament; had not modern society so rudely and abruptly dismissed its use of coal, it might have had a ready alternative to oil. As it was, overnight switchovers by oil-consuming industries to alternative fuels were impossible—coal-burning equipment had long been scrapped, and unexpected problems had developed in the expansion of nuclear energy.

Nuclear energy. Andy laughed whenever he heard the word. "Do you know," he asked, "that these madmen with their slide rules once predicted that nuclear reactors would one day power airplanes the way they do ships at sea? And why not cars? Why not go all the way?"

The OPEC action had brought about drastic changes: Speed limits were lowered, and rationing tickets secretly printed. But what effect it would have on the coal industry was unclear even to Andy. So many domestic oil companies already held coal properties that it was possible the two industries would, in effect, merge. Andy knew only that the oil firms would selfishly guard their profits—this he himself had witnessed—and that the spiraling oil prices would somehow someday have an effect on the price of coal. When that happened, he warned, change would once again come to Coal County.

At the moment Bonnie was not interested in OPEC. "I just stopped by to tell you I'm heading out to that Ratliff clan today," she said. "I don't know when I'll be back."

"And you just might be interested to know that I stopped by to see Porter yesterday," he said.

"You did? What happened?"

"Nothing, unfortunately. I was informing him of our plans, and he seemed to be listening, but then his mother came down and all but kicked me out."

"I guess it stands to reason that Sarah Porter would follow in the footsteps of her husband. It's too bad. Just means there'll be more victims of Porter obstinacy. We have another one in the clinic right now, and he isn't doing so well."

"Who's that?" Andy asked.

"Ernie Jason. The old guy who used to handle the mail. He has emphysema and is struggling for each breath, the poor man. He's gotten so bad we thought we'd better get him out of that old folks' home and into the clinic where the doctor can watch him. He pushed a bed into a corner, and some of the women from the church volunteered to nurse him around the clock. At least the oxygen tent can make things a little easier for him." She walked toward the door. "I'll see you tomorrow, I guess. Don't ruin your eyes with all that reading."

Andy laughed. "You worry about yourself, and be very careful on those mountain roads. And keep Chester's hands off you. He might try to make you his next wife."

Chester Ratliff had been a Porter miner for most of his life. He was a thin man of average build and height, but it was said in the mines that he had the strength of two men. Rules notwithstanding, he had still pulled an occasional work shift past his sixty-fifth birthday. Bonnie believed him now to be well into his seventies. His large family included fourteen sons and daughters, many of them still children, who were born to his fourth wife, a woman in her early thirties. Although he had been employed by the Porter company, Ratliff did not live in Porterville. His ancestry stretched back for four generations in West Virginia. Ratliffs were loners, mountain folk who avoided the company town and resided in seclusion in a small, closely knit colony in a remote section of the Coal County foothills. True to their own tradition of independence, they distrusted physicians. But one young daughter had heard about Bonnie and approached her one day with an appeal for help for her father, who apparently was very sick, perhaps dying. The daughter had said her father would flatly refuse to visit the clinic and asked

377

if Bonnie perhaps could visit him at their homestead. She had to go alone, that being the only hope that the old man would accept any medical attention.

After leaving the union office, Bonnie hopped into a jeep she had borrowed for her journey to the Ratliffs'. Eleven miles outside Bannerton, she turned off the county road and slowly maneuvered the four-wheel-drive vehicle up a narrow pathway etched into the mountainside. She guided the jeep as deep into the woods as she could until even it could no longer pass through the briars, rock and overgrown brush. She began walking the rest of the way up the winding, barely visible trail leading to the cluster of weatherworn shacks which the Ratliffs claimed as their homes. No one knew how long the family had been living on this same spot. They had been there for as long as anyone could remember, occupying a sliver of flatland on property owned by the Owens Coal Company. John Owens had left the Ratliffs alone. Bonnie doubted if the new owner, Lamon C. Hubbard, was aware that they lived on land that was now his.

With the weather either hot or cold, Chester Ratliff was never seen without his bulky bearskin wrapping, so it was difficult to determine the state of his aging body. His straggly gray beard extended down to his belly, and the unkempt strands of knotted hair that fell from beneath his coonskin cap reached nearly to the small of his back. Since he no longer worked at all in the mines, people outside his immediate family saw him no more than once a year. Each encounter touched off another round of tales and rumors about the reclusive clan that lived on the mountain. Where Chester had found his current wife was unclear and the county education officers were too afraid of him to challenge him about the uninterrupted truancy of his school-age children. What was known was that no other living man in Coal County knew the temperament of the mountains as intimately as he, a fact that by itself kept intruders out.

Bonnie was aware of this, and Chester's known hostility

to visits from outsiders sent a wave of fear through her with each step she took through the brush. But she had made a promise to Chester's daughter, and the least she could do was try. Her best guess was that she had about two miles to walk from where she had left the jeep to the Ratliff compound, but she had never made the trip and was uncertain of the clan's exact location. She suddenly knew she was there, however, when, after she had rounded a bend, a gunshot rang out, grazing a boulder to her side.

"Chester! Hold it! It's Bonnie Fenner," she shouted, throwing her arms into the air with the suspicion that the old man's shot had missed her only because he had intended it that way. At least she now knew he was able to get up and around, an encouraging sign.

"You jist keep yer hands in the air, come slowlike and state yer business," Ratliff ordered, dropping another round into the chamber of his deer rifle.

"I've heard you're not well, Chester. I just want to talk to you about it," Bonnie said, advancing slowly.

"That's enough," the old man shouted, raising the barrel of his rifle when Bonnie came within ten yards of him. "Why you botherin' me?"

"Your family is worried about you," she replied. "And look—I brought you some whiskey." Bonnie reached into her black bag and removed a pint-sized bottle of bourbon, which she raised above her head.

"Make it two bottles, and we can talk," Ratliff said, grinning sufficiently to display his blackened, rotting teeth.

Bonnie laughed. She had anticipated that the mountain man would bargain with her and had brought along two pints. She reached back into the bag, withdrew the other and handed the pair over to him.

After Chester laid his rifle against a tree, the nearby shacks began to empty of other members of the clan. Men and women, children and grandchildren, moved sheepishly and tentatively toward them. Bonnie counted sixteen of them before she stopped. The daughter who had approached her was among them, but Bonnie made no show of recognition. Instead, she moved closer to Chester and began examining as much of him as his heavy clothing revealed. There was a pale, glassy quality to his skin and a shallowness to his eyes, ominous signs. He opened one of the bottles and began taking large swallows from it as she reminded him that she was Duke Shaw's daughter and explained that she was now a nurse. He did not protest when she opened his bearskin garment and the tattered shirt underneath it and examined his sagging folds of skin. He was clearly dehydrated and appeared extremely weak despite his show of defending his compound. There was no one precise symptom to signal the nature of his illness, but Bonnie had little doubt what it was: a failing heart. She had seen the subtle exterior signs of the disease too many times.

"I think you're a very, very sick man, Chester," she told him, speaking softly and noticing that every other member of the clan was silent, waiting apprehensively for her words. "I strongly urge you to go see the doctor in Bannerton. I'm not sure, but I think he might be able to help you—maybe with an operation."

Ratliff took another swig from the open bottle and then spit to the ground. "Like hell I'll see some witch doctor. There's nothing wrong with me. Strong as I ever was and still every inch a man. Just take a look at my missus there." He pointed to a woman Bonnie had assumed to be a daughter or a daughter-in-law. The woman's protruding belly verified her advanced state of pregnancy.

"These diseases can be tricky," Bonnie tried again. "You can feel fine for a month, and then boom"—she clapped her hands—"you're flat on your back. Won't you please come see the doctor? I promise you he won't do anything you don't want. And there'll be no charge." Bonnie noticed the pleading eyes of the young girl who had summoned her. But

Bonnie's urging failed. Ratliff raised one of his heavily scarred, blackened hands to pat the top of her head.

"You're a pretty young un," he said gently. "And I'm plenty grateful fer yer worry. But ya should go on home now. Thar's nothin' here fer ya ta do." He dropped his hand, turned and walked slowly away. One by one, the rest of the clan followed, the girl who had approached Bonnie leaving last, nodding subtly to Bonnie in gratitude for her try.

While Bonnie was off in the mountains meeting with the Ratliffs, Dr. Gordon Spencer drove to the Red Fox Mine to meet with Jim Porter. It had been some time since the physician had last visited the Red Fox, and he found it unusually active, men and equipment everywhere. Jim spotted his car and rushed to greet him. After they shook hands, Spencer recalled that one of his first visits to the Red Fox had come when he was forced to sever Duke Shaw's leg deep within the mine's darkened interior. There no longer were any visible signs remaining of that disaster. The collapsed heading had been sealed, and a new one tunneled along a parallel path to replace it. The accident, the doctor commented, seemed forgotten despite the seven corpses still buried in the rubble.

Jim liked Spencer and often wondered what his relationship was with Bonnie. Surely her beauty had to distract him from his surgery on occasion—look at the interest she had sparked in Hubbard.

Jim handed the physician a safety helmet and escorted him by a railcar six miles into the mine. They stopped at a site where a continuous miner, painted bright yellow, was in operation, chewing at the face of coal like an oversized locust. Jim, unable to speak above the noise, pointed to the front of the machine where a battery of nozzles directed a steady spray of water into the air. When the machine stopped, Jim explained that the machine had been fitted with a water system providing more than double the volume of spray previously available.

"Every twenty minutes or so we shut the thing down, and a safety inspector checks the air with a special meter. If the air's too dirty, we call the men out. If not, they stay. But in either case, we hose the entire area down," he said.

As they headed for another chamber, Jim pointed out how the walls of the shaft had been painted with a layer of whitewash to keep the dust down. The other room was a few yards away and was separated from the work area by a sheet of yellow canvas serving as a barrier to flying particles. Inside, the floor was covered with wooden planking to prevent boots from kicking up additional dust. The room's ceiling and walls also were painted white.

"We juiced up the water spray, put in the hoses and painted the walls almost right after I spoke to you at the clinic," Jim told the doctor. "I've been meaning to show it all to you but just haven't had the time. This room we're in now is the latest antidust measure—the dinner hole. We've got them in every heading for the men to take their food breaks away from the work areas. As you can see, the air is as clear as a spring day in the mountains."

"That's terrific, Jim," Spencer said. "It must have cost you a lot of money."

"After what you showed me, we really didn't have a choice. And I want you to keep me posted on any other ideas you get about fighting black lung. I've read where they're experimenting with face masks and spacesuits. If these work, I want to know about them."

"Actually, I just got a packet of black lung material from the government in the mail. If you'd like, I'll have it delivered to you."

"Look," Jim said, "I'm headed for Bannerton anyway. Why don't I follow you and take a look now?"

"Sure," the doctor replied.

* * *

Ernie Jason, fighting for each breath, was resting on the hospital bed Bonnie and the doctor had managed to squeeze into a corner of the clinic behind a screen. She had just finished checking his oxygen system when she heard the door open. She found Spencer holding the door for Jim Porter. Bonnie knew the look on her face betrayed her surprise.

"I didn't expect you back so soon. How did it go?" Spencer asked.

"Not very well, I'm afraid. That old man won't trust anyone, and he looked pretty bad off to me. But who knows? Maybe his family will go to work on him. It wouldn't surprise me too much to see him walk in here someday," she said.

"Well, Jim and I spent a couple of hours at the Red Fox. You should see all the measures he's taken to cut down on the dust," the doctor said.

Bonnie smiled. "That's good to hear. But I have to wonder if for most of these men it isn't too late."

"Perhaps it is," Spencer responded. "But at least it will cut down the risk for the new generation. You can't blame the mining companies for what happened in the past—we just didn't know."

"Of course," she replied, her tone apologetic. "It's just that it's such a horrible way to die."

"Jim stopped by to look over some material I have on black lung," Spencer said, escorting his visitor to his desk.

"Actually," Jim said, "that's not why I'm here."

Bonnie and the doctor both looked at him curiously.

"The reason I came is to tell both of you I've found a way to help you at least partially finance the building of a new clinic. All you have to do is find some other company to come up with the rest, and you're in business."

Spencer was beaming. "I can't believe I'm hearing this," he said. "You have no idea how much we need a new facility."

Bonnie looked at Jim suspiciously. Was it a coincidence

that the Porter company just happened to find the money for a contribution to a new clinic on the day after Andy warned of the upcoming union campaign? She was weighing whether to remark on this when suddenly a loud clap came from behind the screen blocking off the clinic's one bed. It was a flat noise but powerful enough to rattle the clinic's windows. The three of them rushed toward the screen.

"Oh, my God!" Bonnie cried, looking at the bed. "I tried to warn him. I warned him a dozen times."

The plastic oxygen tent over the severely ill man had melted, and his face and upper torso were seared with second- and third-degree burns. At the side of his pillow, burning a hole into the bed sheet, was a freshly lit cigarette.

"Let's get going on him—fast!" Spencer ordered, slapping an oxygen cup over Jason's blistered lips.

They began the emergency procedures that were the only hope for saving Jason's life and worked on him feverishly for a half hour, but to no avail. With one last rattling gasp, Jason died. Bonnie covered the dead man's face with a sheet. She and the doctor then walked around the screen to where Jim was waiting.

"We lost him," Spencer told him. "I guess I'd better notify the county." He moved to the telephone at his desk.

"Three times I took those cigarettes from him, and each time I warned him that you can't smoke in an oxygen tent. But he wouldn't listen," Bonnie said, fighting back her tears.

Jim walked over to her and placed a hand on her shoulders. "It wasn't your fault. You warned him just like you said. There was nothing else you could do."

Feeling light-headed and fearing she would faint, Bonnie found herself involuntarily collapsing into Jim's arms. She began sobbing.

After Spencer hung up the phone, Jim suggested that Bonnie be allowed to go home. "I'll take her. I'm heading back to Porterville anyway," Jim said.

Spencer nodded. Jim, with his arm around Bonnie, escorted her out of the clinic and to his car.

She sat huddled against the car door for the entire trip, her head buried in her hands. This was unlike her. Working for Spencer, she had witnessed death in many forms, helped treat scores of the most grotesque injuries and displayed only the slightest emotion. But never before had she felt responsible for a patient's setback or death, and at the time of Ernie Jason's freak demise, she was still shaky from her experience with Chester Ratliff and his deer rifle.

When they reached her home, Jim again took Bonnie's arm and led her to the door, which was unlocked. They found no one at home. Bonnie collapsed on the sofa. Jim sat beside her.

"It's such a terrible waste," she said softly, dabbing at her eyes.

"Excuse me?"

"Ernie Jason. He lived here all his life, and what did he have to show for it? Nothing but a squeaky old rocking chair which he wouldn't have had if it had been up to the company."

She was talking more to herself than to Jim. "Looking at him in that bed, his body all bony and crumpled, I tried to imagine how many times he had hauled those mail sacks, and all the time nobody much gave a damn. I bet ninety percent of the mail he carried was mail for the damn company. And in the end, he dies trying to enjoy one of the few pleasures he had left—a lousy cigarette." Her eyes, which had been focused in the distance, turned toward Jim. She sat upright and leaned forward. "You see them come to the clinic one by one, broken men with nothing to their names, their spirits vanquished and not even the slightest urge to go on. Human trash. We might just as well pile them up with the slag. They're about as useless as that, to themselves and their families." She went to the sink in the bathroom to pat cold water on her face. When she returned, she took a seat in a chair across from Jim. The water, although it had soothed her swollen eyes, had done nothing to cool the anger building within her. She pointed a finger at Jim as if she were jabbing him in the chest. "I don't know where your father is, and to be honest, I don't really care if he's alive or dead. But I only wish he could be around Porterville now to see all the harm his greed and insensitivity caused in men like Ernie Jason. My God, that poor man!" She· broke down again, her head falling to her hands. Jim moved over to her and placed a hand on her shoulder. But she abruptly pushed it away and jumped to her feet. "I hate you! Every one of you Porters!" she screamed.

"Wait a minute, Bonnie. Listen to reason," Jim said, taken aback by her outburst.

"Reason? What's more reasonable than just looking at the victims? There's my father. And then my husband. There's Thomason. And seven men never rescued from a roof fall. There was Nelson and poor John Owens. And now Ernie Jason. You can mount them as trophies in your den like stuffed pheasants or nail them up like pictures in some art gallery. And then, Jim, you can add me and my daughter, two more victims of the mighty Porters and their rush for power and money."

"Listen now," Jim snapped. "Just what did I or my father ever do to Mari?"

Bonnie lowered her head and muttered, "Just forget it."

Jim took one of her limp hands. "Can't you see, Bonnie? I'm trying to be your friend," he said softly. "I understand all the hate and anger you have built up inside you, but so many years have passed. This is a new age."

"Please," she said, her head still bowed, "just leave me alone."

Jim dropped her hand and moved slowly to the door. He looked back at her, but her position was unchanged. He left, closing the door gently. As he turned, he bumped into Mari.

"What the hell are you doing here?" she demanded. "Can't you get it through your thick head that all we want is for you and your kind to leave us alone?"

Jim smiled. "You might not believe it, and you probably can't understand, but your mother and I were once very close friends."

Mari hissed at him, "We all make mistakes, don't we?" Then she went inside.

Two weeks later, Jim was returning home from Bannerton when he found Robert Allen waiting at the front door. He went up to the porch to meet him.

"I've just been presented with a proposition that I think you ought to know about right away," Allen said.

"Come on in. You can brief me in the study."

Inside, Allen explained how he had been approached by a man named Joseph Romano representing a New York-based company called Landex International Incorporated and how the firm had set its eyes on acquiring the reserves of the Porter Coal Company. "They've done their homework," Allen said. "I don't know how, but they seem to know as much about our production and financing as you or I."

"Landex. God, that rings a bell with me," Jim said. "Well, it's the first of many."

"Excuse me?"

"The first of many," Jim repeated. "They'll be arriving now like horseflies at a picnic. I've been expecting it."

"What do you mean?"

"The oil raids all over again. After years of coal being next to worthless, this Arab business has made us important again. There are moneymen all over the world now looking at us, and what they are seeing is black gold. Well, the hell with them."

"I think I should emphasize that this guy said Landex was

387

prepared to meet any reasonable price you might set. He seemed to take the position that no matter what we did, he'd move in on us anyway," Allen said.

Jim thought for a few seconds. "How can he? We aren't vulnerable, are we?"

"The company's a public corporation now," Allen replied. "I suppose there's nothing to stop them from going around and buying up the stock we've issued. But as long as you still control more than fifty percent, I don't see how they can gain control merely through a stock raid. Of course, there are a few other ways. It depends on how much coal knowledge and imagination they have."

"Explain that, please."

Allen answered with a nonchalance that irritated Jim. "Oh, if they gained control of enough coal operations in this area, they could try to price you out—lower the price of their coal so much that you and any other holdout owners would be pushed to the brink of bankruptcy. Or they could go after your creditors, bribing them with new lucrative business in return for their turning off the spigots feeding you."

Jim mentally reviewed his company's financial status. Going public and issuing stock had raised a great amount of capital, but the firm still needed to borrow to help finance all the new machinery Allen had ordered. All the outstanding debts seemed manageable except for one loan—a $300,000 note from Raymond Baxley's bank that was due within the month. That would have to be extended. Baxley, despite the growing tension in Jim and Anne's marriage, had not interfered and could be counted upon, Jim thought. He was confident his father-in-law would even increase his support if the company were the object of a corporate raid.

"The fellow said his firm had become very interested in coal and intends to acquire as many reserves as it can get its hands on," Allen said.

"Landex International, is that what you said?" Jim asked.

"That's right. Landex International Limited."

Jim snapped his fingers. "I knew I had heard of it. It was in the paper a few weeks ago. Something about a grand jury in Charleston investigating Landex and a couple of other outfits."

"What for?" Allen asked.

"The mob. The federal government thinks they're arms of the mob."

"You mean the Mafia?"

"That's what the paper said."

"Holy shit," Allen said. "Who'd ever think they'd be interested in something down this way?"

"Well, whoever they are, Bob, you can just tell them no. The company's not for sale."

Allen nodded. "Whatever you say. But if I were you, I'd give it some thought."

"Why?"

"The industry's going to get mean and messy again. As you said, all the signs point to that. Selling would give you an opportunity to get out with a bundle of money. You could live in peace and not have to deal with it anymore. Of course, I would hate to see that happen out of my own selfishness. I happen to like my job. I was just thinking of you."

Jim smiled, believing Allen to be sincere. "Thank you, Bob. But my family's been in the coal business for three generations, and I'm not going to be the one to leave it. Not now."

Allen rose from his seat, preparing to leave the study. "There's just one more thing I think I should tell you," he said, pausing at the door.

"Yes?"

"I met with this Romano at the motel in Bannerton. When we were finished, he walked me out of his room and went to the bar. I couldn't see too well in the darkness, but he took a seat at a table across from another man. All I could make out was the back of his head. They were talking like they'd known each other for some time or had some kind of partnership or deal together. I suspect this guy's a local man legging for him, Jim. I'm sorry, but I didn't think it was wise to stick around to see who it was."

"I see," Jim said, rubbing his chin. "Well, thanks for telling me."

"Romano said he'd call me. I'll tell him your decision," Allen said. Jim escorted him to the door.

CHAPTER 14 _____

Fog rolled through the hollows and valleys almost every morning, and there had been a record amount of rain. Tourists had heard about ramps and now joined the mountain folk in their rite of spring. The ramps harvest was poor as a result —too many of the visitors failed to leave one plant standing in each patch so that the ramps would propagate the next year. And the sassafras tea used to wash down the ramps no longer tasted the same. A group of medical researchers had reported their suspicion that the root of the sassafras tree might be a cause of cancer. Few Coal County residents paid any attention to the warning, and there had been no noticeable cutback in the consumption of the tea, but it seemed to have a different, more bitter taste. In 1974 it was a depressing spring.

The fog had lifted by the time Bonnie arrived at the clinic, but the sky remained overcast and the wind was blowing. The dreariness of winter refused to relinquish its hold.

The new clinic was constructed of brick and cinder block, and unlike the shack formerly used, it did not sway with each breeze. Jim Porter had come through with his promised financial help, and Lamon C. Hubbard had also made a substantial donation—somewhat out of character—to make the new clinic possible. Once the money was available, the structure had been built in less than two months, largely through the volunteer help of dozens of miners. With its increased capacity, the clinic now was able to support a full-time registered nurse. Bonnie, who had never obtained a formal nursing license, assumed the role of administrator, handling the paperwork, ordering supplies and performing most of the other nonmedical tasks necessary to keep the clinic running smoothly.

Bonnie waited in Dr. Spencer's neatly furnished office for him to finish his rounds in the twelve-bed ward at the rear of the one-story building. Only four of the beds and one of the two private rooms were occupied. Bonnie pressed her face to the window. Through a cut in the hills she could view what had been a thick forest until the trees and brush had been taken away. Workmen were busy rolling the land, removing rocks and planting grass seed for the Coal County Country Club golf course. Like the Trap and Skeet Club, the golf course was primarily the project of out-of-town business executives who had come to Coal County as their firms took over various coal properties. It was the first golf course in the county. Bonnie watched a tractor pull a wide roller back and forth over the undulating land which someday would be a fairway. The construction made her sad; she already missed the trees.

She heard a noise at the door. Assuming it to be the doctor, she asked, "Do you want me to begin sterilizing now?"

"Not until you first say hello," came the response. It was Andy LeGrande.

"What are you doing here?" Bonnie asked. "I figured you'd be so busy today I wouldn't get to see you."

"Everything's as set as it could be," he replied. "So I thought I would brief you on it."

Andy, at last, was making a direct move against the Porter Coal Company. To kick it off, he had scheduled a large rally in the Porterville town square for that afternoon. Immediately following the rally, he planned to establish a picket line at one of the Porter mines. He had selected Cedar Ridge.

"Andy LeGrande has done it again," he told Bonnie. "We're going to have a good turnout today from the other companies."

"I should hope so after all the work you did with those men."

"It's not easy to convince men working at unionized companies that it's very much in their direct interest to organize elsewhere. But I think I pulled it off. We should have a hell of a crowd. Are you ready to sing?"

"Unless something happens around here, yes. But I still don't like the idea. I haven't sung in years, and I'm scared of an audience this big."

He moved closer to her. "Look, honey, there's nothing to be afraid of. Just strum a couple of those labor numbers I taught you, and pretend nobody's there. You'll do fine."

The doctor entered the room. "Oh, hi, Doc," Andy said. "I was just leaving. I'll give you back your little nurse."

"Don't go because of me," Spencer said.

"I've got a few things to check before our rally. You going to be there, Doc?"

Spencer shook his head. "Not unless I'm professionally required, which I hope won't be the case."

"Naw. Don't worry about that. These things are peaceful. I make sure of that," Andy said, smiling and departing.

Bonnie returned to the window. Spencer watched her for a moment and then asked, "Bonnie, is there anything wrong?"

"Oh, I'm sorry," she said, stepping away from the window pane. "Just daydreaming, I guess." She paused. "Actually, it's Mari, my daughter."

"What's happened? Nothing serious, I hope," he said.

"I don't know. All she does is mope around. Won't take a

393

job or go to school or even give me and my ma a hand around the house. I don't know what to do." Bonnie walked to the coffeepot kept in a corner of the office and poured herself a cup. She looked at Spencer to see if he wanted one, but he shook his head. "Then she started hanging around with this long-haired crowd. Fell right in with them and decided that I don't know what I'm talking about and neither do her grandparents. She started ranting and raving about capitalists and the exploiting of little people and told Andy that he and his union are just as corrupt and spineless as the companies they're supposedly fighting." She paused for a sip of coffee. "We don't see much of her at all. Spends most of her time with those hippies. There's a colony of them, you know. They live in tents and a couple of old trailers out in the hills off the county highway. Some of them have started showing up in town. As far as I know, not one of them works, and no one seems to know where they're getting their money. Each time Mari comes home, the first thing I do is fill her full of food. You should see her. She's so skinny."

Spencer looked at her compassionately. "I'm sorry to hear that, Bonnie. But maybe this is just something she'll grow out of."

"I hope so," Bonnie said.

The doctor moved behind his desk. "These are different times, I guess. There've been some tremendous changes in Coal County. Augustus Porter is gone or dead. John Owens has moved to Florida. In Porterville the company store shuts down, then burns to the ground and now is a field of rubble. The oil crisis comes, and the coal economy starts to pick up again but too late for the mineowners who sold out for a pittance and too late for all the miners who moved away. They're not a part of it anymore." He shook his head. "Now I hear there's some outside firm trying to buy out Jim Porter. Landex International, it's called. I didn't think too much of it until I picked up the paper the other day and read how there're grand juries sitting in at least four states now investigating the spread of organized crime into the coalfields."

"Organized crime?"

"Apparently they're running these companies as fronts. Anyway, Landex was on the list. And I was just becoming accustomed to the Texans." They both laughed.

"You know, you and I have been working too hard," Spencer continued. "We need a break. Maybe if the weather clears, we'll take a picnic lunch up into the mountains and get some of that good air. Nothing like it for recharging old batteries." It was not an unusual proposal from Spencer. He was happily married and did not pursue Bonnie as a lover, but he had grown very close to her. Their friendship was deep and sincere.

"That seems fine to me but—" Bonnie's words were cut short by the approach of a helicopter. The sounds of the chopping blades of helicopters were no longer rare in Coal County skies. The county airport had a fleet of the machines for lease or rent, and would-be investors used them to avoid the tedious mountain roads in their searches for potential mining properties. The chopper Bonnie and Spencer heard hovered loudly above the clinic and landed on a nearby field. Through the aircraft's plastic bubble they saw the face of Sheriff Thad Carter. He hopped out and walked toward the clinic door.

Visits from the sheriff were frequent, and Bonnie's first assumption was that he was coming to complete the paperwork on the Chester Ratliff case. She went to get the Ratliff file.

Bonnie had heard nothing from the Ratliff clan after her visit to their mountain enclave until a week earlier, when the old man appeared without warning at the clinic. He was accompanied by three of his older sons. It took only a brief examination by Spencer for him to conclude that the case was hopeless. Ratliff's arteries were almost fully blocked, and tests indicated his heart had suffered severe damage. Upon questioning, the mountain man admitted having had several episodes of chest pain. Spencer suspected he had probably suffered two or three minor heart attacks. There was nothing the doctor could do beyond administering sedatives to make Ratliff's death a little easier. One of the private rooms was vacant, so the doctor put his unexpected patient in there to pass his final days.

Spencer had been direct and honest in his assessment of the old man's condition, with both him and the three-member delegation his clan had sent with him. In both instances, the news was accepted stoically as confirmation of what they already knew: Chester was dying. One son proposed that it would be best his father return home to the mountains to die, but Spencer argued against it, saying that it would be wise for Chester to have round-the-clock medical attention. When Bonnie voiced the same argument, the family decided to leave Chester in the clinic.

The next day brought an unusual ritual. The entire Ratliff clan appeared at the clinic to pay homage to their dying patriarch. There were more than thirty of them, children, grandchildren and others of uncertain relationship, ranging in age from infancy to their fifties. In groups of three and four, they filed into Chester's room and stood at his bedside. Most were embarrassingly direct in seeking his wishes and in extending final farewells. His wife, Alma, entered last. She was alone. As the others loitered in the clinic waiting area, she spent an hour with her husband. She emerged strangely calm, chin up, face proud, and walked through a path cleared for her to the center of the family. Reaching into a pocket of her dress, she removed a pipe, packed it full of Prince Albert tobacco and put a match to it. She stood amid the others, smoking in silence, not one of the group giving any indication of intending to leave. Bonnie, watching them, was puzzled. Then a shot rang out from Chester's room. Bonnie rushed in, Spencer right behind her. There was nothing they could do— Chester had done the job expertly and cleanly. The pistol shot to his temple had killed him instantly. In shock, Bonnie and the doctor returned to the waiting area to speak to Chester's widow. But she and the others were gone. Looking out a window, Bonnie saw them slowly piling back into the two ancient trucks that had brought them to the clinic.

The suicide had necessitated the convening of a coroner's jury. Bonnie and Spencer related what had happened. The jurors, in turn, asked each of them the same question: Who had supplied Chester with the gun? Neither knew for sure.

Later Carter had lectured Bonnie and the doctor on improving the security at the clinic, but he didn't press the point, it being understood by each of them that there was little one could do to stifle the plans of determined mountain folk. Now Bonnie guessed that Carter was stopping by to complete his final report. With that done, the case of Chester Ratliff would be closed. She met the sheriff at the door.

"I've already pulled the file on Chester," she told him.

"That's not why I'm here, Bonnie," Carter said grimly. "I'll need the doc to come along with me if he doesn't mind." Bonnie knew what that meant. The county coroner, who was not a physician, often asked Spencer to examine death scenes and perform autopsies.

Spencer, walking toward them, also assumed this was what Carter had in mind. "What do you have?" he asked. "Can't you bring the body in?"

"Not this time," Carter replied, shaking his head. "This is one you'd better have a look at right at the scene."

"Okay," Spencer said. He turned to Bonnie. "Please get my bag. And why don't you come along and get yourself some fresh air?" He told the new nurse where they were going.

They could hardly hear each other above the noise of the helicopter, so Spencer shouted when he asked what it was Carter was taking them to.

"A skeleton," the sheriff yelled back. "A couple of hunters found it way the hell up by Paw Paw Pinnacle. All that's left are bones and some rotting shreds of clothing and shoes."

The helicopter made a precarious landing on a small, round

ledge extending from the side of the mountain. Carter led Spencer and Bonnie for several yards along a narrow rocky path until they came to another patch of nearly level land filled with cedar trees. In the center of the tree stand, partially covered by a layer of decaying leaves, was the skeleton.

"I didn't touch it," Carter said. "Wanted you to see it just as it was."

Spencer bent over the collection of bones and brushed away the leaves. Only a few strands of dried tissue remained. It looked as if the vultures had long ago made a meal of the other edible remains. The doctor said the skeleton appeared to be that of a male. A cursory examination found no broken or shattered bones. "I don't think he was shot," Spencer said. "It looks to me like he was at an advanced age when he died."

The physician fingered the jaw and told the others that the teeth were in good condition and showed evidence of expensive dental work. Then, around what remained of a finger on the left hand, he noticed a ring. Spencer removed it and lifted the band into the sunlight. It was a gold ring, seemingly very expensive. Etched onto a flattened portion of its surface was the letter *P*. Spencer showed the ring to the others and then told them, "I think we'd better have a talk with Jim Porter."

The wind kicked up again and sent a sharp, cold breeze against Bonnie's face. She shivered, but she wasn't certain if it was caused by the wind or the eerie feeling she had at that moment. After nearly two years the mystery of Augustus Porter was solved.

The sheriff photographed the site, having trouble calculating the proper exposures. Then Spencer, with Bonnie's help, carefully packed the remains into a plastic body bag. They were returning to the helicopter and its waiting pilot when Bonnie stumbled on something protruding from a clump of grass. She reached down and found a heavily scarred axhead covered with a patina of encrusted dirt and corrosion. As she scraped the soil away, the outlines of an engraving appeared. But the

398

characters were still too obscured to be read.

Carter instructed the pilot to head to Porterville. A few minutes later they landed on a patch of flatland on the edge of town.

"If you don't mind," Bonnie said, "I'd rather not go with you to the Porters'. I promised Andy LeGrande I'd help him at his rally."

"Of course, Bonnie. You go ahead," Spencer said.

He and the sheriff headed for the Porter mansion. Bonnie left for the square, where she could see a group of men already collecting.

The square had been little used in recent years. The carnival no longer came to Porterville, and there had been no ceremonies welcoming home the GIs of the Vietnam War. The treasury at the American Legion post had shrunk with the depression in the coal industry, and the post had dropped its subsidizing of the weekly outdoor movies in the summer. And it was so rare that an outdoor dance was held that no one bothered to maintain the dance floor—it was crisscrossed with grass-filled cracks.

Some local union officials had expressed fear that the organizing rally would be a flop, that the morale of the mining men in the region was so low they had given up on the union as a source of strength and hope. But Andy suspected otherwise. His confidence proved justified. The square was packed with miners, both unorganized Porter men and union members from other companies.

Behind Andy's belief that the rally would strike a responsive chord was the appearance of a new breed of mining man. A stranger observing the faces of the men attending the rally might have had the feeling he was at a student protest in some city rather than a gathering of workers in the heart of coal country. Most were young—in their twenties—and they had the look of San Francisco's North Beach or Manhattan's East Village. Their hair was long, in some cases tied in ponytails.

Full face beards and long, droopy mustaches were plentiful. And their colorful shirts, vests and headbands contrasted sharply with the miner's normal garb of coveralls and baseball cap.

Nearly all were Vietnam veterans, home from the war embittered about the two, three or four years chopped from their lives while others had avoided service. While slogging their way through rice paddies, their fellow youth were getting stoned regularly and enjoying the other easy pleasures of "flower society." Upon their release from the military, many veterans sought to catch up on all the joy they had missed. They grew their hair long, although long hair on the college campuses and urban streets was rapidly becoming out of style, and they latched onto the revolutionary rhetoric and fervor that had produced so much free love for their civilian counterparts. Most encountered trouble finding jobs. When they did find work, they were at the bottom of seniority lists and at the mercy of an unaccommodating coal economy. For those working for unionized companies, the union had succeeded in raising wages, demanding new safety measures and improving health, disability and pension benefits. Under Lamon C. Hubbard, even the old Owens company had joined the national mineowners' bargaining group, allowed the union to organize its workers and accepted the national contract hammered out in Washington. Now these Vietnam-era miners, many of them entering mines in the footsteps of their fathers and grandfathers, were intent on preserving these hard-won benefits locally. To do so, Andy told them, they would have to organize the Porter mines.

"I was afraid you were pooping out on me," Andy said when he spotted Bonnie.

"We had a coroner's case up in the mountains," she answered. "Turns out it was Augustus Porter's skeleton."

"Well, I'll be damned. You mean he was dead all these years? I had him figured for living it up in Rio."

"Looks like he just went off either drunk or crazy or both

400

into the mountains, and eventually the elements got him," Bonnie theorized.

The gathered men were growing impatient, some of them shouting at Andy to get the rally going.

He motioned toward a makeshift wooden stage situated in a corner of the park between two cone-shaped public address speakers. "I've got your backup there all set to go," he said, pointing to three musicians—a fiddler, a guitarist and a wash-tub bass player—waiting with their instruments. "Let's get started. And don't be nervous—these guys are all behind you," he said, handing her her guitar.

They climbed onto the stage. While Andy was calling for quiet and introducing her, Bonnie inspected the crowd. Youthful faces dominated the gathering, but there also was a large number of old-timers. Many were retired but still wore their miner's attire. They had witnessed the organizing of other Coal County companies years earlier, and when Bonnie launched her medley of Joe Hill and Woody Guthrie labor tunes, many of them remembered the words and sang along. Notably absent from the rally were miners in their forties and fifties. This was the generation hit hardest by the coal industry depression, and Bonnie understood that their broken spirits had left them bitter and suspicious men—men no longer capable of hope.

Bonnie's singing was well received by the rallying miners. The cheering and applause grew louder with each song. After her second number, she spotted her father in the first row, whistling, clapping and cheering more vigorously than any of the others. Her performance set the tone for the rally, and when she was finished, the crowd's energy was well primed. They cheered wildly when Andy moved to the microphone, adjusted his feathered hat so that it was cocked at an angle and began his address.

"Hello, miners," he shouted, a broad grin on his face. The salutation was greeted by more loud cheering and applause. "That's right," Andy continued. "You're miners, and that's a fact of which you should be very, very proud." There was another round of cheering. Then he lowered his voice. "You don't have to look hard at the history of this country to see the role the miner has played. Your fathers and your grandfathers did their share. Now it's your turn. And you're going to do it, but by God, you're going to get your fair compensation."

Andy had a natural talent for public speaking. His style was electric. He paced his words, pausing just at the right moment, and delivered his message in a rhythm one could clap to.

Andy told the crowd it was time for miners to be justly compensated for their risks and backbreaking labor so they could live a decent middle-class life. To ensure this, they needed a union that was strong. The assembled miners cheered. To achieve strength, he continued, the union required county-wide unity—no more working at fluctuating pay on a per diem basis so that no benefits were awarded and no more walking into mines so dangerous that their shorings wobbled. This must end, he shouted, because each time a miner sells his soul, miners a generation later, whether unionized or not, pay the price. The cheering echoed up and down Porterville's hollows.

"Now here's what we're going to do," Andy said, appearing confident he had won not only the men's ears but their spirits. "We're going to pick one of those Porter mines—we'll announce which one later—and we're going to put up a picket line as close as we can get to the portal and keep it there around the clock, seven days a week, until there isn't a miner left who can walk in there for work and still hold up his head." They cheered their loudest yet, and Andy had to pause fully a minute before it was quiet enough for him to continue. Bonnie, moved by the outburst of support for Andy, felt tears form in her eyes. "Now there's just one more thing I want to talk to you about, and that's violence," Andy continued. "We don't want it. More important, we don't need it. For every fist that's thrown, for every shot fired or rock that's picked up, we're going to alienate one of our non-union brothers. And then we may never get that man."

"Screw you, LeGrande," came a shout from the middle of the crowd.

"Yeah, the hell with that," yelled another.

"Burn the mother. Bomb Porter's mines," screamed another voice from the corner. Andy appeared confused.

Bonnie, rising to her toes, tried to spot who was doing the yelling, but the shouts came too quickly. She was unable to spot the hecklers until she saw a short, skinny young man at the rear of the crowd chanting in a high-pitched voice, "Burn 'em, burn 'em, burn 'em."

The agitator appeared to be about twenty-one or twenty-two. He had a pale, beardless face and thick red hair, which hung to his shoulders. A heavy work shirt failed to conceal his rounded, almost feminine shoulders. Wire-frame glasses with pink-tinted lenses added to his fragile appearance and served to camouflage his face.

Bonnie, despite the distance between her and the redhead, was certain she had seen the youth previously but couldn't pinpoint where. The young man's features, what Bonnie could see of them, were familiar. Probably one of the hippies from the colony outside Bannerton. Maybe a friend of Mari's.

Andy tried to ignore the interruptions. Bending close to the microphone, he shouted, "We'll begin tomorrow morning. We'll have picket schedules and details at the union office." Then he signaled to Bonnie and the other musicians to resume their playing. They tried. But the sounds of their instruments couldn't carry above the heckling, which had increased in its frequency and loudness.

Shouts of "Cedar Ridge" and "Cedar Ridge now" came from the crowd. The shouts evolved into a chant, and soon the agitators had succeeded in forming a procession out of the park, its members moving in twos and threes in the direction of Cedar Ridge.

Bonnie dropped the guitar to her side. The other musicians also gave up on their playing. Andy returned to the microphone and shouted, "Hold it! We're not ready for this!"

"Screw you!" the redhead yelled back at him.

Andy retreated to Bonnie's side. "There's nothing I can do to stop them now. Might just as well head out there and see what happens."

"I think I've seen that redhead," Bonnie told him. "Who were the others with him?"

"Damned if I know," he replied. "Never saw them before. But it's not the first time radicals have taken over a union rally."

"What do they want?"

"Most of them are city kids, bomb throwers who had the hell kicked out of them trying to organize factories. They've decided the coalfields are their best shot at revolutionizing the country, at leading workers to pick up arms to take over the government. The union's their tool. They're all in favor of it. The only problem is guys like me, the union leadership."

Duke called from the foot of the stage, "What do you do now, Andy?"

"We get out to Cedar Ridge," he answered nonchalantly. "Come on, I'll get us a ride."

Jim was worried about his mother. He knew that from the windows in her bedroom she could see the town square at the far end of the hollow. The sight of the union rally would upset her, he was certain, and he didn't want her to watch it. But Sarah had locked the door and wouldn't open it when Jim asked her to come out.

Jim was still standing outside the master bedroom when he heard the doorbell downstairs. In a moment, Marie, the maid, appeared to announce the visitors as Sheriff Carter and Dr. Spencer.

Jim had an uneasy feeling as he went downstairs to meet

them. If the sheriff had been alone, Jim would have associated his visit with the rally under way in the square. But it didn't follow that the doctor would be with him. The fact that Carter and Spencer were together signaled a different kind of trouble, no doubt involving injury or death. Jim nervously shook their hands and motioned them into the parlor.

"Jim, can you please take a look at this ring?" Carter said, getting right to the point.

Jim accepted it from the sheriff and turned it around in his fingers for a few seconds, pausing to look twice at the letter engraved on the flat portion of its surface. His hand began to shake. He looked up and spoke softly, "That's his. Where did you find it?"

"Hunters found the remains near Paw Paw Pinnacle," Carter explained.

"I see," Jim said, rising from his chair. He paced silently back and forth for a while, digesting the information that ended a mystery of almost two years' duration. Turning to Spencer, he asked, "How did he die?"

"I don't know pending a detailed examination, but my guess is that he succumbed to the elements. Exposure. There's no sign of violence—or suicide."

"The way I figure it," the sheriff said, rubbing his chin, "your pa wandered off that night, and he just wasn't himself, wasn't thinking right, and he ended up in the mountains with no coat and no food and just got lost. It's just a goddamned shame we couldn't find him."

"I can see your reasoning, Sheriff, but what I still don't understand is the fire," Jim said. "Remember the fire in the bedroom wastebasket? I don't have to tell you my father had a lot of enemies, a lot of people who would have wanted him out of the way. And—"

The sheriff interrupted him. "Jim, there was just no way. There's no evidence whatsoever that anyone had anything to do with your pa's disappearance that night except he himself. As I recall, he was mad at all of us, including you and your mother, for putting him in bed, right?" Jim nodded. "Well, he probably set that fire himself, thinking he could get even. Or maybe he was seeing some kind of demons. As I said, he wasn't thinking right and I've seen this demon thing before with men who liked their drink."

"You mean the DTs?"

"If that's what you want to call it," Carter replied.

Jim felt numb. Strangely, he was neither saddened nor relieved at that moment—the news carried by the sheriff and the doctor was too anticlimactic. Almost from the first day of his father's mysterious disappearance Jim had assumed he was dead. But not so his mother. In her withdrawn state she had wavered between referring to Augustus in the present and past tenses, one day believing her husband lost forever, the next expecting him to come staggering home from the Club Havana any minute and demanding a drink. Jim worried now how he would break the news to his mother and how she would take it. "When can I claim the body?" he asked. "We'd like to give him a decent Christian burial."

"That's up to the doc, but I don't think it will be more than a day," the sheriff said.

Spencer nodded. "Just a day or two, Jim. But I'm trained to be very cautious, and while I think it's very probable that the remains are those of your father, I'd like to be certain. Can you tell me where he had his dental work done?"

Jim supplied the name of a dentist in Livingston.

The two visitors thanked him and offered their condolences. "Well," said the sheriff, "I guess that's that. Now I'd better have a little look at that rally down the way."

They were moving into the foyer when the physician remembered the axhead he was carrying in a plastic bag. "Hey, Thad, what about the ax?" he asked the sheriff.

"I forgot about that," Carter replied. "Guess I really don't need it for evidence. Might as well give it to you now, Jim." Spencer handed the axhead to Jim, who immediately recognized it. There could be no doubt now that the dead man was Augustus. Jim thanked the sheriff and doctor once more and slowly closed the door behind them. Raising the axhead to look at it again, Jim turned around and then froze. Standing there was his mother.

"Ma, I didn't hear you come down," Jim heard himself saying, his mind racing for the words to tell her the tragic news.

"It's your pa, isn't it?" she said in what was a conclusion more than a question. Jim nodded and waited for her reaction, ready to move quickly if she should start to faint. But Sarah remained motionless, her expression unchanged until very, very slowly a smile came to her face. Walking as if in a trance, she moved into the parlor.

"You know, sometimes I really hated that man. But I also loved him," she said, speaking very softly and slowly. "I understood your father. He was a man's man. And I guess I've known in my heart all along that he was dead." Her words stopped, her eyes, still dry, peering out the window.

"The doctor said that the death was probably caused by—"

Sarah raised a hand. "Please, Jim," she said, "there's no need to tell me. All that matters is that he is dead." The sounds of hooting and cheering filtered through the window. Jim watched his mother's eyes and face for a change, but none came. Her lips were still taut in a smile, and her expression was almost cheerful. Her eyes conveyed pride, and she presented an aura of determination and strength. "He demanded a lot from people, including you and me," she continued, "but he also gave. He held this company and town together at times when neither job was very easy." She reached out and took Jim's hand. Moving closer and looking up into his eyes, she said, "Your father did what had to be done, and now so must we."

The sounds of another cheer wafted up to the mansion as Jim guided his mother to a seat on the sofa. He poured each of them a drink. By the time Anne returned home from what she said was a meeting of her club's executive committee in

Livingston, Jim and Sarah had quietly made plans for a brief and private church service, to be followed by burial in the town graveyard in a plot adjoining that of Colonel James T. Porter.

The procession of miners marching to Cedar Ridge blocked the roadway, and Andy, Bonnie and Duke had to follow them slowly at the end of their line in the car Andy had borrowed. It was not until the group reached the floor of the valley at the base of the ridge that Andy was able to pull around them. Sheriff Carter apparently had radioed ahead because two patrol cars, their red lights flashing, were waiting at the bridge. Under the direction of the redhead and the other militants, the men moved into a long, shuffling picket line a few yards from the patrol cars.

The Cedar Ridge Mine was not the biggest of the Porter company's properties, but it was active, and the approach to the portal lent itself to an effective picket line—there was no way for Porter miners to report for work without passing the cut in the foothills and walking through the picketing union men. In addition, Hubbard had closed the old Owens mine at that site; that meant there would be no interference with that recently unionized company.

The men on the line were boisterous. Over the next few minutes their number grew as word spread to other Coal County mines that a showdown was under way at Cedar Ridge. Beer was distributed, and the militants stoked the crowd's anger with fiery rhetoric: "You're being exploited while fatcats like Porter get rich." "Porter's sippin' tea while you're breathin' air as black as the coal you dig." "Power to the men with the shovels!" "We want ours—NOW!"

Within an hour a mob of nearly 300 men, most of them union members on the payrolls of other companies and many of them already intoxicated, had assembled on the roadway leading toward the bridge.

Bonnie, Duke and Andy stood to the side, nervously watch-the angry group of demonstrators. The chanting and catcalls grew louder and continued without interruption until the sound of a helicopter filled the valley. The chopper put down near the portal on the other side of the creek, and Robert Allen hopped out. Almost with his arrival, the five dozen or so men working inside the mine began to appear in groups of four and five at the portal. There was an authority to their steps as they strutted out of the darkness, threw their food buckets into a heap at the base of the small tipple and gathered into an angry group.

Andy was confused as he watched Allen talking to the men, his hands spread in innocence while the men raised fists to him. "I can't figure this," he told Bonnie and Duke. "I'd sign up those men in a minute, give them membership cards right on the spot, but I don't think the union's the reason they came marching out of there."

"Join us! Join us! Join us!" the redhead began chanting. The other militants picked it up, and soon most of the picketing miners were shouting the invitation across the creek to the assembled Porter men.

In a few minutes a half dozen of the Porter workers did cross the bridge and join the picket line. Duke walked over to ask one of them what had happened.

It obviously was part of a complex plan hammered out well ahead of time to the smallest detail. Just as the marchers arrived from Porterville, a group of younger miners inside the mine had begun spreading the word that a particular heading—number three—had dangerously sagged and Porter was attempting to conceal the fact from the men. "The roof's shifted. You can see the damn cracks, but these bastards sent us in anyway," went the story as it spread from one bent miner to the next, fanning out to each section of the mine. Memories were rekindled of the time the roof did collapse in the Red Fox and of the toll in death and injuries it had taken. If the allegation was true—and for some men, there was no reason to doubt it in view of the company's past history—then the concealment of the hazard was unconscionable, a crime bordering on homicide. A small group of militants, strategically scattered among the miners, fed their collective anger with rhetoric until finally, in one seemingly spontaneous mass action, the men dropped their tools, abandoned their machines and paraded out of the portal in what had the effect of a wildcat strike.

Allen, attempting to learn the cause of the work stoppage, encountered an angry mob waving their fists and shouting obscenities at him, the safety engineer and Jim Porter.

"Hold on! Hold on!" he shouted. "I can't hear you all at once. Now would one of you be kind enough to tell me what this is all about?"

A young miner, less than two years on the job, stepped forward. He was one of the Vietnam vets, a fact conveyed by his long hair, full-faced beard and maritime tattoo. "The roof's fallin' in number three, and you mothers didn't think twice about sending us in there," he charged.

"The roof?" Allen asked in confusion. "What's wrong with the roof?"

"It's shifted. There're cracks in the wall, and the ribs are getting ready to pop. But do you think you give a damn?" the young miner gibed.

Allen called for the safety engineer. "What about it?" he asked.

"Nothing wrong with that ceiling that I could see," the engineer replied.

Allen turned to the men and announced, "That ceiling passed a safety inspection only this morning." They responded with a chorus of catcalls, threats and boos.

"Hold on! Hold on, I said!" Allen shouted angrily. "I'm going in there and look at it myself. A couple of you men come along and show me where you think the problem is."

Allen, accompanied by the safety engineer and two miners, one of them the young man who had spoken, rode into the

410

far reaches of the disputed heading. There the two miners pointed to a small spider web of cracks along one wall near its connection with the ceiling. "That?" the engineer asked incredulously. "That's been there for more than two weeks. It doesn't mean a damn thing. You know that."

Allen looked at the miners. "Both of you men have been mining long enough to know that a flaw like that is common and doesn't threaten anybody's safety so long as the pillars are tight."

"Bullshit!" said the miner who was the self-appointed spokesman.

"That's right," said the other. "We ain't workin' this mine till we get our own safety men in here to look at it. You know what I mean, inspectors from the union."

"That's fine with me," Allen said. "But you don't have to pull out of the other headings. They're not affected by this."

"The hell they ain't," said the miners' spokesman. "How many other safety risks are you bastards hiding? And not just at Cedar Ridge here. What about the others? What about the Red Fox? We're stayin' out till this whole thing's settled."

"For chrissake," Allen said, deciding he had heard enough. He turned his back on them and marched off to the manager's shack. Inside, he could be seen picking up the telephone. In a few minutes he was back again. "Okay. I just talked to Mr. Porter, and we'll play your silly game," Allen announced. "How long will it take to get the union inspectors here?"

"Tomorrow—at the earliest."

"That's fine with me, buddy. But let me tell you one thing: Don't let these men get any notion that they're getting paid for this time. It won't happen."

Allen turned abruptly and went to the helicopter. In a moment he was airborne.

"They're making a big mistake," Andy told Duke and Bonnie. "They don't know it, but they're playing right into the company's hands. After the men realize how they've been used by these punks, our cause will be set back further than Porter might have dreamed of."

"I don't understand," Duke said.

"First, I'm not about to allow any union inspectors to go into that heading. They're not using me like that. And secondly, you just don't cry wolf or yell fire in a theater. Wait until these Porter men learn that their fears were raised over nothing." He pointed to the picket line, the members of which were still chanting loudly. "You see this? This is not real labor movement strategy. This is like a carnival . . . a ball game . . . a panty raid. Nothing more than a one-shot emotional binge. Pretty soon the fun will wear thin, and the liquor will tire these men. We'll be lucky to have three pickets left. Organizing a mine is serious and demanding. It's hard work."

Andy was right. Fortified by the beer, the men walked the line briskly, singing labor songs now and then and raising their fists for the news photographer from the Bannerton *Tribune*. After a few hours, however, the picketing on the hard, rocky soil became tedious. Feet hurt. The photographer departed. So did most of the pickets. The dedicated dozen or so who remained paced back and forth slowly and, for the most part, silently. Their energy returned only when a Porter worker happened by en route home from the other side of the creek. Then two or three union men would grab him and politely state their case for organizing the company. "I gotta work," was the typical response. "What are you guys gonna do about feeding my family?" The union men didn't argue. They handed him literature and asked him to think it over, to try to comprehend that he was being exploited and to understand that it was in his long-term interest to unite with his brother miners.

Andy, Bonnie and Duke had remained in the background observing the demonstration and its loss of momentum. By the time they were ready to leave only a dozen pickets remained. "Don't worry," Bonnie told Andy, trying to cheer him. "Something like this takes time."

But after watching the events of the day, Bonnie wondered if there was any chance of winning over men who had been beaten so badly financially they would almost pay to have a job. The Porter company's manipulation of them over the years had made the men cynical, and many saw the union as little more than a dues-collecting body with no muscle. This, she told herself, was an image that would not be changed overnight.

As they walked toward their car, Duke spotted the red-headed agitator. "There's that ringleader now," he said, pointing.

"I want to have a talk with you," Andy yelled to the youth, who was resting against the trunk of a dead tree.

Bonnie tugged at Andy's arm. "Now don't hurt him, Andy. You don't want trouble," she said.

"Just leave this guy to me," Andy said, his expression furious. Cocking his hat on his head, he strode toward the redhead and asked, "Just who the hell are you, my friend?"

"Who the hell are *you?*" the youth retorted.

"If you don't mind, it'll be me asking the questions. Who are you?" Andy demanded.

"Pete Foster. What's it to you?"

"You a union member?"

The young man pulled a well-worn membership card from his pocket. Andy inspected it carefully and then showed it to Duke and Bonnie. It had been issued in Indiana in the name of Peter E. Foster and appeared to be authentic.

"If you're from Indiana, what the hell are you doing here?" Andy asked.

"I'm here to help with the struggle," Foster replied. "Some of you thickheaded so-called union leaders might not know it, but you're in a war between classes." He scratched his head through his mop of long hair. "It's the workingman against the owning class, the imperialists. The fight's not in the factories or the farm fields or the streets of cities but right here in the mines. Most of you red-neck alleged union leaders are too ignorant to see it. You've sold out the men."

Andy inched threateningly toward Foster, but Bonnie again took his arm and squeezed. Andy slapped his thigh, as if to shake the anger out of him, and told Foster softly but authoritatively to move on and not return to Cedar Ridge.

"Why?" Foster demanded. "And what if I don't?"

Andy spread his arms and began shooing the redhead away. "I'm not going to argue with you, and I'm not going to wring your goddamned neck like I should. Somebody else can do that and probably will. Now move on. You and your friends get out of here the same way you came."

Foster backtracked, swearing at Andy as he retreated. "You haven't heard the last of us, pig," he shouted.

The sun streaking through the window of the study played a harsh game on Sarah's face. She was sixty-four years old but looked eighty, having aged with shocking speed after her husband's disappearance. But her eyes remained alert, as they had been since Augustus's death had been ruled official; her normal voice had returned, and she had acted decisively during the first week of the union's picket line at Cedar Ridge.

Jim marveled at how his mother had responded to the union's challenge, easing him aside and stepping right in to take control of the situation. The union, she declared again and again, would not intimidate the Porter Coal Company, no matter what the price, and she had developed a strategy of defenses that bore the marks of a talented, no-nonsense businesswoman. Against Jim's protests that perhaps the company should bargain with the union, Sarah ordered Allen to hire a small army of security guards to post at Cedar Ridge and the other Porter mines. She instructed that coal trucks be used to transport miners willing to work through the picket line and authorized the recruitment of out-of-town men to replace the Porter employees who had joined the pickets.

The situation at Cedar Ridge remained as it had been since the second day of picketing—a stalemate. A half-dozen Porter miners, moved by the arguments of Andy LeGrande and others, had dropped out of the work force; two of them promptly joined the picket line. After Andy refused to authorize the union inspectors, the working miners quietly forgot about the alleged safety violations and dropped their demand for an inspection. The mine was back in operation. At the beginning of each shift the pickets silently parted their ranks to allow the Porter trucks to pass carrying the miners who were working. The confrontation between them and the union men had been reduced to a battle of glares instead of the shouts of "scab" and "Judas" that had characterized the first few days. The two sides knew each other well, most of them having lived among one another for years. Several had been high school classmates in Bannerton. Until the union issue separated them, some had been close friends. The conflict had yet to pit one brother against another, but Jim suspected it wouldn't be long before that happened.

There had been no violence or major trouble until the incident of the truck, which Allen was now outlining to Sarah and Jim in the study.

The truck had picked up twenty-one miners and was headed for Cedar Ridge when it happened, Allen told them. The driver ran up and down the gears as the vehicle made its way over the winding and hilly gravel road. About two miles outside town he slowed the truck almost to a stop to negotiate a sharp, descending curve skirting the side of a cliff. When the truck swung around the pillar of rock and into the straightaway again, he slammed on the air brakes. The road was blocked by two cars, one a sedan, the other, a station wagon. They were parked nose to nose. Eight men, heavily armed with rifles and shotguns, jumped from behind the cars and from the brush at the side of the road.

"Get out of the truck!" shouted one of them, a young man with long red hair and rose-tinted glasses, whom some of the

Porter miners recognized as having been at Cedar Ridge on the first day of picketing. "Get out, I said. And I don't want to say it again," the redhead ordered.

The men climbed slowly from the truck. The driver hopped down from his cab. They gathered in a group on the road surrounded by the armed men. Three of the gunmen were recognized as young miners from unionized Coal County mines; the others were strangers to the Porter workers.

The short, skinny redheaded leader stepped in front of them. "You're here to listen to a discussion about morality and how you're screwing your fellow workingman," he declared in a shrill voice, smiling smugly. For the next fifteen minutes or so he delivered a harangue, talking of a forthcoming workers' revolution and how those who didn't join the cause would someday be in plenty of trouble.

"I'm sure you all understand logic and reason and that what I've just said has gotten through your thick heads," he said. "So I don't see any reason to waste any more time. Raise your right hands, and Jamie here will read you the oath."

Two of the Porter miners balked at raising their hands, but jabs from the rifles prompted them to comply with the redhead's order. A fat, bearded youth stepped forward and read from a piece of paper. It was, he said, a fidelity oath.

"Congratulations!" the redhead shouted in mock joy after the oath had been delivered. "Now you're all good union men." His colleagues began circulating among the miners, shaking hands with each. "Jamie will get your names and addresses. You'll get your membership cards later. For now, you're on strike. So just get back in your truck and go home."

The Porter men, most of them seething at their humiliation of the past few moments, climbed back into the truck. The driver turned it around and headed back to Porterville.

Jim shook his head when Allen had completed his report on the incident. "Who the hell are these guys?" he asked.

"Commies. Bona fide, card-carrying Reds. Little college boys who call themselves Maoists," Allen replied, his voice grim. "I've run across them here and there. Ever since they got the shit beat out of them. . . . Oh, excuse me, Mrs. Porter. I mean, ever since they got whipped in the factories, they've decided we coalmen are the ones ready for the revolution." He smiled sarcastically.

"The next time I see one, I'm going to run him right out of town," Jim said, slamming his fist against the top of his father's old chestnut desk.

"Oh, no. Don't do that," Allen said. "That would be playing right into their hands. Leave them be. They may make a lot of noise and prove a nuisance now and then, but mostly they're harmless." His expression grew serious. "What you've got to worry about is the potential audience these hippies can win if you give them the chance."

"What do you mean?" Jim asked.

"There's a whole new generation of miner now. These kids are tough. Most of them fought in Vietnam, and they're mad. They want theirs, and they're going to get it no matter who they have to kick. They're not illiterate immigrants just off the boat like the men your father and grandfather used to deal with. These guys are for real." He bent forward and in almost a whisper added, "And some of them are crazy."

"Arm the trucks," said Sarah, whose expression had remained unchanged throughout the discussion.

"Excuse me, ma'am?" Allen asked.

"I said arm the trucks. Put armed guards in each of them and move them in convoys," she said.

Jim looked at his mother. It was another of her calm, nononsense business decisions. "That might be inviting violence, Ma. There must be another way," Jim protested.

"Just do as I say," she said sternly to Allen. "Since when have the lives of mining men become the playthings of spoiled adolescents who wouldn't know a piece of coal from the hashish they smoke?"

Allen left to carry out Sarah's order. She retired upstairs

for a nap. Jim was about to depart for Cedar Ridge when the maid told him a visitor had just arrived. She had shown him into the parlor. He was Lamon C. Hubbard, the lumberman who had bought the Club Havana and, later, the Owens mines.

From what Jim knew about Hubbard, the lumber business had made him quite rich, and now that the oil situation was pushing the price of coal upward, his new company was adding to his wealth. He owned two Rolls-Royces and was rumored to have ordered a third. And his bank account was believed to be the largest administered by Baxley. It galled Jim that Hubbard managed to make money even off the club.

Jim also was bothered by Hubbard's approach to the coal business. Shortly after the doubling of worldwide oil prices, the price of coal began to climb as the nation's industries and utilities switched from one fuel to the other wherever they could. Jim, as his company's chief salesman, played conservatively, seeking out long-term contracts, which, while netting less money per ton than spot orders, provided the stability he sought to pacify his creditors. Others played the game more radically, diving into the volatile spot market and holding out for the highest bids. Among them was Hubbard. Behaving in the spot market like a poker player with unlimited resources and a hell-be-damned attitude, Hubbard stockpiled his coal as if there would be no tomorrow—he wanted to be prepared to ship instantly each time he collared a desperate spot market buyer. This action locked up business that otherwise might have gone to Jim when he sought a spot order to fill a hole in his production schedule.

"Good morning, Lamon," Jim said, entering the parlor.

Hubbard didn't bother to respond. Jim noticed a track of dust across the carpet from Hubbard's battered boots. The lumberman's mouth was stuffed with chewing tobacco. When Jim walked to him and offered his right hand, Hubbard shook it cursorily from his seated position. "What can I do for you?" Jim asked.

"The first thing you can do is get me somethin' for this here tobacco juice. That's too pretty a rug you got there for me to mess it up."

Jim handed him a silver bowl Anne had imported from England. Hubbard shot a stream of brown juice through the space between his two front teeth into the bowl and then placed it on the floor beside his chair. Jim sat down opposite him and studied his visitor. The tall, lanky, sixty-three-year-old lumberman was a study in contrasts. He still wore the faded and torn old blue jeans that had become his trademark in the timber business. His shirt was a ragged and ill-fitting woolen plaid he probably had picked up in a Bannerton discount store. But three of his fingers were adorned with diamond rings of one karat or more.

"There I was this morning out at the airport waiting for my plane, and the fog was so thick you couldn't see the tip of your nose," Hubbard said. Jim knew Hubbard was speaking of his private plane, a twin-engine propeller-driven aircraft. According to the rumors, he had tried a small jet for a while but found it unable to land on many of the short mountain runways such as the one at Bannerton Airport, which was just a sliver of flat land between two mountains. The four-seater he now owned could land anywhere, provided the runway wasn't engulfed in fog. "I have a fat contract waiting for me in Florida if I can get down there, see, so I tell the tower to tell that goddamned pilot of mine to try to land. Sure enough, I hear him coming, buzz, buzz, buzz. But then the son of a bitch chickens out and pulls out of his dive. So I figures instead of wasting the day, I'd come by to see you."

"And now you're here," Jim said, irritated by the rambling introduction to their talk.

"I think you know me well enough now, Porter, to know that I don't beat around the bush. I've got a proposition to offer you, and you can either take it or leave it—I really don't give much of a damn." Jim's face began to flush. Bargaining between two traditional coalmen was almost a religious experience—a soft-spoken ritual in which matters of substance were dealt with circuitously, one man always displaying his respect for the other. Hubbard might have thought his approach was direct. In reality, it was ill-camouflaged pomposity, and it instantly alienated Jim. A very stupid man, Jim thought before telling his visitor, "I'm listening. Go on."

"As you may know, I've gone very deep into the spot market. That's where the money is but it has its dangers. You can wake up one morning and need fifteen hundred tons to be shipped that afternoon. If you don't have it, tough shit, brother, you can kiss an eighty-dollar-a-ton spot contract good-bye." Jim didn't need Hubbard's elucidation; he was very well aware of the mechanics of the spot market, and he knew Hubbard had just told half the story. While the mine-owner could find himself with an immediate need for 1,500 tons of coal, he could also find himself with 1,500 tons stockpiled and nowhere to ship it.

Hubbard continued. "Under my present setup, I've reached a limit, a plateau. My sales potential on any given day is much bigger than my production capacity. I have to expand, and that's why I'm here. Porter, I wanna take over two of your mines."

"Which ones?"

"Cedar Ridge—there's still some coal left in my own property there."

"And the other?"

"The Red Fox. It's the only mine around here big enough to satisfy my needs." Hubbard paused to bite off another chunk of his Red Man tobacco plug. It was a strategic pause, intended to allow the enormousness of his proposal to sink in. "That would leave you with your three other mines and any other leases you've acquired to develop," Hubbard continued. "You'd still be in the coal business, and from what I know of your situation, it'd be the first time in a long while that you had some money in the bank. And a lot of money, I might add. All in cash. I'm prepared to offer you—"

"No deal, Lamon," Jim said, rising to his feet. "Don't even bother with a figure. I don't want to hear it. The Porter mines are not for sale." Having heard enough, Jim walked toward his visitor and extended his right hand to signal an end to the conversation. "I'm sorry, but as I'm sure you know, I have some picketing going on and a lot of work to do."

Hubbard stood. "Like I said, Porter, it's up to you. I don't give a damn. You're not the only mineowner in these parts." He strutted toward the door.

Hubbard's chauffeur, seeing him approach, started the Rolls and jumped out of the car to open the passenger door. Hubbard paused before climbing in and yelled back to Jim, "Don't be so haughty, Porter. You know we're thinking of dedicating a room at my club to the memory of your father. Now there was a man with class."

Jim closed the door gently and moved to the study. He sat in his father's high-backed chair and lifted his legs onto the chestnut desk. Jim grinned. No fool like Hubbard could bait him—not anymore. He was more amused at the lumberman than insulted or angry. But he was also worried. He knew that as the price of coal climbed, however artificially, there would be an increasing number of offers to buy his mines. There would be numerous pressures put upon him, and some of the offers would be thinly disguised raids. Already the rising coal prices had attracted a first wave of outside fastbuck artists to the region. One didn't have to see them to know they were around. The sounds of helicopters crisscrossing the sky told of their presence. They seemed to view themselves as archangels sent from the heavens to redeem those backwards mineowning hillbillies.

"Well, we'll see," Jim said to himself as he thought of Romano, the man from Landex International, and Hubbard, the *nouveau riche* lumberman. "We'll see."

Despite the hindrance of the picketing under way at Cedar Ridge, the condition of the Porter Coal Company was improving. All five mines were now in operation, and orders were arriving unsolicited. Its debt was under control, except for the $300,000 note soon due Baxley's bank, which no doubt would be extended. Jim had felt so confident of the firm's growing strength that he had approached a banker in Cardiff City for even another loan, this one very modest in size. But something puzzling had happened. Although the loan was relatively small and the company's financial picture had improved, the Cardiff City banker balked at making it. Jim had expected the approval to be automatic. The banker asked a series of seemingly irrelevant questions about the firm's current operation and then said no. When Jim asked him why, the banker was evasive. He acted as if there were something he knew about the company but was not at liberty to tell.

Jim looked for a connection between that banker and Romano or Hubbard but found none. This left him uneasy. He was considering whether to approach Baxley for help in clearing up the mystery behind the other banker's rejection when the telephone rang. The call was long distance and person to person.

"Yes, this is Jim Porter speaking," he told the long-distance operator.

A male voice came on the line. "You don't know me, and you've probably never seen my name," the caller began. "My name is Peter DeLupo, and I'm calling from my home in Shaker Heights in Ohio."

"Yes," Jim said suspiciously. The caller was correct—he had never heard of him. Jim braced himself for what he anticipated would be yet another stranger's bid for ownership of the Porter mines.

"I'm a stockholder of yours, Mr. Porter. Bought twenty shares a year ago. I'm retired, you see, and usually I'm a very cautious man, but I thought I'd take a flyer buying in with you, and I must say I've watched you improve the firm."

"Well, thank you, Mr. DeLupo, was it? What can I do for you now?"

"Answer a couple of questions for me, would you, please? I don't want you to get the wrong idea. I'm not pumping you for inside information or trying to do anything illegal. I just want to know where I stand."

"Go on, sir."

"You don't have to answer completely, if you like, but just in general terms."

Jim was growing impatient. "Ask your questions, Mr. DeLupo. I'll answer them if I can."

"Well . . . are you planning any major announcement in the near future, something, perhaps, that hasn't been expected?"

Jim was confused. "I'm not sure I know what you mean."

"I'm not sure I do either. I guess what I'm getting at is whether there've been any major developments like, you know, the discovery of oil or something on one of your properties."

"Oil? No, we haven't found any oil. And even if we did, our leases don't give us oil rights on any of the land we mine, Mr. DeLupo. What is it that would prompt you to ask such a question?"

"Oh, intuition. A gut feeling, that's all. I dabble in the market a bit, and I'm an investor who follows his feelings." DeLupo wouldn't be pinned down. He returned to his own line of questioning. "If I read you right, Mr. Porter, then there's no impending major announcement that would likely affect the value of my stock."

"No, sir. None that I'm aware of."

"Either up or down?"

"Nothing, Mr. DeLupo. There's absolutely nothing like that in the works."

"Well, thank you, Mr. Porter. I appreciate your giving me your time. Good-bye."

"Wait a second!" Jim shouted into the phone, hoping to learn the source of the caller's curiosity.

"Yes, sir?" he heard DeLupo ask.

"Look, I've been candid with you. Now you be honest with me. What's this all about?"

It sounded as if DeLupo were cupping his hand over the phone. His voice was muffled. "Look, I can't talk freely just now. There's a man in the next room here wanting to buy my stock. He says you're in trouble, that you're about to default on a three-hundred-thousand-dollar note that won't be renewed. But when a big New York conglomerate is after my stock, I smell something else—like oil. Of course, I know about your strip mining plans. . . ."

"What conglomerate?" Jim asked urgently.

"I'm sorry . . . I've got to go now." The telephone clicked.

Jim returned the phone to its cradle slowly. What was that all about? Was DeLupo a worried minor-league investor fearful for the integrity of his small nest egg, or was some conglomerate knocking on his door? Jim picked up a pen and jotted down a few notes summarizing the call. He had the suspicion that Mr. DeLupo and his mysterious questions would return to haunt him. Then he called the Cedar Ridge mine in search of Allen.

"Bob, just a couple of quick questions," he said when Allen came to the line.

"Sure, Jim. Shoot."

"Did you ever hear of a stockholder of ours named De-Lupo? He lives somewhere in Ohio."

There was a pause. "No, Jim. Can't say I have. Why?"

Jim's mother appeared at the study's door, her nap over. He motioned her to sit down. "Oh, nothing," he told Allen. "But I also was curious about whatever happened with that pompous fellow who wanted to buy us out. Landex, I think the name of the firm was. The thought occurred to me that we never heard back from him."

"I did what you told me to do," Allen replied. "When I next heard from him, I told him you weren't interested. He said, in so many words, that he didn't care, that you were the loser, not he. And I haven't heard from him since. But he did say if you were ever interested to give him a call, although he couldn't guarantee the same price." Allen paused. "You haven't changed your mind, have you? I still believe it's something you might have given some thought to, even though I personally would hate to see the company change like that."

"No. There's no change. I was just curious why I never heard about him again. Thanks, Bob."

Jim hung up the phone. He lowered his head, his mind searching for a pattern to what he was certain was an organized challenge to his ownership of the company. The enemy was no longer merely a shrinking coal economy. Nor did the threat come from greedy oilmen, easily identifiable in their Stetsons and high-topped boots. Instead, companies such as Jim's were the targets of well-concealed forces, octopuslike conglomerates with an army of faceless officers or obscure holding companies the existence of which went little beyond the paper that certified them. Behind them were powers on Wall Street or foreign money or, if one believed the newspapers, Mafia chieftains in places like St. Louis and Chicago. No matter how hard he tried, Jim could identify no specific assault on the company other than the two overt offers. But he saw a number of ominous signs.

"What is it, Jim?" his mother asked.

Jim locked eyes with his mother. His expression was grave; his voice, subdued. "I can't prove it, Ma, but as sure as I'm sitting here, I'm convinced we're being betrayed."

"Well, if you want to call this union business a betrayal, but I don't think—"

"Not the union, Ma," he interrupted. "It's something else. I just received a call from a man who owns some of our stock. I've never even heard of him, and neither has Allen—or so he says. Yet this fellow knew a couple of things that only someone in the company or very close to it would know."

"Like what, son?"

"Like our preliminary plans to do some strip mining and like our note due Baxley. He not only knew the amount but also said it wouldn't be renewed."

"That's ridiculous!" Sarah responded. "Ray Baxley happens to be your father-in-law and a longtime friend of mine. There is no way he won't go along with a renewal."

"You're probably right, Ma, but that doesn't diminish the fact that this DeLupo fellow has inside information. The question is how . . . and from whom?"

Both were silent for a few moments. Then Sarah asked, "What about Allen? To be honest, there's always been something I haven't liked about that man."

"I've thought of him. He's extreme at times, but I've seen nothing to suggest he isn't loyal."

"Well, what do we do?" she asked.

"We don't waste time, for one thing. I'll head right over now and see Baxley about the note. Get it over with before there're any other surprises," Jim said. He rose from his seat, looking down on his mother, who at this moment seemed smaller than usual. "It's not the same anymore, is it, Ma?" he said.

She nodded knowingly. "Your pa used to say it would come to this, the outsiders taking control and all the coal families being forced out. He fought it, but in the end he thought they would win."

"Well, it's not all bad news. The work has picked up, and folks who moved away are coming back. That's good."

"But it's still the outsiders running more and more of the companies," she said. "We can't let that happen to us, son, not if we can help it."

The generally deteriorating quality of life in Livingston did not taint Raymond Baxley's life-style. Baxley was not only unaffected by coal industry troubles but actually appeared to prosper from them. No one knew for certain his net worth, but he was sufficiently wealthy to afford a new

Continental every year as well as a new wing to his mansion.

Baxley met Jim at the door and then took him around the side of the house to view the foundation for the new wing. They stood a few yards from the footbridge, and Jim could see Anne's playhouse partially obscured by trees and bushes across the ravine. The playhouse appeared freshly painted and well maintained almost as if it were still in use every day by a young girl fond of her collection of dolls.

Even as he proudly pointed out the new construction, Baxley did not seem to be his normal self. There was an awkwardness to his words, and his eyes shunned all contact with those of his son-in-law. He avoided all talk of business until both were inside and the bourbon had been poured. Then he gave it to Jim straight: The bank's board of directors had decided the Porter Coal Company was too heavily financed. They ordered . . . repeat, ordered . . . Baxley to reject either an extension or a renewal of the note. He didn't agree, and he had argued valiantly with them but to no avail. The note would be due as scheduled in less than three months. He was sorry, but there was nothing he could do. He would, of course, help Jim search for other financing. What would happen if none was found? Default, he was afraid. And the bank unfortunately would have to claim the Porter family stock it was holding as collateral. He knew that this was a portion of the stock bequeathed to Jim and his mother by Augustus. And yes, he also realized that this stock represented the control of the company if it was in certain hands. And this whole business was especially rough on him because Jim was the husband of his daughter and he considered Jim as he would a son.

Jim, feeling his face drain of blood, could find nothing to say. DeLupo had been right. The note would not be renewed. In one sense, Baxley's disclosure was anticlimactic, and it was not until Jim was halfway back to Porterville that the anger began to build inside him. By the time he reached the driveway to his mansion he was ready to explode.

"Where's Anne?" he asked his mother, hoping maybe his wife somehow could shed some light on this deplorable, incomprehensible action by her father. Board of directors, my ass, Jim thought. There's not one person in Coal County who doesn't know Baxley owns the soul of every so-called member of that board. The refusal to renew was his and his alone.

"She's gone," Sarah replied. "Said she had a meeting of the garden club or something."

"The garden club!" Jim shouted, slamming his fist into the foyer's wall. "Is she married to those goddamned clubs or is she married to me?"

Anne had, in fact, become an absentee wife. It seemed as if every day of the week she had one obligation or another to claim her time. Once he had given thought to the possibility that she had acquired a lover, that she was engaged in an affair. She had been acting strangely at times, becoming much, much too pleasant with him. It was almost as if her efforts at cordiality stemmed from the anticipation of a pleasurable afternoon in bed. But Jim dismissed this prospect. She no longer was very attractive. To pursue her for sexual favor, a man would have to have another motive in mind.

"We'd better talk, Ma. We're in serious trouble," Jim said, leading her back to the study.

He told her of Baxley's decision. She, too, found it difficult to believe. And then the two of them reviewed each aspect of the puzzle that had so abruptly developed, pushing them to the edge of panic.

Whether they could salvage their ownership of the company, Jim wasn't sure. But what he did know was that as a first step they would have to get the union off their backs. He proposed a peace offering to Andy LeGrande.

Sarah stood. Her face was bright red. "Absolutely not!" she shouted. "I'd rather lose everything we own than do that to the memory of your father." With that she marched from the room.

Jim took every precaution he could to keep the meeting secret. He insisted that it take place on a lonely back road far into the foothills well past sunset. The stakes were very high for his talk with Andy LeGrande, and it was best for both of them that no one else know they had met.

They stood between their parked cars, each resting against one of the vehicles, the full moon lighting their faces, their voices soft. Jim decided he had to be honest about Baxley's foreclosure on the $300,000 loan and the existence of a traitor.

"As you may know, the Porter Coal Company is the object of a raid," Jim began, filled with distaste for what he was doing. "A firm by the name of Landex International has bought several of the outstanding shares and is working with someone in or very close to the company. At least I think it's Landex behind the move." Andy nodded, suggesting he had heard of the firm. "As it is now, I still have control, but there's been a recent development to jeopardize that. Ray Baxley holds a three-hundred-thousand-dollar note against the company. Unfortunately he says his board of directors won't go along with a renewal or even a short extension. They want it paid in full in less than ninety days, and there's no way I can raise that kind of money in so little time." Jim paused, studying the union man before he went on. Andy's expression was one of curiosity. "What it boils down to is this: If the bank takes the stock I put up as collateral and if that stock gets into the hands of the outside firm that I believe is running around the country buying up all our outstanding paper, then my mother and I will lose the company. That's it, unless you and the union can help me. That's why I'm here —to ask for your help." Jim paused, but Andy said nothing. There was no hint in the bearded union man's expression of his reaction to Jim's humbling himself before him. Jim, straightening his back, continued, "My proposal simply is this: The union comes in immediately. You can write your own terms. In return, you extend me a line of credit and a pass if any strike develops next year."

It was a bold proposal, but Jim knew that such action by the union would not be unprecedented. The union had gone to the aid of companies in the past but did not care to publicize it. The assistance usually came in the form of a low-interest loan from union pension funds. And on some occasions an individual coal company with a history of co-operating with the union had been given a one- or two-week reprieve during a national strike. National contract negotiations were scheduled for Washington in the following year, and to most coalmen, a walkout seemed inevitable. The Porter Coal Company could benefit from both forms of assistance.

"It seems to me that it would be in the interest of you and the men for the company to remain in local hands rather than have to deal with some anonymous corporation five hundred miles away and a parade of officials who have no notion of what it's like down here," Jim argued.

Andy fingered his beard and then adjusted his hat. Jim braced for the lecture he was certain would come. But Andy remained calm, his voice soft, even sympathetic. "I admire you," the union man said. "It took guts for you to do what you just did. I'd like to help, but I'm afraid I can't."

"Does that mean a flat no?"

Andy moved away from his car and stood face to face with Jim. They were almost the same height, and they stared at each other eye to eye. A breeze rustled the leaves in the stand of trees to the side of the road.

"You don't understand labor, Jim," Andy declared. "It's not you we have to win. Believe me, we could bring you to your knees if we had to. Under federal law, you can't stop an affiliation election, even though you may think you can. It's the men we have to win, their hearts and their minds and their souls. You can't hand the union to them; they've got to fight

430

for it. Like a baby learning to walk. You can hold his hand, but ultimately he's got to take that first step himself. And then he never loses the taste of success that was his in that moment."

Jim, although he didn't want to, understood the union man. Put that way, his argument could not be challenged. But there was something wrong. Andy had been too courteous, too reasonable. There had been no questioning of what Jim's proposal would mean for him.

Jim shook Andy's hand. "Thanks for the meeting," Jim said, opening the door to his car.

When he was behind the wheel, Andy lowered his head to the open window. "You mentioned a traitor in your company," he said. "I'm just curious—do you know who it is?"

Jim shook his head.

It was past midnight. The mansion was still. The air was chilly. Jim, feeling numb and defeated, moved into the parlor and collapsed onto the sofa facing the darkened fireplace. He lifted his long legs onto the top of the Early American coffee table Anne had recently purchased. And he closed his eyes.

Anne was upstairs—but maybe she wasn't. It didn't matter. Sarah, he hoped, was free of her worry and sleeping peacefully. At least, as things had turned out, she would not have to be told of his peace gesture to the union. Who was the traitor? Robert Allen, the smooth-talking, ambitious business-man? Doubtful. It just didn't fit. Andy LeGrande, as always, merited special vigilance. The explanation of his rejection of the compromise proposal had seemed rational. But something else besides logic, something devious, had to be behind any decision from the union man. Baxley's behavior also had been bothersome—how sneaky and dishonest he had seemed when announcing his action that amounted to betrayal. How embarrassing to sulk in defeat from the Baxley mansion, his tail between his legs. If only he could do it over again, he'd let Baxley know just what he thought of him. Maybe if he got angry enough, he'd even pop him, just once, right on the chin with the proper touch to send the son of a bitch sprawling.

Jim opened his eyes. Strangely, despite all that had happened, he did not feel angry. There was no tension in his body. He was filled with a growing wave of tranquillity, an inner peace totally incongruous with the war he was waging. Was this the same almost mystical experience found on death row in the hours before a hanging?

He looked above the fireplace at the portrait of Augustus now hanging there. His mother had commissioned it shortly after the burial. The image was unlike Augustus, neither scowling nor grinning. Too serious. And almost saintly. The artist was far off his mark. Underneath the portrait's frame, the head of the pickax was back in its place. *Ex Disciplina Venit Libertas*. But no amount of discipline or hard work would by itself salvage the company now. Such virtues, in the era of cartels and conglomerates, were irrelevant.

There had been the colonel. Then the major. He himself was supposedly the captain. If he lost the company, would he be busted to PFC? He removed his legs from the table and straightened his back. The lineage had come to an end. There were no more Porters. He was the last. And whatever did or did not happen to the Porter Coal Company now would mean nothing twenty, thirty or forty years later, when the name Porter survived only as a chiseled block of letters on a bank of tombstones.

Anne wouldn't understand this—she was concerned only about the present, and left thinking about the future to the men. Bonnie, however, would know what he meant when he said that the Porter dynasty didn't matter anymore, that there were more important things than one's pedigree. Bonnie would. . . .

A thought suddenly came to him. He rose to his feet. It was a startling revelation, yet it was so clear. And it had been there all the while, just waiting for him to acknowledge it.

He needed a drink. As he poured the bourbon into the glass,

he shook his head, bemused. Sometimes one arrived at such insights through a long and agonizing process of deduction, the laborious sorting out of facts and alternatives. Other times the knowledge came in a burst of serendipity, an answer that was suddenly there without warning.

In an instant of inspiration, many things had fallen into place; many things now could be understood. He knew that he would have to discard the past and acknowledge what fate had cast for him. He knew now the mandate facing him.

The lineage had not come to an end.

CHAPTER 15 _____

The sky was crystal blue and cloudless, the sun shining warm and brightly on the kind of rare summer day that turns the mountain ranges into glistening jewels of refracted sunbeams and inspires lethargy in even the most motivated of workers. Main Street and the town square were full of people moving at lazy paces. Several young boys rested their backs against the park's trees. It was not a day for worry.

Bonnie was at the wheel of a jeep. She was dressed in her nurse's whites, the starched material radiating brightly in the sunlight. As she looked at the kids in the park, she was filled with envy, thinking how nice it would feel to sit under a tree, her legs stretched out in the grass with no concern other than what she would eat for lunch. As it was, she had little more than one hour to visit Andy LeGrande at Cedar Ridge before reporting to her shift at the clinic. She wanted to see Andy to invite him to dinner.

When an oldie by the late hillbilly Hank Williams came over the jeep's radio, Bonnie joined in, humming. She felt exhilarated, almost giddy, and as the road took her higher, the clear mountain air refreshed her and filled her with energy. Here and there the sun struck a house window or car and reflected in a sparkle bright enough to force Bonnie to avert her eyes. It was cooler at the higher elevations, and a soft breeze occasionally brushed her face, but the rock absorbed the sun, and she could feel the heat from the passing palisades. The valleys and hollows off to the side of the roadway appeared inordinately lush in the bright light, patterned in incandescent greens and yellows. Birds of numerous sizes and species soared over the countryside, and in the distance, a long coal train of at least 120 cars snaked its way toward the Red Fox tipple.

By the third week of the picketing the men walking the line at Cedar Ridge had begun to see their spirits fluctuate. On most days now, there were seldom more than a half dozen pickets pacing back and forth along the sheriff's wooden barriers. On some occasions, especially late at night, the number fell to two or three lonely men. At such times the pickets parted ranks without reluctance to permit the heavy coal trucks bearing the Porter workers to pass. Their enthusiasm had been sapped so much by the tediousness and apparent futility of their demonstration that they merely stood to the side, allowing the convoy to crawl past them under the watchful eyes of the Porter security guards. However, the union's cause sometimes aroused the interest of a greater number of men for reasons not entirely clear. When it did, two dozen or more pickets appeared. The line assumed a rebellious flavor, and the hard-core union men knew more than ever that what they were doing was right and necessary. As she rounded the bend for the descent to the Cedar Ridge Valley, Bonnie saw that this was the case now. More than thirty-five men were walking the line or sitting to the side out of the sun.

She found Andy propped against an empty oil drum in the shade of a tree with five men scattered around him. As usual, he was lecturing. "You bastards can laugh now, but I'll have the last laugh when they take your jobs away and start mining coal like it was gas."

435

"I still say it's bullshit," one of the miners said.

"You just listen to Andy LeGrande. I'm telling you thick-headed SOBs that they've already got a dozen ways of gasifying coal," Andy said. "And now there's a scientist right here in West Virginia who's got a plan to set coal on fire right in the vein."

"You're kiddin'? What good would that do?" asked Duke Shaw, joining the group.

"What good would it do?" Andy repeated. "Don't you see? It would do away with the need to extract coal. There'd be no mining anymore, and simpleminded bastards like these guys would be out of a job," he said.

"How could they do it, this here burning?" Duke asked.

"Like the oil rigs, I think. They'd drill one hole to pump pressurized air into the vein and then drill another for the hot gases from the burning coal to escape. The gases would power turbines, which in turn would run generators for electricity," Andy explained.

"Another pipe dream," said one of the other miners.

"Maybe so. But you can never tell, and this professor says they've already got the microwave machines to keep track of where the fire spreads underground," Andy said.

"How does the good professor propose to stop the flames at a lease line—with fire hoses?" one of the men asked, laughing derisively.

Andy looked at him in a combination of condescension and sympathy. "I'm surprised at you, Pete. You ought to know by now that if there's a way to do something cheaply and save a buck, these mineowners won't let anything stand in their way, least of all a lease line. They'd work something out."

Andy had started to relate other advances in the gasification of coal when the growling of a convoy of Porter trucks could be heard from around the bend. It was the arrival of the day shift.

Without comment, Andy and the other men moved to the

picket line. In a few moments the convoy appeared, a sheriff's patrol car in the lead. The line of trucks came to a stop, waiting for the pickets to part. None of the union men moved. Although no words had been exchanged, and no orders given, the group of unionized miners had reached a point of collective frustration that inspired impulsive defiance, defiance in the form of a wall of men, two and three deep, who did not break for the powerful diesel trucks and who stood there, silently immobile, blocking the trucks from the bridge that would take the Porter men and the out-of-town scabs to the portal.

The two deputies in the patrol car sounded their siren. Still, the men did not move. Then, grabbing their batons, the deputies left their vehicle and strutted authoritatively toward the balking union men.

Bonnie, standing to the side, did not watch what happened next. Her eyes had caught sight of the uniformed guard sitting in the cab of the second truck. He was a huge black man, and when he removed his hat to pat the sweat from his balding head with a blue handkerchief, she was sure—it was Will Thomason.

"Will!" she called out, advancing toward the truck. "Will Thomason, is that you?"

The guard peered out at her, craning his neck to see who had called out his name. When he spotted Bonnie, he pushed his head out the open window and grinned.

"Well, I'll be damned," he said. "I know you—you're Duke Shaw's little girl, aren't you?"

She nodded. "I didn't think I'd ever see you again, Will. Didn't figure you'd ever come back to Porterville."

"Yeah, I thought that myself for a while. Didn't think I'd get out of that prison alive. But here I am."

Bonnie was startled at how much Will had aged. The band of hair around the side of his head was pure gray. His face was heavily furrowed, and a thick scar ran across his left cheek. But he still seemed solid, and she guessed that he had probably lost little, if any, of his strength.

"How's your family, Will? How's the wife?" she asked.

Will's expression changed. He no longer was smiling. "She won't have me. Not that she doesn't have good reason. Took all my money. And believe me, I had quite a little nest egg."

"I'm sorry, Will. But maybe if you get settled down again you'll win her back. She's a good woman, that wife of yours." She moved closer and took hold of his thick forearm. Her voice grew softer. "Don't you know what you're doing, Will, working at this place? Don't you know why the men are out here?"

"Yeah, one of these union boys collared me in town and tried to give me religion. But Porter's payin' a lot of money—more than twenty thousand dollars a year with overtime—and you know I need it if there's any hope for me getting my old lady back. I'm an ex-con, child. An ex-con."

"But, Will, can't you see it's for your own good? You don't need to wear that uniform; you can get your old job back in the mines."

"Too old for that," he said.

"Well, maybe the union would hire you."

Will smiled. His mouth opened to respond. But no words came. Bonnie heard a slight, almost inaudible thud. A blotch of bright red appeared on Will's forehead. His neck snapped back, and his face froze in the grotesque shape of instant death. In what seemed several minutes but was only a split second, Bonnie heard the report of the rifle.

Two more shots rang out. The side window of the lead coal truck shattered.

"The cliff!" one of the pickets screamed. As Bonnie turned to look at the wall of rock above and behind her, the line of security guards across the creek opened fire, peppering the cliff with one volley after another. Bonnie thought she saw a mop of red hair on one of the fleeing gunmen. She had seen at least three of them.

Bonnie fell face down to the ground. Andy, panic on his

face, was yelling to the others, "Stay down. Don't move. You get up, and they'll blast you."

Bedlam let loose as terrified Porter miners jumped in desperation from the vulnerable open bins of the coal trucks. The guards from the trucks and the two deputies charged into the prone union men, their clubs and blackjacks swinging. A roar of pained screams and battle whoops filled the valley.

Andy, clubbed in the back of his knees and head, crumpled. Bonnie crawled toward him.

The guards across the creek, incensed at seeing the sniper's murder of Thomason, lowered their line of fire from the cliff to the roadway. Shots ricocheted all around the brawling truck guards and union men. One deputy shouted to the other to summon the sheriff by radio. The second deputy scurried toward the patrol car but was cut down by a shot from the cliff above.

Bonnie looked for her father. Just as she spotted him, a fist from an enraged guard caught Duke in the mouth, impaling his lower lip on his teeth and sending him sprawling, his blood spraying the air as he fell. From the background, Bonnie heard a voice coming over the trucks' CB radios: "Get the bastards, dammit! Kill! Kill! Kill!"

Andy, whose head was bleeding, pushed Bonnie's hand away. "These sons of bitches!" he muttered.

"You've got to do something, Andy!" Bonnie begged him. "Stop it before everyone's killed. They've already hurt my father."

"What can I do? What can anyone do?"

Before she could respond, Bonnie heard the sound of a helicopter growing louder over the ridge. Soon the aircraft landed across the creek. Through its bubble she could see Jim Porter and Robert Allen.

The noisy arrival of the chopper brought a halt to the gunfire. Bonnie didn't wait to see how long the peace would last. Her steps came automatically. She heard nothing and saw nothing except the bridge that crossed the creek between her and the Cedar Ridge portal. The image of Will Thomason's grimace of death and the circle of blood splotched on his forehead returned to her and stayed, as real as it was in the millisecond it happened. Thomason was dead, Andy clubbed, her father beaten, and a half dozen others were wounded or killed already. The violence had to stop. Jim could stop it. She would cross the bridge to Jim Porter and beg him to do something to end it.

Bonnie didn't hear Andy and Duke shouting to her to come back, to get out of the line of fire. She didn't see Jim Porter frantically waving to her to get down. In her bloodstained nurses' uniform she ran across the bridge to Jim, who jumped from the chopper, grabbed her by the arm and pulled her to safety behind a truck.

"Jesus Christ, Bonnie! Are you crazy?" he screamed at her, still gripping her forearm forcefully.

"You must stop this, Jim. It's got to end," she pleaded, her eyes wide and imploring.

"Didn't he tell you?"

"Didn't who tell me?"

"Your friend LeGrande. I met with him and tried to make peace. I told him the union could come in on whatever terms he wanted. I've got enough trouble with some New York outfit named Landex International that's trying to steal the company from me."

"You offered to let the union in?" Bonnie asked incredulously.

"I did. And he turned me down. Said he didn't want it that way. And this happened. I came here as soon as I could to try to stop it."

Bonnie was furious. She believed Jim. He had nothing to gain by lying. She broke his grasp and sprinted back across the bridge to confront Andy. But when she reached the roadway, she found the sheriff leading Andy away. Other uniformed men were searching the cliff where the initial shots had come from. It was all over. The gunmen had fled.

"Where are you taking him, sheriff? Is he under arrest?" Bonnie asked Carter while he shoved Andy into the back seat of his patrol car.

"Not under arrest. At least not yet," the sheriff replied. "Just say he and I are goin' to have a little talk about all this. I won't have it in my county." He climbed into the car and drove away.

Bonnie's questioning of Andy would have to wait; she had to tend to her father. When she found Duke being treated by Dr. Spencer, she began circulating to comfort the other wounded and injured. The area looked like a battlefield. The odor of gunpowder lingered. Except for the rumbling of the trucks and an occasional moan of pain, it was eerily silent.

Later, Bonnie helped place the bloodied body of Will Thomason onto a stretcher and tenderly covered his lifeless form with a blanket.

Jim Porter spent the next morning meeting with Robert Allen at the company office trying to decide what to do about the picketing at Cedar Ridge and the bloodshed that had resulted. Jim felt helpless. He was not to blame that LeGrande had rejected his settlement offer, and it was not Jim's men who had fired from the cliff, touching off the violence. Still, he had to try something to end it. The best idea he and Allen could come up with was to make yet another peace gesture to Andy LeGrande.

Jim decided to forget the request for financial help and simply propose that the company and the union end their battle and get on with the business of extracting coal. First, however, he wanted to talk to his mother. His conscience had been bothering him, and he didn't want to make a move behind her back again.

Marie met Jim at the mansion's door. "Do you know where my mother is?" he asked her.

"She's gone, sir. Went to consult with the minister," the maid replied.

"And how about my wife? Where is she?"

"Upstairs. She's napping, sir. She said she wasn't feeling very well," the servant said.

Jim started to climb the stairs, but a shout from the maid stopped him. "Mr. Porter! Just a minute, sir!" she yelled.

"What is it, Marie?" Jim asked, irritated.

"Ah . . . the stove, sir. We've been having trouble with the stove. Perhaps you could have a look at it, please?" the woman suggested.

"Of course, I'll get to it a little later," Jim responded, continuing on upstairs.

"No, Mr. Porter! No!" Marie shouted, her voice frantic.

"What's the matter with you, Marie? I've never seen you like this."

The maid was embarrassed. She lowered her head and softened her voice, answering him like a child caught in a forbidden act. "I don't think you want to go up there, Mr. Porter. That's all I can tell you," she said.

Bonnie had had trouble sleeping, and although the clinic was busy treating some of the injured from the previous day's battle, she found herself unable to concentrate on her work. She was preoccupied with thoughts about Andy. It made more and more sense to her. She turned the evidence over and over in her mind: Andy's rejection of the peace offer; Jim's revelation about the raid on his company; the bloodshed and its effect on the company's production. It looked like Andy had refused to end the picketing because of some alliance with the firm seeking to take over the Porter Coal Company. It was logical. Still, she didn't want to believe it. Andy seemed too honest to resort to such a tactic. She had to see him.

Instead of taking a lunch hour, Bonnie walked to the

union office. Yes, a man there told her, Andy had been released by the sheriff. In fact, she had just missed him. He
had concluded a meeting only a few minutes ago.

"A meeting with whom?" she asked.

"Some fellow named Romani or something like that. I
think he had a New York accent."

"Where did Andy go?"

"To the Porter house, I believe," the man replied. "I think
he said he had to speak to Jim Porter."

"Thanks," Bonnie replied. She ran back to the clinic and
borrowed Spencer's jeep. With the accelerator pressed nearly
to the floor, she raced to Porterville. Jim had to be warned.

The maid's strange behavior and her expression of panic
communicated more than her words. "What the hell is going
on here?" he said, racing up the stairs, taking the steps two
at a time. The door to the bedroom was closed. He slapped
his palm against the doorknob, twisted it with a jerk and
kicked the door open.

A shirtless man was seated on the edge of the bed with his
back to the door. Anne, wearing only a bra and panties, was
massaging the back of his neck. Startled by the noise from
the door, both snapped their heads around to face Jim.

Andy's expression immediately signaled his surrender. His
talent with words could not possibly help him now. Saying
nothing, he moved to a chair and retrieved his shirt.

"Get dressed, and get your fat ass out of here!" Jim shouted
to him, his eyes never leaving the figure of his wife, who
remained on the bed looking alternately between Jim and
Andy.

The union man, moving quickly, slipped into his plaid
shirt but didn't bother to button it. He stepped into his boots
and grabbed his hat from the dresser. He started to leave but
Anne motioned him to stay. He did.

Jim glared at Anne. She stared back at him. Despite the

443

scene he had walked into, he didn't feel angry. She was too pitiful for hate. He didn't care. He didn't care what happened to Anne Baxley Porter anymore.

"Why?" he asked her. "Can you tell me that much?"

She smiled arrogantly. "Because I wanted to."

The anger that had been absent from him a second before suddenly exploded. Jim moved to the bed, grabbed her arm and lifted her to her feet. "You goddamned spoiled, selfish bitch!" He shouted, clenching his fist and cocking his arm. Anne began to quiver, her face filling with fear. But Jim didn't hit her. He released his grip on her arm, and she fell to the bed, pulling the sheet to cover her.

Jim brushed past Andy, moved to the door and called loudly for the maid.

Marie timidly appeared at the bedroom door. "Pack a couple of bags for Mrs. Porter," Jim ordered. "She'll be leaving."

Anne, lifting the sheet to cover her breasts, sat up abruptly. "What do you think you're doing?"

"I don't know. I honestly don't know what I'm going to do about you. But one thing I do know is that I want you out of my sight. There's no whore going to live in this house. When your bags are packed, you're going home to your mother, so you might as well get dressed." He yanked a dress from her closet and threw it at her. "And right here in our own bed," he said, disgust thick in his voice.

"Not always, my Jim," she said, smirking. "Sometimes we'd sneak into my old playhouse just like you and me, remember?" Her smile disappeared. She buried her face in the dress and began to sob.

Jim ignored her. He turned to Andy. "Just get the hell out of my house, would you?"

"I think you should know that . . ." Andy started.

"I don't want to know one damned thing from you," Jim shot back, grabbing the folds of Andy's shirt and pulling him out of the bedroom.

Bonnie had a strange feeling as she drove into Porterville. The thought of the huge polished oak door of the Porter mansion intimidated her. Recalling the time her father had stood on the porch and pleaded with Augustus Porter for a job for T.C., she had the impulse to go around to the back and use the servants' entrance. But she drove right up the driveway to the front door.

She took a deep breath. Then, she spotted Andy's car pulling out from behind the Porter mansion. Her jeep screeched to a halt when she recognized the man behind the wheel.

Bonnie hopped out of the jeep and moved to the car. "I have just one question for you," she told the startled union organizer through the open window, her voice shaking. "Did you reject Jim Porter's offer of a settlement because of some kind of deal with that Landex company?"

Andy looked away. His voice was distant. "A long, long time ago, I did give a damn. I was an idealistic young man. But then one day I started to get tired of the union this and the union that, giving up my personal life for the cause of men who, with their overtime now, earn more than double what they see fit to pay me. The ungrateful sons of bitches. They didn't deserve my talents, my dedication. It was time for me to get mine."

Bonnie's eyes were wide. "But I believed in you. I thought you actually cared about the men, about fairness, about me."

"You see this?" he said, raising his hand to display his diamond ring. "Do you want to know how I really got this? A dozen payments from mineowners anxious to keep me happy. And there's more, a lot more, stashed away in a bank vault in Charleston."

"I can vouch for that," came a voice from behind Bonnie. She turned around. It was Jim. "He tried to put the bite on me."

"Jim," Bonnie began, "while his men were lying bloodied

all over Cedar Ridge, this modern-day John L. Lewis was all the time conspiring with some official at Landex. I don't understand how he did it."

"Easy, Bonnie," Jim replied. "It's like this. Your bearded friend here is approached by Landex International and goes on their payroll. He needs an insider, so he comes here, ostensibly looking for me, and lets his twinkling eyes enrapture my wife. My faithful wife is one step away from working for Mae Sexton, so naturally she bites the bait. And while they're enjoying themselves here and Lord knows where else, she fills his ears with all sorts of little tidbits about the company. And before the sun sets, that information is in the hands of Landex."

"You mean he was seeing your wife?" Bonnie asked incredulously.

"Seeing her? My God, the windows are still steamed upstairs." Jim's voice changed. "And in the meantime, my wonderful father-in-law also strikes up a cozy deal with Landex. God knows *his* price."

Bonnie turned to Andy. She was seething. "How could you?" she demanded. "You make me sick!" Her eyes filled with hate. She cocked her arm as if to slap him on the face. But he reached for the ignition key, turned it and sped away.

"Whew!" Jim sighed, shaking his head. "It's going to take me a few minutes to sort this one out. Jeez, could I use a drink! How about you?"

"Don't ask twice," she replied.

He led her into the mansion and invited her to sit on the sofa in the parlor. He then went to the kitchen for ice and returned with two chilled glasses of bourbon and water. Both took large gulps.

Jim's anger was spent. Surprisingly his thoughts were relatively clear. "LeGrande," he told Bonnie. "It wasn't really his fault . . . not with that conniving wife of mine."

446

"He sure had me fooled, all his talk of the labor move-ment and workers' rights and fair pay. . . ." Her words trailed away.

Suddenly Jim burst out laughing. "Who would have fig-ured it? Hah! That big grizzly-bear friend of yours and my wife! Can you imagine a more unlikely conspiracy? I just wish my father were still around—he'd drink straight for a month."

Bonnie smiled, and for a few moments neither said any-thing. Jim busied himself with his pipe. Bonnie fingered the collar of her uniform.

"Tell me," Jim said finally, "where do you think I went wrong?"

"Who says you went wrong?" she asked him.

"It seems like only yesterday that we were holding hands and talking of the future, and now I look in the mirror and I see an old man. Where did it all go?" He turned away from her, his fingers fondling the bowl of his pipe. "I've got no children. My so-called wife turns out to be a selfish bore who never knew the meaning of the word 'love,' sleeps with a man out to get me and spends so much money an entire family fortune starts flowing down the drain."

Bonnie searched for a way to respond. She was spared when both of them were distracted by the sounds of luggage being pushed down the stairs. In a moment the front door slammed shut. Anne was gone.

Jim sighed. He wanted to forget the past few minutes. He looked at Bonnie and smiled. "What about you? How's that arts and crafts project going?"

Bonnie stammered, caught off guard by his sudden change in subject. In the context of what had just happened, the question was trivial. But she shared his desire to turn their attention to something else. "Well, last year a man visited one of our fairs who happened to be a storeowner from New York. He liked what he saw and made us a proposition: If we shipped him our goods, he'd display them on consignment.

447

They've been selling like crazy ever since—right in the heart of famous Madison Avenue between all those fancy art galleries and boutiques you read about."

"That's great, Bonnie. I'm proud of you," he said. "Those crafts represent important skills to this area. It's good that the rest of the country is starting to see what we can do."

Bonnie nodded energetically. "You know, sometimes for the heck of it, I make it a point to have lunch alone at the motel in Bannerton. I like to listen to the traveling salesmen and what they have to say about us. 'These people are something else,' I heard this one man say the last time I was there. His companion asked what he meant. 'Well, I stopped in this gas station and asked for directions. There were three of them there, all doing nothing, and nobody said a thing.' He went on to tell how he stood there until finally a young fellow says to an old-timer, 'You'd better tell 'im, Jonas. I'll only git 'im lost.' The salesman looked up from his food and said, 'They're ignorant and rude, I tell you.'

"Jim, I wanted to scream. I wanted to stand up and tell them that it's not rudeness—it's just the way, that's all. The way people get after two centuries of poverty and the memories of maiming and death under the watch of a stern God and the humility a person gets when he measures his life in tons of coal. But how could they possibly understand?"

"I don't know, Bonnie," Jim said, made reticent by the intensity of her feelings.

She looked at him. "I never thought I would say this, Jim —not to the son of Augustus Porter—but I've been watching you, and I actually think that now you yourself understand it. And that makes you a better man."

Jim turned from her. For a moment he was pensive. Then, his eyes wide and unblinking, he looked at her again and said, "And now the company is facing the greatest challenge in its history, just as we're starting to get somewhere. It's a damn shame, too. Because it's not only the company, it's a tradition." Bonnie touched his arm. He bent forward, and his eyes narrowed. "But as sure as I'm sitting here, that company is going to survive."

"You'll do it, Jim. I know you will. You must," she told him. Her eyes grew misty and distant. "Sometimes I think I liked it more the way it used to be, despite the fact that no miner had much money."

Jim nodded. "Me, too. The days when Porterville was like a secluded little village nestled into the mountains. There was a certain peacefulness then, no hustle, no greed." He paused to fill his pipe, the aroma of his tobacco filling the room as soon as he zipped open its pouch. "Remember the day we met at Blakely's? Your father and the other fellows had just buried someone's thumb. What was that man's name? Evans! That's it. That's whose thumb it was."

Bonnie smiled with the memory.

"Lou Greentree was his classic self that day. I don't think I'll ever forget it," Jim continued. It had been years since he had given any thought to his drinking sessions with the mining men at Blakely's. The store didn't exist anymore; a fire had gutted the building, and it had been paved over into a small parking lot. "Then we went berry picking, do you remember that?" he asked. Bonnie, still grinning, nodded. "I ended up sitting in the creek, and if my memory's right, you ended up a little wet, too. And then the carnival. It's too bad they don't have them anymore. Say, whatever happened to that duck? Do you remember the duck? I gave him to you. The poor thing was your responsibility."

"I was afraid you'd ask that. The duck ran away," she said, her eyes distant. "I never saw him again."

Jim edged closer to her, his face inches from hers. "And the belfry. The day we climbed to the church tower. That was the most beautiful moment of my life, Bonnie." His voice became lower and he spoke slowly. "What happened, Bonnie? What happened to us?"

She turned toward him. "Why did you have to say it, Jim? Why did you have to tell your pa you were only using me?"

He pulled back slightly. Then, speaking more to himself than to her, he answered, "At the time I didn't think I had a choice. But they were only words. They weren't true." Both were silent, their memories seeming to hang in the air as each pondered the forces that had pulled them apart in one climactic breakdown in communication.

Finally, Jim pressed close to her again and took her hand. "It doesn't have to be. You know that, Bonnie. You're a free woman. As soon as the judge signs the papers, I'll be a free man. We could give it a try." A tear rolled down her cheek. Moving slowly, he tenderly kissed the teardrop away. Her eyes opened wide, and she looked at him searchingly, a middle-aged woman who had, in that instant, the vulnerability of a teenaged girl. Jim kissed her again, this time on the lips, and they fell into an embrace. He tightened his grip on her hand. She shuddered. For the moment he felt as if they had been moved back in time to a day when their drives and emotions were still youthful and clear, not yet fogged by reality and years.

Then she stopped it. "No," she said, pushing him away. "It's not the time, Jim. Maybe someday . . . but not now."

He fell back on the sofa, feeling embarrassment more than defeat and surprised at how he had acted upon impulse. He resumed his busywork with his pipe while Bonnie ran her hands through her hair and straightened herself in her seat.

After a few moments Jim rose, took a deep breath and stretched his arms. "I guess I'd better be going," he said, starting for the foyer.

"Where?" she asked.

"To Cedar Ridge. I want to be the one who tells those pickets how Andy LeGrande sold them out. I want to see their faces when they hear about his little sweetheart deal. They'll run him out of the county if he's not already gone."

They had passed through the foyer and reached the porch. "I'll go with you," Bonnie said.

"No. It's best you don't. They might not believe me, and then things could get a little wild," he said from the steps.

Acting on impulse, she bent forward and kissed him on the cheek. "Be careful," she said, standing on the steps and watching him walk to his car parked a few yards down the circular driveway.

CHAPTER 16 ⎯⎯⎯⎯⎯⎯⎯⎯

Bonnie was awakened by the sound of a bird outside her window. Not yet wanting to surrender the peace sleep had brought her, she kept her eyes closed. She curled up on her side and cuddled the pillow, hoping to delay her return to the world as long as possible. When the bird finished its chirping and flew away, she reached to her left, but her fingers failed to find Jim. All she felt was the silk sheet, the smoothness of which she still couldn't adjust to.

It was hard to believe. They had been married two days short of a month. Mrs. Bonnie Porter. It sounded so strange and unlikely, as unlikely as the thought that she would wind up living in an eighteen-room mansion with five baths and a bedroom as large as her entire former home.

It had happened so quickly, and as she stretched on the silk sheets, opening her eyes to the light of a new day, she relived the moment, a moment she would remember always.

Jim had come to her the day after discovering Anne and Andy in the bedroom of his house. It was late—nearly midnight—and his knocking at the window of her home startled her.

"What in the world are you doing?" she asked incredulously when she met him at the door.

"I've got to talk to you, Bonnie. I can't stand it anymore."

She was confused. "Okay. Come on in."

"No. I don't want to wake your parents. I've brought my car. I thought maybe you could throw on a coat and take a ride with me."

In a few moments she was seated beside him in Jim's car, and they were heading slowly out of Porterville.

"I couldn't sleep at all last night, and I've been pacing the floor all today. I had to see you, Bonnie," Jim said.

From the light cast by the passing lampposts, Bonnie could see that Jim did look weary. "Well, that's understandable, I think. After all, a lot of things happened to you yesterday. I mean, with your wife and all."

"It's not that," he said. "It's us. You and me, Bonnie. We've been lying to each other for twenty years."

"What do you mean?"

A rabbit scampered through the beams of the car's headlights. They were on the road to Bannerton. "It's not hard to explain. For years you've been walking around thinking conceited old Jim Porter, the son of a mineowner, wanted nothing to do with you because you were an immigrant miner's girl except to lure you to a church belfry. And I've been assuming that because of one stupid mistake on my part, I could never win you back." He took his eyes off the road and glanced toward her. "As I see it, we've both been fools. It doesn't have to be that way."

Bonnie was suspicious. She had fallen for a Porter's pitch once too often and had vowed to herself that it would never happen again. "I just don't know, Jim," she heard herself saying. "It all happened so long ago, and when I think about it, I wonder if it just wasn't meant to be, that you and I were hoping for too much when we thought it might work. We were kids, Jim. We're not kids anymore."

"I know now how I hurt you, Bonnie, and I'm sorry. I hurt a lot of people, I guess. But it wasn't intentional. I didn't mean it—or even understand what was happening. I just played by what I thought were the rules—what they told me were the rules." His voice began to crack. "I could have had it all. I could have had you. But I walked away. And what happened? I ended up marrying a brick wall in as barren a marriage as one can have, no children, no laughter, no love. I don't think I knew how to love—at least not after losing you."

Even the dim light from the dashboard was sufficient to reveal that tears were rolling down his cheeks. "Stop it, Jim. You don't have to be so hard on yourself."

They had reached the outskirts of Bannerton. Jim pulled the car to the side of the road and shut off the engine. He turned to face Bonnie. "Can't we give it a try, one more time before it's too late?"

He took her hand. Bonnie coughed nervously. "Jim, there's something I think you should know."

"What's that?"

There was no answer. Bonnie couldn't say it, couldn't tell him. Not at that moment. She coughed again to fill the void. "Life is never very simple," she said finally, stumbling over the words. "You may think you alone are responsible for this or responsible for that, but it's not so—there are too many outside forces at work on our lives. Especially here in Coal County. We've become the world's pawns."

His arm moved around her, and against all the force of her logic and the warnings from the past, she allowed him to pull her head to his chest. In a moment he was kissing her, the bristles of his mustache pressing against her skin. She could smell his after-shave lotion and found it a familiar scent. Could it possibly be the same one he had worn so many years earlier on carnival day? Through his shirt she could feel his biceps and huge pectoral muscles, as hard as ever, but there was still a gentleness to his touch as he ran his fingers up and down the back of her neck. Despite all her bitterness at seeing Porters victimize her father, her husband, herself, despite all the hatred the years had built into her soul, Bonnie now locked her arms around Jim Porter, clinging to him in an embrace that electrified every nerve in her body, an embrace that contradicted everything she had said since her last visit to the mountaintop, every promise she had made. She clung to him and wanted never to let go.

Suddenly, however, Jim moved away. He took a deep breath. "I don't think we can stay here," he said softly. "If one of the sheriff's men comes along . . . well, we're not exactly teenagers."

Bonnie laughed. "Can't we pretend?"

"Well, we can't go to your place—your folks are there. And my ma's at my house."

"We're being silly, aren't we? Two people our age in search of a lover's lane." She giggled.

"I've got it!" he announced, starting the car and throwing it into gear.

"Where?"

"You just leave it to me."

They drove through the deserted downtown area of Bannerton and turned right after passing the cinema with its darkened marquee. It was a narrow, winding road that led to . . . the Club Havana!

"Hey," Bonnie protested, "you're not taking me in there."

"Hush," he shot back.

A half dozen cars were parked in front of the club. Jim drove by them and pulled to a spot at the rear of the one-time railroad hotel. Taking Bonnie's hand, he pulled her toward the rear door. She protested each step of the way.

Bonnie couldn't see who answered Jim's knock. "Get Mae," he said. "Tell her Jim Porter's here."

In a moment an elderly woman with large circles of rouge on her face was at the door. Her hair was paper white and piled high in a mound of small curls.

"Jimmy!" the woman exclaimed. "My God, I thought you were dead for all the years since I last saw you. Don't you still have a spot in your heart for poor old Mae?"

"You told me once that if I ever needed anything, I could come to you," Jim said.

"Of course, Jim. What do you need?"

"A room."

"A room?" she asked, bewildered. Then she broke into a grin. "Oh, I see. Yes, a room. I got just the one for you."

The old woman escorted them up a rear stairway to the second floor and to a door midway down a long hall. Opening it, she swept her hand to usher them inside. "Anything you want, you just yell. Jeez, it's good to see you, Jim." She pinched his cheek and gently closed the door.

Bonnie could sense that the room was large. A single candle burned in a tall glass chimney on a table in a corner, and the room was almost completely dark. It took a few seconds for her eyes to adjust and see that the walls were paneled in dark red padded velvet. Her feet sank into a thick shag rug that was pure white. A huge oval mirror in a gilded frame was hung on the wall across from the bed. It was a Victorian bed with four tall posts and a canopy as white as the carpet. It was the biggest bed she had ever seen.

Jim guided her to the bed, and they sat on its red silk sheet. As Bonnie ran her fingers across the smooth fabric, he asked, "How's this?"

She giggled. "You have no idea how being in this place makes me feel." Then her expression grew serious. "I must ask you how it is you happen to know that lady?"

He laughed. "Mae and I go back a long time. She was one of the nicest results of my father's streak of craziness and we—"

There was a soft knocking at the door. Jim went to answer

it. He accepted a tray and bucket from someone Bonnie couldn't see. The door closed, and Jim moved to a table.

"Champagne," he announced. "Compliments of Mae."

Bonnie heard the pop of the cork, and in a moment Jim was handing her a chilled long-stemmed glass. He sat beside her.

"To us," he proposed. "Two children of the mountains who aren't intelligent enough to grow old."

They clicked glasses and sipped. The taste of the champagne mixed with the rose perfume of the room. To Bonnie's surprise, the bubbly liquid felt good to her tongue—she had never tasted champagne before.

As they sipped from the crystal glasses, Jim massaged Bonnie's back. Neither said a word until Jim took her glass and set it with his on a side table. Then he fell to one knee in front of her and took one of her hands. Bonnie, her throat still tingling from the champagne, laughed at the sight.

"Don't laugh," he scolded. "This is serious. I'm falling to my knees before you to ask you for your hand." Then he returned to her side. His grip on her hand tightened. "I mean it, Bonnie. For one of the few moments in my life I'm being deadly serious. I want you to marry me. I've already talked to Judge Hemphill, and he's assured me that for the proper considerations he can wrap up my divorce in less than three weeks. He'll marry us the day the divorce becomes final. And you can move right into my home and get out of that firetrap you're in now. Your parents can come, too, of course. And Mari. She needs a father anyway. And there's nothing more that I'd like than to be her father. Will you, Bonnie? Please say yes."

Her head turned to the side. "Jim, I just don't know. I mean, you're springing this on me. I haven't had time to catch my breath." Her mind flashed with memories—Jim splashing in a creek, a crazy duck tied to a tether, a moment in a church belfry never to be forgotten—and she heard herself saying, "Yes."

Jim took her in his arms and they both fell backward to the silk sheets of the bed. When his lips left hers for a moment, she said, "I wonder how many girls have said yes to a marriage proposal on the second floor of a brothel."

Jim didn't answer, but reached for the top button of her blouse. In a moment they were undressed. "I'll never hurt you again, Bonnie. On my life I make that promise," he whispered. And they made love.

The rose fragrance of the red-walled room at the Club Havana lingered even as Bonnie awoke on the silk sheets in their bedroom in the Porter mansion nearly two months later. Jim had been right. The divorce had proceeded expeditiously. Duke and Liz, however, had elected to remain in their own home. They did consent to accepting Jim's gift of the deed to their lot. Workmen, paid by Jim, were putting the finishing touches to a virtual rebuilding of the house, inside and out. Mari also had refused to move into the Porter household. And that was still a problem Bonnie had to deal with. "He's not my father," the young woman had declared. "I hate him. And I hate you for marrying him. He's exploited every decent person in this county at one time or another."

Bonnie wasn't certain how to handle Mari. Nor had she gotten up the courage to tell Jim what she had started to say on the day the conspiracy by Anne and Andy was uncovered. But there was no hurry. Bonnie had the time to come up with the answers.

The door to the bedroom opened. It was Jim. He was dressed in a suit and carried a tray. On it was Bonnie's breakfast.

After setting the tray on her lap, he bent to kiss her and then sat by her covered feet. "Are you happy?" he asked.

"Yes."

"No regrets?"

"No."

"That's good. And there won't be any."

She drank from her glass of orange juice. "Why are you up and at it so early today?" she asked.

"A meeting. I've talked my way into an appointment with a banker in Bloomington. He's my last hope. The clock keeps ticking."

Bonnie felt sorry for Jim. He had tried so hard to raise the financing to meet the note payment due to Raymond Baxley. Only four days remained before the deadline. Jim had tried every tactic he could think of, and they had even given up their honeymoon for him to make the effort. He had promised to make it up to her as soon as possible with a trip to Paris.

Financing was not Jim's only business problem. Andy LeGrande had left Coal County for Pennsylvania and the company had been peacefully unionized, but the violent radicals remained. Thus far, their efforts at inciting the Porter miners had failed, but who knew what they would try next to launch their coalfield revolution.

"I had trouble sleeping last night," Jim said. "I'm not sure exactly why. I had this sort of premonition, a sense of foreboding."

"It's just your nerves, Jim."

"No, I think it's more than that." He rose from the bed and moved to the windows to open the curtains. "I never used to believe in such things until one day I had to go visit the Nelson widow to tell her her husband had died. And do you know what, that woman had known the instant of the accident that he was dead. I saw it with my own eyes." He stared through the window for a moment and then said, "Well, I'm driving, so I'd better be going."

"You'll work it out. Maybe this banker will make the loan," she said cheerfully.

"We'll find out soon enough." He returned to the bed and kissed her. "Whatever happens, I love you."

"And I love you."

When Bonnie heard the front door shut, she moved to

the window to wave as he got into the car. Just as she reached the glass, her body froze. Her eyes had caught a glimpse of two bent figures scurrying through the brush away from Jim's car. One of the fleeing figures had bright red hair.

"No, Jim! Wait!" she screamed. But it was too late. He had already turned the ignition key.

The blast sent a ball of fire into the sky, its force rattling the windowpanes. When she recovered from her initial shock, she saw the car a mass of shriveled metal, smoke pouring from what remained of its hood, the heat so intense she could see its currents.

"Oh, my God, no!" she screamed. "No, no, no!" And then she began shouting for help.

Jim did not hear his bride's urgent warning; the bedroom window had been tightly closed. The boom of the explosion reverberated through his head, reducing him to deafness. A warm, wet feeling enveloped his body. The brilliant flash of the dynamite had left him blind, and all he saw was a field of white. But then his mind filled the void with an image of a hand. The hand was wrapped around the grip of a gun, a shotgun exploding time and time again, spraying the air with pellets and snapping Jim's head back with each shot. He heard a voice. "Get down here, Owens, goddammit," it yelled. And he recognized it as his father's. While he felt his body being lifted and eased into the back seat of a car, he heard Augustus over and over again curse Dan Owens. "He's dead, Pa," Jim tried to shout, but he found himself unable to move his mouth. The blasts came faster and faster. Then, as quickly as the first one had come at the twist of his car key, they stopped. The image of his father's hand instantly dissolved, replaced by a dark void growing blacker and blacker. Jim heard what he thought was Bonnie's voice, a startled voice, her panicked words mixed with weeping. He felt the touch of her hand, and his lips sensed the warmth of her kiss, a pleasing sensation that stayed with him until a prick on his arm told him he was receiving some kind of injection. "There's no hope," he heard someone say. And then Bonnie's voice again: "Can I have a moment alone with him?" Now he was certain it was her fingers that were caressing his face, and he worked hard to remember in the enclosing darkness the features of her face, the long jet black hair as soft as silk to the touch and the tenderness of her smile. "I'm sorry," he heard her say, her voice shaken with a sorrow which seemed so inappropriate when he considered the strength and determination that characterized her life. She began talking of a child. "Your daughter," he heard her say. Daughter? What daughter? He tried hard to concentrate, to interpret her words, to remember, but the advancing darkness took her voice away.

He felt himself rising. The blackness, like the early-morning fog, began to roll 'away, burned off by the growing warmth of a spectacular sunrise which filled the sky with a fantail of reds, yellows and orange. As he looked around, he saw that an overnight snowfall had bleached the foothills and mountains sparkling white. The mountain air was fragrant with moisture, and except for the call of an occasional passing bird, there was silence—total silence. When he reached the top of a peak, he sat down and took two deep breaths to clear his lungs. The fresh air, which he felt now like never before, sent a charge of energy through the muscles of his body. He rubbed his eyes and scanned the vista, finding it a sea of rolling land painted white by the newly fallen snow. Below him were Porterville, Bannerton and Livingston, a meandering railroad track connecting the three. Off in the distance was Paw Paw Pinnacle, the county's highest and most majestic peak. As he watched it, the peak moved closer. His vision blurred. He felt dizzy and light-headed, as if he had levitated into the air and were flying like a bird, soaring through the clear blue sky, sweeping over the villages and foothills and the mines with their towering tipples. All the while Paw Paw Pinnacle loomed closer. With one last effort he swept upward, arching his back as he glided toward the very top. He threw back his head until he saw no more of the gray rock. The pinnacle disappeared, leaving only the infinite blue of the West Virginia sky.

Dr. Spencer reentered the room. With him was Sarah Porter. He gently pulled Bonnie off the body. Her clothes were dark with the stains of blood. Her hands were shaking. She watched motionlessly as the doctor rolled a sheet over the mutilated body. Then she and Sarah fell into a silent embrace. Spencer, taking Bonnie's hand, led her from the room, leaving the older woman alone with the remains of her son.

The doctor escorted Bonnie to his office. He offered her a seat, but she declined, moving instead to the window. The sky, which had been so crystal clear earlier in the day, was overcast and gray now. Bonnie searched for a break in the cloud cover but found none. She then switched her gaze to the cut in the foothills toward the Coal County Country Club golf course. Although its fairways were more rocky soil than grass, the golf course had been opened for play. Most of the seventh green and the tee for the following hole could be seen in the narrow view from the clinic.

The golf course was popular. Bonnie, in her moments at the window, had watched the newest wave of coal industry executives, bankers and potential customers parade by while conducting their business between swings of their golf clubs. She didn't recognize most of the golfers. An increasing number of players putting out on the seventh green and teeing off a few yards away appeared to be from out of town, some of them even looked like foreigners.

Bonnie had to do something to occupy her mind, to stave off her grief, to drive away the image of Jim's broken body. So she watched the golf course. She saw three conservatively attired Orientals approach the green with cautious shots. They were accompanied by an American. Japanese, she suspected, thinking that it wasn't too many years earlier that it would have been impossible to escort such a group into the coal-fields—in the 1940s the memories of World War II were too fresh, and later the Japanese bore too striking a resemblance to Koreans. But now, in the arena of international coal trade, the Japanese held the aces. They set the market's pace. The French, Italians, Dutch and others fell into line.

Observing the foursome from the distance, Bonnie was struck by the irony of the Japanese's visit and the welcome extended to them. Fewer than four decades earlier it was a lack of coal that had helped bring the Nippon war machine to defeat. Many of West Virginia's miners were the sons of men who had fought and died at the hands of that machine. Now three Japanese executives were standing on a golf course in the midst of an American coalfield with a local coalman kowtowing to them.

"We're come full circle," she said.

A hand touched her shoulder, surprising her and causing her to stiffen. She turned around. It was Lou Greentree. His expression was grave.

"Bonnie, you have to come with me . . . now," he told her.

"Why, Lou? What's happened?"

"Just come along, would you? The sheriff sent me to fetch you. Don't make it hard on me, please."

Bonnie was mad. "Come on, Lou. Level with me. What is it, my dad?"

He shook his head. "I don't know how to tell you this but . . . well, we tracked those two bombers up into the hills, and they've holed up in a closed mine. . . ."

"Well?"

"Well, one of them is that redheaded radical that's been causing all the trouble, and the other . . . the other is Mari." He looked in her eyes. "I'm sorry, Bonnie."

For a moment she thought she would faint. But then, for the second time within minutes, Bonnie suppressed her emotions. She knew once again what would have to be done. She and Lou rushed from the clinic and raced off in a jeep to an abandoned mine far in the foothills.

About a dozen men were positioned around the portal, crouched behind boulders, slag and rusting machinery for cover. Bonnie saw Hargrave with two of his dogs. Nearby was Sheriff Thad Carter.

The sheriff, seeing her, rushed to her side and took her by the arm. "I formed a posse as soon as I got the call. Grabbed everybody I saw. One of those radicals dropped a pistol near the car. The dogs picked up the scent and took us up here. We almost lost them at the creek, but the hounds picked up the trail again on the other side. They're pinned inside this mine. Lou and I moved in there behind a coal car, and each time we showed our faces, they triggered a shot. Then, when I asked them who the hell they were, one of them, a male, tells me to drop dead. The other one, however, yells back that she's your daughter." He tightened his grip on her arm. "I'm very sorry, Bonnie. I knew she was hanging around with all those hippies, but I never thought it would come to this. Anyway, we don't want anyone to get hurt. I sent Lou for you because I thought maybe you could talk your daughter out. Want to give it a try?"

Bonnie nodded. She was too shaken to talk.

He led her to the rear of a coal car. Lou joined them. They began pushing the car slowly along the track leading to the portal. When the car nudged the partially opened gate, Carter stuck his head around the corner and yelled, "Hey, you in there, the portal's blocked. There's no way for you to get out. Spare yourself, friends, and drop that gun. Raise your hands, and walk on out."

There was no response.

Using a long piece of lumber, Carter reached around the car and pushed the gate open. With the car as cover, they advanced slowly into the mine. "Stay as quiet as you can," the sheriff whispered. "And watch out, for chrissake. Watch out."

The car, trailed closely by the sheriff, Lou and Bonnie, rolled five to ten yards at a time and then paused while they scanned the area ahead. Sufficient light seeped through the portal, so they had no need yet to use the flashlights the men carried. As they rounded a bend, however, the area ahead of them was in nearly total darkness. Carter flipped on his flashlight and swept its beam in front of the car. Seeing no sign of the two fugitives, he signaled to the others to resume pushing the car. They had just started to move again when a shot rang out.

"Stay down!" Carter shouted, quickly flicking his light off. "Anybody hit?"

The others replied negatively.

"Sounds like a pistol," Lou whispered. "A thirty-eight, maybe."

"All right, you," Carter shouted into the black heading. "Let me lay it out. You've got one way out of here, and there are enough armed men blocking it to fight the Civil War again. Lay down your weapon, raise your hands and walk toward us before both of you get shot."

The fugitives answered with another round. "Damn," Lou said in frustration. "They just won't give up."

From the flash of the last shot, Carter said, he had pinpointed the gunman about twenty yards ahead of them. Still very much in control of the situation, the sheriff decided it was time to try another tactic. He moved closer to Bonnie. "The important thing is that nobody gets hurt, Bonnie," he said. "Why don't you just talk to her gentlelike? I'd sure hate to have to fire at that daughter of yours." Bonnie nodded.

"This is your mother, Mari," she called from behind the car. "I understand what you did and why, but there's no sense in anyone getting shot. So drop the gun and come out of there now."

There was no answer. Instead, they heard a male voice: "Mari, throw me that gun!"

"No!" came the response. "I'm keeping it. I can handle all of them."

"It sounds like it's your daughter with the weapon," Carter whispered. "Try it again."

"Mari, I know what you've been through, and it hasn't been easy—" Suddenly Bonnie stood up and walked from behind the car.

"Bonnie, get back! Get back!" Carter shouted, reaching without success to pull her back. "She's disturbed. You don't know what she'll do!"

Bonnie ignored him. "First you lose T.C., and then you lose your hope," she continued, her voice soft as she advanced slowly through the darkness toward her daughter.

"It's suicide," she heard Carter whisper to Lou back at the car.

"I'm angry and bitter, too, Mari. But what is done is done. There's still time to repair the damage, to make it work. Now come to me and give me the gun."

Mari didn't respond.

"There have been injustices and abuses, but there are ways to deal with them besides a gun." Bonnie continued walking. "If you come to me now you'll get help. The sheriff promised me that."

Still no sound from ahead.

"Mari, you're my daughter and I love you. For God's sake, come out!"

Suddenly Mari bolted from the shadows. She held the pistol above her head. Her eyes were shut. She gritted her teeth and pulled the trigger again and again, sending one shot after another into the ceiling of the shaft until the gun merely clicked. It was empty.

"Mari?" Bonnie whispered, holding out her hand.

The two women, both motionless, stared into each other's eyes, the pain of a young girl's lifetime of death, violence and hate passing between them. Mari's eyes began to cloud. Then, moving slowly, she dropped her arm, pointing the pistol toward the ground. Behind her, now cowering in fear, was the redhead, who, for the first time, seemed to have nothing to say.

Bonnie moved forward and took the gun from her daughter's hand. As Lou and the sheriff arrived and roughly hand-cuffed Foster, Bonnie and Mari fell into each other's arms. Both were crying.

The Porter Coal Company, in a notice signed by Executive Vice-president Robert Allen, announced that its mines would be shut down for three days out of respect to its late president, James T. Porter II. The company office was draped in black and the town of Porterville took on the appearances of mourning. The Bannerton *Tribune* devoted two full columns on its front page to Jim's obituary.

On the surface, Coal County reacted to Jim's death as coal communities traditionally had responded to the demise of a coal baron, when an entire region would be thrown into economic turmoil while their sole source of livelihood was passed from one generation to the next. But this was deceiving. As they had with the death of Jim's grandfather nearly four decades earlier, the Porter miners almost immediately upon learning of the death headed en masse to the foothills, seeking fish and game. But this time they had no urgent need to stockpile foodstuffs for their families; they hunted and fished because they enjoyed it, and as a result of the three-day shutdown, they had the time. Similarly the bankers and other creditors with funds still tied up in the company made their appearances. But their concern was not so much for the safety of their money as it was with adhering to time-honored formalities. Neither the capitalist nor the miner was worried about the durability of the Porter Coal Company. The only question was who would take Jim's place at the helm.

The body of Jim Porter lay in repose for two nights, not

at his home in the traditional manner but in a recently opened funeral parlor in Bannerton. Raymond Baxley and the other moneymen were among the first to pay their respects. They then retired to the Club Havana, where Jim's sometimes odd behavior of the past few months was discussed over freely flowing liquor. The nights also were filled with alcohol and a degree of merriment at the homes of the Porter miners as the workingmen, back from the foothills, passed jugs of bootleg in impromptu festive gatherings celebrating their unexpected free time. If there was any evidence that a mineowner no longer ruled as an ironfisted feudal lord, it was there in Porterville in the days after Jim Porter died.

Bonnie was numb. She had witnessed the death of a man she once loved, later hated and finally married in what had seemed to be the beginning of the happiest period of her life. And her daughter had been arrested for destroying that dream in one flash of dynamite, and was now officially described as a conspirator and murderer. Bonnie braced herself with each of the blows, proceeding, as she always did, with the tasks that had to be done. Introspection could come later. At the base of her stoicism was a concession that nothing, absolutely nothing, was immune to change in her life.

Bonnie's first impulse was to protect her daughter, to shield her from society's wrath at her alleged despicable acts. As a mother Bonnie was confused, her emotions torn between love and anger. She realized deep down that despite her devotion to Mari, it had been years since she had really known her daughter.

What Bonnie dreaded most was the revelation that would have to be made to Jim's mother. Sarah had accepted Jim's marriage to Bonnie with grave misgivings, suspecting, Bonnie was certain, that her motivation was the Porter fortune. But Sarah had not directly challenged Bonnie's sincerity. "I believe in my son and his judgment," she had said instead. "If this is his decision, I won't stand in the way." Sarah welcomed Bonnie into the Porter household with restrained cordiality, and despite their brief embrace at the side of Jim's deathbed in the clinic, she kept her distance from Bonnie during the two days of Jim's wake. After all, it had been Bonnie's daughter who was at least partially responsible for the murder.

Then, after she and Bonnie had taken their last looks at Jim's body and the casket was eternally closed, Sarah made a surprising request. "I was just wondering if I might ask you to sing at the funeral," she asked softly. "Jim told me that one of the things he liked best about you was your excellent voice."

"Of course," Bonnie responded. "I'll do anything you want." Sarah reached out and squeezed her hand.

The next morning the sheriff allowed Bonnie to visit Mari. She waited until he had relocked the cell door behind him before saying anything to her daughter. Then, staring unblinkingly at Mari, she asked, "Did you do it? Did you plant that bomb?"

"I'm not talking," Mari replied defiantly.

"But, Mari, I'm your mother," Bonnie said gently.

Mari spoke slowly. "He was a pompous, greedy capitalist who exploited the sweat and muscle of everyone around him—"

"I know you feel all that," Bonnie interrupted. "But my God, did you have to kill him?"

"He wasn't human, Mother. He was a pig. He didn't deserve to live." Bonnie was shaking her head. "I suppose you're going to his funeral?" Mari asked. Bonnie didn't answer.

"Daddy would have hated you for this!" Mari shouted, rising to her feet.

"What do you mean?"

"Going to a Porter funeral after what they did to us. I hate them. I hate them all."

Anger was building within Bonnie, but she knew her daughter was sick. Mari needed to be treated with understanding and compassion. "Jim Porter was a greater man than you realize, honey," Bonnie said softly. "Please try to understand."

"Understand what? How he used you?"

"Let me tell you something. Jim Porter set up a pension for the Nelson widow at a time when he wasn't sure if the company would live another week."

"So?"

"And it was Jim Porter who was paying the room and board for Ernie Jason at the old folks' home and doing it anonymously. Does that sound like a capitalist pig?"

"That was peanuts for him, Mother."

Bonnie was getting madder. Her voice was rising. She knew she was losing control. "And let me tell you one more thing, young lady," she began, but stopped herself. No, not now.

Bonnie kissed her daughter's forehead. "Don't worry, child. Somehow we'll get you the help you need," she said, then turned and knocked on the door to signal the sheriff.

As the time for the funeral service approached, the gray overcast was replaced by a radiantly blue summer sky, interrupted only by an occasional passing puff of cloud. The Porterville First Christian Church was filled to capacity, and Bonnie felt all eyes upon her as she, Sarah, Duke and Liz moved up the aisle to the family's pew at the front.

Jim's casket, beautifully designed and crafted from hand-polished mahogany, was placed to the side of the pulpit. It was covered with a U.S. flag and a modest bouquet of flowers picked in the mountains that morning. The organist played a selection from Bach. When it was finished, the Reverend Weatherson solemnly ascended the steps to the pulpit. He paused for a moment to inspect the faces of the congregation spread below him and then began his eulogy softly. "The Lord giveth and . . ."

As the preacher spoke, a woman attired in an ill-fitting

navy blue dress opened one of the heavy church doors. At first only the mourners in the rear of the church noticed her, but as she made her way slowly up the center aisle, nearly every head turned. As more and more of those present became aware of who she was, a chorus of whispers drifted forward to the pulpit, and the Reverend Weatherson stumbled over his words. The woman, walking with a strut and her chin raised, moved to the front pew across the aisle from Bonnie and took a seat. Bonnie, who had struggled to keep her eyes ahead while hearing the murmurs behind her, now saw the cause of them—Anne Baxley Porter.

Sarah leaned toward Bonnie. "The nerve of her," she whispered. "She could have sat right here with us if she'd given me the courtesy of stopping by the funeral parlor."

The minister's talk lasted about a half hour. When he had finished, he signaled to Bonnie, who then moved to his place in the pulpit. He handed up her guitar, which had been resting out of sight against the pulpit steps.

The church was quiet as Bonnie began softly picking the strings of the instrument. She sang the hymn at half its normal tempo, drawing out each word, letting each note float to the church's wooden rafters. "Amazing grace . . . how sweet the sound . . . that saved a wretch like me," she sang, her voice as clear as mountain air, her guitar responding to her fingertips with haunting sharpness. The congregation, hesitantly at first, began to join in, and when the hymn was over, there was not a dry eye in the church.

The casket was carried in a procession to the small cemetery adjacent to the church. The six pallbearers included Robert Allen, Dr. Gordon Spencer, Henry Crawford, Duke Shaw, Bill Bergen and Lou Greentree. The preacher led a brief graveside service; the casket was lowered, and the service was over, except for the bell, the renewed tolling of which echoed off the walls of the hollows and out into the countryside.

Bonnie, who had held up in the church, finally broke

down at the grave. Sarah took her by the arm and was leading her away when a woman stepped in front of them.

"Just who in the hell do you think you are?" Anne demanded of both of them. "The man's body isn't cold yet, and already you're picking over the spoils." Anne raised her right arm and pointed, her finger only inches from Bonnie's face. "You're trash, that's what you are. You're nothing but a whore." She dropped her arm and turned to Sarah. "I was James Porter's wife," she declared. "His shares in the company belong to me, and don't you forget it!" She turned and walked away, her head held high.

Trash. A tomboy once had taunted Mari with such slander. Now, like her daughter, Bonnie wanted to strike back. "Let's be calm about this and simply walk away," Sarah instructed, taking Bonnie's arm. "I talked to the judge about that woman. She might have some claim, but the judge said there's no way she'll get her hands on the company."

"She can have whatever she wants," Bonnie said emotionlessly. "I don't care."

"Hush, dear," Sarah scolded. "Your home is on that hill now. Don't you forget that. Jim wanted it that way."

As the bell above them continued its pealing, the mourners one by one approached Sarah and Bonnie. There was Robert Allen, looking stunned. Lou Greentree, his embrace powerful and full of emotion. The widow Nelson, her eyes sharing their grief. Axel Blackwood, who also knew the pain of a spouse's unnecessary death. Dr. Spencer, his handshake firm and words touching. The Reverend Weatherson and old red-nosed Blakely, both fingering their chins nervously. A black woman, whom Bonnie didn't recognize until she introduced herself as Will Thomason's widow. Even Mae Sexton, aided by two young women, her rouge streaked from her weeping. And stranger still, Lamon Hubbard, looking worried.

Bonnie and Sarah greeted and thanked each of them. Then, trailed by Bonnie's parents, they walked arm in arm to the mansion.

As was the custom, Bonnie and Sarah received the mourners at the mansion. By dinnertime all had left except Bonnie's parents and Judge Sebastian Hemphill, whom Sarah unexplainedly invited to stay.

"It's all happened so fast I don't know what to think," Bonnie said when they had seated themselves at the dinner table. "All I know is how sad I feel."

"It'll take time to get over it," said her mother.

"First things first, I guess," Duke said wearily. "Mari will need a lawyer."

"We'll get her the best we can find in the state," Sarah said, passing the platter of sliced roast beef to Duke. She cleared her throat. "I've asked the judge to join us tonight because he tells me how Jim placed a very odd reference in his will not too long ago."

"What was that?" Liz asked.

Sarah motioned to Hemphill, who until now had remained silent. "Tell them," she instructed.

Hemphill looked toward Bonnie. "Well, not so long ago, just a day or two after your marriage, Jim came to me. I was kind of his personal lawyer just like I served his father. I don't do much of that now, however, since I'm on the bench. I only make exceptions—"

Sarah coughed impatiently.

"Well, as I was saying, he came to me and asked me to change his will. He named me executor, of course, and while the will won't be probated for some while, I thought it best that you know what Jim did. You see, when Augustus was declared legally dead, Sarah here received half of the family's interest in the company and Jim got the other fifty percent. Now, under the terms of the revised will, you, Bonnie, are to receive every share of the company that Jim Porter owned."

Bonnie had given little thought to the company since Jim's death, but, of course, she had been his wife and would inherit his share of the ownership. The notion filled her with fear. But the judge wasn't finished.

"And Jim further stipulated that upon your death, his estate should be left to your daughter, Mari. He said—and I quote—'Mari Fenner, whose mandate it is to pass on the blood of the Porters.'"

Bonnie's face turned pale. Jim had known. But how? And for how long?

"You see, dear, I was hoping perhaps you could explain that to me," Sarah said. She and the others waited for an answer.

Bonnie cautiously formed each word in her mind before speaking. "I have no idea," she would say. Nothing more than that. Let it remain a mystery. But then it occurred to her that by avoiding an honest answer she would be denying Jim in much the same way he had once denied her. Besides, times had changed—it no longer was as shameful to make love out of wedlock as it once was. No, she decided, she wouldn't lie. She would tell them the truth.

"Mari was Jim's daughter."

Liz's fork crashed onto her plate. Duke gulped. Sarah nodded to indicate her suspicion was now confirmed.

"Bonnie, I think you'd better explain," Duke suggested.

She spoke slowly, measuring her words. "You might remember that Jim and I were seeing each other before he went to London. Well, we made love . . . just once. And I got pregnant."

"And T.C. never knew?" Liz asked, her face white.

"No."

"My God, Bonnie. And all these years you held that inside you?" Duke said, reaching for her hand.

"How did Jim learn of this?" Sarah asked.

"I don't know. Sometimes when we'd bump into him, I'd notice him inspecting Mari very closely," Bonnie replied. "But I didn't think he knew—at least until I tried to tell him on his deathbed. Obviously, I was wrong."

Sarah, having somehow absorbed the fact that Mari, the alleged killer of her son, was her own granddaughter, moved to Bonnie's side, put her arm around her shoulder and said, "My God, child, what you've been through. But enough—we've got the future ahead of us. We'll be a team. Sarah and Bonnie Porter. We'll turn this company around. What the heck, they even have women working inside the mines these days right along with the men. You and me, we can do it. We certainly know more about mining than these outsiders moving here." She patted Bonnie on the back. "And already our first problem's solved."

"Our first problem?" Bonnie asked in a hoarse, broken voice.

"As you know, the company owes that money to Baxley's bank, and they're demanding payment. Three hundred thousand dollars. Jim was afraid we'd lose the company because of it. He didn't see a way to raise the money. But I got a telephone call last night from John Owens down in Florida. He had heard about Jim's death, and he wanted to express his condolences. Well, we got to talking about how things are changing, and I mentioned our little problem with Baxley. Guess what? John said he'd finance us to whatever extent is needed. Said he'd do anything to get back in the coal business. But he told me not to expect him up here. He's having too much fun puttering around in his yacht. Even got himself a commodore's suit." Sarah laughed.

Bonnie stared at the woman, guessing that maybe it was the years waiting for word on what had happened to her husband that made her so capable of dealing with grief. "I don't know what to say," Bonnie told her.

"Don't worry about that now, dear. We've got plenty of time."

Bonnie found it hard to think of the future with such optimism. Jim had left her a coal company and the unknown burdens that came with it. There was nothing in her genes to prepare her for the role of mineowner. In Sarah's—and

475

even Mari's, perhaps—but not hers. What did she really know about the coal business? What did she know about management or selling? Was her life henceforth to be dictated by the requirements of boring tunnels into the sides of mountains? Could two women—she and Sarah—survive in a world almost exclusively controlled by men? The questions stayed with her, one leading to another, until she heard her father asking if she'd like to go for a walk.

"It's very pleasant outside," he told her. "It would do you some good."

They rose from the table.

About a third of the old company homes had been torn down, many of them replaced by new structures or large house trailers financed through the new prosperity brought on by overtime. Almost all seemed to have at least one car, camper or pickup truck parked in front. On the roof of each was a television antenna. To the sides of a few were fancy boats. Until now Bonnie had not really noticed how much Porterville had changed in recent months, the result of the increasing demand—and rising price—of coal.

Most families were indoors finishing their meals, and the street was nearly deserted. Although the sun had dropped below the horizon, the sky retained a glow of red and yellow, and they could see the silhouetted range of mountains in the distance. Gravel crunched under their feet as they walked, and sometimes they could smell the odors of freshly cooked meat or homemade soup.

"How do you think it happened? How did I lose my daughter?" Bonnie asked after a few minutes.

Duke shook his head. "I don't think anyone can answer that for sure. Maybe drugs had something to do with it. That whole group uses them, from what I hear." He paused for a moment. "Sometimes God's way is not for us to understand."

They walked on for several minutes without speaking. Then Duke pulled a cigar from his pocket.

"You know," he said, stopping to light the tobacco, "it used to be some mineowners were so greedy that they'd con a farmer into selling his coal rights for a flat seventy-five dollars. The farmer would spend the money right away, of course, and soon mining cars and machinery would be tearing up his land, and he'd have no choice but to go work in the mines himself on the very land he owned."

"I've heard that that happened," Bonnie commented.

"Now I hear about these same farmers looking for outsiders and selling them rights they don't even own." Duke chuckled. "Guess one group's as mean and greedy as the other. Things always seem to even out in the end."

They had reached the church at the end of the hollow. Bonnie spotted the fresh mound of dirt at Jim's grave. She stopped. "If you don't mind, Pa, I think I'd like to be alone for a while," she said.

"Sure, honey. I understand. I'll head back." He turned and hobbled back up the hollow, puffing on his cigar.

When Duke had disappeared into the shadows, Bonnie walked to Jim's grave. She stood beside the mound and prayed. After a few moments she returned to the front of the church and climbed the stairs. She tried the doors. They were unlocked. She opened one just wide enough for her to slip inside. Feeling her way in the darkness, she found the small door leading to the belfry. It opened with a squeak. The wooden ladder was more wobbly than Bonnie remembered it to be. Was it the same ladder she had used when she last climbed to the belfry with Jim and a tethered duck? A pigeon flapped its wings loudly in panicked flight when she reached the top, and the musty odor of the belfry filled her nostrils. She moved to one of the slatted windows and peered down at the two hollows of Porterville.

A gentle breeze stirred the dust on the road below, and the moon, in its first quarter, began to peek from behind an unseen passing cloud. The reddish glow had disappeared from the sky, and except for the moonlight and the yellowish flickering from the windows in the long rows of houses, it was dark now. Bonnie stared at the distant shadow of Newcastle Peak, which she could barely discern. The mountain had failed her once. Now she asked it a question: Had her fate, like that of a man she had loved, been cast millions of years earlier, when unknown gods, playfully perhaps, had laid beneath the West Virginia countryside an undulating bed of coal? Coal was as black as anything on earth. It absorbed the full spectrum of the light cast upon it, sucking in its energy and heat and giving none of it back. Maybe extracting coal, freeing it from its chamber of darkness, was a violation of nature or, at the very least, a tampering with time, the interrupting of processes begun millennia before the appearance of man. As she peered from the church belfry where her child had been conceived and pondered the claims on her, on Jim, on Mari, indeed on all Coal County, Bonnie wondered if it wasn't best that coal be left alone, that it rest unhindered in its eternal prison beneath the mountain range. Left untouched, coal could claim no revenge.

But a decision had been made. It was not Bonnie's decision. Nevertheless, it had been made. The coal was to be taken from the mountain, drilled, blasted, hammered and shoveled until it was free. More than ever the civilized world depended upon it. As with the bloody but necessary butchering of a helpless cow, the mining had to be done. But it was important that it be accomplished by people who understood its essence, who respected it, who cared.

In the moments after Jim's coffin had been lowered into the earth, Bonnie was so numb that she could not concentrate on the condolences offered her by the many persons at graveside. Now, alone in the belfry, their words came to her. Robert Allen saying "Whatever help you need." The Reverend Weatherson: "It's more than just the company at stake." Mrs. Will Thomason: "We're praying for you, all of us." Mae Sexton: "You can do it, dearie. This old lady knows." And Gordon Spencer: "The torch has been passed to you."

They were right. A battle was raging over a way of life, and it was her lot, one determined, perhaps, long, long ago, to lead the fight, to preserve a heritage, to rally a people. The challenge left her neither sad nor scared. She felt as calm as she ever had in her life. In this same loft she had given Jim Porter a gift; now he had given her one, equally precious, equally irrevocable. With it came an inner peace, the joy in knowing the direction the rest of her life would take, the delight in understanding her destiny and the pride in seeing the source of her ultimate fulfillment.

As the distant shadow of Newcastle Peak blended into the darkness of the night, Bonnie was smiling. She was happier than she had ever hoped. Her contentment, almost mystical in its nature, seemed to touch her soul. After all the love and hate, the laughter and song, the bloodshed and bitterness, she and the mountain were in accord.